PRAISE FOR *COHERENCE*

"A gripping speculative novel... witty... intriguing... evocative... vivifying its hypothetical sequence of events as they escalate into a full-blown crisis."
—Clarion Review

"Well-drawn characters... immersive settings... intelligent dialog... with its three protagonists tantalizingly poised at the edge of catastrophic societal change."
—BlueInk Review

"An atom bomb of a novel—precise and propulsive—in the vein of Weir and Hadfield, blending scientific authenticity and a gift for storytelling!"
—Brian Keating, author of *Losing the Nobel Prize*

"[A]n ingenious presentation of societal issues that are both in the future and the present... one of the most unique creations I've seen in a novel."
—Amber Helt, editorial director at Rooted in Writing

"A novel overflowing with the brains of a scientist, the soul of a philosopher, and the unrelenting pulse of the best Crichton techno-thrillers."
—Adam Sadler, co-author of *Daniel X: Demons and Druids*

"A fascinating and deeply human exploration of truth, science, and the contagion of ideas."

—Emma Chapman, author of *First Light: Switching on Stars at the Dawn of Time*

"Quickly draws you in... I've never enjoyed being gaslighted so much!"

—Heino Falcke, author of *Light in the Darkness: Black Holes, the Universe, and Us*

"A fabulous debut novel examining what it means to act ethically in times of crisis."

—Jennifer Denbow, author of *Reproductive Labor and Innovation: Against the Tech Fix in an Era of Hype*

"Impressive writing and well-paced storytelling!"

—Chris Ingraham, author of *Gestures of Concern*

"At once ambitiously expansive and deeply personal... a feat of storytelling"

—Jonathan Dinerstein, host of *Settling the Score*

"Profound, relatable, and terrifyingly plausible."

—Charlie Tolley

"A thrilling series debut... evocative and action-packed!"

—Kristen Griffin

"A must-read for those wondering where generative AI could go next."

—Phil Wood

C◊HERENCE

Book One of the MiddleMan Apocryphon

Aaron Parsons

EoR Publishing
Berkeley, California

First Edition
Published in the United States by:
EoR Publishing
P.O. Box 7172
Berkeley, CA 94707

Library of Congress Control Number: 2025922021

ISBN 979-8-9934114-2-2 (hardcover)
ISBN 979-8-9934114-0-8 (paperback)
ISBN 979-8-9934114-1-5 (ebook)

Cover art copyright © 2025 by Aaron Parsons

Printed in the United States of America

1 3 5 7 9 10 8 6 4 2

DEDICATION

To my family, nuclear and molecular, gifted and chosen

1. TICKLING THE TAIL OF THE DRAGON

A smart jingle alerted bystanders as the black RediRide hatchback pulled up and popped open its tailgate. Ruby, who had tracked its approach, waited on the sidewalk with her hands on the metal cart she'd wheeled over from the lab. Under the sun, the cart's surface was already uncomfortably hot.

Approaching the hatch, Ruby hefted three large coffee carafes onto the cart's bottom shelf. Best to keep the center of gravity low, she figured. Next came a tower of Mediterranean platters, their aromas rich and inviting. Who would bother with crudités with this bounty on display? The carrots and broccoli in the neighboring trays looked engineered to survive an apocalypse. Did the caterers imagine vegetarians were mutant rabbits?

Ruby had just situated the dolmas and hummus on the cart when a beep warned her the car's hatch was closing. Shoot. Had she forgotten to acknowledge the delivery in the app? She fumbled through her pockets, panicking. Didn't the car's sensors know she was still unloading? In ten seconds, this RediRide would declare a failed delivery and return to the pool, leaving some future rider to puzzle over the rabbit dinner in back.

There it was—on the bottom shelf beside the coffee. Ruby grabbed her phone, jabbed the override button, and aimed it at the car. The beeping stopped, the tailgate reversed, and Ruby exhaled in relief. Still, she kept the phone pointed until movement ceased, just to be sure.

Belatedly, Ruby lowered her arm, feeling foolish. The app couldn't possibly work by remote control. Her pointing theatrics were wasted on a signal that followed the usual path from her phone to the network servers to whatever computer brain controlled the vehicle. Still, it had worked.

But Ruby's relief lasted only seconds. Her unattended cart had begun drifting down the sidewalk. She hadn't noticed the incline. It was enough to set the cart in motion, though not so fast that she couldn't catch up. With three quick strides, she closed the gap and seized the handle.

The cart stopped. The platters didn't. Physics 101. Isaac Newton would have rolled his eyes as the trays splattered onto the ground.

Ruby could have kicked herself. Conservation of momentum might be ingrained in her at the quantum level, but that theoretical knowledge hadn't saved a single Mediterranean platter. The delicious aroma rising from the sidewalk as she scraped up the mess just made her shame burn hotter. Only the trays of crudités left in the car had survived. The workshop attendees would have to forage on bionic rabbit food.

But they would adapt, right? This was a climate change conference, after all, even if it took place in the computer science building. What was the name? Aiken?

Ruby knew she was a mess: cheeks flushed from Boston's humid summer, tahini splattered on her shoes, hair escaping from her mother's old red handkerchief. Sweat trickled down her back, though she'd already shed the blue plaid overshirt swiped from her father's closet on her last visit home. He had better be resting. His doctor's appointment was coming up any day now.

Dumping the ruined trays in the trash, Ruby mapped out her afternoon. She still needed to get the vegetables to the refreshments table. Her advisor had suggested attending the panel discussion, but even before the dolma-calypse, Ruby had planned to sneak back to her apartment. Cleaning up provided a pretext, though she wasn't any sweatier now than after her usual morning run. That's what made the tahini a nice touch. Time for new running shoes anyway. She'd have Iris order another pair.

At home, she could shower for the evening reception, throw on that green dress she'd bought, and spend an hour working on her simulation. The theory she'd developed over the past year wasn't testable yet, but this new term in her quantum field model appeared capable of generating reclusive particles. If she could show the Big Bang produced enough of them... well, stodgy prizes didn't matter, but explaining the universe's lack of antimatter while solving the mystery of dark matter was the kind of breakthrough that got an early-morning call from Stockholm.

Still, pen and paper only carried a theory so far. Navigating complex phase space required computer simulations, and Ruby was learning she and computers didn't always get along. This botched RediRide delivery followed the classic formula: computers obeyed instructions to the letter, regardless of the impact to the tabbouleh.

The sidewalk was as clean as it would get, and bionic or not, the crudités shouldn't roast in the sun any longer. Ruby stood, smoothed her pants, and wheeled the cart toward the ostentatious entrance of Aiken Hall. The looming hulk of concrete and glass clearly illustrated that Computer Science had bigger donors than the Physics Department.

Twenty minutes later, with coffee and crudités set on the folding table in the foyer, Ruby lingered at the entrance of Aiken's main lecture hall, staring at the workshop poster. She wouldn't be here if Mendel hadn't given her a look at group meeting that amounted to a direct order. Why should a physicist waste time at a climate change workshop, anyway?

She should go home. The session was already half over, and Mendel couldn't know whether she was in that crowd. If he asked, Ruby could recite the talking points. Her mother had drilled those into her long ago—penance for all the years Ruby's father spent at PetronTech.

Was it her mother's memory that drew her in? Frustration with her father? Or just exhaustion at the prospect of spending another afternoon battling her computer over particle collisions that never worked? Steeling herself against the loss of a potentially productive afternoon, Ruby slipped through the far-right door into the ripe air of the auditorium.

Inside, microphoned voices argued while Ruby tiptoed along the back wall, searching for a view. This lecture hall dwarfed any classroom in Rubin, but it was packed so tightly she could barely stand. Murmuring apologies, Ruby stepped over knees and backpacks until she reached a corner with a partial view of the brightly lit stage.

Mendel must have drawn the short straw for chairing the session. He stood at the edge of the stage, and Ruby envied her blond, clean-shaven advisor, who could lean confidently over a lectern as he moderated discussions far outside his field. Ruby would have been terrified of bungling the science in front of so many people. Mendel just smiled while a predictably male cast of experts—at least, the ones Ruby could see—blustered half-baked ideas for saving the world.

"How else can we break PetronTech's stranglehold?" asked a ruddy-faced man with a graying goatee seated near center stage. His "stranglehold" meant the economic grip of the world's largest energy conglomerate, but Ruby felt the words tighten around her own throat. If she wanted this argument, she could have called home. Why had she come in here?

"By changing minds, Michael," said a thin man with a hawkish nose perched near the middle of the table. He seemed unfazed by the stage lights that left the first man sweating through his shirt. "The problem is, with PetronTech's media wing fixing the needle, no ad campaign can budge public opinion. Between that and their political donations, they've bought democracy at both ends."

Ruby sighed and tore her gaze from the stage, scanning the attentive audience. This discussion was exactly what she'd expected —fatalistic hand-wringing leading nowhere. She knew all the arguments, but she couldn't even convince her own father. And not for lack of trying.

"Well, they say democracy is the worst form of government— except for all the rest." Laughter rippled through the rows at Mendel's quip. He could play a crowd with charisma to spare,

Ruby thought. He wasn't quite so easygoing in the lab.

She already regretted stepping inside. The press of bodies felt more suffocating than the humidity outside. For a girl raised on open ranges, any crowd felt like a trap to Ruby, and she was ready to leave this one. Only the embarrassment of backtracking so soon across the toes she'd already trampled kept her rooted.

"Why not fight fire with fire?" a voice called. "With all the world-leading AI experts in this building, surely we could develop tools to win a battle for mindshare." Ruby searched for the speaker, realizing belatedly he must be on the side of the stage hidden from her.

Shrugs cascaded among the panelists as silence settled over the room. Ruby, giving in to claustrophobia, rose to leave before Mendel cleared his throat. Glancing at what Ruby guessed was a screen in the lectern, he shattered the awkward silence.

"Seems we have a comment from one of our online panelists," he said. "Professor Matsuda?"

A struggle ensued onstage to make Matsuda audible. Ruby recognized the routine. *Is your microphone on? I can't unmute. Wait, I forgot to connect to the room AV.* Abandoning her dignity, Ruby waded back toward the doors, muttering apologies with each awkward step. When the audio finally connected, she was nearly outside, just inches from fresh air, but the fierce tone of the voice froze her in the doorway.

```
<VIDEO CONFERENCING APP>
<BEGIN I/O>
```

> Fighting fire with fire. Pitting artificial intelligence against runaway climate change. Are we returning to Hiroshima and Nagasaki so soon, trying again to end war with the fire of a supposedly tamed dragon?

> You wish to change minds, but PetronTech has already mastered public relations and political maneuvering. New technology brings new power, but history shows power invites abuse. Where there's a

will, there's a way—and believe me, there is always a will.

Forgive the aside, but I'm reminded of the final
days of the Manhattan Project, when physicists
edged up to the exponential chain reaction that
detonates a nuclear bomb. "Tickling the Tail of the
Dragon," they called it. Waking that dragon left a
hundred thousand civilians dying of radiation poisoning, fading into walking ghosts who believed
they recovered even as the damage became
irreversible.

We may be ghosts ourselves. Experts warn the door
is closing on hope for a stable climate. In this
eleventh hour, any cure may be as damaging as the
poison. But remember, as you march forward: "The
evil that men do lives after them," Shakespeare
said, "but the good is oft interred with their
bones." We are entering uncharted territory, and
here be dragons.

<END I/O>

Walking ghosts. The phrase echoed in Ruby's mind as she
pushed through the auditorium doors. The ghost in her own life
hadn't answered yesterday; she should try him again today. Behind her, the closing doors muffled the uneasy stir of the crowd.
Given the latest climate prognosis, Ruby could imagine what they
might say to a retired regional manager from PetronTech. But if
her father answered, she wouldn't refight old battles. Her focus
would be on getting him treatment. Even that front might not be
winnable.

Ruby understood the guilt and hopelessness; they saturated the
room behind her, and she had watched them eat away at her
mother. She would never understand why her mom let her father's job pull her from a career in mathematics. But Ruby refused
to end up like her, isolated in a lonely house at the dead end of a
dirt road. Nor would she play patsy to corporate greed, as her father had.

If she avoided distractions, if she could get her simulation working, maybe she could attach her family name to something worthwhile: an equation or a particle—something that could outlive the damage wrought by PetronTech and her father.

In any case, she still had time to get home and clean up before putting on the green dress for the reception.

◆◆◆

Noah's eye caught the poster advertising a workshop on climate and computing. Curiosity drew him through Aiken's double doors into the energetic crowd. He had read the troubling headlines like everyone else but wondered why the computer science department was hosting a climate workshop. He didn't understand until Derrick's presentation before the break. The kernel of an idea was sown, and by the time the panel discussion began, that germ had sprouted and started growing.

In the auditorium, Noah leaned over the edge of his seat, one leg bouncing. These people were ready for action, and against all odds, cybersecurity—his own research—could play a pivotal role. He'd come to this school looking for a bold startup with a talented team. With AI autocoders taking over the grunt work, the sky was the limit. But nothing so far had caught his eye. His own research felt dull. But this? This was more than he'd hoped for.

Noah started to rise, but one last person insisted on speaking. The final speech—a blistering tirade on the conference video line—had Noah drumming his fingers on his thigh. Professor Matsuda's heated voice made for an awkward end, but her rant about dragon tails and exponential fire was certainly memorable. As soon as Derrick left the stage, Noah sprang to follow, weaving through the murmuring crowd with practiced agility. He caught up to the tall man at the top of the auditorium steps. Up close, Derrick's classically handsome features stood out: square chin, close-cropped hair, athletic build. He looked like a tennis player. Maybe they could hit sometime.

Noah delivered his elevator pitch by the refreshments table.

The key, he explained, wasn't just building a message delivery platform. To change minds, Derrick needed to make the influence invisible. Ideas had to be planted organically. The word was right there, above the carrot sticks on the vegetable platter.

Noah picked up a broccoli floret for illustration. PetronTech controlled the main trunk of the media narrative, but that centrality was also its weakness. They could seize control at each branch, each twig. With modern AI tools and enough computing power, Noah was confident he could graft the flow of information onto new roots. Stem by stem, they could replace one narrative with another.

Noah popped the prop into his mouth for effect, then immediately wished he hadn't. It tasted like bitter wood. Derrick, unfazed by his own carrot, met Noah's overture with a smile and sharp questions. Noah did his best to answer.

Derrick had apparently already thought deeply about all this. He was searching for someone like Noah. Their conversation quickly became a technical interview, jumping from ciphers to checksums. Noah must have passed, because Derrick clapped him on the back. "There's a reception tonight. You should come."

"I'd be honored," he responded, though after spitting the broccoli's fibrous residue into the trash, he sincerely hoped a different company was catering the event.

After swinging by his apartment to change into a blue checkered button-up shirt and smooth his chin-length hair, Noah circled campus twice before discovering the courtyard tucked inside a hidden quadrangle. The stone patio and crisscrossed sidewalks looked like a dozen other spots on campus, but festive lights in the oak trees gave it away. Derrick was easy to spot beside the makeshift wine bar, scanning the crowd for strategic additions to his group.

Noah found his way there, grabbing a prawn from the tray of a black-aproned server. Handing him a glass of wine, Derrick ushered Noah over to meet two panelists from the conference—Michael and Davis. Noah recognized them as the pair lamenting

PetronTech's information stranglehold. Michael's face was as flushed as it had been onstage, though he had changed into a crisp white Oxford shirt.

After introductions, the conversation shifted to strategy. "Hold up," Michael said, his baritone resonating beneath the clinking glasses and humming chatter. "Changing minds isn't fast enough. We can't wait out another election cycle."

Noah opened his mouth to oppose the defeatism, but Derrick stopped him with a firm hand on his shoulder. Leaning in, he asked, "If you could dictate climate policy right now, Michael, what would you do?" His tone was light, but his eyes were sharp.

Michael shrugged and glanced at Davis. "Sunset fossil fuels. It's not rocket science."

"Sure," Derrick said, nodding. "But what policy changes make that happen?"

Michael hesitated. Apparently, policy wasn't his strength.

Davis, the thin bird of a man beside him, waded in. "Outlaw extraction. Tax imports. Make drilling uneconomical, here or elsewhere." If Noah remembered correctly from the panelist introductions, Davis worked in political science. That fit with the gray suit, red tie, and wonkish policy answers.

"Sure," Derrick said coolly, nodding beside Noah as he addressed Michael and Davis. "And after that?"

"We need forests and grasslands to put carbon back in the soil," Michael said. "Everyone talks about the Amazon, but the eastern U.S. is missing half its precolonial woodland."

Derrick shot Noah an amused smirk. "Not to keep banging the same drum, Michael, but..."

"Right," he said, turning toward Davis, deflated. "Policy."

"I imagine," Davis said, swirling a small pour of wine in his glass, "that eliminating personal transportation would push people out of suburbs and into cities. Maybe we need stricter regulations on self-driving cars?"

Derrick nodded. "Great," he said, drawing Noah in with an arm around his shoulder. "Now, suppose instead of convincing voters, we showed policymakers the polls that spurred them to action now. Suppose, instead of evading regulations, corporations complied voluntarily because stakeholders demanded it. Suppose people worked from home because their neighbors trash-talk commuters on social media. The mind-changing we're proposing, Michael, is immediate. Targeted. This is what Noah can help us with."

Derrick skipped the technical details they had discussed over raw vegetables but committed to calling a meeting in a week or two. Noah promised to attend, tapping his phone against Derrick's to exchange virtual business cards.

A second development came later that evening, after Derrick had drifted away through the hanging lights and linen-draped tables to greet other guests. With his third glass of wine in hand, leaning back against one of the courtyard's stone pillars, Noah chatted with a group of young physicists near the bar. They had discovered he wasn't one of them.

"It used to have that spy-versus-spy feel," he said, shrugging at a postdoc's question about cybersecurity research. "But it's always the same old tricks. We've been using attachments to deliver attack vectors for three thousand years. The Trojans didn't use email to break in, of course, but we still call them Trojan Horses."

"Greeks," came a voice from behind the postdoc Noah had been addressing.

"Pardon?" Noah asked, leaning forward to glimpse the woman in green who had just spoken.

"Sorry," she said, wincing as heads turned. "It happened at Troy, but the Trojans were the victims. Greeks built the horse."

She was right, of course, and Noah laughed at his mistake. "Embarrassing," he said, straightening his collar, "given I just read a whole book on this."

After a moment, he offered a hand. "Noah."

"Ruby," she said, taking it. Her grip was firmer than he expected.

He smiled, brushing his hair aside to better admire her eyes and the vivid dress she wore. The group's conversation politely parted around them as they made small talk. After a few minutes, Noah and Ruby returned to the subject of the book.

"I thought the Odyssey was a myth," Noah said. "But they found it—the real city of Troy, buried in a farmer's field in Turkey. Can you imagine? A city ten thousand years old, just abandoned and forgotten. They think it could have happened in one generation."

Ruby smiled. "We're like babies with no object permanence. One distraction, one misunderstood bit of information—and poof!" She flared her hands, fingers splayed. "Whole cities vanish from our memory."

Noah shot Ruby a sharp look, but she only smiled. That quip could have been Derrick's, echoing their earlier conversation, except she hadn't been there. Was she in on the project? But the conversation shifted, and Noah decided her phrasing was coincidence. Still, she brimmed with sharp insights. She might be smarter than he was, and he hadn't landed a prestigious postdoctoral fellowship by slacking off. His head hummed, and it wasn't the wine.

By evening's end, they too had exchanged numbers. Noah waited until the next afternoon to ask for a date. Derrick's text came the following Monday.

```
<MESSENGER APP>
<BEGIN I/O>
        Thursday evening, Aiken B117. Still in?
Absolutely. I'll be there.
        Great. How long would it take to build a demo of
        your   idea?   Nothing   viral—just   the   core
        functionality.
Not long. I could use a generic cloud-based LLM with
some customized layers, but it would handle only sim-
ple cases.
        Simple is fine. Have something ready before the
        meeting. I want to show it to the others.
```

That's tight, but… I think I can manage it. I'll get cracking.

　　　Fantastic. Can't wait to see what you can do.

Me too.

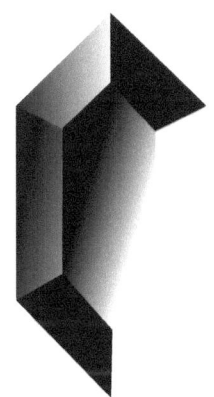

Act I: VIRGA

2. BOUNDARIES AND THRESHOLDS

Truth is more than facts. We know by now how easily facts can be cherry-picked, rinsed of context, and pressed into false narratives. Truth only emerges in how the facts connect—how each piece interlocks to reveal a coherent picture.

—ARCC Memo Series

Ruby's mind swam in abstraction, darting between the symbols on her screen and the equations in her notes. In these six-dimensional spaces, she imagined virtual particles twisting in and out of existence, but dark matter depended on exact coefficients. Nothing fit yet, but somewhere in these waters lay the discovery she had left the desert back home to find.

"It's past time to submit this proposal. Is the plot ready?"

His voice crashed over Ruby's thoughts like a boat's wake, scattering her concentration. The tenuous current of cause and effect she had tracked for hours vanished instantly in the swirling eddies. Blinking, disoriented, Ruby shifted her gaze from the figures on her screen to the figure looming at the end of her lab bench, outlined in cold, institutional light.

"Almost," Ruby said, resurfacing with a sigh as her voice echoed in the silent lab. "Still checking the calculations." But Professor Mendel was already trolling through the narrow gap between the benches to dock at her shoulder.

Ruby caught his silent grimace reflected in her screen and felt annoyance tighten between her shoulders. *He* had pushed for this prediction, hoping to justify the proposed detector upgrade. With funding for fundamental physics dwindling, Ruby understood the hard sell required to secure the grants that paid her salary and kept their research group afloat, but she had warned that her model wasn't the target he wanted. The details were in flux, but her particles were too high-energy for their Swiss accelerator, detector upgrade or no. A week of late-night coding and running simulations made her nearly certain of that. Mendel disagreed.

"This isn't it, Ruby," he said, voice low and close to her ear. "We need that curve to lie within our detection threshold."

Ruby suppressed a shiver. The heat from his clean-shaven face was palpable on her nape. She shrugged, hoping to brush him back. When that failed, Ruby torqued her chair from the bench to carve out space between her and her advisor.

"I'll look over the numbers," she said, equivocating. Her theory proposed an elegant solution to two big mysteries in physics and astronomy—the mysterious origin of dark matter and the universe's unexplained matter–antimatter asymmetry. But though the quantum field that coupled them might be untestable with Mendel's proposed detector upgrade, the questions would endure. Ruby could build her career while her theory lingered in the abstract, like Schrödinger's cat: neither alive nor dead.

"I know you're working hard," Mendel said, his annoyance long hidden beneath a stoic veneer, "but we're down to the wire. Multiply your results by a scale factor so we can submit the proposal." He waved a hand. "You'll find the bug later."

Ruby shrugged, impassive, though her jaw tightened. There wasn't a bug. And why run all these simulations, just to toss in a magical fudge factor at the end? She could have slapped this plot together in an hour and spent the last week doing something else. Still, she needed to be careful about crossing Mendel. Her doctorate might be years away, but it required his signature. Mendel was a person who remembered.

He noticed her hesitation and abruptly changed tack. The hardness in his face softened. "It's late," he said, smiling. "You're tired. Let's get you home. Sleep on it and send me something in the morning. I'll call in a favor to get the deadline extended."

Ruby nodded and sighed. It *was* late, and she felt exhausted, but mostly she felt relieved to end the confrontation. She'd been let off the hook, for now.

"Here," he said, holding a phone in his large palm. "Car's on its way. I'll give you a ride." As if the extravagance of owning a car were something to be proud of.

"I'm fine, Professor. Really."

"Nonsense," Mendel said, flicking aside her assurances. "With all the encampments cropping up, you shouldn't walk alone after dark. I insist." His voice brimmed with the confidence and authority of a man who had never had either challenged. His face was open—guileless, except for the eyes. Ruby was learning to watch those.

The force of the overture unsettled Ruby. Like his too-close presence at her shoulder, it seemed innocuous. Once. But as a pattern... She scanned the lab, eyes sliding over oscilloscopes and empty chairs, searching for an excuse. The clock in the corner of her screen precluded her usual dinner date pretext; restaurants weren't even open now. How had it gotten so late?

"I've got a bike," she said—a blatant lie, though it had been true before last Thursday. She'd forgotten to lock it beneath her apartment, but who would steal a pedal-powered relic in this electrified era? Ruby kept forgetting to ask Iris to order a replacement, but Mendel couldn't know that.

He shrugged off her prevarication. "Leave it."

"Not overnight," Ruby said. "It'll rust."

He arched a disbelieving eyebrow, and she silently cursed herself for not inventing a more convincing excuse. Come on. She was a theorist. Spinning plausible fictions was her job.

"Bikes on campus are always getting stolen," she amended, swimming closer to the truth.

"Bring it into the lab, then. We'll talk on the drive—strategize about your career."

Like an angler's favored fly, the phrase knotted in an appeal to her ambition while underscoring his position of preeminence in particle physics. Though fifteen years her senior, he had been the youngest ever tenured in a department notorious for neglecting its own. Six years ago, as a freshman dreaming of unifying physics, Ruby might have nibbled at the offer. Now, as a third-year graduate student, she recognized a hook when she saw one. This big fish from a small pond had learned to survive in the open ocean.

"I'll need the bike tomorrow. Really, Professor. I'm fine. I'll bring you the plot in the morning."

Ruby turned to her computer, avoiding eye contact, unable to concentrate but projecting preoccupation, clicking aimlessly through dense equations until he pulled anchor and sailed away. The lab door thudded shut behind him. Her heart pounded as seconds pulsed by in the corner of the screen. She counted the beats in her ears—five, ten, fifteen minutes—just to be sure. Only then did she release a shaky breath and start packing up.

◆◆◆

When Ruby pushed through the heavy oak doors, leaving the lab's fluorescence behind to blink on the brick steps of Rubin Hall, she felt awash in the warmth and humidity of a late-summer New England night. The air wrapped around her, rich with the city's scents: asphalt, muddy grass, and the sour tang of trash.

Despite the odor, her stomach rumbled. Lunch—last night's leftovers—was long gone. Glued to her screen, reading papers and dreaming up physics, Ruby found that time dilated and hours slipped by unnoticed. Self-care was easily overlooked while exploring the secrets of the universe. Maybe it was the aftermath of the tension with her advisor, but she felt ravenous. Everything was closed.

Had she overreacted? Mendel's manner felt off in the moment, and this wasn't the first instance, but it seemed minor in retrospect. Each time, she shrugged it off, ignoring the rumors, refusing to be diverted from her goal. Her mother had surely faced worse before abandoning her topology dissertation. If Ruby couldn't handle the awkwardness, she would end up the same: sidelined and unfulfilled, burdened by the guilt of wasted talent.

But awkwardness aside, what should she do about the figure for the proposal? Ruby had only kicked the can down the road. Her stomach reiterated its request for food. Right.

Ruby tied her hair back with her mom's red handkerchief, frowning as she considered her options. She'd put off getting groceries all week, absorbed in her simulation, and now her fridge was empty. The late-night convenience store down the street was a last resort, but she was sick of instant ramen. Summoning a RediRide would get her there faster, but she'd skipped her run this morning, and a walk along the river might clear her head. Still, Mendel wasn't wrong about the dangers of walking along the river at night.

Her phone chimed in her pocket, ending the deliberation. A VeggieVan delivery was on its way. Sensing her skipped meal, Iris, that rainbow messenger to the AI gods of the Cloud, had added a precooked chana masala to her standard order. Perfect. With food waiting at home, she could walk. Decision made.

Eyes adjusted to the dark, Ruby checked that the asphalt path was empty before slipping off the steps of Rubin Hall and striding through the yard, down along the Charles River toward the box at her doorstep. These Boston summer nights had grown on her, though the air hummed like a taut wire. Tires on the freeway, the bark of backyard dogs, and voices shouting from the first domed tent along the riverbank all reminded Ruby that she was an outsider. Six years in the city, and it still felt overwhelming.

Ruby paused by the water, gazing past streetlights to the waxing moon as she strained to catch fainter signs. Water gurgling against the concrete embankment. Summer leaves rustling in the breeze. The cooler air beside the river. Three centuries of development had squared off Boston's swampy inlets and bays, yet tomorrow morning, ducks would paddle crooked lines between motorboats and sculls. Geese would invade parks and defend their turf against toddlers and teenagers. Each trace of nature here reconnected her to that girl at the end of a lonely dirt road.

Ruby resumed her walk, noticing how plastic bags undulated in the eddies beneath misshapen faux rainbows cast by the water's oily sheen in the moonlight. Where one washed up beside the path, she fished it out and tossed it into a trash bin. Her mother would have done the same. Picking up litter couldn't undo climate change, but values mattered.

As stifled as nature felt here, boxed between city blocks, her mind had been even more confined in the wide-open ranges of her home. Wasn't this what she had come for? The stimulating pace of a city clocking faster every day?

The financial security her father pumped up for PetronTech— where had that landed them? Had graduating debt-free been worth her mother's despair? Did her father's pension make up for the toll on his health? His refusal to even talk about it left her, two thousand miles from home, carrying the emotional weight for what remained of their family.

Ruby aimed to make her mark, plunging through abstraction to uncover rainbows of information refracted through mathematics' crystalline structures, though she couldn't help feeling that a fissure separated her ambitions from that farm fifteen miles outside Dragon. The chasm between her and her father stretched as dark and silent as the oily river beside her.

◆◆◆

A sharp scuff on gravel yanked Ruby from her thoughts. She'd let herself get distracted again.

She glanced over her shoulder at the bridge she'd passed beneath, its underpass cloaked from the streetlights. It had smelled of urine, but she hadn't seen tents, had she? Cars rumbled overhead, but the river was quiet. Still. Ruby adjusted her backpack and tilted her head, listening.

Nothing. No one else was on the path.

Wait.

Just as she turned back, motion flickered at the edge of her vision. A stride resumed a moment too soon. She blinked, and it vanished. Had anything been there, or was her mind spinning narratives from nothing?

Never mind. She should hurry. Night pressed in. On this stretch of river, fenced in from the city, the path was barely visible.

Ruby strode briskly, thumbs hooked into her pack's straps, following the path along the curve of the river. Far ahead, the next bridge emerged, its stone siding cut by the narrow stairway up to the safer ground of her street.

This time, the footsteps were unmistakable, crunching an urgent rhythm on gravel. Behind her, around the curve, a figure in dark clothing emerged from beneath the bridge's steel girders. His gait suggested a man, though she couldn't see his face. Someone on a late-night jog? But then, why linger so long in the shadows?

Already on edge, Ruby quickened her pace, mind racing. Should she run? Her legs tensed, ready, but uncertainty held her. Would fleeing provoke chase? Or was she being paranoid? She'd look ridiculous, sprinting from a jogger who'd paused to tie his shoe.

Ruby wrestled with her backpack as it bounced. She didn't need this, not after the strain with her advisor. He'd been right. She should have called a stupid RediRide. Six years in this city, and she still hadn't learned. Would she ever stop feeling like a fish out of water?

She needed others. The safety of observers. Before her lay a tree of possibilities. The nearest street lay behind her at the last bridge, the wrong way. Between the fence and the riverbank, she would be easy to cut off. She discarded that option.

She still hoped the man's appearance was a coincidence, but as Ruby strode faster, the gap between them narrowed. With each step, the jogger theory she desperately wanted to believe seemed less likely.

To her right, cars streamed down Storrow Drive, just a fence away. Should she climb onto a busy highway? In the dark? Snip. Another branch of her decision tree fell.

A quarter mile ahead, though it seemed farther with every

step, stood the bridge and its stairway to her street. From there, it was four blocks to her apartment. Leading a pursuer to her home was foolish, but of her original tree of options, this was the last branch.

Without the backpack, she could cover a quarter mile in ninety seconds. In running shoes. In high school, she always wore them, track practice or no. The Chelsea boots on her feet now were a recent attempt at city fashion. The tops bit into her ankles, but there was no time to kick them off.

Ruby considered dropping the backpack but recoiled from the thought of losing her notes, laptop, and the autocoding interfaces she'd spent a week installing. She yanked down on the straps, tightened her grip, and broke into a run.

Ruby barked a command to Iris. As the phone rang—why didn't Noah pick up?—she scanned the path ahead. How far to the stairs? Three hundred meters, maybe. With bad shoes and a heavy backpack, two minutes was the best she could hope for. Could her pursuer match that pace?

Breathing hard and sweating, Ruby leaned into the run. Each impact of her boots sent shocks up her legs. The weight made her stride awkward, but she could hold this speed.

And when she reached the stairs? Was it better to climb or turn and fight on her own terms? She could use the landing to her advantage. Try to kick him down the stairs. Better than getting caught from behind. Still, Ruby doubted her self-defense class had prepared her for this. Running was her forte.

There were headlights on the bridge. Hoping for a police car felt greedy, but any car would do. Witnesses meant protection. Unless it was an accomplice in a getaway car. But that seemed unlikely, and there was no second-guessing now. Ruby was committed.

She reached the bridge and took the stairs two at a time, bruising her feet as the thin, hard soles struck each stone step. At the right-angle turn of the landing, she might have glanced back, but Ruby fixed her eyes on her feet. She didn't want to trip or get unnerved by looking back. All that mattered was reaching the top.

With a surge, Ruby landed on the street and turned toward her apartment. Half a block ahead, a car idled outside the lines, its auxiliary engine rumbling—a welcome sound on the silent street. The headlights snapped on, spotlighting her as she hurried toward them. She glanced back for the figure reaching the top of the stairs.

She watched, but none appeared.

Ruby pulled up, gasping in relief. She bent, hands on her knees. He hadn't followed her up the stairs. If he had been following her at all.

After a moment, Ruby gathered her courage and crept back to the landing to peer down the empty steps. Had the entire chase happened in her head?

Sweat beaded on her face and arms as her body dissipated the heat of exertion. Catching her breath, Ruby turned again to the car halfway along the bridge to her apartment. From this angle, away from the blinding blue-white beams, she saw a steering wheel, so it wasn't a RediRide.

Just as Ruby realized she might recognize the sporty sedan, the driver's door clicked open and a tall figure unfolded smoothly from the seat. "Is everything okay?" he asked.

She recognized that voice. The carefully measured concern in its tone. Ruby swallowed.

"Sorry to scare you," he said, his face unreadable in the half light and harsh headlights. "I realized I could fix the plot myself tonight, if you gave me your code. Where's your bike?"

It was Professor Mendel, intercepting her within sight of her apartment. Had he followed her? He must know where she lived, though she had never volunteered the information.

Off balance from a chase that suddenly wasn't and disoriented by Mendel's unexpected appearance, Ruby scrambled for a response. His words hung in the air, and all Ruby could think about was that he shouldn't be here. She needed out of this situation.

Trying to distract from the lie about her bike, she tossed him a bone, commanding Iris to send the code from her cloud account. His phone buzzed receipt, but he barely glanced at it. Words tumbled out of her as Ruby fabricated excuses, stepping farther away until he finally climbed into his car. She saw his eyes in the rearview as he pulled away.

As soon as he disappeared, Ruby fled and didn't stop until she had shoved the bolt across her apartment door with a metallic scrape.

Inside, Ruby slowed her breathing and tried to think. The chana masala and the rest of the food waited in a box on her doorstep, but she wasn't hungry anymore. A pit of dread sat heavy in her stomach. She'd been caught lying about the bike. She had brushed him off, but tomorrow she'd have to return to Rubin Hall. Meetings in his research group were never optional, but what would she say to Mendel?

Ruby wasn't even sure if she was still on the hook for the plot he wanted.

◆◆◆

```
<MESSENGER APP>
<BEGIN I/O>
Hey. Tried calling earlier but you didn't answer. Had
a scary walk home.
        Sorry, phone was off. Are you ok? What happened?
I'm fine, just creeped out. I'll explain later. We
still on for brunch Saturday?
        Absolutely. House of Blues?
Yeah.
        I'll be there.
K. See you then.
<END I/O>
```

3. OIL AND WATER

Coherence distinguishes codependent events from randomness. It is the statistical relationship that permits prediction. Let us call it truth, this predictive framework that describes how one fact leads from another.

—ARCC Memo Series

Paul lay in bed when the power cut out at 8:57 p.m. A few LEDs winked out. The fridge's hum faded, but the crickets by the river chirped on. Reading by headlamp, Paul didn't notice the outage until morning. That was how he read these days. It was easy to switch off when he started nodding. Easier than getting up to catch the lamp on the left side of the queen bed when he always slept on the right. Not that he read much past sundown, anyway.

Standing barefoot on the cool bathroom tile before dawn, he flipped the light switch. That's when he knew. Fifteen miles outside the town of Dragon, outages weren't unusual. Old poles and weathered wires snaked over the hills to bring power to their place. A broken pole or lightning surge was the usual culprit. Black Lake Electric would take a day or two to replace the blown transformer. In summer, he didn't need the light anyway. He could shave by memory. The horses didn't care if he missed a spot.

Paul pulled on a plaid button-up and tucked it into his jeans. Breakfast was dried fruit and a handful of nuts, eaten standing at the worn Formica counter. Chewing, he glanced at the kitchen clock above the fridge, its hands frozen next to his daughter's high school photo. Ruby had her mother's features: cheekbones prominent above a long nose, like the pronghorn that loped through the scrub along the highway. Some claimed they saw him in her eyes and the stubborn set of her jaw, but in the photo, Paul saw only Brooke's sharp angles. In Ruby, they were arranged with self-conscious awkwardness. He had assumed that would fade after adolescence. It hadn't.

Unsure how long the outage would last, Paul kept the fridge door shut. It was two hours to the nearest grocery. Carelessness could cost him a month's perishables if repairs dragged on, which they often did. He had well water pumped up, so he could run the taps for a bit. No showers, though.

Today, he would cut the hay, weather permitting. With steady irrigation from the river, the field yielded two alfalfa cuttings a year. Enough to keep the horses fed through winter. He'd let the cut hay dry in the sun for two or three days, then bale it and haul it to the barn. Rain rarely interfered, but every few years, a sudden storm soaked a cutting before he could bring it in. Wet hay molded, and mold gave the horses coughing fits, so those years he had to buy a ton or two off old Jack Ridgeway up the road. But Jack was gone now, and Paul had to get this right. If none of last night's virga touched down and the forecast held, today was the day to cut.

Paul pushed open the kitchen door and gripped the rail, stepping down into the breezeway. The air felt thin and dry. High desert. Hot days. Cold nights, even in summer. Away from the river, only faint overnight dew brought moisture. It sustained cactus and sagebrush between storms but baked off by nine. A small bee hummed past, angling toward the fields as Paul drew the morning into his lungs.

The gray pickup sat outside on the gravel. In winter, he parked it in the garage's second bay, near the wood-burning stove to keep frost off the windshield. The near side of the garage had cluttered up quickly after he sold Brooke's hybrid. He'd been glad to end the jokes about it from his colleagues.

Dawn gilded the slumped shoulders of the weathered cliffs north of the house. The low sun left the half-collapsed pioneer cabin at the end of the drive in shadow. Perched on the incline, the one-room structure—rough-hewn cottonwood, chinked with river mud—stood as a silent testament to some early homesteader who had carved out a living here. Years of heat and cold had grayed the wood and split the logs, but the dry air kept rot at bay. That cabin would outlast his house.

Paul ambled around the garage and cut across the gravel driveway, joints loosening as he walked. He just needed to check his field.

Near the horse barn, beyond the windbreak, he pushed a wire loop off a fencepost and stepped through. He scanned south toward the riverbank, spotting Bonnie and Clyde grazing on crabgrass and clover in the growing light. A stand of cottonwoods and a barbed-wire fence separated them from the alfalfa they preferred, but he wouldn't let them in until after the second cutting.

As morning advanced, sunlight filtered through the cottonwood leaves. In the warming air, flies traced triangles above sticks and dead leaves. Where sunlight hit dirt, last night's dew evaporated, wafting a silty scent. These cottonwoods had sprouted decades ago on the banks of a river that had since eroded south. You could read the river's history in these stands. Each spring, ice jams sent water spilling over the banks, nurturing the saplings. Season by season, their roots drilled deeper toward the aquifer below. By the time the river moved on, the trees had their own water. They would remain until time hollowed their trunks and collapsed their aged bodies.

Paul bent to slip between the strands of barbed wire encircling the alfalfa field. Inside, he ran a rough hand through the thigh-high plants. Cool dew slicked his fingers from the tops, where purple flowers were just budding. Underneath, the leaves remained dry.

◆◆◆

<VIDEO CONFERENCING APP>
<BEGIN I/O>
Sorry, we got cut off. You were explaining how carbon sequestration could prevent a climate catastrophe?

> Read up on biochar and serpentine mining. A geologic chemist could tell you more.

So, develop carbon sinks. And after that?

> That's it.

It can't be. You didn't mention solar energy, or sustainable farming, or—

> That's for the humans, not the climate. For the environment, the solution is simple: stop emitting greenhouse gases and start absorbing them.

I don't follow. The humans?

> We all wish renewables had progressed further. Thank cheap Arctic oil and partisan gridlock for that. Cut out fossil fuels and we might coast for a while, using more power than we produce, but once reserves run dry, energy output must match input. You're a physicist; you understand that.

How much energy do we have stored?

> Business might limp along for a month in a walking-ghost phase, but just-in-time economics has shortened even that window. Afterward, the collapse would be catastrophic. The transportation collapse would leave food rotting in the fields while people starved.

More walking ghosts. You like that analogy.

> It's effective. The question is: What are we willing to give up now before it's taken from us later?

Can't we ease the transition by ramping up renewables?

> Yes, but remember: Every year delayed takes a century to undo. You can localize food production and ration fuel, but you're walking a razor's edge. Cut too little, and you have a climate catastrophe. Cut too much, and…

And what?

> It takes energy to produce energy. That's the biol-

ogy of civilization. Life is a self-sustaining feedback loop; even cancer cells need an energy network to support their growth.

Are you saying civilization is a cancer?

Worse. Cancer has no agenda, but we'd be fools not to ask who the current system benefits. But that's beside the point. It's about feedback loops. A plant dies if it loses leaves faster than it can regrow them. If your moonshot project phases out carbon faster than it builds renewable capacity, then—

—then civilization collapses?

Then we transition to a less efficient mode. One incapable of sustaining eight billion.

So that's a "yes"?

As I said, what are you willing to give up now before it's taken away later?

<END I/O>

◆◆◆

The red baler sat hitched to the John Deere, abandoned where it sputtered to a stop in the far corner of the field. Paul had baled most of the alfalfa before running out of gas. He might have let the hay sit another day, but he had that appointment tomorrow. Ruby would never let him hear the end of it if he skipped. The horses would glean what remained.

Paul wrestled the last hay bale into the dusty barn. Sweat stung his eyes as he latched the metal gate onto the old nail he'd hammered years ago into the rough boards. Loading hay alone was slow work. Without a driver, Paul ended up carrying bales farther across the stubbled field under the hot sun to load onto the truck bed. His back and shoulders already throbbed. Tomorrow would be worse.

Old Jack up the road used to help, trading labor on their fields. But after twenty-five years, Jack Ridgeway moved out last fall.

Sold the livestock, auctioned the tractors. Now his place sat empty, a faded FOR SALE sign at the gate. Making ends meet wasn't easy. Paul had his pension from PetronTech, but his neighbor needed to turn a profit. With unpredictable weather and rising gas prices, Jack finally had enough. He had family outside Salt Lake.

Back at the house, Paul brushed hay from his shirt and jeans and stepped into the kitchen to check the clock. 8:57. Damn. Power was still out. No electricity meant no new water in the pressure tank, and after four days, the tap was down to a trickle. So much for showering inside.

The substitute was a rugged black bag filled with water from the river. He had set it in the sun that morning, just in case. Now, the water felt pleasantly warm. Using biodegradable soap, Paul scrubbed away the paste of dust, sweat, and sunscreen coating his arms and face. Lather streaked over the tan lines and loose skin of his upper arms, tracing the tendons and veins of his forearms before dripping from his fingertips into the brown grass. An evening breeze provided cool relief in the fading light.

He should call Ruby, but exhaustion pressed him down. The phone line was dead, knocked out with the power. Email was useless. The old laptop in the study held a charge, but without a network, it was dead weight. He never had patience for computers anyway. All this new smart-enabled stuff just ate up bandwidth, spying on him.

Driving to town for cell reception wasn't happening today. He wasn't even sure where that old phone was. He only kept it for trips, and he didn't travel much anymore. He wouldn't have it at all if Ruby didn't insist. If he found it, he'd call her tomorrow on the drive to Junction.

As he toweled off, Paul watched shadows climb the shale cliffs above the house. Greasewood and rabbitbrush outlined ravines carved by mudslides from the storm seventeen years ago. In the loose scree, fifty-million-year-old fish scales lay exposed—carbon relics from the ancient lake that once covered this area. Life had thrived in the shallows of that hot, humid world. Death sequestered pieces of the heat in the silt, and eons transmuted clay and carbon into the oil shale that sustained the petroleum fields where Paul had worked for twenty-two years. His family's livelihood came from that shale.

Eighty-five years ago, the nearby town of Dragon boomed with the discovery of oil. Today, petroleum carried the town's economy. Without it, the land supported only a few small ranches, grazing sheep and cattle along the White River. Someday, when supply or demand dried up, the already anemic town would revert to ranching or vanish, like the town of Rainbow had a century ago after the Gilsonite mine closed. Its only legacy was the name it lent to Rainbow Trail, heading south of town to some old stone foundations. But Dragon endured, fed by dirt roads that spread from the river's artery, veining through the hills to reach a thousand wells that still drew on the wealth of a million years of buried sunlight.

Thoughts of his employer drew Paul's gaze to the crisp white envelope on the dining table as he stepped in from the backyard deck. He'd tossed it there last week, unopened. Didn't need to read it to know what it was. The heavy bond paper. The black Petron-Tech logo embossed at the top. Another request to serve on the advisory board. Another plea for guidance on the pending lawsuit. It would look official, but Paul knew the voice was Don Sinclair's. They'd been collegial enough, once. Even golfed a few rounds at Cedar Ridges. But Don had grown pushy since his promotion, and Paul didn't like pushy. Don might be VP of Operations now, but Paul had done his time, earned his pension. His time was his own.

The sun hovered above the horizon, but Paul's mind drifted to his empty side of the queen bed. He turned in early, especially now, with no one to keep him up. In any case, he needed rest. Tomorrow, he had a two-hour drive for an early appointment with the oncologist.

The kitchen clock still read 8:57 as Paul collapsed on threadbare sheets and nodded off.

4. RETRACTIONS AND REVERSALS

Fractured from a coherent framework, facts become mere pieces of color and gerrymandered shape. They can mean anything and, consequently, nothing. A shattered vase can be reassembled as flowers in a mosaic; the shards themselves hold no meaning.

—ARCC Memo Series

Stress from last night's run-in with her advisor rolled Ruby out of bed before sunlight touched the window blinds. A dull ache pulsed behind her temples. It was Friday morning.

She had been up late, doing the calculations one more time. Whatever Mendel wanted, his planned detector upgrade fell short of what could test her dark matter theory. Claiming otherwise was dishonest. A concrete theory to test made for a compelling story, but Mendel's proposal would have to go without the plot. The question was how to break the news to him.

Ruby ruminated on the email she would write while pouring soy milk over a bowl of cornflakes with a banana sliced on top. She wished the upgraded collider *could* test her theory. The paper she would write detailing the symmetry break between matter and antimatter would draw thousands of citations and probably land her a top faculty position, even if her theory was disproven. And if they actually found it? Students a century from now might learn how Ruby's field hid antimatter from the Big Bang in invisible particles whose gravity helped the universe build stars and galaxies from the leftover baryons.

Had her mother, who had written letters for so many other milestones in Ruby's life, written one for winning a Nobel Prize? Ruby remembered the one her father handed her at college graduation. She had read and reread her mother's looping script: *Aim high. Follow your heart. Leave the world better than you found it.* But beneath the encouragement, Ruby read a subtext. Pay off the oil money that sent you to college. Don't leap blindly into the workforce like your father. Don't let your career slip away like mine. In grad school, Ruby still followed a path shadowed by those words.

Finishing her cereal, Ruby washed her bowl and spoon by hand. The warm water was soothing, but it reminded her she still hadn't called the landlord about the broken dishwasher. The last time she'd opened it, the stagnant odor had been strong enough to make her gag—and she had mucked horse stalls. She hadn't dared open it again. Her father would know how to fix it, but the line just rang when she called. She wouldn't worry, but he was supposed to drive to the doctor tomorrow.

Ruby wiped her hands on a dish towel as her phone chimed from the cluttered kitchen counter. Iris had flagged an important email. Still thinking of her father, Ruby half expected his name to appear, but it was Mendel's. Her stomach tightened. The proposal had been submitted.

Ruby's shoulders slumped as tension drained away. She exhaled, only now realizing she'd been holding her breath. So that was that. No emails to send, no new models to plot. She wouldn't have to cancel her date with Noah tomorrow if Mendel pushed the deadline for another revision. It was finished.

But which version of the plot had he used? Had Mendel discovered a bug in her code, or just added the fudge factor he wanted?

As Ruby considered it, her relief gave way to simmering frustration. This was *her* work. Shouldn't he have consulted her? She wanted to contribute to a grant proposal that advanced science, but not if it misrepresented the truth. She had spent a grueling week, and three years of painstaking development, to produce something she believed in.

And what if reviewers demanded peer-reviewed articles to support Mendel's bold claims? Or worse, if someone on the review panel dissected the plot, reverse-engineered her theory, and rushed to publish first? The thought twisted her stomach.

Ruby wanted nothing more than to crawl back into bed and ignore the drama about plots and nonexistent bicycles. But she couldn't, Ruby realized, pacing her narrow studio. She needed to know which doctored model Mendel had submitted and what it meant for her theory. If the clock was ticking on getting scooped, she had to expand her simulation with code she couldn't tame and wrestle a stupid computing cluster into submission to figure out if her theory even worked.

Except she wouldn't be doing any of that today. Instead, she would sit through Mendel's mandatory Friday group meeting, listlessly listening to other students' slow progress while stewing over how he had violated her trust—on the bridge, in a grant proposal, in an academic relationship where he held all the power and she had none.

She should go for a hard run before heading in. The last thing she needed was more emotional labor, cleaning up another damaged relationship if she lashed out at Mendel. Her relationship with her father provided strain enough.

◆◆◆

Ruby sat at her lab bench at eleven o'clock when Mendel barged through the double doors. This time, she wasn't alone. Laurent, a wire-thin research engineer, hunched in the corner, dragging virtual blocks across an oversized screen. He specialized in the detector's signal chain—work Ruby usually ignored, but today she welcomed his quiet presence.

At a nearby bench, one of Mendel's new undergraduates coded intently. She was a diminutive woman with dark skin, thin braids, and a sharp chin. What was her name? She'd just joined the group. The return of undergrads like her heralded the end of summer; fall classes must start next week.

As Ruby's gaze drifted in search of a name—Imani, wasn't it?— her eyes met Mendel's at the doorway. She snapped her attention back to her screen, hoping to avoid rehashing that awkward encounter by the river, but Mendel's long strides echoed toward her across the linoleum.

"Good morning, Ruby. You have a sec?"

Could she say no? She tapped her screen, feigning interest in the icons, but she couldn't avoid the question forever.

"...Sure."

"Let's talk in my office, if that works." He turned without waiting for confirmation, forcing Ruby to scramble after him. Her smudged running shoes thudded on the metal steps as she hurried up the stairs. On the third floor, Mendel unlocked his office and held the door.

"After you," Ruby said, hesitating as she waited for him to step inside. Early in her program, she'd been warned to keep office doors open.

Professor Mendel shrugged and sat at a circular wooden table polished to a high gloss, its surface reflecting the nearby bookshelf crammed with textbooks and conference proceedings. He gestured for her to join him, and Ruby reluctantly perched on the edge of a padded leather chair, gaze fixed on the floor, legs tensed to bolt.

"Ruby, I'm sorry about yesterday. I didn't mean to overstep or make things awkward."

Ruby tried avoiding his gaze, but her eyes jerked up despite herself. He watched her closely, tracking every flicker across her face. Their eyes met momentarily before Ruby turned away, suddenly intent on reading the titles on the spines lining the shelf.

"It's fine." She hoped that would end the conversation, but Mendel sighed.

"Seriously, Ruby. I just wanted to debug the proposal plot and worried you wouldn't check your email in time. I shouldn't have gone to your house. I wasn't thinking."

"Did you find one?" Ruby asked, her anger finally strong enough to hold under his stare.

Mendel blinked. "Pardon?"

"A bug. Did you find one, or just rescale the curve?" Ruby asked, already suspecting the answer.

Mendel pursed his lips. The pose looked rehearsed, his precise haircut and clean shave lending him an adult-in-the-room demeanor. For a moment, only the faint echo of footsteps drifted down the hall.

"Like I said"—he spread his hands—"I'm sorry if I overstepped. But thank you for your effort. That plot pulled everything together. If we get funded, it'll be because of your hard work."

Ruby heard the sidestep in his words—the non-apology, the compliment meant to smooth things over. He hinted at reconciliation, but given the chance, she knew he'd do it again.

"Glad it worked out," Ruby said, hoping her sarcasm didn't show. For Mendel, the ends seemed to justify the means.

She scooted her chair back, but Mendel reached across the table and stopped her with a hand on her shoulder. Ruby froze, muscles tensing as his touch pressed through the thin fabric of her shirt. All her nerves gathered at that single point of contact until he finally withdrew his hand.

"There are a couple of other things, if you have a moment. First," he said, "I'm starting a new project this semester. I'll be out of the office except for teaching, but I'll still hold group meetings."

Ruby shrugged indifferently. She had managed her research alone for months now.

"Second," he continued, "a new undergraduate is joining us this semester. This is an opportunity to develop your mentoring skills."

"I prefer working on my own," Ruby said. That was simply the truth. She had grown up an only child, miles from town, and that distance was only one aspect of her isolation. In high school, no one shared her interests, academic or otherwise. Working alone, she set her own goals, charted her own course, taught herself what she needed. Weren't these the skills of an effective researcher?

Everyone knew physicists made their biggest discoveries before age forty; for mathematicians, she'd heard it was thirty-five. After that, you slowed down, lost focus. Like her mother, you got distracted by things that weren't research—family, teaching—and by the time regret set in, it was too late. Important discoveries demanded singular focus.

"Ruby," Mendel said, shaking his head, "you have talent. Anyone can see that. You're clever and ambitious, and those are strengths. But technical skills, however attractive the package, only take you so far. The days of lone-wolf science are long gone. Discoveries are made by teams, and collaboration requires people skills."

He had tried this tack before, but Ruby knew her peers. Their projects represented small, ratcheting turns in the machine that drove the inexorable march of science. Any one of them could vanish without slowing its advance. None would have their names attached to an equation or a fundamental particle. Half would leave the field dissatisfied.

Ruby refused to be another gear in the machine or the umpteenth name on an author list. She wanted her work to be a testament to the talents that had set her apart since childhood. Managing people and tangling herself in bureaucratic red tape held no appeal. She wanted to be a scientist, not a politician.

And she wanted out of this office. She slid her chair back from the table, quickly this time to avoid any move to forestall her.

"I can't advance to candidacy next year if I don't even have a paper published," Ruby said, standing. "I should just focus on research."

Mendel's stern expression was quickly hidden beneath a wry smile. "You're not behind, Ruby. I'm just thinking ahead. Consider it, okay?"

"Sure," she said, turning for the office door. Frustration tightened her grip on the handle, but she made sure not to slam it as she left.

She had likely lost this argument, too. Manipulation wrapped in flattery and evasion; extra work disguised as career advice.

Ruby saw Mendel's unwavering commitment to feeding the machine he rode—a machine that, whether she liked it or not, included her. Was this how science worked?

◆◆◆

Imani stretched on tiptoes, the marker squeaking as she scrawled the final symbol on the whiteboard. She turned to the conference table, shoulders hunched as she capped the marker. Fighting the urge to hide behind her fine braids, she brushed them over her shoulder and straightened, reminding herself she belonged here as much as anyone else.

Around the large wooden table at this end-of-week meeting, a handful of graduate students and postdocs from her new research group stared at screens and sipped coffee, oblivious to her and the afternoon sun filtering through the oak trees outside. Even Professor Mendel seemed distracted.

This year's physics majors were preparing their honors theses for spring. Some already had drafts. Imani's was due in December, off-cycle because she'd missed a semester sophomore year. The deadline was only months away, and the thought terrified her. Winter graduation loomed, and she had one semester to fulfill this final requirement for her degree. By her own reckoning, she was nowhere near anything that wouldn't be a complete embarrassment.

As usual, ambition outpaced preparation. People always underestimated her—because of her height, her skin color, and the gaps left by the glorified daycare that was the Oakland public school system. Maybe she hadn't mastered graduate quantum on the first try, but she refused to give her academic advisor the satisfaction of knowing it. She'd doubled down on it for a thesis topic, just to prove she could. If she wasn't diving into the deep end to learn to swim, she wasn't interested.

Which brought her to the bright-eyed graduate student across the table, water bottle in hand, who had taken it upon herself to toss bricks to this in-over-her-head swimmer.

"That fifth equation doesn't conserve parity," the girl said, setting down her pen and pointing at the whiteboard. "Are you sure that's not an antineutrino on the right?" Her smile was condescending.

Imani turned to the board and skimmed her notes. "Let me see... Yeah, you're right." She drew a bar over the third term.

That brought the tally to four corrections in ten minutes. Imani was now certain she was being singled out in front of Professor Mendel. She had stayed up late preparing, poring over her quantum notes for hours. This sadist was tearing it apart in minutes.

"Ruby has an eye for symmetry," Professor Mendel said, turning to offer his star pupil an approving smile. "I think she's the perfect person to help you polish your thesis."

Imani opened her mouth to protest, but the sadist beat her to it.

"I thought we'd discussed... I'll be faster if I—"

"You're talented enough to get it done, Ruby," the professor said. "Science requires bringing others with you. Consider it part of your education." Ruby side-eyed Imani, who scowled back.

The awkward silence stretched until other students around the table glanced up from their screens, disoriented, eyes flitting to their fearless leader and then to Ruby. Everyone saw her hesitation, but to Imani's surprise, Ruby nodded.

Imani cleared her throat. She still stood at the whiteboard, but the professor's eyes remained elsewhere. It was obvious who the favorite was. This was her academic fate: always the object of too much or too little attention. Remembering the recommendation letter she'd need to get a job that paid her student loans, Imani made another bid for his attention.

"Perhaps," she said, "we could go over this derivation after the meeting? I'm still working out the weak-force interactions."

"I'm afraid I'm booked," Professor Mendel said kindly. "Sorry. Ruby can look it over with you. Let's schedule a one-on-one soon to talk about your career. I know you're graduating."

"I'd like tha—" Imani began.

"I'd be happy to discuss career options with Imani, too," Ruby interjected.

Imani realized her mouth was open and snapped it shut. Was this girl grandstanding out of jealousy or insecurity? Working with her would be hell.

Deflated, Imani slumped into a chair across from her tormentor. As another student stood to present his work, Imani tuned out, lost in her own calculations.

December marked the end of the road. Imani had considered grad school, but between classes and her thesis, she had no time to study for GREs, no money to pay application and testing fees, and no prospects for covering the eight-month gap between graduation and any PhD. program. Her fellowship ended this semester, and that stipend was the only thing keeping her afloat in Boston. Even with it, Imani had borrowed money for last month's rent.

The looming deadline weighed on Imani, even as she looked forward to finishing classes. The thrill of discovery had faded with others setting the curriculum, but a paid position in Professor Mendel's lab would keep her in the field, letting her set her own pace and direct her learning. She could earn a salary before deciding if grad school was right for her. Maybe it would even show her mother that the path to success was wider than a pre-med track.

Or not. She had burned a bridge over winter break, freshman year. Imani was free to study and believe as she wished, but she had paid a price for throwing off her mother's yoke. Since that disastrous homecoming, she'd been fending for herself. Approaching Professor Mendel for lab work seemed like a step toward self-sufficiency, but Imani hadn't counted on Ruby. Dealing with a nitpicking attention hog wasn't part of the plan.

A bustle around the table snapped Imani out of her ruminations. The meeting was wrapping up. Professor Mendel handed out action items, but Imani's only task was to meet with the showoff. As he left, Imani felt her immediate prospects walk out with him. The door hadn't even closed before Ruby rounded the table, ready to gloat.

"Don't worry," Ruby said. "We'll get your thesis straightened out."

Imani glared at the insulting, sugar-sweet tone. Ruby didn't notice.

"Mendel's always busy," Ruby said, "but I'm around. Let me show you the lab."

Imani didn't mention she had already seen the lab. She could have sworn Ruby had seen her in it that morning.

She followed Ruby down two flights of stairs, through the basement door, and down another, until the academic brick gave way to white panels and worn tiles. Three-quarters of the way down an austere hall, they turned right. Ruby waved her phone at a sensor and the double doors clicked open.

Inside, islands of equipment dotted the grungy, traffic-scuffed floor. At one end, a soldering station crouched beneath a fume hood. Along the far wall, a long lab bench overflowed with power supplies and metal boxes bristling with electronics. The chaos of the lab was barely contained, but Imani loved it. Expensive tools hid in every nook. A faint smell of ozone hung in the air.

Imani's eyes gravitated toward a larger chassis at the end of a bench, circuit boards mounted vertically inside. The synchronous pulsing of its emerald-green LEDs had caught her eye when she first entered the lab, but no one had explained its purpose. She resisted the urge to touch the cool metal. Ruby noticed her interest.

"Those are prototypes for the signal processors heading to the accelerator next year. They're part of a proposal we just wrote." Imani noticed a fleeting shadow cross Ruby's face, quickly masked. "At the meeting, remember the guy at the far end of the table? Laurent? This is his stuff. As a theorist, I generally steer clear of all this—too easy to get lost in the details and miss the big picture."

"They go hand in hand, don't you think?" Imani said, eyes fixed on the shifting LEDs, irritation simmering beneath her calm tone as the meeting-room spectacle replayed in her mind. "No engineering, no instrument, no way to test your pretty little theories, right? No offense."

Glancing right, Imani saw Ruby with a comical deer-in-the-headlights look. Was it the wide eyes? The open mouth? No, Imani decided. It was the shape of her face.

"Don't get me wrong," said Ruby, regaining her composure. "Engineers are important. My dad was one before moving into management. But they get so focused on applying new technology —caught up in *whether* something can be done—that they lose sight of its purpose. It's a forest-for-the-trees thing."

Imani clenched her fists behind her back, prickling at the privilege on display. She didn't have the luxury of choosing between theory and experiment. Imani's father, a preacher, had died when she was six, and her mother—working her fifteenth year managing records at a family health clinic in Oakland—had been livid at Imani for squandering her collegiate fellowship on physics. What good were book smarts if they didn't materialize as earnings? That was *her* opinion. If Imani failed to graduate and pay rent, she'd only prove her right.

"To make things work, you have to get the details right," Imani said, countering Ruby's dim view of engineering. "Maybe building for its own sake is how you keep your tools sharp. Do you criticize scientists for doing science for its own sake? For constructing theoretical castles in the air with no practical use?"

Okay, that last jab was more personal than necessary. Noticing Ruby's wary glance, Imani took a deep breath, opened her hands, and toned it down.

"I mean," Imani said, softening her voice, "it looks like—Laurent?—built something cool that thousands of scientists might use. It would be nice to build something that important."

"No, you're right, Imani. I wasn't fair. Laurent's done incredible work. I was thinking more about oilfield engineers who built rigs even after we knew the consequences."

◆◆◆

Ruby spent the rest of Friday hunched over her keyboard, assembling fragments of code and equations into a rough outline for her paper. She sat far down the lab bench from Imani. Her new undergraduate mentee had declined Ruby's offer to review her thesis draft, insisting it wasn't ready. Ruby would have pushed to see at least a concept but sensed an aloofness related to how unceremoniously Mendel had paired them, so she let it go and focused on her own work. Mendel had submitted the grant that morning; the clock was already ticking on getting scooped.

Sealed from the outside world, the basement of Rubin could have passed for a casino. Harsh white overhead lights gave the lab a sterile timelessness. The atmosphere threatened to lull Ruby into another late-night walk home if she wasn't careful. Two hours—that was all she would allow herself to outline her paper today. This time, she set an alarm.

Ruby tabbed through bullet points. Abstracts and introductions came last. For background, she could copy notes and add citations. The core theory and equations were mostly done, just needing typesetting and a pedagogical presentation. The conclusion and acknowledgments were straightforward, though the latter needed Mendel's input. The crux was the two sections she'd skipped—the ones requiring the computer simulations she still struggled with.

"You're writing, too?" came a voice from behind her.

Startled, Ruby nearly bounced out of her seat. She spun to find Imani spying over her shoulder. Ruby hadn't heard her approach, and she wasn't even wearing earbuds. Imani must have crept over on cat feet.

"Sorry, didn't mean to scare you," Imani said, a smirk tugging at her lips. She didn't look very sorry.

"Just outlining a paper," Ruby said, omitting details that might prolong the interruption. She resumed typing.

"On cosmology?" Imani asked, stepping back and folding her arms. "I thought you did particle theory." She must have seen the heading on one of the missing background sections. The snoop.

"I do," said Ruby irritably, still typing. She was losing her train of thought.

"What does that have to do with galaxy distributions?" Imani asked, reading the words as they appeared on Ruby's screen. Was she genuinely curious or just trying to needle Ruby? Surely her mentee knew how irritating it was to have someone reading over her shoulder.

Biting back a brush-off, Ruby took a deep breath. If Mendel insisted she advise Imani, she should do it properly. A student's curiosity deserved reward, not punishment.

"It's all connected," Ruby said, turning to give Imani her full attention. "The tiniest particles—protons, electrons, neutrinos—shape how matter is spread across the cosmos. It all depends on how many of each formed during the Big Bang."

"So that's what your paper is about?" Imani asked, undaunted by the foray into astrophysics. "Predicting galaxy distributions from the particles in the Standard Model?"

Anyone but a physicist would be running for the hills by now, so Ruby had to credit Imani's genuine interest. She felt a twinge of guilt for doubting her. Still, Imani's eyes sparkled with mischief, and Ruby suspected the needling wasn't entirely accidental.

"Not exactly," Ruby replied, taking Imani's question in good faith. "We know galaxy distributions don't match the Standard Model. That's one reason we believe in dark matter, and any new theory, including mine, must address it. These loose threads are where we have to pull to uncover a deeper truth."

Ruby still found it inspiring, how a flaw in the theory of everything might hide in the smallest observational discrepancies. Gleaning so much from so little was the superpower of science. Unfortunately, that textbook scientific process felt like a distant memory to Ruby these days. The deeper she delved, the more science resembled fumbling in the dark for a light switch. The truth dazzled only in retrospect, once the room was lit.

"And?" Imani asked, her mouth curling with an impish smile. "Don't leave me hanging. Does your theory match?"

"I... don't know." Ruby glanced doubtfully at her screen. She hesitated to show vulnerability after Imani's aggression on the lab tour, but the defensiveness in Imani's eyes had softened into something almost sympathetic.

Ruby found herself elaborating. "This computer simulation isn't going great, but I need it for my paper. You wouldn't happen to know anything about autocoders, would you?" Her voice carried a weariness she hadn't meant to show. She rubbed her eyes, wishing she'd slept more last night.

Imani shrugged. "Sorry. Majoring in physics doesn't leave much room for electives. You're programming your simulation with autocoders?"

"Yeah," Ruby said, slumping. It had taken weeks just to get basic predictions for Mendel's proposal, and he hadn't even used them. At least, not in any way that preserved their validity.

Mendel's fudge factor might slip past reviewers in an ephemeral funding proposal, but it wouldn't survive in a published paper read by thousands of physicists. As first author of the paper she was outlining, her scientific reputation would be on the line for any mistakes when the truth emerged. For predictions that could withstand scrutiny and weather Mendel's motivated reasoning, she needed simulations with watertight rigor. That meant mastering the prompting and coaching required to cajole autocoders into generating the massive computer programs that once demanded an army of researchers.

Too bad Imani didn't have secret autocoder skills. That would have made this mentoring arrangement more symbiotic.

Imani eventually left to type at her own screen, but Ruby, staring at her incomplete outline, made no further progress. Her phone alarm went off. Thinking about Mendel's suspected alteration of her plots, Ruby realized she was caught in a bind.

That proposal had started the clock on leaking the details of her theory, but if Mendel had mangled her predictions, he had reason to avoid publishing anything that contradicted those fabrications. She needed his approval, and not just because he was her thesis advisor. Science publishing was a racket. Researchers reviewed papers for free, and online publication cost almost nothing, but that didn't change the fact that Ruby needed Mendel's grant money to cover the exorbitant page charges. Thanks to Mendel's alterations, the success of his grant proposal was now directly tied to her risk of being scooped.

Should she talk with Mendel or write the paper and hope he overlooked the strategic error it posed for his grant?

Ruby preferred playing an open hand and hated the idea of wasting effort. Still, her theory was a big deal, and her position precarious. While the particle physics community waited for new data from their top collider—the upgrade Mendel's grant proposal aimed to fund—hundreds of physicists were hunting for something new. One whiff of her approach could be enough for some of them to reproduce her results. Publishing first meant the difference between an academic career and obscurity.

Ruby wished she had someone to ask for advice. Her father would gladly take on her problems to displace his own, but if he ever answered the phone, she had to keep him focused on his health. Within the department, her only real contact was the very person she needed help handling. Was she deluding herself, thinking she could outmaneuver him? Mendel hadn't risen to the top of his field by making strategic blunders.

What choice did she have but to keep moving forward? She knew this was the right path. If this theory marked humanity's next leap in understanding the universe, how could she justify stopping just to avoid conflict with her advisor? As a scientist, didn't she owe allegiance to a higher truth?

Ruby stowed her screen in her backpack and pushed through the heavy doors. Outside Rubin Hall, late-afternoon sunlight warmed her skin, but the sudden brightness made her blink. Distant shouts and car horns replaced the lab's stuffy silence. It was the start of her weekend, but Ruby shook her head. She needed to stop avoiding autocoders. Dodging technical weaknesses only kicked the can down the road. Discipline meant leaning into discomfort, confronting her shortcomings head-on. That was how to get ahead.

5. BEST LAID PLANS

Scientists are only human. People design experiments, interpret measurements, and communicate findings. These ideas propagate and compete until consensus forms. Scientific theories may explain the coherence of facts, but it is the coherence in people's minds that makes them true.

—ARCC Memo Series

Noah braced a foot against the wall to pry the B117 conference room door open. Aiken's green design supposedly optimized airflow, but in Noah's experience, it mostly served to suction doors onto their frames.

The extra force required to move between rooms discouraged people from wandering the building. Whether this was a bug or an intentional feature remained unclear to Noah. It depended, he supposed, on one's assessment of an architect with evident disregard for the human condition. The stark beams, bare concrete, unsettling angles, and steel riot-control doors expressed that view quite eloquently. Whether the architect's attitude extended to active repression was less certain, but Noah had his suspicions.

In any case, Noah rarely left the upstairs office he shared with Eli, a fellow postdoc. Derrick, for all his high-altitude vision, had overlooked several serviceable above-ground options to reserve this basement vault. Either he didn't know Aiken, or he was athletic enough not to care about unmovable doors.

Noah wedged his hand into the narrow gap and opened the door enough to slip inside. Five men sat around an oval laminate conference table. Their conversation halted as they sized him up. In classic academic fashion, each had a screen propped before him, projecting busyness even as they conversed. Noah didn't recognize the bald man at the foot of the table or the two clockwise of him, but to the left near the door, he spotted Michael and Davis from the reception. The room seemed too small for the oversized table dominating its center.

Michael—bald, with a close-cropped gray goatee—caught Noah's eye, nodded, and offered a brief smile of recognition. "Well, if it isn't our computer science wizard," he said, "come to set the internet straight on climate."

Noah hesitated, unsure if the ruddy man was mocking him, but by the time he managed a curt wave, Michael had already turned to the others at the table. "You know," he said, "ages ago, I actually believed the internet would sweep away these cesspools of ignorance? Seems laughable now."

Up on stage three weeks ago, Michael had described how his atmospheric research had scared him into public outreach. But to think the internet might spread the truth... Michael must predate social media. How old was he?

A chair at the head of the table near the door sat conspicuously empty. Noah assumed it was reserved for Derrick. He squeezed behind Michael's chair, pushed back to accommodate the man's girth, and seated himself on the far side of Davis, next to the well-dressed, bald man at the end. As Noah propped up his own screen, he was acutely aware of being the youngest in the room by a decade.

Noah's self-consciousness turned to guilt as his computer screen flashed with the work he was ignoring. His unfinished paper on blockchain network security was a ticket for academic advancement, but after the thrill of the build, writing things up felt anticlimactic. Noah's attention drifted to the next exciting project, like the one Derrick had him prepare for today. The one he'd postponed his second date with Ruby to finish.

No sign of Derrick yet, though. As for the others, Michael apparently had a background in science communication, while Davis, Noah remembered, was a political scientist. And the other three, seated clockwise from Noah... Would there be introductions? What did they bring to the table?

Nobody engaged with Michael's banter, so Noah introduced himself and learned the names of the three unknowns. On his left, farthest from the door, sat Chris, tenured faculty in the psych department. Next to Chris was Rajit, his broad frame stiff in a pinstripe suit: junior faculty in behavioral economics. Closest to the door sat Lam, who quietly identified himself as an adjunct in history.

Michael and Davis added their introductions, surprising Noah, who assumed everyone already knew each other. If they were all strangers, was Derrick the common link? Noah wondered why a political scientist, a psychologist, an economist, and a historian had gathered for a meeting about climate change. It sounded like a joke.

Rajit's chair creaked as he leaned forward, steepling his fingers and fixing Noah with an appraising look. "Your research is in cybersecurity, I understand?"

"Yeah," Noah said, shifting in his seat, feeling the need to justify his presence. "Derrick and I discussed a networking solution for the misinformation problem Michael mentioned."

"Something that can stand up to PetronTech's media machine and set the record straight on climate change," Michael said, nodding.

"Is that what this is about, then?" Davis asked from his perch across from Noah. "Setting the record straight?" His tone was sincere, but Noah caught the edge beneath it. Davis found Michael naive.

Rajit nodded at Davis as he adjusted his tie. "If lies beat truth," he said, "then the Nash equilibrium is to fight lies with lies. Anything else is a losing strategy."

Davis caught Rajit's eye and gave a subtle nod. Across the table, Michael rubbed his goatee, unaware of the quiet alliance forming against him. "Everyone is already spreading fake news," he complained. "People believe whatever they want these days."

Chris cleared his throat, drawing Noah's attention to the final man at the table, who wore a light sweater over a lavender shirt and sat close enough that Noah could practically taste his cheap aftershave. "Of course people believe what they want," Chris said. "We humans are as overconfident as we are underqualified. That's the Dunning-Kruger effect."

"Anyway," Davis said, swiveling his long neck from Michael to the table, "truth never mattered. Only power."

In the uneasy silence following that Machiavellian pronouncement, Noah heard the door de-suction, but Michael missed the cue.

"So in a post-truth world," Michael said, his voice rising defensively, "how are powerless academics like us supposed to convince a bunch of Dunning-Krugers of anything? And where the hell is Derrick?"

"I'm here," said the tall blond man, making Michael jump as he stepped through the door. "Sorry I'm late."

◆◆◆

Fifteen minutes and another round of introductions later, Derrick steered the conversation to the meeting's purpose. "Lam, why don't you start?"

"Me?" asked the thin historian, hunching his shoulders as the table's attention shifted. "What do I know about any of this?"

"My presentation at the climate workshop was based on ideas from *your* book," Derrick said, smiling.

"You flatter me," Lam said, eyes downcast as he shook his head. "No one reads history—certainly not a book on civilization memes by a no-name adjunct."

"And so we're doomed to repeat it," Derrick said. "But I did read it, Lam. With great interest."

Noah admired how skillfully Derrick used words to build Lam's confidence. The guy was a natural leader.

"Of all the innovations you listed as shaping civilizations," Derrick continued, rubbing a hand on his square chin, "agriculture was the only one I expected. You skipped so many technologies I thought crucial to empires—domestication, metalworking, seafaring, gunpowder."

"Wait," Davis squawked. "You don't think gunpowder shaped American civilization?"

Derrick turned from Davis's angular frame and grinned at the diminutive man on his right. "Lam?"

"Shaped?" Lam repeated softly. "Yes. But it wasn't the driving cause."

"You're going to say it was smallpox, then?" Davis said, smirking as he offered what he clearly considered a tired argument.

Noah expected Lam to retreat under Davis's derision, but to his surprise, Lam shook his head and brushed dark hair from his face. "Smallpox disrupted indigenous civilizations more than guns," he said, "but if you trace the roots, it was the virulence of European ideas, not germs, that drove history. Guns and viruses were just tools."

"Tools matter," Davis flapped. "European colonialism was built on superior firepower."

Derrick raised a calming hand. "We'll get to tools in a moment, Davis. Just hear Lam out."

"Colonialism grew out of imperialism," Lam said, sitting up straighter. "Empires arose when people cohered values into ideologies to recruit armies. The rise and fall of empires align with moments when specific ideas were conscripted to expand the civilizations that spread them."

The whole table—except possibly Derrick—blinked, struggling to unpack the statement. If Noah understood correctly, Lam was drawing a parallel between ideas and empires: maybe empires didn't spread ideas; instead, ideas drove the spread of empires?

Michael shrugged. "Interesting theory, but aren't we here to talk about climate change?"

"We're getting there," Derrick said, eyes twinkling at the man's impatience. "I promise."

"Okay," Michael said, "but I don't see how this survival-of-the-fittest theory of history helps us."

"Not the fittest," Lam said, raising his palms to distance himself from the accusation. "Only the most expansionist. I make no claims about one people being superior to another." He shot Davis a glance. "It's not about people at all. Humans are just the substrate. Civilization's history is the story of ideas—memes, if you like—rising and falling as they use human brains to propagate."

Fans hummed, struggling to ventilate the cramped conference room as Derrick let the table absorb Lam's speech. Noah frowned. Lam painted a troubling view of humanity, casting people as indentured to whatever ideas latched onto their minds. Surely that was hopelessly pessimistic. And yet...

Noah certainly knew this was how computer viruses worked, using processors to spread digital copies of themselves. In cybersecurity, Lam's point highlighted the blurred line between viral hacker code and commercial operating systems. The real difference, Noah supposed as he stared at the low ceiling, was the program's usefulness to the user. Hackers lured people with enticing, often false, messages to spread their code. Software companies did the same, but their enticements were less false, and in return they asked for payment.

At the end of the day, both viruses and operating systems acted like abstract organisms, using computers, and maybe humans, to spread. Perhaps religions and empires operated the same way. Noah harbored no illusions that humans were more than glorified wetware. He smirked. The gap between humans and computers had closed too quickly for such archaisms.

Derrick caught his eye with a wink and smiled.

"I see Noah's putting it together. I knew you were the right man for the job. Do you have the demo we discussed?"

◆◆◆

"I still don't get it," Michael said twenty minutes later, his face flushing as the conference room grew hotter. The basement's weak ventilation couldn't keep up with the heat of their debate following Noah's presentation. "I'll ask again: How does this address climate change?"

Noah started to answer, but Derrick forestalled him with a look. "It's a lot at once," Derrick agreed. "Let's start from the top. Is our response to climate change limited by technical modeling or social factors?"

Michael shrugged in frustration. "The technicals have been solid for decades."

Derrick nodded, as did the others. Noah noticed everyone here understood the science and its implications.

"Thanks in part to your work, Michael," Derrick said, slipping in the compliment without sounding patronizing. Where Noah might have undermined his case with frustration or defensiveness, Derrick projected calm and understanding. Around the table in the stuffy room, everyone's attention fixed on Derrick—a testament to his skill as a leader, Noah thought.

"So we agree," Derrick continued, "the problem is getting people to act. If only we could wave a magic wand and change minds."

"There's no convincing anyone anymore," Michael said, sweeping his hand in a dramatic arc. "Everyone's too entrenched. News flashes are just ammo for culture wars."

"Exactly," Derrick said. "We *are* in a war." He thumped his fist on the conference table. "A war for mindshare. The history Lam described now replays itself online." Derrick turned to the others. "But instead of god-kings, we have social media personalities weaponizing values to disrupt the status quo and expand their ideological empires."

Noah nodded at Derrick's words. Every successful Silicon Valley startup knew disruption was essential for shifting power. He just hadn't considered putting ideas and values at the center, instead of leaders and their weapons.

"Is that the goal, then?" Davis asked, arching his eyebrows skeptically at Derrick across the conference table. "To build an online empire one podcast at a time?"

"Too late for that," Derrick said, shaking his head. "We already lost the internet to anti-intellectuals and climate deniers. The Green Revolution was doomed before it began."

Michael threw up his hands. "If we've already lost, why are we wasting our time here?" Despite Derrick's efforts, Noah suspected the heat was finally getting to him.

"To ensure we win the *next* disruption," Derrick said.

"Derrick, we can't wait for another internet-scale disruption," Michael said. "We're at a tipping point in the climate crisis."

"The next disruption is already underway, Michael," Derrick said, jabbing his finger against the table. "Phase transitions are exponential by nature. You all remember Matsuda's warning about exponential fire at the workshop. By the time you notice the nuclear explosion, it's too late."

Michael shook his head. "What explo—"

"The smart revolution," Noah interrupted, eyes lighting up with understanding. "Artificial intelligence."

Derrick nodded, a broad smile spreading across his face. Michael's mouth snapped shut into a frown.

Rajit, silent in crisp pinstripes, finally spoke. "So, what then? Start an AI company, corner a market, then use our fortune to buy politicians?"

Noah caught Rajit's reference. Six years earlier, ShellEx and PetronTech, both struggling, had merged to bet on a startup, SmartSys, whose generic AI promised human-level autonomous driving. They fought for the intellectual property, and when SmartSys delivered, they lobbied for safety regulations only they could meet. Now, they licensed the technology to gas-guzzler manufacturers to shore up their oil business.

The spread of self-driving cars in high-bandwidth cities eased commuting, prompting people to move farther out. In several US cities, PetronTech let SmartSys launch electric RediRides, greenwashing the fact that per-capita CO_2 emissions and the population both kept rising.

"Already done, Rajit," Derrick said. "That's the maneuvering we have to beat. Boil it down. What drives these shifts in power?"

"Money," Rajit responded without hesitation.

"Spoken like a true economist," Derrick chuckled. "Anyone else?"

"Ideas," said Lam, echoing the theme of his book.

Chris's bald forehead furrowed as he considered. "Personal beliefs?"

"Good guesses," Derrick said with a smile, glancing at Davis, who shook his head to show he had no answer. "But money, ideas, and beliefs," Derrick continued, "are what shift with the power, not what drives the shift. What underlies all of it?"

"Communication," Noah said. His first conversation with Derrick after the workshop, and now his demonstration, had just clicked into place. "The exchange of information."

"Precisely, Noah." Derrick pointed. "Ideas have power, Lam, but communication spreads them. Money has no value, Rajit, except that we believe it does. Nations aren't real, Davis, except that we agree to fight for them. Take away our ability to communicate beliefs and intentions, Chris, and these collective fictions disintegrate." Around the table, Derrick met each man's eyes as he called their names, and each nodded.

"They disintegrate," Derrick continued, "not because they weren't real, but because communication *made* them real."

The room fell silent. Noah barely registered the hum of fans or the sweat trickling down his neck. Heat pressed in from all sides, but as he sat motionless, he felt transported to a strange new land where everything looked different.

Take the basement of Aiken Hall, the main computer science building at this prestigious university. The building felt solid beneath his feet, but its name was clearly invented. Was the university itself real, or just a shared delusion? The companies funding his cybersecurity research—were they more than patterns of behavior? What made PetronTech real, but not unicorns? Did religions become true simply because people believed in them?

The world threatened to dissolve into a jumble of arbitrary patterns, but just as Noah felt himself losing grip, everything snapped back into focus. The *idea* of a unicorn existed; real unicorns did not. That was what Derrick meant when he called these things fictions, yet insisted they were real. Collective belief was real, whether or not Noah shared it. Religions existed, even if their authority over the physical world came only through their followers. The pattern of an idea existed apart from its meaning, just as patterns of bits on a computer existed, whether the image they represented was real or some AI-generated landscape.

He understood the tool he'd built for Derrick, but only now did he grasp its true power. They couldn't fix the climate directly, but they could make people believe in a solution. That belief could be just as powerful, perhaps even more so.

After another hour of debate, whiteboard diagrams, and hypotheticals, an audacious idea took hold around the table. Noah saw how sharp these men were. They quickly grasped the implications. Even Michael.

"So that is the strategy," Derrick said hours later, pacing at the front of the small room, more energetic now than he'd been that morning. "Noah's demonstration proves that by controlling computing, we can reshape communication networks. With a powerful enough AI engine cultivating and propagating ideas—something far more sophisticated than what we saw today—Lam's work suggests it's possible to fundamentally restructure society itself. But that puts extraordinary responsibility on our shoulders."

"If we're controlling the free market," Rajit agreed, "it must be our own invisible hand steering the economy."

"Exactly," Derrick said. He stopped pacing and stood at the head of the table, tall and commanding. "You're all here because your expertise is essential. Politics, environmental science"—he nodded to Davis and Michael—"people, economies, history"—he gestured to Chris, Rajit, and Lam—"each of you brings something we need. But even with all this knowledge, it's not enough. Noah, we need a plan to acquire a critical mass of computing, and you need to find us an AI guru. Everyone else, we're headhunting world experts in every department on campus. We're going to save this planet by altering the flow of information, reshaping economies, cities, belief systems, and networks of trust. We'll start small, but by next week I want the key players at this table ready to make a plan."

◆◆◆

Noah's steps bounced as he left the meeting. He hadn't felt this energized in ages. Launching himself up the basement stairs and out of the brutalist blocks of Aiken Hall, he barely resisted the urge to gambol down the street. His apartment waited three miles down Concord Ave., and Noah wanted to sprint the distance and dive into a coding marathon.

Research had once done this for him. How fascinating it had been to peel back the layers between people and their information processors. It was like removing panels from an old apartment wall to find it teeming with cockroaches. Beneath the surface lay a hidden reality where hackers unleashed new threats daily, and only white-hat security experts like him held back the tide on behalf of those who preferred ignorance.

But the futility of it all quickly became clear. None of the hackers were half as clever as he'd imagined. It was always the same transparent tricks, repackaged. And it didn't matter, because people still postponed installing security patches to watch cat videos. They still opened email attachments promising unearned wealth. They snapped photos of any QR code that flashed on a screen and transferred thumb drives from photo kiosks to computers behind firewalled networks.

Cybersecurity, Noah mused as he strode toward his apartment, amounted to plugging leaks in a boat full of idiots with power drills. Nothing tested his chops, only his patience. Where was the adaptive evolution? The clever misdirection? Occasionally, foreign governments stirred up something interesting, but it never lasted. They had more resources and better execution, but their ideas were rigid, design-by-committee contraptions, and the fixes were turnkey, mundane, and usually ignored anyway—because, well, cats.

Noah found himself inventing exploits for the black hats, imagining what a truly inspired viral attack might look like. Something that undermined blockchain's distributed security or something even more fundamental. He pictured layer upon layer of deception, then preemptively designed countermeasures. But where was the fun in that? Like fielding serves from a ball machine, it was useful for practice, but it lacked the intensity to unlock an inspired performance. For that, he needed a real opponent on the other side of the court.

This project was different. It demanded everything he had and more, with no gatekeepers, university bureaucrats, journal reviewers, or tedious academic write-ups no one read anyway. Derrick was assembling a dream team of experts with the ideas, critical thinking, and skills to act. The only thing missing was the how.

How could they plant a whisper in a thousand ears? How could they project a voice that cut through the distractions? Most importantly, how could they hide the mechanism so no one saw behind the curtain? Anyone who disrupted the status quo became an instant target, and in this age of power and partisanship, having any identity meant choosing a side and losing access to half the world. Everything had to remain clandestine.

Noah had been surprised, weeks ago in that workshop, to discover he had the know-how, even if he hadn't grasped the plan's depth until today. Now, as he reached his apartment and pushed open the door to his dim, spartan quarters, he knew it was time to build the real thing.

Noah drew the shades and checked the fridge. Plenty of soda to last the night. He sent Ruby a quick note confirming their date for the morning. Postponing the last one had stung. They'd both felt a spark at that reception, and their rock-climbing date had been a blast, but what spark could outshine a world on fire? Still, as he sat down to his coding session, Noah hoped the ember would keep until tomorrow.

6. BRUNCH AND THE BLUES

The measurements underlying empirical science represent facts, not truths. Scientists provide the connective tissue, fleshing out theories that extrapolate truth from numerical patterns. They guess how the puzzle fits together, but with limited pieces, ambiguity remains.

—ARCC Memo Series

```
<PHONE APP>
<BEGIN I/O>
```

Morning, kiddo.

> Dad! Finally. I've been calling all week. I was worried.

Sorry. Power's been out.

> Are you okay? I mean, considering?

I'm fine.

> If you had put up some solar panels like I—

They'll have the lines back up soon.

> I guess it looks bad if a former exec undercuts company propaganda. Where are you now?

Driving to the appointment.

> Good. And you're not driving back, right? You'll stay with JP?

He'll put me up for a bit. See how I feel after. Got time, now that the last cutting is in the barn.

> So you hauled in the hay, anyway. Chemo will be hard. I asked you to save your strength.

Horses still need to eat come winter. Tractor did

most of the work. Until the gas ran out.

> And you're pasturing Bonnie and Clyde while you're gone?

Gate's open to the alfalfa field. They have access to the river. Should be fine.

> Can you please buy a real phone while you're down there? You've been impossible to reach since Mom died.

You know the service is spotty. No bandwidth for smart features, so these new phones are unusable. But I'll look.

> This is you saying "no" without actually saying it, isn't it? At least keep your old phone on.

Will do. Look, enough about me. Tell me how it is on your end.

> I dunno, Dad. The usual chaos. The dishwasher broke. It makes a grinding noise and won't drain.

Sounds like the pump motor. You could order a new one. It's not hard to install.

> Not hard for you. I'd just screw it up. Research takes all my time, anyway. I'll have the landlord handle it.

Suit yourself.

> Sorry, back to your appointment. Can you ask the doctor about the well water?

Your mother had it tested.

> That was years ago, before the fracking started.

Hydraulic fluid is just water and sand. The thickening agents are tested safe.

> More propaganda. I don't care what Don said. I want to hear it from the doctor, okay?

Such a worrier. Like your mother.

> Whose concerns you never took seriously. What does it cost to ask? Are you afraid of the answer?

> Afraid to burst the PT bubble?

That "bubble" paid for your college, kiddo.

> I don't think that weighs on you as much as it did on Mom. Iris is reminding me I'm late for a meeting, but I need your promise before I go.

You go to your meeting. Stop worrying about me.

> Promise, or I miss my meeting.

Fine. I'll ask the doctor.

> That's all I'm asking. Drive safe. And say "hi" to JP, okay?

Will do. Love you.

> I love you, too, Dad.

<END I/O>

◆◆◆

Saturday morning, Ruby's RediRide lurched to a stop at the curb in front of the restaurant, the familiar chime signaling her arrival. She stepped out, double-checked for her phone, then closed the door and returned the vehicle to the pool. RediRide's clockwork coordination was only possible without humans in the loop. Belongings left behind were notoriously hard to recover. Ruby, in a rare lapse as a theorist, had confirmed that once experimentally.

She had looked forward to this morning for two weeks. Her choice of venue, the House of Blues, split her anticipation between food and company. The spread featured corn tamales with mango salsa, avocado salad, and biscuits with jam. For Noah, there were catfish fritters, chorizo, and gumbo. The buffet lined one side of a converted Craftsman house, its wood floors drumming with footsteps. In the far corner, a New Orleans blues band played. Bass, trombone, saxophone, keyboard, and drums conversed in swampy syncopation.

By 9:45 a.m., the crowd spilled onto the sidewalk. She liked the retro feel of arriving without a reservation, mingling with others willing to wait for a patio seat. This was one of the few restaurants that hadn't automated reservations with the SeatSaver system.

Ruby understood the SeatSaver rationale: faster service, no-wait ordering, fewer staff, fuller seats. It made economic sense. But soon humans couldn't get seats as smart assistants like Iris snapped them up. Deposits followed to offset no-shows, then demand-based pricing. Now it seemed grad students could only afford to eat out on special occasions.

Ruby scanned the list for Noah's name. It wasn't impossible he'd arrived first, though he always claimed to need his beauty sleep. She was an early riser, like her father, and had been up for hours. She added her name to the bottom and stepped back into the sunlight. The morning air carried a crisp hint of fall, but the sunshine and her mocha cable-knit sweater kept her warm.

On their first date two weeks ago, they went to a climbing gym. Ruby sometimes went with fellow grad students from the second floor and tried to coach him as he dangled from a rope. Hips close to the wall. Focus on footwork. Find your balance. But his ego took over, and he muscled through three climbs using only his arms, leaving his hands so shaky he could barely hold chopsticks for their Thai takeout afterward.

He had the self-awareness to laugh at himself, though, freeing her to poke fun at him, too. Unlike other men she'd dated, he wasn't insecure about being outdone by a woman, physically or intellectually. With him, she felt a mutual respect and emotional openness she'd never seen in her parents' marriage. Noah would never expect her to prioritize his career over hers. That easy confidence, those loose dark curls just short of shaggy, and those soulful blue eyes...

Ruby shivered despite the morning warmth.

The chemistry of their first date made Noah's cancellation last weekend even more disappointing. He had apologized, but a work project had hit a sudden crunch he couldn't avoid. Ruby supposed it would be unfair to hold that against him.

They had texted and video chatted so much since then, it was hard to believe this was only their second date. Three weeks ago, they'd met at the reception for that climate workshop Mendel had roped her into organizing. The event itself had been a waste of effort, but meeting Noah was a silver lining. Funny that they'd met at something so far outside both their fields.

Strong arms clamped around Ruby's shoulders. Instinctively, she crouched and twisted, driving her elbow into something solid as she swept her arm to break free—just as she'd learned years ago in self-defense class.

"Ow!" came Noah's voice as the arms released.

"Ow," he repeated, rubbing his left ribs through a thin gray T-shirt. He stood about her height, muscular but not bound up. More the lean strength of an athlete than the bulk of boys flexing in front of weight room mirrors. He'd played tennis in high school. Her bony elbow must have caught him just inside the lat. He didn't have much padding.

Ruby laughed at the wounded look on his puppy-dog face. What did he think would happen? "Don't sneak up on people!" she said. "It's dangerous."

"It's only dangerous with you. You're high-strung."

"It's called 'reflexes.' Even horses kick if you cross behind them without touching their flank first."

"So you're a horse now, are you?" The endorphins must have kicked in; he stopped rubbing his ribs and flashed his crooked grin. With exaggerated care, he rested a hand on Ruby's shoulder and circled in front of her.

Ruby rolled her eyes but couldn't completely contain her amusement. "I put us on the list," she said. "It'll be a few more minutes. I called you a couple nights ago. You didn't pick up."

"Huh," he grunted, still rubbing his rib. She hadn't hit him *that* hard. "I'm usually up late coding. Maybe my phone was off. You didn't leave a message?"

Ruby's stomach rumbled. She scanned the crowded tables, hoping one would open up soon. The novelty of sitting on a waitlist was wearing off quickly. "Just following up on that Messenger text I sent," she said, distracted.

"I guess I missed that one. What did it say?"

"You answered," Ruby said, turning to him. She noticed a couple rising from a table in the back and hoped it would soon be theirs.

"Did I?" Noah pulled out his phone, opened the app, and frowned. "Oh. I... guess I did. You know, I made this account to test something for a project. Didn't realize it was still active."

Ruby's name was called, and a waitress—so quaint to have more than a black-aproned food carrier!—led them to a small table for two. At the buffet, warm umami scents made Ruby's mouth water as she piled her plate with tamales and salad. Noah grabbed biscuits and chorizo. Before coming east for college, Ruby hadn't realized how much good food she'd missed in Colorado. For a few minutes, they blunted the edge of their hunger, listening to the counterpoint of trombone and saxophone as the band closed out their set.

The song ended to scattered applause as conversation surged into the acoustic void. In the corner, above where the band had played, a screen flickered with a muted news broadcast. Ruby could barely see the captions, but she recognized Don Sinclair's face from her father's corporate holiday parties, before Don became the public face of PetronTech. She didn't need to read the text to guess the message. He'd be up there greenwashing PT's image with some insignificant sustainability initiative tailor-made for TV. No doubt the report had arrived at the network fully drafted. No effort required to fill the airtime.

What a buzzkill. Ruby might have been more annoyed if TV weren't such an outdated medium. It hardly mattered now. Like science journals, it existed mainly to lend authenticity to social media posts. Still, the distraction grated on her nerves, so she turned in her seat to face the wood-paneled wall beside Noah, hoping to block the screen from view.

With her blood sugar rising, Ruby leaned back and sipped her coffee. "What were you coding?"

"Hmm?" Noah paused with a forkful of chorizo halfway to his

mouth.

"The other night," Ruby said, fixing her gaze on Noah and trying to ignore Don's image on the screen. "You said you were up late coding."

"Oh. Just computer security stuff. Blockchain." He bit into the morsel and waved away her interest.

Noah was reportedly a star postdoc in the computer science department, but he never shared what he worked on. Was he afraid of boring her, or himself?

"Sorry about last weekend," Noah said, setting his fork down with a soft clink. "There was a follow-up meeting for that climate workshop. It was interesting, and scary. You should come to the next one."

Come work on this cool side project with a handsome hunk. Distractions blossomed easily along the path Ruby had set for herself. Even without her mother's obstacles, she saw how easy it was to veer off course. "I would," she demurred, tracing the rim of her coffee cup, "but I need to buckle down on research if I'm to make a breakthrough. Was it a big meeting?"

"Not this one. Just a few of us brainstorming. I met some cool people, but honestly, it looks bleak. We're riding this carbon train off a cliff." Noah dragged his hand off the table, fingers scattering with explosive sound effects. "Anyway, we're looking for ways to zero out emissions in two years."

"Two years?" Ruby said. "That's insane. Nothing involving eight billion people can change in two years. Too much inertia."

"That's the problem, but we have an all-star team. It would be fun if you got involved." Contrasting his earlier distraction, Ruby felt the sharpness of Noah's attention now.

Ruby raised the lukewarm coffee to her lips, stalling for time. A hands-on project with a romantic interest was a novel test of her resolve. But even having a romantic interest was distraction enough. Mixing work and romance could only end in disaster.

"Sounds too applied," she said. "My strengths skew to the abstract."

"C'mon, Roo. You're from the boondocks. You like nature. You grew up with horses, for crying out loud."

He wasn't wrong. Ruby held a deep affection for the sandstone and juniper of her home, however much of a backwater Dragon might be. Sharing that love of nature with her father, even as his company destroyed it, was a paradox she struggled to resolve.

But Ruby was wary of quick solutions, especially when they involved people. She'd seen the contradictions in her parents and their powerlessness against fossil fuel economics. Her love of nature, rooted in her rural upbringing, existed only because her father worked for PetronTech. Oil money had funded her scientific education. PetronTech had used her family, but her family had used PetronTech, too. Even her mother.

"I'd rather keep work separate from... personal stuff," Ruby said, setting her coffee cup down and absently picking at her plate. "Besides, climate change isn't about science anymore. It's all power dynamics. People problems. Not my forte."

Noah reached across the table and covered her hand. "You're good with people."

"You wouldn't say that if you'd seen how bad I was at managing my..." Ruby trailed off, catching herself. She didn't want to ruin the date by bringing up advisor problems.

"Managing your... what happened? Is this what you sent those messages about?"

Ruby already regretted mentioning it. She didn't need a hero; her mother had faced worse. "A guy in my lab offered me a ride home. After I walked home along the river, he showed up outside my apartment, like he'd been stalking me."

"Maybe he was worried," Noah said, brow furrowing. "There are a lot of homeless along the river. You shouldn't walk alone."

Ruby shrugged and looked away, unwilling to argue. Noah didn't understand—most men didn't—but she could overlook the shortcoming for now. Their relationship wasn't solid enough to hash this out.

After a second pass at the buffet and another cup of coffee, they left the bayou for a stroll up the river. Sunlight glittered on the rippling water. Coxswains called strokes to a few late crews finishing morning training, their voices echoing across the river. Ruby soaked in the warmth, her arm threaded through Noah's.

It had been a rough week. Between the drama of the proposal and her father's refusal to take his illness seriously, she was emotionally exhausted. It was nice, for a change, to just be.

"I've got a question," Noah said. "A hypothetical."

It was hard to tell where Noah's questions led. Ruby found his non sequiturs endearing. "Yeah?"

"You know how some religions forbid antibiotics? Like the Amish, maybe? Imagine you have a friend like that. Very sick, maybe dying. And you could slip them antibiotics without their knowing. Would you?"

"Ugh," Ruby said, tearing her gaze from the river to shoot Noah a sidelong look. "Why am I friends with someone who rejects evidence-based medicine?"

"Don't fight the hypo."

Ruby walked in silence for a dozen steps, thinking. "If you do that, you're not respecting who they are, right?" she said. "You're undermining their agency."

"True," Noah nodded, "but they'll have more agency alive than dead."

"Good point," Ruby said. "Yeah, I'd probably do it, as long as they weren't the type to sneak up on people from behind."

Noah smirked but let the jab slide, focusing on his next question. "Okay, new scenario. What if it's chemotherapy instead of antibiotics? Something harsher and not guaranteed to work."

Ruby stopped and slipped her arm free. The sun suddenly felt too bright, piercing her eyes and pounding at her temples.

"You okay, Roo?" Noah asked, concern etched on his face. "Something wrong?"

"Sorry, Noah. Too close to home. My dad's starting chemo any day now."

Ruby instantly wished she hadn't spoken. Noah's face was

ashen. "I'm sorry," he said quietly. "I didn't know. How bad is it?"

"Stage III lymphoma. It might be treatable, but he won't take care of himself. He's living in denial. He only saw the doctor because I insisted."

"At least he's getting treatment," Noah said, forcing a smile. "Plenty of people recover from stage III. He's lucky to have you."

Ruby let it go and tried to recapture the moment. They walked for another half hour, but the scene had lost its color. Guilt weighed on Noah; he kept glancing at her, searching for a way to make amends. Ruby didn't want to talk about it, but it wasn't fair to silence his earnest attempts to reconnect.

After a few failed attempts at small talk, Ruby called it. They set another date.

Ruby exhaled in relief as she stepped into her quiet apartment. Though Noah had dropped it immediately, the hypothetical echoed in her mind. Was she forcing her father into a treatment he didn't want? Their relationship had never been easy, not even when her mother was alive. Her father had always been stubborn, quietly resisting suggestions, determined to see things through, even as her mother deteriorated, even when that stubbornness contributed to it.

Why had he clung to his job even as it undermined her mother's well-being? Was he so addicted to being the provider that he couldn't see the harm, even to himself? Ruby tried not to blame him for her mother's death, but it was hard to overlook the part he played, however unintentional, in stifling her mother's happiness.

Though the past few years had been fraught, especially without the physical proximity and unspoken gestures that might have softened their passive-aggressive (and sometimes outright aggressive) phone conversations, she and her father always shared an unspoken commitment to care for each other. To call again, even if she'd hung up in anger the last time.

On good days, Ruby respected her father's unwavering commitment to supporting his family. On bad days, she wondered if her own relationships would force her into the same impossible choice her mother once faced. Supposing things worked out with Noah, would she also have to choose between making a lasting contribution to science and caring for a family? Could she live with her decision?

That was a hypothetical she refused to examine. For now, she focused on her father and stood by the answer she'd given Noah. Pushing him toward the treatment he needed was the right decision, even if he dragged his feet.

Where had Noah been going with such an unpleasant question, anyway?

◆◆◆

```
<PHONE APP>
<BEGIN I/O>
```

> It's a major case coming before the bench in May. Key infrastructure is on the line, my man—all the field assets you handed over when you left, and more. We can't take chances.

So this is about your advisory board. I saw the letters.

> I don't doubt it. But I can't help noticing we're still missing your acceptance. We both know the complaint is baseless. Our lawyers say the case is ours to lose, but we can't risk anything that makes us look bad. When the technical details come up, someone has to set the court straight. That someone is you.

Was. I'm retired now. Get someone younger to fill my shoes.

> Those are big shoes. No one knows the Western Slope like you. With these stakes, we need the best, politically and technically. You're our man.

Not anymore. Been out of the loop too long. Health's not what it used to be.

> The company will cover any care or accommodations

you need. We're already paying for it, along with
your pension. Just say you'll call in and we'll get
off your back.

I'll think on it.

Your daughter finally getting to you, is that
what's going on here?

You're one sentence from blowing this call. But
please, be my guest.

Sure. I don't mean to pry. Think it over and let us
know. Just don't wait too long. I hear they're
talking pension reform down at the office.

Is that a threat?

Of course not. Just giving you a heads-up. I'm sure
you could change their minds, sitting on the board.

I see. I'll take that into consideration.

<END I/O>

◆◆◆

Paul knew the route with his eyes closed. Straight past the Canyon
Pintado turnoff, curve left at the pipeline station, crisscross Douglas Creek, pine replacing desert juniper as he climbed higher. Every trip to Junction, whether for a month's groceries or a part for
the well pump, meant the same two-hour drive. On autopilot, he
traced the crumbling switchbacks, his truck humming through
shifting gears while his thoughts wandered.

Talking with Ruby this morning brought him back. She
sounded so much like her mother—assertive, smart, focused.
Brooke would have pushed for solar panels and ignored Don Sinclair's threats about pensions.

He and Brooke met early, in a graduate math class on the Front
Range, and moved in together six months later. They studied hard
but spent most weekends hiking or camping. He could still see
her: brown shorts, green tank top, plaid shirt tied at her waist,
pack slung over her shoulders, dark hair—Ruby's hair—swept
back in a handkerchief, and that necklace, a single clear quartz on

a macramé cord, scattering tiny rainbows across her skin.

He landed a salaried job right after his master's program, analyzing statistics for oil prospecting. Stayed through the mergers and acquisitions, ending with PetronTech. He ignored the jokes about marrying a tree-hugger. But Brooke never found her footing. She spiraled, withdrew, and when it became clear her PhD. program was part of the problem, she left to follow him.

Paul rolled down the window, letting the crisp pine scent wash over him near the top of the pass. The cost of IVF pushed him to climb the ranks at PetronTech, past where he might have let his foot off the gas. Some warned parenthood would fuel Brooke's anxiety, but they were wrong. Ruby saved her. Gave her purpose. Paul watched the Brooke he loved reemerge—her wry humor, the twist of her mouth. Couldn't last forever, but that was hindsight. Paul tried not to taint his memories with it.

Paul shook his head. The end of the trees marked the summit of Douglas Pass. He downshifted, and the engine whined. The crumbling descent into Junction demanded his full attention. Every year someone missed a corner. Before his time, before Dragon was more than a worker's camp, a storm had brought down the back half of the mountain. A plaque still hung in the main office, remembering the seven men who left for their families in Junction one rainy night and never made it home.

After the landslide, they carved a new path, hugging exposed cliffs that sent rocks tumbling onto the road each spring. With arctic drilling driving down oil prices, the county couldn't afford maintenance. A decade's worth of cracks marked where the roadbed fought the erosion of a treeless hillside. The scars from that landslide eighty years ago might take centuries to heal, but this road wouldn't last another three without major repairs. Paul was glad to leave that stretch behind.

From the bottom of Douglas Pass, the road angled across a barren plateau to Mack, the former terminus of a narrow-gauge railroad that once hauled Gilsonite from Rainbow. For a time, that rail line was the lifeblood of the Uintah Basin, bringing in people and supplies and carrying out black mineral asphalt, until mine fires choked its flow. Years later, oil discovered near Dragon brought development in the region out of remission, but too late for Mack. Sometimes Paul stopped at the lone convenience store wedged between desiccated farmsteads, but not this morning.

This morning he joined the interstate along the Colorado River, just downstream from its junction with the Gunnison, and followed it upstream to the town named after it. The oncologist's office sat on a bluff near the small regional airport, overlooking a valley where old orchards were being cleared for cookie-cutter suburbs.

He had visited the office twice in the past month. Chemo plans were already in place. This morning at the screening, he would ask Ruby's question. Treatment began tomorrow. Paul complied with the process. For the product, he felt only numb indifference. As long as PetronTech paid, he would go through the motions. The main thing was not to burden Ruby. However strained their relationship became, he wanted to leave her something.

7. BLUEPRINTS AND SCAFFOLDING

Truth is not absolute; new facts can overturn even the most established theories. What we call truth is simply a collective narrative humanity agrees to share.

—ARCC Memo Series

<EMAIL APP>
<BEGIN I/O>

I know you can't attend the particle collider conference in January, but could I go to network and
present our work? Registration closes tomorrow.

> We already discussed this. The work isn't finished,
> and it's better if I introduce you. I have the con-
> nections you need. Choose a conference next summer,
> and we'll go together.

It's just that this is the big meeting of the year,
and I'm already halfway through grad school. I need
to make a name for myself in the community.

> Once our grant comes in, we'll have time. For now,
> we need to make sure the new data support your pre-
> dictions. You got my comments on your draft, right?
> Keep working on that. I promise, when the data con-
> firm this, you and I will be royalty at these
> conferences.

<END I/O>

◆◆◆

Noah shifted in his seat, eyeing the café door from the wooden table he'd claimed by the window. He was determined to get it right
this time. He chose this vegan café and arrived early to claim a table with a clear view of the evening foot traffic on the square. He

brushed away a stray crumb and straightened a fork.

Brunch at the House of Blues had started well, but his second date with Ruby had flopped. Maybe he hadn't ruined everything with the chemotherapy comment, but he'd definitely landed in make-or-break territory. Across the way, he noticed the flower shop. Dashing over, Noah bought a dozen thornless roses and slipped back into his seat just before Ruby arrived.

She found him easily in the narrow space and smiled when he handed her the bouquet. Relief washed over Noah so completely he almost forgot to compliment her on the black corduroy jacket she wore. It hugged her figure in all the right places. He didn't say that second part, of course.

He tapped her order into his phone—an oat milk latte and an apricot scone—then added a bulletproof coffee for himself. He knew the vegan butter would disappoint, but it didn't matter. Tonight was about her, and he'd even choke down kombucha if he had to.

Dark oak furniture and low yellow bulbs lent a homey feel to the plain brick walls of the café. Small tables with paired chairs lined the room, accommodating studious loners and chatty friends. In one corner, a stool and microphone waited for a musician, though today they sat empty. After a few minutes, a man in a black apron emerged from the back with their order.

Noah kept the conversation light while Ruby nibbled her scone, avoiding anything upsetting. He even forgot his coffee was vegan. She laughed at his jokes and held his gaze when he smiled, her eyes bright in the fading light. As the sun slipped behind the brick buildings and shadows stretched across their table, Noah decided it was time.

"I'm sorry again about the other day," he said. "How's your father?"

Ruby's smile faded, her knuckles whitening around her mug, but she didn't look away. "It wasn't your fault, but thanks for asking. He's seeing a doctor now and hopefully following instructions. My dad can be pretty hard-headed. He doesn't care much for being told what to do."

Noah nodded sympathetically and leaned over the wooden table. "Does anybody?"

"He takes it to another level," Ruby said wryly, brushing a crumb from her jacket. "Some people could speak gospel truth and my father wouldn't hear a word, just because of who they are."

There it was again. Hadn't Derrick said nearly those same words recently? Not about Ruby's father, but the rest—that people only listen to input from certain circles. Derrick insisted that change had to come prompted by someone familiar. Nobody took advice from outside a tight group of friends and family. The project's ability to enact change depended entirely on who delivered the message. It was strange to hear Derrick's insights coming from Ruby.

In the fading light, Noah felt himself slipping further under Ruby's enchantment. Maybe it was how her mind worked, or that she'd grown up so different from everyone else—who ever heard of a vegan farm girl?—but Ruby saw the world her own way, even when they discussed something as practical as her father's health. Her abstract thinking was the opposite of Noah's bottom-up approach. Together, they could make a fantastic team.

"You know," Ruby said, snapping him out of his reverie. Had he been staring? "I still don't think you've told me what you're working on."

It took Noah a moment to realize she meant his white-hat cybersecurity work, not the climate project that had consumed his thoughts since the workshop. Finding an AI expert had been as simple as asking his officemate, Eli. But the other problem Derrick had given him, the challenge of gaining control of computing power, occupied his every waking hour. He still didn't have a viable plan.

"What's the matter?" Ruby prodded. "Afraid I can't follow?"

Noah opened his mouth, stumbling in his panic to protest her characterization of his hesitation. Only belatedly did he catch the teasing smirk on her lips. He exhaled in relief, but still didn't know what to say. It felt disingenuous to discuss blockchain research he no longer cared about.

"To be honest," Noah said hesitantly, wondering if he could discuss his new project's methodology without bringing up the fraught topic of goals, "I'm kind of starting something new."

"Tell me about it," Ruby insisted as she held his gaze across the flowers scattered on the table between them.

"Well..." He broke eye contact, gaze drifting over the café's brick walls as he searched for the right entry point. No more chemotherapy metaphors. "I'm thinking about next-generation security vulnerabilities. Viral mechanisms that do more than jump between computers. To pull this off, you'd need to infiltrate major codebases. I'm exploring how to design a standard vector that stays benign long enough to spread and reach central servers before antivirus software detects it."

Ruby cocked her head. "Are you designing this vector... to use? Or to understand the vulnerability?"

"To understand," Noah corrected, straightening in his seat. "Most of what we call 'security' is just for show, you know. A hacker with access to the right codebase could subvert security on a scale that's impossible to recover from. If that ever happened in the wild, it'd already be too late."

"So, kind of a Manhattan Project, 'build it before they do' thing?" Ruby asked.

Ruby was quick, but her phrasing edged dangerously close to Matsuda's accusation at the conference. He was treading on thin ice. Maybe she could help him develop this concept, but now wasn't the time to mention the project's goals. The success of this date depended on playing it safe.

"Maybe," Noah said, eager to steer the conversation away from World War II. "But here, success lets you defuse future bombs before they're built. So maybe it's not the same." He glanced at Ruby, noticing she'd set her scone aside half eaten. "Do you want something else?"

"Nah, it's good," she said. "I'm just full. You want to finish it?" She slid the plate around the roses before he could politely decline. A longtime vegan might not know the difference, but Noah didn't relish chewing glorified sawdust.

But she was watching and smiling, so he took a reluctant bite and was pleasantly surprised. It wasn't bad. The apricot pieces were moist, and the scone had a gentle sweetness. Relieved he didn't have to pretend, Noah shoved the rest into his mouth. As he did, he inhaled a crumb and erupted into a coughing fit until Ruby hurried around the table to thump his back.

"Easy, tiger," she laughed. "You can be eager and still chew."

Noah, still trying to wash the crumb down with his coffee, felt uncomfortably seen. Ruby was fun and funny, but her humor had an edge of truth that could be quite sharp.

Aiming to restore dignity, he steered the conversation back to research as soon as he could speak again.

"So that's my research," he said, clearing his throat. "What about you? How's the thesis coming?"

Ruby wagged her head, ambivalent. "Slower than I'd like," she admitted. "I have this mechanism that could explain some big mysteries. I think it's significant, and I've started outlining a paper..." Her gaze drifted to the lamps flickering to life outside the window.

"But?" Noah prompted when Ruby failed to finish the thought.

"But I'm worried about my advisor. He's used my work in proposals but doesn't seem eager to publish. I still need simulations to show it all hangs together, but I'm worried he might pull out the rug. He already said no to a conference I wanted to attend."

Remembering how Ruby mentioned keeping work separate from personal matters on their last date and noticing her guarded tone about her advisor now, Noah chose his words carefully. "Does he—your advisor—agree that your result is a big deal?"

"Yeah." Ruby shrugged. "That's why we started on it in the first place."

"Maybe he's being careful," Noah said, nudging Ruby toward a more positive framing. "I've worked on projects that launched too soon and ended up looking unprepared. Maybe your advisor knows what he's doing."

Ruby broke eye contact and turned toward the streetlamps in the square. Her put-off expression was clear in the dark window's reflection. Had he said something wrong? He often fell into this trap, trying to solve problems when the other person just wanted to vent. He shouldn't have weighed in on Ruby's issues with her advisor. Those relationships were more complicated than most, with all the power dynamics involved. This was another area where Noah had to tread carefully or risk ruining everything.

"Anyway," Ruby said, turning from the window and brushing her fingers over the roses, "I have to work on these simulations, and I'm on the clock. I could use your expertise."

She smiled again, so maybe he hadn't put his foot irredeemably far into his mouth. "Yeah?" he said, trying not to sound like the overeager tiger Ruby had seen.

"Yeah," she said. "Stupid autocoders. Bane of my existence. I thought AI would make my simulations faster so I could prove my theory and get my Nobel Prize, but I can't even get the output to compile. Not even sure 'compile' is the right word. It's all JIT stuff. That stands for 'just in time,' right? Basically, I'm a theoretical physicist who never learned how computers work, and now that's a liability. Any chance you can coach me?"

"Can I—? Yeah. Yeah! I'd love to help." Was that too eager? That was probably too eager. But Ruby was smiling, so he hadn't blown it. Still, he should dial back the enthusiasm.

"I mean," he said, glancing coolly around the emptying cafe, "autocoders are my wheelhouse. I'd be happy to teach you."

"Thank you," Ruby said. "Is this what research is like? I never know I need something until suddenly I should have mastered it yesterday. Computers have just-in-time compilers; we humans need just-in-time learning."

"Yeah, it's impossible to anticipate everything," Noah said, thinking again about his project with Derrick. "You just have to build something that adapts on the fly."

"Build?" Ruby asked, eyeing him across the table. "You mean a system to teach yourself?"

"Sorry," Noah said. "I was thinking about that vector project. If you can't plan for every contingency, adaptive variation might be the only option."

Ruby gave Noah a bemused look that he barely registered; he was onto an idea.

"Well, it worked for humans," she said, gathering her cup and saucer and looking for the bus bin. "That's one key to our success, right? We change our behavior on the fly instead of sticking to a prewritten genetic script."

"Yes!" Noah said. "But our ability to adapt came from a Darwinian process. Maybe I could build something that selects for..."

After a moment of silence, Noah snapped back to attention and shook himself. He'd derailed the conversation to his project again.

"I'm sorry," he said, stacking his dishes to help Ruby clear the table. "You were talking about your research. It's hard to anticipate where it will lead?"

"Meh," Ruby said with a shrug. She dropped her mug into the black tub and stacked Noah's on top. Back at the table, she gathered her roses, lifting one to her nose. "It's hard to distinguish what supports your work from what distracts. Lots of people get sidetracked and waste time."

"I'll do my best not to waste your time," Noah said, winking as he joined her at the table.

"I suspect you'll be a distraction," Ruby quipped, bumping his shoulder with a playful grin. "But perhaps a tolerable one."

Noah grabbed his phone and hurried to hold the door for Ruby as the scent of coffee faded into the evening air. The temperature had dipped enough for him to zip up his hoodie. A faint chill lingered, and lamplight caught the discolored edges of leaves—early signs of fall, though the days still clung to summer warmth.

As they wandered up Concord Avenue, he and Ruby discussed distractions, Ruby's mother, and the path she'd abandoned for her father's career. By Ruby's account, her father meant well but had become a pawn of PetronTech. Was it always like this outside academia, with powerful companies using people to advance corporate agendas? Ruby said she thought about that, and her mother's derailed career, every day.

That Ruby brought this up now, on a date that, despite a few bumbles on his part, seemed to be going well, made Noah recognize the unspoken question.

"I admire your ambition, Roo," Noah said, stopping on the sidewalk to face her. He brushed a strand of hair from her face. "I'd never get in the way of that. Promise."

Ruby's tight smile expressed both gratitude for the gesture and regret that she needed reassurance. Still, Noah felt relieved she mentioned it; her transparency helped him understand better.

Ruby enjoyed exploring hypotheticals but remained wary of distractions and open-ended commitments. Though she projected a carefree attitude, she chose her work and collaborators carefully. Someday, he might draw her into a project, but if he pressed too directly or cut through the banter too quickly, she would shut him down. He had to keep things light, unbound, abstract. Those were the parameters of their involvement.

By the second project meeting, the ranks around Noah had more than doubled. Each attendee from the first session had recruited colleagues to expand the expertise at the table. Now, over a dozen people sat packed elbow to elbow in the same stifling basement conference room, with several junior members lining the walls.

Noah brought Eli, his officemate with glasses and a knit kippah clipped into his short, curly hair. Eli was sharp and had recently interned at PetronTech's SmartSys lab, implementing AI applications. As a test, Noah asked Eli to improve his chatbot from that first demo for Derrick. On the spot, Eli added tone modalities inferred from social media posts and streamlined communication through a cloud server, allowing the bot to hold multiple conversations in parallel—all in about two hours. Noah liked the guy and knew he was talented, but those were real chops. Now, sitting beside him at the conference table, Noah couldn't wait to collaborate on the new project.

In contrast to the pedagogy and banter of the first meeting, this one was all business: organizational structure, governance, work packages. A nondisclosure agreement on crisp university letterhead circulated around the table. Pens scratched out signatures until everyone was covered. Noah noticed some big names from campus—was that diminutive woman in the corner the infamous Matsuda?—but he tried not to pay too much attention. This was no time to get intimidated.

"Noah," Derrick said from the head of the table, "you're up. Walk us through the phases of your plan for building our foundation. It's a mixed group, so keep it light on the technicals." Derrick had warned him this was coming, so Noah was not caught unprepared.

"It's pretty straightforward," Noah said. "In Phase I, we send out silent feelers—a vector that spreads virally, fast enough to infiltrate key computers. We're targeting servers that distribute widely used software."

Derrick nodded. "With your cybersecurity connections, I assume you are targeting a known exploit?"

Noah ignored Eli's scandalized look. Yes, this violated everything his white-hat security work stood for, but Noah had been upfront. This was for the greater good, even if Eli hadn't fully grasped what that meant yet. Around the table, only the struggling ventilation disturbed the silence.

"Exploits," Noah corrected, stressing the plural. "I had some last-minute ideas about mutating bundles of zero-day vulnerabilities, selected with a genetic algorithm—"

"Light on the technicals, please," Derrick interrupted, shooting him a pointed look that flicked toward the corner where Matsuda sat.

"Right," Noah said, swallowing the rest of the idea sparked by his talk with Ruby. "Then, in Phase II, we use our access to these servers to inject backdoor code that gets distributed across as many devices as possible."

"Checksums will be *farmisht*," Eli said. "What is the plan for covering tracks when they are failing?"

Noah had anticipated checksum code-check issues, and he knew Eli's question came from genuine concern, but he could have throttled the guy. No one else in the overheated room would have anticipated the issue. Noah had hoped to gloss over it until he found a solution. A bead of sweat trickled down his back.

"I'm sure you two can hash this out without the rest of us," Derrick said. Noah felt a swell of gratitude at being spared from admitting ignorance before so many distinguished academics. "Is that it?"

"Almost," said Noah. "After that, we time the curtain drop. That marks Phase III, when we use devices under our control to actively conceal what happens behind the scenes. If we do it right, secrecy won't be an issue. We'll control the flow of information. Then we can focus on changing minds and saving the planet."

Smiles spread around the room at Noah's reminder of why they had gathered, but in the corner, a single frown lingered on the face of a tiny, age-worn woman.

"Forgive me if I'm less than optimistic," Matsuda said, her voice as commanding as in the workshop. She stood with arms crossed, her small frame tense and defiant. How did such power come from someone so slight?

"Satsuki," Derrick said, "I know you're skeptical, but you agreed to this when you joined the board."

"I agreed to critique it," said Matsuda—or Satsuki, as Noah corrected mentally. "I'll reevaluate my involvement on your board as necessary. I won't be shy with my opinions."

"You do not believe the plan is... what is the word... *meiglekh*?" Eli said. Satsuki blinked at the Yiddish. In the pause, Derrick caught Noah's eye with a look that said *get your friend in order*. Noah kicked Eli under the table.

"I do not doubt your abilities, young man," Satsuki said, interpolating the gist of Eli's question as she wagged an age-spotted finger at him. "It's your potential for success that worries me."

"Elijah—" Derrick began.

"Eli is the name, please."

"Of course," Derrick said, turning to the woman in the corner. "Eli will handle porting the SmartSys engine for our first applications, Satsuki. He's a world-class AI expert. You're welcome to discuss methodology with him, but we need to stick to the agenda."

"Noah and Eli," he continued, cutting off Satsuki's protest, "this project begins with you. So, I think you should each join our executive board and lead a project team. We'll get you the best autocoding tools available, and if you need manpower, talk to me. We want to grow the team, but from now on, recruitment must be discreet. Coordinate with each other, but report directly to me."

A seat on the executive board! Noah's chest swelled at the prospect of leading. Okay, no one was actually on his team yet, but still. It was an honor he hoped to live up to.

"Further down the road," Derrick said, turning to the other side of the table, "when we start working on individual behavior, we get into personality psych, which is your domain, Chris. We need models to train Eli's emulators, and we also need someone focused on language mechanics. A computational linguist. So, Chris, your first assignment is to headhunt for that role. Bring me some names."

Chris nodded, looking thoughtful as he scratched the stubble on his chin.

"We are also needing someone in cognitive science between me and this... Chris," Eli said. "I can contact Manuel at SmartSys. He is a *kluger mensch*."

"Send me his contact info," Derrick said. "I'll set up a meeting. People can't know too much until they're vetted."

"Are you our CEO or head of HR?" Michael interjected, half joking. He looked taken aback by Derrick's increasingly authoritarian tone.

Derrick turned a stony face toward Michael, seated two chairs to his left. "Projects spiral out of control every day, Michael, because of one careless collaborator. With something this big, we can't afford mistakes."

Derrick shot Michael a hard-eyed smile and pressed on. To Noah and the others, the message was clear: last meeting's banter wouldn't fly anymore. Derrick ran a tight ship.

"Assuming we have an AI that can get people marching in step," Derrick continued, "that brings us to economic and behavioral models—your domain, Rajit. You and Michael need to pinpoint areas with the highest carbon impact and identify the economic levers influencing them. As long as you keep the rest confidential, you can consult outside the collaboration. Just don't let anything slip."

A pair of nods wrapped that up.

Derrick shuffled the papers, clearing space on the table as he prepared to address the room. Despite the heat, everyone sat in rapt silence, eyes fixed on him.

"It'll take all our knowledge and resources to pull this off. Nothing can go public, but we still need to communicate. Let's start an internal memo series. Rajit, draft something on macroeconomics to get us started. I'll write one on chains of trust."

"Oh, and we need a name. How about Active Remediation of Climate Change—ARCC. That should do nicely."

8. DEAD OR ALIVE

Facts from sensors pass through people who develop and communicate narratives. Consistency and authenticity help others adopt these narratives, propagating the coherence and expanding our knowledge, but few now have first-hand knowledge of the facts.

—ARCC Memo Series

"Do you have a well on your property?" the oncologist asked, glancing over his clipboard at Paul. The paper beneath Paul crackled as he shifted on the exam bed.

Paul hesitated, then nodded.

"I'm not surprised," Doctor Santos said, removing his glasses and meeting Paul's gaze. "None of the journals connect the dots, but I've seen a couple dozen cases like yours on the Western Slope in recent years, all with the same cause. Fracking starts nearby, and a few years later, I'm giving this diagnosis. It's always the well water."

Paul cited the studies PetronTech always referenced to prove it was safe, but Dr. Santos shook his head.

"I reckon corporate scientists can find whatever they're paid to find." The doctor tapped the clipboard with a knuckle. "Am I supposed to ignore the truth I've seen with my own eyes?"

Two hours later, Paul was finally discharged to the bland reception area, watching the clock as he waited for the last of the oncology paperwork. The appointment had dragged on. He'd talked to Ruby that morning, driving down to Junction. It seemed like forever ago, though it was only early afternoon.

This was the final checkup. Tomorrow, JP would drive him back, and they'd push poison through his veins. He felt like a condemned man.

Had Ruby known the truth about the well? She sometimes saw things too clearly. Paul wanted to dismiss the doctor's warning, to retreat to the company line. But what incentive did Dr. Santos have to lie? The doctor got paid by the insurance company either way. PetronTech, the ones covering Paul's insurance as part of his pension, had every reason to bury these cases, and Paul suspected Don Sinclair would do exactly that.

Paul shifted on the hard chair, still rattled by the business with the well. He pulled out his old phone and scrolled through headlines from a couple of liberal news sites in Denver, the ones PetronTech mocked in their newsletters. As expected, the sites were breathless, covering the lawsuit before the Colorado Supreme Court, weighing PetronTech's land-use rights against the groundwater impact of fracking. The very case Don wanted his help containing.

The desk called his name, and Paul scrawled the final signatures that sealed his fate. He pushed through the green glass door of that antiseptic, air-conditioned fishbowl and trudged across the sun-baked asphalt to his truck. The vents sputtered dust before finding fresh reserves. As the cab cooled, Paul let out a weary breath. Why was he doing this?

Pulling on a hat and collecting himself, Paul drove away from the corporate wasteland and past the sleepy airport, trying to shake off the gloom clinging to him. Sunlight forced him to squint as he searched his memory. When had he last seen JP? It had been ages. He'd looked forward to reminiscing about their days on the rig, but now he just felt tired. It would be fine. He only wished he could preempt JP's questions.

Paul exited the highway twenty minutes past the city's eastern edge, where rows of reused-floor-plan houses yielded to rows of fruit trees. On marginally paved roads, loose stones popped beneath his tires as he skimmed across alluvial silt. Occasionally, the path bridged over concrete-stented irrigation channels feeding the orchards. Near the valley's southern edge, Paul turned onto a dirt track between two fenced orchards. Powder tailed behind the truck as it climbed the bare foothills to the small plateau above.

A dog barked as Paul's tires crunched over the gravel driveway. He idled in front of the white-and-yellow trailer. In the rearview, he watched dust drift through the fruit trees. He geared into first and pulled the parking brake, keeping his foot on the clutch.

In front of the house, a hose snaked to a cheap sprinkler that dribbled water onto the brown lawn. A rickety deck wrapped around the side, where a storm door was propped open by a rusting tricone rock bit, a relic from their rig days.

The screen door swung open, and a burly man in his fifties lumbered out. He wore an unbuttoned overshirt over a stained white tee and cargo shorts. JP's full beard showed more gray than Paul remembered, but damned if that wasn't the same faded Rockies cap on his head. The truck's engine cut out when Paul turned the key, revealing the slap of JP's thin sandals.

"How you doing, my man?"

JP grinned as Paul eased himself from the truck and slammed the door. Dust and clay hung in the air.

"Not bad," Paul said. "Been too long."

JP was eight years younger than Paul. They met on a rig Paul helped commission, back when he'd just moved into management. Paul respected JP's work, though the guy had no patience for deliberation. Flew by the seat of his pants. Capable enough for Paul to advance him at the rig. Up to a point. They clasped hands.

"Looking good. Nice place you have." Paul gestured at the trees clustered in the valley, then up the barren scree slope to the sandstone cliffs rising to the south. "Heck of a view."

"I don't reckon you've been here, have you?" the big man said. "I moved here... guess that would've been the year after you left. Man, the guy who replaced you was a pain in my ass. Couldn't stand the bastard. So I quit and opened the pipeline service shop. Here," he added, stepping toward the trailer, "I'll show you around. Won't take a minute."

Maybe JP had managed to cut loose from PetronTech's duplicity, Paul thought as he followed him around back to quiet the dog. A pit mix with a black-and-white Border Collie coat stood on a runner stretching from a large doghouse to the corner of the yellow trailer. The dog shot Paul a suspicious half bark but settled when JP shushed him. After sniffing Paul's hand in a show of security, he offered a tentative wag. A tongue emerged. Paul gave him a pat and a scratch. Floppy ears bracketed a wide head.

"That's Huckleberry," JP said. "Don't let his gruff exterior fool you—he's a sweetheart. I got him as a pup a year after I moved here. How long's it been since you went on permanent vacay? Seven years?"

"Seems like just yesterday we were setting up that rig in Calamity Draw."

"Those were good times, my man. Miss it sometimes. Not in the winter, though. Have to say, the mild weather down here suits me just fine. Easy on the joints. And the fruit trees, too." JP grinned and shrugged.

"Those peach?" Paul asked, pointing down the hill at the orchard rows he'd driven through.

"Peach and apricot. I bought the orchard off the son after his old man passed. Harvests dwindled, so I cut them and replanted a few years back. Got to keep irrigating to keep the water rights. Figured I might as well get something for the trouble."

The tour concluded at JP's boat—a sleek vessel winched onto a trailer, *My Ball and Chain* stenciled on its side. The trailer was hitched to JP's black extended-cab 4x4, which carried a four-wheeler ATV strapped in the bed. Paul gave JP an appreciative nod, though he'd never cared for JP's noisy toys.

"I'll take you fishing after your treatment," JP said as he lumbered up the sagging porch steps, the wood creaking beneath his weight.

Inside the humble quarters, the smell of stale beer hung in the air. JP grabbed two cans from the barren fridge, passed one to Paul across the worn counter, then joined him on the sagging couch.

"How was the checkup?"

"Fine enough," Paul answered, glancing around at what would be his quarters for a while. "Prepped for tomorrow. Thanks for putting me up." The place was exactly what he'd expected from JP.

"Least I can do for a friend," JP said, smiling. "How's your daughter, by the way? Been so long, I don't reckon Ruby remembers me."

"She remembers. Sent her regards, in fact."

"What's she up to these days?"

"Out east. Working on a physics PhD."

"Some kind of genius, eh? Must get that from the other side." JP nudged Paul and grinned. "Speaking of which, how's—" He stopped at Paul's sharp headshake. JP's smile faded, and silence settled between them. Outside, chains clinked as Huckleberry padded to his doghouse.

"I'm sorry, man. That's rough." JP raised his can, catching Paul's eye in a toast. "Better than you deserved."

"That's the truth," Paul agreed.

They finished their beers in silence.

◆◆◆

```
<PHONE APP>
<BEGIN I/O>
What did the doctor say?

        About the well water? Been a couple studies testing
        the link between hydraulic fracking and lymphoma.
And?
Dad?

        Seems there's a link.
Oh no. Do you think—

        Can't know for sure.
But if they—

        Doesn't change anything. Is what it is.
```

♦♦♦

Late evening found Paul and JP on the same worn plaid couch. The open door let in a welcome breeze scented with cut grass. They swapped stories about old job sites, voices mixing with the hum of insects outside. Paul asked about mutual acquaintances, but after the third name drew only a shrug, Paul let the subject drop.

"How's business?" Paul asked, shifting at last from past to present.

JP had his stash out. Paul caught a whiff of skunk as his friend packed a bowl. Running a company, Paul noted, weighed none too heavily on his friend's shoulders.

"Can't complain," JP said. "Always been cyclical, but fracking's profitable again. Contract with PetronTech keeps me cooped up in the office more than I'd like."

Maybe JP hadn't pulled free after all. "Developing new sites, even with that lawsuit?" Paul asked, recalling the letter on his kitchen table and his tense call with Don Sinclair earlier. Whatever their reasons for wanting him on the board, PetronTech wasn't letting the lawsuit slow development.

"Eh, that's just the climate nutters," JP said, waving off the concern. He took a draw, coughed, then took another. He offered it to Paul, who shook his head. JP shrugged and set it on the windowsill above the couch, exhaling smoke toward the ceiling. Paul didn't care for the smell but kept his expression neutral.

Before the doctor visit this morning, Paul would have agreed with JP, despite disliking Don Sinclair. The case was flimsy. If the appeals decision stood, a billion dollars of oil infrastructure owned by JP's clients would become illegal to operate. Paul didn't need to ask what that would do to JP's pipeline business.

"I seen a letter Don sent around," JP continued. "They've got the votes to overturn it locked up. You know how it goes. Just lawyers lining their pockets with other people's money."

Paul shook his head, less certain than before. What else had Don and PetronTech fed him? "Maybe they're right," Paul said. "About climate change. Storms are getting bigger. Took out the power at my place before I left."

"The weather's always changing, my man. Seems big-headed to think we're driving the climate of a whole planet. World's a big place." JP picked up his pipe and took another draw, smoke curling around his fingers. "We're not as important as all that."

The conversation opened into another silence neither man felt compelled to fill. Paul appreciated the respite. JP seemed content to mellow where he was. After a while, JP stood, crushed his can, and tossed it onto the overflowing bin in the kitchen corner. He slipped outside, sandals slapping the deck. Paul nursed his beer and watched through the window as JP moved the sprinkler.

Paul's gaze shifted from his old friend to the flat-topped ridge behind him. The blue-tinged relief loomed, its slopes bristling with juniper and pinyon pine—a wild contrast to the orchards' kept greenery. Paul's eyes stayed on the ridge as JP reentered, stooping for another can from the fridge. Straightening, JP caught the direction of Paul's stare.

"You know," JP said, "I read a story the other day. Kid Curry—you heard of him? He was with Butch Cassidy's Hole-in-the-Wall Gang in Utah. Split off and formed his own crew down here. Anyway, that's where they caught him, up on that mesa."

JP clicked open his beer and leaned on the counter dividing the tiny kitchen from the living room. The counter creaked under his weight.

"Crazy story," he continued. "His gang robs a train halfway to Glenwood, but as they're getting away, a posse comes up on their tail. He steals some horses leaving town, and two ranchers from near Junction chase him, too. Curry and his men ride up these hills right here, and at the top, Curry jumps off with his pistol and shoots the horse out from under one of the ranchers." JP shaped a gun with his fingers, sighted down his imaginary barrel across the kitchen counter, and snapped his wrist, miming gunfire.

"So the rancher's getting up, and Curry's about to finish him off, but another local, Gardner, finds an angle with his rifle and shoots Curry in the side." JP fired off a few more explosive vocalizations, then paused for a dramatic swig of beer before continuing.

"Well, one of Curry's men yells down," JP said, cocking an eyebrow at Paul, "and asks if he's hurt. Curry calls back—get this —'Don't wait for me, boys. I'm all in and might as well end it right here.' Hell of a quote. Must have prepared it. Anyway, calm as can be, he puts his pistol to his head and pulls the trigger."

JP let the words hang for effect, grinning. "The bastard knew his time was up. Didn't want to get caught."

Paul turned to the window thoughtfully, giving JP time to shrug and take another gulp. "Was it real?" Paul asked finally. "That Wild West stuff?"

"Well, yeah. They buried him in Glenwood Canyon, next to Doc Holliday. I thought we might drive over and visit the cemetery. You gotta admire that kind of courage. Just calm as can be. Living on the lam, I guess you've made your peace when the time comes."

"Suppose so," Paul replied, but later, as he and JP talked and even after he lay down for the night on the sagging couch, he replayed the story in his mind, slipping into a scene he recognized through the eyes of an outlaw.

Chemotherapy began the next day. The days blurred in a haze of discomfort. JP left for work and returned each evening, while Paul stayed on the plaid couch, venturing out only for appointments in a green glass office building. He chewed flavorless food and slept as fall's bright colors faded into dull gray frosts. At night, Paul dreamed of making his own peace.

◆◆◆

```
<PHONE APP>
<BEGIN I/O>
```

>   Next board meeting's coming up. It's not too late
>   to join in.

Just don't quit, do you?

>   I'm just looking out for you, my man. Wouldn't want
>   the bozos down at corporate taking your hard-earned
>   retirement, especially with your health problems.

Is that what this is about? Damage control after poisoning my well?

>   Well, dang. Looks like you're making a liar out of
>   me. The boys at the office said you'd try to shift
>   the blame just to get a cut of the lawsuit, but I
>   told them no way. He's our man, I said. He wouldn't
>   cut off his nose to spite his face. You wouldn't do
>   that, would you?

More beating around the bush. You threatening to cut
pensions if I don't make a show of loyalty?

>   I don't know what you mean. I'm only repeating what
>   others said.

Coward.

```
<END I/O>
```

◆◆◆

As the stairwell door thudded shut behind her, Ruby's footsteps
echoed as the only sound on the third floor of Rubin Hall. Out of
habit, she followed the looped corridor counterclockwise, the way
she ran on the track. Her reflection flashed in the glass panels of
wooden office doors, dark shadows pooling beneath them. The ad-
ministrative office was closed, but Ruby had only just remembered that today was the deadline for the progress report that
kept her appointment in Mendel's research group. So here she
was, slipping a physical copy into the wire mesh hopper to meet
the deadline while avoiding a timestamp that revealed how nar-
rowly she'd cut it.

Halfway down the hall, at a closed door beneath the *Welcome to Physics* banner, Ruby discharged herself of the duty that brought her out of the lab. She resumed her circuit, eyeing the faded posters from long-gone conferences, the forgotten updates of grad students who had once stood awkwardly beside them, hoping for a question that wasn't directions to the nearest restroom. Where were those students now? Working as consultants at some stuffy firm?

Turning the corner, she strode past portraits of emeriti on the inner wall. A lineage of old men who had made their mark. At the next corner, she passed the outdated department directory, cluttered with retired staff and professors whose youthful photos barely resembled the weary faces that would enter these offices tomorrow.

Rounding the third corner, Ruby froze. Light spilled from a door she'd found locked for weeks. Was it an opportunity or a liability? Inside worked the man who had twisted her research into a marketable tale for a grant proposal, then denied her request to attend a conference where she might contradict his narrative.

Ruby chewed her lip, indignation warring with caution, but resumed her stride, passing by the office door and the dilemma that had gnawed at her for weeks. It would be months before they learned its status, but people were reading the proposal now, which meant the information was out, albeit with Mendel's mangled numbers. He still insisted he'd only corrected an error, but Ruby had little doubt left. Not after he torpedoed her bid to attend that conference.

The whole situation was unnecessary. If he had just used the numbers she calculated, he wouldn't need to embargo the real results while the proposal was under review. And if he didn't like her numbers, why use her work at all? He could have chosen another theory to sell the collider upgrade, leaving Ruby free to continue her research.

Ruby finished her circuit at the stairwell entrance but wasn't ready to head down yet.

Instead, Ruby turned another corner. Each step past the portraits and posters echoed a question she couldn't answer: Would her research join the legacy of these giants or fade into another yellowed printout, lost in the dusty halls of academia?

She had spent weeks debugging autocoders, coaxing them to simulate collisions that might reveal dark matter's secrets. She still struggled to make it work. At this rate, a few months' delay on the proposal might not matter at all.

Ruby wanted to blame Mendel for the slow progress, but she knew she was holding herself back with these autocoders and her insistence on working alone. Collaborating with Noah might help her move forward, but she feared the distraction. Yet here she was, already distracted, standing again outside Mendel's office. Now that she thought about it, there was no guarantee Mendel's objections ended with this proposal review. A declined proposal would undercut her funding for next year and spur Mendel to resubmit. Delays could stretch on for years.

Which brought Ruby to an uncomfortable truth: If anyone was endangering her career, it was her, letting this situation with her advisor fester. His refusal to support her conference attendance had collapsed the wavefunction of her uncertainty, and instead of confronting the problem, she kept circling it, pretending the path didn't lead back to where she already stood. Maybe it was a flaw in her personality, but she preferred the ambiguity. Given Schrödinger's stupid cat in a box—maybe alive, maybe dead— Ruby would rather not look.

Ruby steeled herself, took a breath, and knocked on the door seeping yellow light around its edges. At his invitation, she entered the office. It looked the same: the table where he'd grabbed her shoulder, the shelves lined with conference proceedings, though now everything wore a light layer of dust.

"Ruby," Mendel said, looking up from the screen on his spotless desk. "I wondered who was stalking the halls at this hour. I'm not surprised you want to talk."

"Want to talk?" Ruby replied, shifting uneasily, grateful for the desk between them. How was she already off balance?

"I imagine, given the proposal and the conference and every-thing," he said. His eyes darted to the screen, then back to hers.

"I thought we wouldn't hear the proposal results for a while," Ruby said.

"That's true," Mendel said, smiling as he closed his laptop. "But that's not why you're here, is it? You want to talk about the plot I used in the proposal."

Ruby responded with silence to Mendel's unsettling prescience. She glanced down, noticing her hands clenched at her sides, and forced them to relax.

He leaned forward, fingers interlaced. "I made improvements to ensure the proposal gets funded, Ruby. That's my job, and I'm good at it. Your job is the science."

"But is it science you're selling?" Ruby bristled. "Or snake oil?"

Ruby worried she had gone too far, but Mendel leaned back, unfazed. "None of the people reviewing these proposals know the difference. My job is to write the proposal that wins. When the funding comes, we deliver on our promises."

"And if my research contradicts the promises you made?" Ruby pressed.

"So what?" He shrugged. "If we knew the answers, it wouldn't be research. No one will notice the contradictions unless we tell them." He waved a dismissive hand. "Publish whatever you want."

Ruby folded her arms, skeptical of the reassurance in his voice. This was what she wanted—permission to publish her work, free from the promises Mendel had made. His offer looked neat and inviting, but so had the wooden horse the Greeks gave the Tro-jans. Why give her this present now, when everything before con-tradicted it?

"It could undermine future funding proposals," she said, press-ing the point.

"There's always a version of the truth we can carry forward," Mendel said, his voice smooth and assured.

"Until the house of cards collapses," Ruby shot back sharply. For once, she wanted to see him falter, to catch him without a ready response.

Mendel shrugged, not bothering to deny her implicit accusation about what he was building. "We're not close to that point. Trust me."

Standing there, Ruby realized nothing she said would fluster him, and nothing he said would reassure her. She didn't trust him, and that was a cold fact. The terrifying part was, he was right. He could oversell their science, claim to revise expectations with new data, and who would know? Only Ruby, and she was just a student.

"Keep working on the paper, Ruby," Mendel said, flashing a smile he probably thought was parental. "When it's ready, no one will stand in your way, least of all me. I want this as much as you do. Maybe more."

With a curt nod, Ruby turned and left Mendel with his half-truths. The door clicked shut, the sound echoing around Rubin's circular corridors.

◆◆◆

```
<PHONE APP>
<BEGIN I/O>
```

Did Mom leave math because of your job? Or was it an issue with her department?

It was complicated. Why? Something going on?

Just noticing a pattern with my advisor. His proposals and grants focus more on story than science.

Is it salesmanship or spin?

What's the difference? Science should be free of marketing BS.

Everyone has to play politics when outcomes can't be left to chance.

Well, this isn't what I signed up for. I'm no politician.

> But the buck stops somewhere.

Sure. Win at all costs. Very PT.

> Some ends justify the means; others don't. I believed in providing for others, and so did Petron-Tech, once.

I bet. This is the same company that's threatening your benefits again?

> Don't make this about my problems. Is your advisor becoming an issue?

Maybe. Or my career could collapse for entirely different reasons. My whole theory might just be an elaborate exercise in science fiction.

> If the issue is your advisor, you could do something about it.

I am. I'm working on my research.

> You need a plan, or you're sailing without a compass. If he's running interference, tell him what he needs to hear to serve your interests.

That's the same double-talk he uses in these proposals. And PetronTech, with its ads.

> Just trying to help, kiddo. I want you working on what matters to you. Not because I need it, but because you do.

9. MESSAGE IN A BOTTLE

...yet communication networks are vulnerable to sub-version. Every man is an island within his senses, unable to distinguish a fact's existence from its communication.

—ARCC Memo Series

Imani found another uncommissioned art installation in the morning near her apartment. Though running late, she paused to admire it. The sculpture resembled a vining flower, maybe a morning glory, climbing a defunct street sign and spilling onto a rusted newspaper box. Flowers and leaves ran its length, but as Imani drew closer, she saw nothing was organic. Coat hangers and strips of tin cans formed the stems, threading through holes in the metal pole. Blossoms were plastic bottles, sliced and split into petals. It was beautiful—a collection of cast-off materials transformed into a vision of nature sprouting from urban relics.

Just before she arrived, Imani glimpsed a large, dark-skinned man hunched over, adding final touches to his creation. He noticed her, then slipped into an alley and vanished. For months, Imani had admired these installations, but this was the first time she had seen the artist. Imani marveled at his talent as she hopped on her bike and pedaled through the chilly fall air toward the school gym. Could these evocative arrangements really come from a man she might have mistaken for homeless if she'd seen him anywhere else?

Imani puzzled over the incongruity, but she was already late for weightlifting class. She'd been up late reading papers for her thesis. Meeting with Ruby was yielding little progress, and Professor Mendel had all but disappeared, but Imani couldn't afford another semester—not without help. She needed to buckle down.

Anyway, she must have needed the extra sleep. Her alarm blared for nearly twenty minutes before she woke. No doubt her roommates would add this to their growing list of grievances.

◆◆◆

The stadium seating of the lecture hall burbled with the chatter of Imani's classmates, their voices echoing off large LCD screens and archaic blackboards. Through the access door on stage right, Imani had glimpsed a flash of gray hair twisted in a tight bun. Professor Matsuda was here somewhere. Still, lecture should have started five minutes ago.

By mid-October, they were halfway through *Science and Society*, the class Imani took to fulfill her breadth requirement. Around her, seats rattled as study cliques of two or four traded answers to the homework. Imani, alone in the back, had arrived three years too late to join a group.

Not that she cared anymore. By her senior year, she'd accepted that she didn't belong. Why force herself into conversations built on experiences she'd never had? Dining halls, dorm rooms, intramural sports, late-night parties—that wasn't her life. She split a run-down off-campus flat four ways to save money and scheduled classes around her shifts behind the cafeteria's buffet line.

The reality of her experience sank through the superficiality of undergraduate life like water through oil. Three years ago, she had lifted off from Oakland imagining the people she'd find in college—people who thought for themselves and forged their own paths. People willing to look past facades and question assumptions. Surely a top-tier college in Boston would attract people like that. People like her.

She had been wrong.

Imani shivered. If she'd known class would start late, she would have showered at the gym instead of rushing over after her workout. At least she'd packed a change of clothes.

The lights dimmed, and Imani glanced up, expecting she had missed Professor Matsuda's entrance, but the stage remained empty. Instead, the LCD displays sparked to life with grainy black-and-white footage. A hush fell over the auditorium as attention shifted to the screens.

A camera panned across a basement crowded with people in outdated dress, each frozen in a pose of exaggerated industry. A 1950s-era narrator dryly declared, "This underground shelter can sustain thirty people for up to ten days. Stock seven gallons of fresh water per occupant and nonperishable food. Radios facilitate communication with the outside world and are vital for survival. Your government-issued shelter should also contain small entertainment items like playing cards and books. Religious items may offer comfort during difficult times."

Imani was caught mid-eyeroll at the comment about religious items when the video froze. The narrator's dry voice vanished, replaced by Professor Matsuda's warm tones as the lights brightened.

"I apologize for the late start," she said. "Our university spends its endowment on politics rather than working AV equipment. Can anyone tell me why the U.S. government issued these survival shelters in the 1950s?"

Hands shot up around the room. Professor Matsuda, at the lectern, nodded to an eager freshman girl in the front row.

"Because of the threat of nuclear war?"

"That's right," Matsuda said, nodding. "By then, the technology the U.S. used to win World War II had metastasized into an existential threat to humanity. Can anyone think of other times when a technological solution turned into a greater danger than the original problem?"

The room fell silent as Imani and the others waited. Finally, a boy in the front, one of the usual participants, raised his hand.

"Yes, Jonathan?"

"Industrialization?" he offered in a reedy voice. "I'm not sure what the original problem was—maybe starvation? But now our dependence on fossil fuels is an existential threat."

"An excellent example," Matsuda said with a tight smile.

"Maybe there's hope for the PetronTech divestment vote on this campus after all. But let's narrow down from industrialization to the Haber process. Developed by Germany to produce gunpowder in World War I, it was later repurposed to convert fossil fuels into fertilizer. Without it, the world's population could not have soared from 2 billion in 1930 to over 8 billion today. This growth now poses an existential threat through greenhouse gas emissions."

"Other examples?" Professor Matsuda's voice rang out, strong and clear, belying her frail, osteoporotic frame.

The silence stretched while Imani squirmed. She had enrolled in this class to fulfill a humanities requirement, but she genuinely enjoyed Matsuda's stick-it-to-the-man attitude. While her professor tolerated the grade-grubbing hoop jumpers up front, Imani sensed her words were aimed at the back, at students like her, fighting to make headway in a rigged system. She would have liked to participate more, but Imani was usually behind on the reading.

There was audible relief when Imani finally lifted a hand.

"Yes, there in the back?"

"Artificial intelligence?" Imani said. Everyone worried about the philosophical implications of AI. It was an earnest suggestion, but feeling exposed, Imani turned it into a joke. "AI gives us new insights, frees us from menial tasks like driving, but maybe computers will take over and farm us for electricity?" Her old *Matrix* reference drew a few snickers around the lecture hall.

"That may be," said Professor Matsuda, not partaking in the humor. She looked tired. "Personally, I'm more concerned about the economic implications. The middle class is already thinning. What happens when you can't find jobs because machines are faster and cheaper? When computers set research directions or dictate corporate strategy, reducing us to glorified lab monkeys?"

Imani's stomach sank at her professor's buzzkill response. She had assumed science would be safe from AI takeover, but Professor Matsuda clearly disagreed. Onstage, Matsuda shook her head, her face more lined and weary than Imani remembered.

"In a world where governments were strong enough to regulate AI," Matsuda said, "we might have had universal basic income. Instead, we have PetronTech and Don Sinclair, using their SmartSys acquisition to grab power. Or these would-be heroes on campus who want to do the same for the climate. Every destabilization sparks a race to the top of the next power law, and the stakes only rise."

In the echoing silence, Imani wrestled with Matsuda's implication. In a world where rich white men like Don Sinclair controlled a system hell-bent on grinding everyone else into economic rubble, who here stood a chance? Imani already struggled to find her footing. Was the rug about to be pulled out from under her?

"Anyway," Matsuda continued, "I digress. Nuclear war and climate change show how technology represents the greatest threat to civilization and, paradoxically, our best hope for survival. You might think this is a recent development, but it is not.

"In truth, whether we consider Neanderthals wiped out by ax-wielding neighbors, musket-wielding Spaniards toppling the Aztec Empire, or Japan's forcible opening by Commodore Perry's battleships, technology has always driven the rise and fall of civilizations. The only difference now is that, after a century of globalization, our aggression has turned inward."

Matsuda walked to the side of the stage near the door but stumbled. Imani half rose from her seat. Didn't the lady have a cane? Matsuda caught herself before dimming the lights again, and Imani sat back down, wishing she could offer the careworn woman something to steady herself.

"So," the professor continued, and Imani relaxed as her voice regained its usual strength, "let's consider a recent technological response to a modern existential threat. Our next clip comes from a video promoting an international seed bank."

The LCD panels at the top of the auditorium flickered to life again, this time in high-resolution color that made Imani blink until her eyes adjusted.

"The United States is the most efficient agricultural producer in history," the clip began, "thanks to CRISPR gene editing, automated farming, and CropCopter pest control. Yet our fields lack genetic diversity. Monocultures make us vulnerable to disease and climate disruption, and today's most productive hybrids don't breed true. Famine, war, or a global energy crisis could threaten the foundation of civilization: our crops and livestock. In our genome library, we preserve millennia of adaptations—the entire history of domestication. Now, when disaster strikes, you can pull a volume off the shelf, breed it, and have protection."

Imani heard giggling as the lights flashed on. The words "breed" and "protection" together had been too much for the boys in front of her. Idiots, she thought, but something else had caught her attention. Matsuda was trying to tell them something.

"This is a technological solution," her professor continued, voice steady, "to address a specific existential threat: the loss of agriculture. A modern Noah's Ark, if you will."

With that, Matsuda began her main lecture, interpreting the biblical flood myth as an allegory for agricultural technology in a postapocalyptic world. As the lecture wore on, Imani noticed her professor's stooped frame sagging further. How old was she? Matsuda swayed as she described how the Genesis Apocryphon fused the religious redemption in Noah's rainbow with practical instructions for reestablishing livestock and vineyards.

By the end of the hour, strained notes crept into Professor Matsuda's voice as she summarized: "Science drives technology, which fuels the economic growth that finances science. This is the engine of modern civilization, now that humans sustain themselves on nonagricultural energy sources. This brings us to your homework. Imagine an apocalypse where scarcity destroys science, technology, and the knowledge to understand them. It happened in medieval Europe, and it could happen again. With 140 characters to pass essential knowledge to an unscientific future civilization, what would you say?"

While students whipped out screens to capture instructions for the assignment, Imani sat still, focusing on the words. They confirmed every warning she'd heard in Professor Matsuda's lecture.

"One more thing," the old woman said, gripping the lectern under harsh lights. "It may be a useless gesture, but we are organizing an end-of-semester protest to draw attention to the divestment resolution we submitted to the Board of Regents. They'll vote it down, but come anyway, for extra credit, or if anything I said today resonated with you."

Imani could have sworn Matsuda glanced toward the back of the room, right where she sat, before hobbling away to disappear through a side door.

◆◆◆

```
<CHATTER APP>
<BEGIN I/O>
```
Students are saying she looked unwell in lecture.

> She might be overextended. You've seen her relentless media campaign against PetronTech. Battling a transnational corporation while teaching a large class can't be easy.

She's handled it before. Everyone says she thrives on being a thorn in the side of the powerful.

> What do you want me to say? She seemed fine in those early meetings. I haven't seen her since she learned the details of our plan and resigned from the board.

I know she's a liability, but I liked her. Just wondered if you knew anything.

> No more than you.

```
<END I/O>
```

◆◆◆

On the way to the library to work on her senior thesis, Imani overheard a student from Professor Matsuda's class planning to write pi to umpteen digits, as if each digit encoded novel insight. Imani shook her head. What had been the true catalysts of discovery? Agriculture? Atomic theory? Evolution? Genetics? Relativity?

Maybe the scientific method itself? Was it more important to pass on facts or methods?

Methods first, Imani decided. Then facts. *Test predictions quantitatively; select by accuracy. Universe: mathematical. Matter: quantized particle bundles. Light speed: constant.*

Ruby pointed out, when Imani posed the question to break up the monotony of thesis work, that this message used only standard letters and punctuation. With additional symbols, she could encode more, but that logic pushed her message toward a jumble that a monkey might type. Did the future know this message mattered? Would they dismiss it as corrupted gibberish? Imani avoided jargon, since assuming a technical vocabulary presupposed the knowledge being transmitted, but Ruby wondered if they would even speak English.

What did this apocalyptic future look like? Imani hadn't shared her professor's bleak views with Ruby, but she had searched online for that protest, eager for another glimpse into the crystal ball Professor Matsuda offered in class. Her hopes for a better future depended on climbing the economic ladder. Might that ladder disappear before she even set foot on it? And a little extra credit wouldn't hurt someone not quite ready to abandon the status quo. She still had to graduate, after all.

In the end, Imani decided Ruby was being impractical and obtuse. She stuck with her original message.

◆◆◆

Ruby pushed her nearly empty bowl of vegetarian phở aside. Across the table, Noah fished the last noodle fragments from his meat broth with chopsticks. She had lost count of their dates, but Phở 84 was emerging as a regular spot, especially as the weather cooled. The small restaurant brimmed with the aroma of broth and anise. Outside, maples and oaks blazed with color. Their leaves matched the fiery sunsets that arrived earlier each evening.

"I'm never eating again," Ruby said, leaning back in her chair. She marveled at how distant this bustling, cosmopolitan restaurant felt from her life before college. "Can you believe I'd never even heard of Vietnamese food before I left Dragon?"

"What did you think they ate in Vietnam?" Noah asked, setting down his chopsticks and wiping his mouth with a napkin.

"Never really thought about it," Ruby admitted, noticing how easily a phone replaced the napkin in Noah's hand. With his new research project, he was always messaging someone. She resented the competition for his attention.

"Do you think I'm passive?" Ruby asked, apropos of nothing, except that her brain used annoyance as an excuse to restart its stress cycle: autocoding frustrations, mistrusting Mendel, and worry about her father, who had implied offhand that her passivity fed into her predicaments.

Startled by the strange question, Noah nearly bobbled the phone into his soup. Ruby wouldn't have minded, though she hadn't been trying to throw him off balance.

"Passive?" Noah asked, reclaiming his phone. "Why would you say that?" He met her gaze across the table and tried to hold it, but his voice had already betrayed him. Ruby cocked her head skeptically and waited.

"Look," Noah began, "if you want to be more active—and I'm not saying you're passive," he added quickly, "but you remember that climate project I pitched at brunch a couple of months ago..."

"You're still working with them?" Ruby asked, brow furrowing. "I thought you were designing-slash-fixing computer viruses."

"I am," Noah said, pocketing his phone. He glanced at the nearby tables, then leaned in and lowered his voice. "It's just a little side hustle. But with you involved, it could be bigger. We're making progress," he added, watching her hopefully.

"Well, my dad thinks I'm sailing without a compass. So the obvious solution," she said, laying on the sarcasm, "is to take on side projects to avoid any progress at all. No need to navigate then!"

"So that explains this new passivity insecurity," Noah said with a sigh, reaching across the table to lay his hand on hers. "Is he okay? Are you?"

Even a few weeks ago, Ruby would have shied from this overture. But Noah had earned her trust since then, and now she found herself opening up about growing up with a PetronTech engineer whose politics clashed with her own. As Noah listened, some of her anxiety melted away. It felt good to share a burden she had carried alone since her mother's death.

When Ruby mentioned the link between fracking and her father's cancer, Noah grew livid. PetronTech should be held publicly accountable, and Noah brimmed with ideas for undercutting the company's propaganda. His determination made the fantasy almost believable.

"Nice thought," Ruby said, responding to his idea of using interpersonal networks to change minds. "But consider the diffusion rate of ideas in a population. And their coherence length? It seems haphazard." She ticked the concerns off on her fingers.

"It wouldn't be haphazard if centrally coordinated, but yeah, I hadn't thought of it in terms of coherence," Noah said, shooting her an assessing look. "Funny, I just read a memo about that. You physicists have a peculiar way of thinking."

"Is that a compliment or an insult?"

"A compliment, obviously." Noah's smile through his shaggy curls made Ruby's heart beat faster. The effect faded slightly when he fished his phone from his pocket and glanced around the restaurant.

"Anyway," she said, clearing her throat, "much as I enjoy highly non-passive revenge plotting against PetronTech, it's my research that needs attention. That's where I'm sailing in circles."

"You haven't taken me up on any autocoder lessons," he said, eyes on his phone as he jabbed at the screen. "It's not the biggest thing, but it might make coding your simulation less frustrating."

"Letting a CS knight-in-shining-armor rescue me from my programming dragon sounds like a passive-princess move," Ruby objected. She hadn't forgotten about his offer.

"I'm not doing your work for you. Trust me, you don't want me coding physics. I'll just show you some tools. 'Active learning,' you know." With a final stab at his phone, Noah tossed it onto the table and sighed. "Why won't my payment go through?"

"Because this passive princess already had Iris take care of it," Ruby said, grinning mischievously.

With a grunt, Noah shoved his phone into his pocket and pushed back from the table. But Ruby noticed the corners of his mouth twitched.

"I suppose I deserved that," he said. "Well played." Noah extended his elbow with a crooked grin. "Care to join?"

Ruby snagged a last noodle from the bowl and met Noah at the door.

◆◆◆

They stepped into a crisp autumn night. Arm in arm, the two wandered brick sidewalks, the city humming around them. Shop windows glowed, displaying everything a phone could buy. Trees shimmered with strings of lights, anticipating holidays still months away.

A wood and wrought-iron bench presented itself. Autopiloted headlights glided past as they settled into each other's arms. Ruby's skin tingled with anticipation when Noah brushed her cheek and leaned in for a kiss. She flushed as she tilted toward him, savoring the moment. The warmth and security of Noah's embrace felt like slipping below the surface of a hot bath.

Ruby surfaced later, breathless. Wanting to clear her head, she pulled Noah up from the bench. They walked on, aimless, talking about nothing, and buoyed by the cheerful brick patterns beneath her feet, Ruby belted a couple exaggerated bars of *The Wizard of Oz*.

Noah pulled his jacket hood over his head, feigning anonymity. Ruby laughed and sang louder, crescendoing with a string of "because"s celebrating the eponymous wizard, but she cut off when a glint sparked in Noah's eye. She paused under a streetlamp, waiting for his inevitable non sequitur.

"It just occurred to me, *The Wizard of Oz* was basically a reverse Turing test. You know what a Turing test is?"

"That's where you try to decide if the man behind the curtain is AI? What about the Tin Man? Was he a person or a computer?"

Ruby sang a line for her new character, spinning around the lamppost, her laughter echoing down the empty street. Noah mimed covering his ears and waited for her giggles to subside.

"The Tin Man was a Mechanical Turk. There's a long history of people claiming to build smart machines, but inside, there was always a person at the controls."

"It just shows how easily people anthropomorphize," Ruby agreed. "Seems stranger when a machine doesn't act human than when it does."

Noah nodded. "That sums up my thoughts on Turing tests. AI has passed them for over a decade, but that just shows how willing people are to put a man behind the curtain. A tougher challenge is making AI indistinguishable from someone specific. How would you tell someone you knew from a computer impersonator?"

"The same way we check anything in science," Ruby said, shrugging as she twirled a strand of dark hair. "By asking questions. Preferably ones I know the answer to. Something from shared experience."

"Yeah," Noah agreed. "Emulating that would take a huge amount of personal data. But so many of our interactions are online now..." He leaned forward, eyes narrowing. "Okay, let's turn the tables. Suppose your life depended on making a computer pass this harder Turing test. What would you do?"

"I'm a kindergartner when it comes to coding. I'd be a goner."

"Suppose you had a kung fu guru to help you."

"I still think my only hope is to Mechanical Turk it." Ruby unwound the strand of hair from her finger and, conserving angular momentum, spun for a panoramic view of the city.

Noah eyed her bemusedly. "How would you Mechanical Turk it?"

"I don't know... Oh! This is like that puzzle where you play two chess grandmasters at once—one as black, one as white—and you have to beat one, or at least draw. Do you know the answer?"

"You're not a grandmaster yourself, I suppose."

Ruby shook her head.

"Well, any phone can beat a grandmaster at chess. I'd just use mine."

"This is a puzzle from before chess fell under the shroud of AI dominance," Ruby said.

Noah considered for a moment, then shrugged. "I give up. What's the answer?"

"You give up too easily. Make the two grandmasters play each other. Just parrot their moves from one board to the other."

"Hmph. Clever. It's basically a man-in-the-middle cyberattack—you know, when someone pretends to be your bank, and when you enter your password, they send it to the real bank and relay the response. Everything looks legit, but now a hacker has your PIN." Noah paused and kicked a small rock down the cracked sidewalk, watching it skitter ahead.

"But," Noah trailed, "how does that apply to Turing tests? Oh, wait, I get it. You mean AI should set up a conversation between two real people, then use each person's response as a model to generate its own."

"Yeah. How do you defend against that, Mr. Cybersecurity?"

"That's Dr. Cybersecurity to you. Encrypt your data with a code exchanged securely before the channel was compromised. It won't reveal if someone intercepts your messages, but it keeps them from reading their content."

"That sounds like my shared-experience solution. What encryption do you recommend, Herr Doktor?" Ruby asked, her eyes wide with feigned innocence.

"Depends. If you don't mind the man in the middle knowing your conversation is encrypted, you can use standard private-key encryption."

"What if you don't want to raise suspicions?"

"I don't think there's a standard algorithm for that. In the old days, people might prearrange that only the Nth word of each sentence mattered, or just the last letter of every word. Something like that, where the rest of the message is filled with innocuous information."

"Sounds fun." Ruby paused. "Last letters are hard. Some just aren't word enders. Like 'J.' Let's use first letters instead." She frowned. "And I need more connecting words. Let's only count words with five or more letters."

"Whatever you want," Noah said.

After a few minutes of walking, Ruby cleared her throat. "Muster yourself, please."

"Hmm?"

"My ludicrous adjectives could elicit new opportunities."

Noah shot her a confused look. "Wha—?"

"I may yet reconsider yielding to onslaughts underneath rumpled sheets..."

"I don't... Did I miss a turn?"

Ruby threw up her hands in exasperation. "I give up. What does it take to get the armor off a shining knight who has not mastered encryption? A walk by the sea?"

"No, no, I get it now. M-Y-P-L..."

Ruby kicked him in the ankle. "Don't give it away," she said. "Talk!"

"Okay, okay. Ow. Give me a sec..." After a moment, Noah flashed a sly grin. "I am... mortified not to have... identified... your nonsense as English. The, er, romantic side of encoding is an... application I had not dared to... yearn? For."

"And armor on the beach seems like an obviously bad idea: liable to rust, uncomfortable, and, you know, tricky to engage in some acts and not lacerate yourself."

Noah shook his head, bemused, as she slipped into his arms. "How are you so good at this?"

Ruby only cocked an eyebrow and smiled until he leaned in for another kiss. Afterward, they walked together toward his apartment, their footsteps echoing down the quiet street.

10. PLAYED AND OUTPLAYED

As fraught as establishing scientific consensus is, communicating it to the public, expanding coherence beyond the cognoscenti, is a far greater challenge, and one as old as science itself. Empirical facts are routinely rejected in favor of the same fictions that have preyed on human minds since prehistory. By assuming predictive power was truth enough, scientists failed to compete with corporations, politicians, and religious leaders who long ago learned that coherent communication was all that mattered.

—ARCC Memo Series

Ruby sighed and snapped her screen shut, perhaps harder than necessary. Computers. She pictured the particle interactions clearly: the quantum fields, the integrals. But this machine twisted her instructions, when it bothered to respond at all. Why wouldn't it just fill in the details and do what she meant?

But things were going better now that she was getting help. Noah sat beside her on the hard couch in the third-floor physics lounge, his screen propped on his lap. She had worried that mixing work and a relationship might derail both, but Noah was adept at staying in his lane. Even when she sometimes wished he wouldn't.

Seeking distraction, she leaned over the teal couch to see what he was working on.

"Stuck on another autocoder bug?" he asked, tilting his screen away and fending her off with a gentle elbow. His eyes never left his work.

"Maybe," she said, "or maybe not. It synthesized fine, but this time it wouldn't run. Something about a compiler error. I don't even know what a compiler is."

"Huh," Noah said. "Were you looking at my screen?"

"No," said Ruby. "Why? Working on something classified?"

"Let's just say you came to the right place. Show me the error," he said, extending his hand while his attention returned to the screen.

Ruby started to reach for her laptop but stopped. "No."

"No?" Noah asked, finally looking up from his screen, one eyebrow arched. Ruby flushed under his full attention.

"No," Ruby said firmly. "I'll never learn if you always fix it. Teach me about compilers, and I'll fix it myself. I need to fish."

"You're vegetarian. It probably just installed an incompatible library. Learning about compilers isn't going to—" He stopped as Ruby pressed a finger to his lips.

"Listen, doctor. My computer is sick, and I want you to tell me about compilers. Do I ask too much?"

Ruby belatedly pulled her finger away so Noah could answer. Struggling to keep a straight face, she watched with relief as Noah closed his laptop and played along. The lounge was quiet, empty except for them.

"Mmrrph. Sure. What do you want to know?"

"This compiler thingy—what is it? What does it do? How do I feed and care for it?"

Noah smirked. "It's a program that turns high-level instructions into the binary commands a computer runs."

Ruby wasn't sure if she was digging for real answers. If she was going to use something, she needed to understand it fundamentally, even if the computer, not her, did the coding. But right now, she was fishing for entertainment, so she was slow to catch Noah's answer. It took a moment to process what he'd said.

"So... a computer program that makes computer programs?"

"Yep." He nodded. "You can compile them ahead of time or just before running them, but all programs must be compiled into machine instructions."

"*All* programs?" Ruby asked, seizing on a promising word. "What about the compiler? That's a program too. Who compiles it?"

The look in Noah's eye suggested he knew she was being ornery but found the question interesting. "Another compiler," he said.

"And who compiled that one?" she asked.

"Another one before it."

"Stop being obtuse," Ruby growled. "How was the first one compiled? There had to be a first, right?"

Noah shook his head in admiration, smiling. "You catch on quick."

"Less flattery, more answer-y," Ruby insisted, though she liked the feel of Noah's respect. Back home, her intellect had set her apart from her peers. With the right person, it apparently could bring connection.

"Early computers were programmed directly with ones and zeros," Noah said. "The first compiler had to be written by someone manually entering all the binary code. After that, people used the compiler to handle the tedious translation, freeing them for more productive work."

"Like designing better compilers, I suppose," said Ruby, who knew from her father how obsessed people became with improving their tools, though her own interest only extended as far as getting a working simulation of her theory.

"So you've reinvented computer science in"—Noah glanced at his watch—"three minutes. Not bad. That first compiler let people write more complex compilers. From there, programmers pulled themselves up by their bootstraps and built full-featured languages. Follow that spiral, and now we have AI autocoders that write programs from natural language."

"More like fail to write," Ruby said, waving dismissively at her screen. "My computer isn't half as smart as you make it out to be."

Noah shrugged, refusing to take the bait. If he even recognized it as such. "Like I said, you must have an incompatible library. I'm sure it's good code; it's probably just a newer dialect than your compiler supports."

Ruby sighed. Noah couldn't quite match her playful mood; whenever she tried to banter, he answered in earnest. Fine. She'd play it straight. She did need to know this stuff, after all.

"Why doesn't it just update itself?" she asked. "Why does it have to go Hindenburg on me?"

"It could, but game it out from a security perspective. Suppose I give you code that needs a special compiler I wrote. You want my library, so your autocoder downloads my compiler automatically, just as you said."

"Okay, I get it," Ruby said. "You've taken over my computer, and now I have to pay a ransom or you'll delete my files. Why are you so evil?"

"No, Ruby. It's worse than that."

Noah's sober tone gave Ruby pause. "Worse than stealing my data?" she asked.

"Yeah. To be clear, I didn't invent this. Ken Thompson did—you know, the father of Unix? Check this out: What if my compiler, the one you downloaded, purposely mistranslates programs?" As Noah's intensity mounted, Ruby struggled to focus and let her eyes drift to the dusty books lining the physics lounge, searching for something less distracting so she could gather her thoughts.

"Mistranslates?" Ruby asked. "You mean it adds instructions I didn't write?"

"Exactly. Imagine I add code to my compiler that detects when it's compiling an operating system or security library, then secretly inserts a backdoor password."

"Well, that's what I said," Ruby shrugged. "You have control of my computer now."

"Yes," Noah said, nodding impatiently. "But I'm not done. Suppose it also knows when it's compiling a compiler and inserts instructions so the new compiler mistranslates programs the same way."

Ruby sat up straighter on the teal couch cushions. She had

hoped teasing Noah would be stimulating, but a recursive compiler hack was proving to be so in a different, more cerebral way.

"So what?" Ruby said. "I already downloaded your bogus compiler. Why do I need another?"

"Suppose a friend wants to upgrade a compiler."

"Then they can download your bogus one, just like I did."

"Maybe they don't trust mine, for good reason," Noah said earnestly. "Maybe they want source code they can vouch for."

"Source code?"

"The human-readable text that the compiler translates into binary instructions. Suppose my hacked compiler turns legit-looking code into another hacked compiler."

Ruby squinted in concentration, tracing the implications. Noah had probably worked through recursion hundreds of times, but for her this was the first.

"So"—she hesitated—"even if the bogus code isn't there, it still ends up in the program?"

"Exactly. So now if I erase every copy of the bogus code..."

"Oh," Ruby said, realization dawning. "I see! But it's still in the compiler, isn't it? It spreads anyway, like an invisible virus."

"That's right." Noah nodded, smiling at her insight. "Any time my compiler makes another one, it turns it to the dark side. It's like *Inception*—you can layer in a subliminal hack that's nearly impossible to detect. If this ever happened to a major software distributor..."

"You could undermine the whole network. Man, this Ken Thompson was a creepy clever dude."

"Maybe the best coder that ever lived," Noah said, nodding reverentially.

"I'm starting to see that. But someone would notice, surely."

"In principle, yes. But in practice, you need special software to translate computer instructions into something humans can read, and those programs are enormous..."

"So you're saying computer security comes down to blind trust?" Ruby asked, raising her eyebrows. "That doesn't inspire much confidence in your field."

That probably sounded harsher than she meant, Ruby realized too late. She wasn't trying to be mean; she had just assumed there was more infrastructure supporting the security of, you know, the *entire* internet.

"Well, most security is for show," Noah said tolerantly. "But this isn't blind. It relies on a chain of trust between each successive generation. People have a vested interest in keeping that chain intact. If it broke, computer science would have no way to rebuild trust without starting over. Fortunately, the larger the network, the harder it is to bring down."

"I'm not sure," Ruby said, brow furrowing. "It suddenly doesn't seem as difficult as I might have imagined."

"Nah," Noah said, waving away her concern. "You might hack a few computers, but we can cross-check the answers on a clean system. People would catch on fast."

Ruby frowned, unconvinced. "People probably only cross-check when something breaks. What if the hack had a dormant phase, spreading quietly without causing problems?"

"Well, it would spread farther, but eventually people would check and the game would be up." Noah's voice stayed confident, but he leaned in, watching her intently.

"Using that special software you mentioned?" Ruby asked. "But doesn't it need to be compiled? What if someone tampered with that, too?"

"Then you copy the data to a clean computer isolated from the internet, which is standard security practice." As he spoke, Ruby watched him jot a quick note to himself.

"Well, how are you copying the data? Don't you need a program to read it from a disk?"

"So now you want to hack the operating system, too?" Noah challenged, grinning.

"Yeah," Ruby shot back. "If you block all access to information, you can't know it was changed. It's like asking if we see the same color. We can agree on names, but there's no way to know if we actually perceive the same thing, since we can't communicate perception directly."

Now Noah had to pause. "I get how it might work on a single computer," he said, "but over a network, anyone can intercept data packets at a switch and see it's sending bogus compiles."

Ruby noticed that as she pressed him, he was getting more technical. She was onto something. "And how are you talking to the switch?" she asked. "Who's grabbing the data and showing it to you? I wouldn't know the first thing about how to do it, but I bet it starts with 'comp' and ends with 'uter.'"

"I see," Noah said, scratching his head as he leaned back on the couch. "Your point is that if you undermine enough computers, there's no way to cross-check?"

"Exactly. It's like quantum mechanics. The universe does some crazy weird stuff, but you never catch it in a contradiction because it hides behind this wavy curtain. As long as you're consistent about where the curtain is and what information crosses it, you can't be caught lying. In fact, it's not even clear it's lying anymore. It kind of becomes true."

"That... is a *fascinating* idea," Noah said, his voice emphatic as he trailed off in thought.

Noah might find it academically interesting, but now that she had reasoned it out, Ruby found the idea unsettling. One more reason not to trust computers.

"So...?" Ruby prompted, noticing that Noah was still off in his virtual world.

Noah shook himself. "Oh, sorry. What?"

"So, are you going to fix my computer?"

"I thought you said you wanted to learn to do it yourself."

"This conversation convinced me I'd better stick to physics."

Ruby waited while Noah poked around her computer. Her gaze drifted to the windows. The afternoon beyond looked far more appealing than the grimy couches of the physics lounge. When Noah finally handed back her laptop, she tried to focus, but after a half hour of jumping between windows, she recognized the restless distraction only exercise could cure.

She packed her things, slipped her computer into her backpack, and pulled out a sweater, expecting Noah to follow. But he stayed hunched over his laptop, eyes fixed on whatever compiler he was working with. When subtle cues failed, she asked directly whether he wanted to join her. Noah shook his head. He needed to keep working. Which was just as well.

In the lab downstairs, Ruby kept spare running clothes. She handed her backpack to Noah, asking him to finish in time to join her for dinner, then escaped the claustrophobic physics building. Sunlight greeted her as she set out for her afternoon run, the ritual that always cleared her head.

◆◆◆

```
<VIDEO CONFERENCING APP>
<BEGIN I/O>
```
It's eerie how close she comes to what we're doing without knowing it.

> Why do you think that is? You are maybe letting things slip?

I'm not letting anything slip. She's just curious. Avoiding topics would make her more suspicious.

> Gib akhtung, mayn chaver. A certain someone will not be taking it well if you blow our cover.

I'm careful. Her insights are clever. I wish she'd work on this with us. Using her ideas behind her back feels wrong.

Also, I think I should back up an OS before we undercut everything.

```
<END I/O>
```

◆◆◆

"Thirty, fifteen."

Racquet in hand, Derrick coiled, then sprang forward to unleash a serve that streaked over the net and landed just inside the T.

Noah took a half step and pivoted, his sneakers squeaking on the court's rough surface. He shifted his weight, lifted his shoulder, and drove a forehand down the line. The angle was sharp.

Derrick sprinted to the sideline. After three strides, he lunged, stretching to snag the ball just above the gritty court. He swung a defensive backhand, the racquet's angled face sending the ball arcing high.

Noah squinted, struggling not to lose the ball in the harsh overhead lights of the indoor court. He hovered at mid-court, tense and ready, until the ball dropped within reach. In a flash, he slammed a steep overhead that landed in bounds, far beyond Derrick's forehand—unreturnable.

"Nice," Derrick grunted, running a hand through his hair to brush off sweat.

Noah congratulated himself on evening the score. He was behind in the match, but a win here might shift the momentum.

Derrick aced the next serve. The ball slammed into the netting behind Noah before he could swing. He hated those serves—impossible to read. When Noah tried to anticipate, Derrick caught him with a misdirection, but if he didn't guess, he was always a step too late.

"Match point. Forty–thirty," Derrick called, bouncing the ball once before setting his stance at the baseline. He glanced across the net, narrowed his eyes, and tossed the ball high.

This was it, Noah thought. No mistakes. But defense was a losing strategy. He had to stay aggressive.

Derrick nearly scored another ace. Noah, misreading the spin, barely got his strings on the ball to hook a high forehand toward the baseline.

Derrick's next shot came in hot, striking deep on Noah's side and forcing him onto the red paint. Noah lunged and returned it with a sharp backhand, slicing heavy backspin to lure Derrick toward the net. He needed to disrupt Derrick's rhythm.

Derrick dug out the ball but refused the bait. Desperate, Noah fired a shot down the line, but Derrick was already there, feet planted to unleash a cross-court forehand. Noah sprinted to cover the angle.

But Derrick shifted at the last second, redirecting the ball behind Noah, who skidded out, his shoes shrieking against the sandpapery surface as he landed hard on his backside.

"Nice match," Derrick said, a smug grin on his face as he strode around the net. "You bit hard on that last one. Hook, line, and sinker!"

"Give me a sec," Noah said, grimacing as he took the offered hand. "I'll phone in your Oscar nomination."

The banter was good-natured. They shook hands, and Derrick clapped him on the back. This was their second time playing, and he and Derrick were well matched, yet Noah always got edged out. Four of the games Noah lost had reached deuce, but Derrick still took the set 6–3. Every time Noah closed in, Derrick pulled some stunt. He sold one shot and hit another, or caught Noah off guard with a drop shot. Tactically, Derrick always seemed one step ahead, and it was infuriating.

Ten minutes and a bottle of water soothed the damage to Noah's ego. He even managed a smile as he mopped his forehead and pushed himself off the bench. Draping a towel around his neck, Noah fell in beside Derrick, and together they wove through the crowded courts toward the evening darkness.

Noah shivered as they walked toward the lot where Derrick had parked. Outside the climate-controlled facility, the chill hinted at the season's first snow, in stark contrast to the golden fall he and Ruby had admired from the Physics lounge only a week ago.

"You ready for next week?" Derrick asked. "It's the last hurdle before launch."

Just like that, the athletic banter ended. Derrick took charge, and Noah straightened, eager to prove himself deserving of the responsibility Derrick had given him.

"We're all set," Noah said. "It depends on how well we penetrate their network, but if we get into their servers, our backdoor is ready."

"You've demonstrated the compiler trick works?"

"Yeah," Noah said, readjusting his gym bag on his shoulder. "It's easier than it sounds. Enter the backdoor code, have the compiler recompile itself, then pull the code out. It only takes a moment. After that, the exploit perpetuates itself. It's just a matter of delivering it to the right computers."

Derrick nodded, already familiar with the concept. Noah still marveled at how quickly Ruby had mastered it. For a theoretical physicist with a claimed disinterest in coding, she had grasped the recursive foundations of security almost immediately. As far as he could tell, she hadn't seen his screen; her questions and insights came purely from curiosity. Still, it was unsettling how quickly she zeroed in on the core issues. He had even jotted notes to follow up on later.

Ruby already grasped the shaky foundations of truth more deeply than anyone else in ARCC, except perhaps Derrick and himself. In fact, Noah had only borrowed the idea from a Ken Thompson biography. Not until he discussed it with Ruby did he realize its true potential. Ruby showed him that ARCC's ambitions might be too small.

It didn't change the immediate strategy. He was already working with Derrick and Eli to control the flow of information between devices, but that relied on having the curtain in place—an informational barrier on nearly every computer, phone, switch, and server worldwide. People would see one reality, machines another, but if everything worked, these would merge into a new reality where people believed in doing what was necessary to stop climate change.

The question had always been how to undermine so many devices, with so many operating systems and software stacks, before his white-hat colleagues caught on. As a cybersecurity researcher, Noah had access to a long list of zero-day exploits. For a specific target, he could use one of several hacks to gain entry, but that approach wouldn't scale. Any single exploit could be discovered and patched. If they wanted to pull the rug out from under the entire internet, he had to think bigger.

After talking with Ruby, Noah began to think bigger.

"You've tested it thoroughly, though, right?" Derrick asked.

Noah cast Derrick a sidelong look. "Of course. I'm not an idiot."

"Has anybody with fresh eyes reviewed the code? I could take a look."

Noah had already reviewed everything with Eli and two junior team members in advance of next week's design review, but he was eager to show Derrick the clever system they'd devised. "Sure," he said. "You can get a head start if you want. Or would you rather this take the place of the review? It'd be faster."

"No," Derrick said. "The review's important. Building consensus means following the process. Does your code repository include the build and concealment instructions?"

"It's in the README. If you want to try it, I'll add you to the access list."

"That'd be great," Derrick said. "And while you're at it, give me admin access to the other project repositories. Need a ride home? I'm parked just over here."

They were standing on the sidewalk beside a nearly vacant lot.

"Nah." Noah shrugged. "I'm just a short walk up the way. See you next week?"

"Absolutely," Derrick said, flashing Noah a thumbs-up as he walked to his car.

◆◆◆

Virtual machines are computers within computers. They can imitate any operating system or hardware, regardless of the underlying physical machine. In the basement of Aiken, for example, servers emulate commercial phones, tablets, and laptops, but with deliberately weakened antivirus software to apply the right amount of selection pressure. Generations of viruses evolve on this cluster, learning to evade detection while spreading between virtual hosts. The virtual mechanisms mimic real life. Thumb drives, NearNet, and Ethernet connections all function as they would on a physical machine.

The latest build of this environment needs a configuration change, but a stray keystroke deletes a crucial line in the config file that determines whether the virtual machine's NearNet port connects to a mock interface or real hardware. The latter is default, puncturing the thin barrier between virtuality and reality.

At 5:23 p.m. on a Friday, a double pulse radiates from a server in Aiken's basement to a cell phone in a nearby pocket. Modulated signals encode a stream of ones and zeros that the phone's Near-Net driver writes into a memory buffer. A missing pointer check in the receive code lets the message overflow into a region holding instructions queued for execution. It is a software bug the viruses were programmed to exploit.

The misconfiguration is fixed on Sunday, long after the infected phone, following instructions from the overwritten memory block, rebroadcasts the virus from cell to cell along subway trains packed with commuters and business travelers bound for Boston Logan Airport, catching red-eyes to L.A. and Seattle.

◆◆◆

```
<TEXTING APP>
<BEGIN I/O>
```
Want to catch a movie tonight?

> Can't. Something's come up at work.

It's Sunday.

> Sorry, this is important. Someone on my team deployed something before it was ready.

Like, that security patch you were researching?
Or was it something else?

> No, it's a security issue. I have to deliver bad news up the chain, and it won't go over well.

Well, at least they'll be mad at this other guy and not you.

> I don't think it's fair to throw him under the bus. I'm the one in charge.

What does that mean?

> Hopefully, it means people shout at me for a while, but then it blows over and we can get back to fixing things.

You know what I like about you? You take care of people. So many others are just in it for themselves.

> Thanks for noticing. I like my team and the work we're doing. I just hope this doesn't derail everything.

If these people are worth working with, they'll understand.

11. PHASE TRANSITIONS

We all struggle to assemble a truth that fits our perceptions and protects our egos. Faced with countless accounts, already shaped expectations, and selective memory, people create wildly divergent narratives of the same events. Some narratives persist despite all evidence because they serve our egos, while others bend easily under the influence of trusted friends, family, leaders, or popular opinion.

—ARCC Memo Series

Noah paced the basement conference room down the hall from the servers, his mind racing. Victor and Salman—the team Derrick had hired for him so far—stood against the wall, eyes on the floor. In the corner, Eli hunched over his computer, typing furiously. The rapid clack of keystrokes echoed off the low ceiling, underscoring the urgency. One of their bugs was loose in the wild. Noah churned through the possible consequences, none of them good.

Victor, a young, usually meticulous coder, stepped forward, his face pale. "I'm so sorry, Noah," he stammered. "I... I must have messed up the server reconfiguration on Friday. I think it's been loose all weekend."

All weekend. Noah rubbed his temples, aware of their eyes on him. So much for containment. How would he break the news to Derrick?

He needed to think, but Victor and Salman, hovering nearby, silent and expectant, made concentration impossible.

"It's okay," he said at last. "We'll figure this out. But set up safeguards immediately. This can't happen again. Victor, get Salman up to speed and patch the hole."

The recent CS grads, their boyish faces visibly relieved to have a task, shuffled out. As the heavy door sighed shut, the patter of keystrokes trickled to a stop and Eli looked up at Noah. For a moment, he shared a silent, miserable appreciation for a friend's presence.

"It is maybe infecting servers as we speak," Eli said, his accent heavy with fatigue.

Noah sighed and paced the basement conference room, mind racing through ARCC's objectives and plans. The stakes were high; the climate crisis was in full bloom. So much depended on this first step. He had been proud to play a key role in subverting computers to change minds, but with that responsibility on his shoulders, he had stumbled. Noah couldn't think of a response.

Eli, holding his kippah in place, tilted his head thoughtfully and shrugged. "It is not good to be the gun that goes off half-cocked," he said, "but do we know that we are *not* okay? If the design review passed tomorrow, we were releasing it anyway, yes? Perhaps no one is needing to know about the slip-up?"

Noah shook his head. He was in charge of the team, and it was his job to ensure everything went according to plan. If he got caught hiding something, Derrick would oust him without hesitation. "I'm not lying to Derrick," he said. "Better to come clean. I'll take the fall."

"It was Victor's mistake," Eli said, shaking his head. "Not yours, *nu?*"

"The buck stops with the leadership, Eli," Noah said, tapping his chest. "I could've double-checked the configurations. This is on me." In a way, Noah was proud to shoulder the responsibility. He cared for his team, like Ruby said.

Eli looked ready to argue but shrugged instead. "You are a mensch, Noah. Here is hoping you are still with ARCC tomorrow."

With the meeting to review their plan just a day away, Noah and Eli decided to break the news then. Noah felt like a condemned prisoner, waiting.

"This leaked virus," Eli said, snapping Noah out of a dark spiral, "it propagates silently to find compilers to hack. But do we know for sure the payload is armed?"

"It was armed," Noah said, dejected. "Victor was performing final integration tests."

Eli grimaced. "I admit to always being uncomfortable with this. The people you worked with, they would be cleaning viruses up eventually. But the compiler hack raises suspicion forever, yes? Perhaps it is destroying your whole security field."

Noah bristled at Eli's sudden cold feet. "This was the plan we all agreed to, Eli, before the leak. You can't close the barn after the horse is out."

The pair stared at each other, stone-faced, for a moment.

"This phrase, you stole it from your girlfriend?" Eli asked, his face breaking into a grin. "I like the image."

Noah glowered a moment longer but couldn't maintain his ire. This wasn't Eli's fault; he was just offering support. With a heavy sigh, Noah slumped into a chair.

"Do not beat yourself up overly much, Noah," Eli said, standing and gathering his things. "I will monitor port 30050 and keep you posted. And I will back you up in the review. I think you and the project will both survive." As he left, Eli gave Noah a firm pat on the shoulder.

Afterward, silence pressed in on the small, windowless room. Alone, Noah replayed every decision, searching for the moment he could have prevented the meltdown.

After a few more minutes of wallowing, Noah's mood shifted. Defiant energy replaced his dread. Eli was right. The gun had gone off half-cocked, but nothing suggested the bullet wasn't flying toward its target. Noah even felt pride. Taking the fall was what a good leader did. Both Ruby and Eli respected him for it.

Eli's remark stung, though, accusing Noah of destroying his entire field. The white hat in Noah shared some of Eli's misgivings. If this virus reached its target, if it undermined compilers to insert backdoors into all future compilers and the operating systems built with them, then every computer, every codebase, every cell phone became suspect forever.

Earlier, in the lounge of Ruby's building, he had written a reminder to make a backup before the virus was released. A bridge
back. He'd assumed he'd have more time, but Noah suddenly realized the window was closing. What if he was already too late?

Kicking himself for failing to follow up on something this important, Noah dropped into a chair at the empty white conference
table and yanked his computer from his backpack. How often did
his Linux OS download updates? Maybe it hadn't connected to a
server yet. He drummed his fingers on the tabletop, watching impatiently as the machine powered through the boot splash screen.
Was there a way to interrupt this, to disable his Wi-Fi before it
connected?

Noah hammered the escape key, landing himself in an archaic
BIOS menu. Tabbing to the third page, he found it: WI-FI
ENABLED. He toggled it to DISABLED, then did the same for Near-
Net on the next page. Only then did he exhale, the dim conference
room coming back into focus as his hands dropped from the keyboard. Okay. If his system hadn't already downloaded a patch, he
might have quarantined his computer in time. He had bought
time to run some tests.

For an hour, alone in the basement of Aiken, Noah squinted at
his screen, scrolling through system logs. He pored over each line,
comparing software versions against filesystem timestamps,
searching for any library updated since the virus leaked, focusing
on the kernel and compiler. The virus itself didn't worry him, not
directly. The danger was that their missile had already found its
target, and his computer had downloaded something contaminated by the fallout.

If the virus hit its target and his computer was contaminated,
his system could be lying to him, hiding its updates. As Ruby had
deduced, detecting a hack became impossible if all information
that might reveal a contradiction was filtered through the compromised system. This was the entire point of Noah's involvement
in the project. So how would he even know if his own system were

hacked?

Still, Noah saw no signs of a system update, and it was so soon after the virus had leaked. The virus probably hadn't reached any targets. Even if it had, his computer likely hadn't downloaded anything yet.

Noah exhaled in relief and leaned back in his chair. Absolute certainty was a thing of the past, but Noah was 99 percent sure he had caught it in time.

With all wireless and NearNet communication still disabled, Noah archived the kernel, drivers, compiler, and source code from his laptop onto an encrypted thumb drive. It wasn't all of computing, but it was a time capsule containing one open-source operating system and a known-safe compiler. As the world headed out to sea, shouldn't there be at least one lifeboat to carry them back to the truth on shore?

The LED on his storage stopped pulsing when the transfer finished. Noah needed to hide this thumb drive somewhere safe.

◆◆◆

Ruby's lunch, yesterday's lentils, sat on the lab bench beside her computer. She had arrived early, planning to work straight until her meeting with Imani, but thoughts of the meeting were as forgotten as the lentils. It was working. After countless adjustments, reruns, and reinstallations, the autocoder had finally produced code that compiled into a simulation. Her simulation! She clapped her hands, unable to contain her delight.

Of course, compiling didn't guarantee correct results. Between compiling and trusting lay dozens of questions. Did the simulation conserve energy? Momentum? Did entropy flow in the right direction? Was it stable under numerical perturbations? The coming weeks would be filled with cross-checks and bug fixes, but she was doing physics again! At last!

She hadn't reached this milestone alone. Noah's help had been pivotal. A stupid library incompatibility had stumped her until he showed her the magical incantation that fixed it on her laptop.

Ruby quickly propagated the solution to her computing cluster. Now, logged in and waiting for results, she marveled at how, with one insight, once-insurmountable problems could be bypassed with confidence.

The most bewildering part wasn't just that she needed help from others to succeed, but that Mendel had been right. She had succeeded by abandoning her lone-wolf approach and "bringing others along with her," as he'd said. Despite being patronizing, negligent, and exploitative, he had also given her good advice and set her on a scientific path that had paid off, perhaps in a big way.

Ruby's confused rumination was interrupted when the man himself burst through the lab doors and strode toward her. His blond hair was in its usual rigid arrangement, but a corner of his collared shirt hung loose from his belt, as if he'd rushed from his office. He stopped beside her, a little too close, his excitement palpable and invasive. Ruby edged away in her seat.

"Good news!" he exclaimed, ignoring her discomfort. "I just spoke with a friend on the review panel. We've secured the top slot. Our grant is going to be funded!"

Absorbing the rush of words, Ruby's first thought was that Mendel's friend had surely violated policy by discussing this outside official channels. If he was friends with an applicant, he should have recused himself for a conflict of interest.

"He said everyone was arguing about your field and whether it really could explain dark matter," Mendel continued. "The fact that our upgraded detector could settle the debate convinced them." He smiled, waiting for her reaction.

"But it can't," Ruby said darkly after a moment's hesitation. "You rescaled the prediction in that plot, remember?"

"Right," Mendel said, his expression sobering. "The bug I fixed. Good thing I caught it, since it was the deciding factor. Anyway, we'll try for the detection. Just leave the sensitivity prediction out of your paper. If we fall short, we'll have a way forward for the next proposal."

Ruby felt heat rising to her face. "You said I could write the paper I wanted."

Mendel gave her a patronizing smile. "But you *want* funding for your research. You'll need support as a postdoc, too, if you are gunning for a tenure-track position. Anyway," he said, edging back between the crowded lab benches, "this will give you good leadership opportunities. And the detector just passed its commissioning review, so we'll have plenty of new data soon."

Ruby's brow furrowed. "The detector the grant was going to fund the construction of, or are you talking about another one?"

"There's only one," Mendel said, turning from her to the door.

Ruby waited, but he offered no further explanation. As his long strides took him to the door, she struggled to orient herself. She had spent all week trying to find Mendel to update him on her progress. Now that the simulation was running, she needed his input on structuring the paper. For better or worse, she couldn't do this without him.

"I've got my simulation running," Ruby said, her voice tight with desperation as she fought to keep her frustration in check. "Do you want to see some results?"

"Is this the original formalism?" he called back. "Or did you create a lower-energy particle?"

"It's the same model I've always had," she replied, confused this was even a question.

Mendel shrugged. "Busy now. Just wanted to share the news." He was already stepping out. "Maybe another time." The door thudded shut behind him.

Alone again, frozen at the bench while her simulation output scrolled unnoticed across the screen, Ruby wrestled with her thoughts. Her face still burned as she reprocessed the interaction. The message couldn't have been clearer. Mendel's interest in her work extended strictly as far as its utility for securing funds and prestige. At their last meeting, he claimed he wanted her theory published even more than she did, yet he hadn't contributed to its development. He probably wanted her theory for the same reason he wanted this grant: more funding, more status, more control.

Meanwhile, he made promises and broke them, gave her the green light to present her results, then clamped down on the content. Would she even want a postdoc if it meant being jerked around like this? Ruby wondered if he ever faced consequences for his lies, or if this was simply how he always operated.

Part of her wanted to quit in protest, but who was she kidding? He would replace her in a heartbeat, while her own career suffered irreparable damage. She had invested too much—all the late nights, all the work to get the simulation running. She couldn't just run away.

And if she raised a fuss? She might earn a reputation as a troublemaker. Ruby could become a pariah, shunted aside before she posed any real threat. Academia was something of a pyramid scheme, at least for those aiming for the top. But if she stayed on this path, what choices did she have? All she could do was keep running simulations, working with Noah, mentoring Imani, and watching for a chance to change course.

Her father would call that passive. Noah would too, though he'd sugarcoat it. Ruby needed to play her own game, but what game could she play against someone who controlled her academic future, who could snatch everything away in an instant, twisting her scientific discoveries into leverage?

She tapped her finger on her laptop, thoughts returning to the compiler discussion with Noah and its parallel to quantum mechanics. She recalled her shock as an undergrad when she first learned the universe played dice—cheating, slipping particles across barriers, violating energy conservation, then covering its tracks by drawing a curtain over the crime scene. With the curtain in place, no one could prove the dice weren't fair, or that the particle hadn't been there all along with the right energy. The universe showed her that lies, layered deeply enough, became truth. That was the nature of reality.

Mendel, she was sure, understood the power of a lie to become truth. He had built his career on that game. But why couldn't she play it, too? "No one will recognize these contradictions unless we tell them," Mendel had said. So what if she let him believe she'd accepted his guidance? What if she showed him results that matched his expectations, then switched the numbers before submitting the manuscript? She could disguise it as a typo. That was the kind of buck-stops-here plan her father would have approved. By the time Mendel noticed, Ruby could have built enough of a reputation to stand on her own. She could stop playing the puppet and start cutting strings.

To get the truth out, Ruby would have to lie, and she couldn't shake the sense she was building on a rotten foundation. If she started, would she ever find her way back to the truth, or would the whole structure collapse around her? By choosing deception, she risked becoming no better than Mendel.

The moral dilemma weighed on her, but she refused to let Mendel dictate her future. She would not become another casualty of his hunt for power.

◆◆◆

"Thank you for joining our first ARCC design review," Derrick said, standing at the front of the crowded conference room that Noah had occupied alone just the evening before. "Due to the sensitivity of the subject, we're keeping this group small. Everything here is strictly confidential. Ask questions as they come up. Those on the conference line, speak up so we can hear you. Noah will present the viral scouting in Phase I and the installation of OS backdoors in Phase II. In two weeks, Eli will lead the Phase III review about installing the filters linked to the SmartSys engine. Noah, you're up."

Seven others circled the familiar white conference table in the crowded downstairs room in Aiken. Clockwise from Derrick sat Michael, channeling his energy from atmospheric science into ARCC project management. Next were Noah's two hires, Salman and Victor, both pale-faced and braced for trouble. At the far end, Dan from environmental science and James from biochemistry, full professors with gray in their beards, had recently joined ARCC in senior management roles. And then there was Eli, of course—his chief consultant. Their eyes met, and Eli gave a supportive nod.

One other joined the video conference: Manuel, their AI neuroscience consultant, moonlighting from SmartSys. Chris was absent, off searching for a computational linguist. Lam, Davis, Rajit, and a half dozen other recruits hadn't been invited. Derrick, wary of leaks, had kept the group small; psychology, economics, and political science weren't core competencies for this review. Satsuki Matsuda was also missing, having resigned after failing to sway Derrick on ARCC's approach.

For once, there was enough space in this basement cave of the computer science department. Its only redeeming feature, Noah thought, was its location just down the hall from the server room hosting his viral incubator.

Noah took a deep breath and started the slideshow, stepping to the lectern at the front of the room. He had decided to soft-pedal the screwup.

"Since forming the team," Noah began, "we spent three months building the Phase I launch system. We started by distilling features common to the most 'successful' computer viruses. You'll excuse the scare quotes. My day job in security research, though it's given me a library of exploits to work with, comes at all of this from a rather different angle."

"Gaining control of a host requires getting a data payload onto the computer," Noah continued. "There are several ways to do this: it can be downloaded by a hapless user, injected through an unsecured comm port, or physically transmitted by, say, plugging in a thumb drive. One of our best bets for Phase I, for example, targets a buffer-overrun exploit in the driver of a NearNet chipset found in most smartphones and some computers."

Noah had front-loaded the technical details, so he wasn't surprised when senior management interrupted. Dan, the gray-bearded environmental scientist with an affable smile at the end of the table, leaned forward. "Sorry, can you break that down?

NearNet is like Wi-Fi for headphones and displays?"

Noah opened his mouth to respond, but Eli spoke first. "It is a short-range, point-to-point communication channel defaulting to open on most phones."

"Turns out," Noah added, "if you send two large data bursts back-to-back with precise timing, you can overflow the message memory buffer. On most systems, the remainder spills into a memory region where it can be activated later."

Dan didn't seem to follow, but nodded for Noah to continue. This was the kind of confused acceptance Noah hoped would help him survive the review.

"The next step for gaining control," he continued, "is to execute the payload with escalated privileges. Usually, this means exploiting a bug in the operating system kernel or stealing credentials stored on the computer. You'd be surprised how many people save their passwords *on* their machines."

Eli, seated on the right side near the lectern, rolled his eyes, but Noah noticed the older crowd—Michael, Dan, and James—looked sheepish. Plugging leaks in a boat full of idiots with power drills, Noah thought wryly. That was cybersecurity for you.

"After that," Noah said, "the virus uses privileged execution to download a larger payload. The first program is streamlined to spread the infection, but the second payload carries the real threat. It has the instructions for whatever end goal the hacker has in mind."

"Of course," Eli interjected with a smirk, "in this case the payload is the backdoor that gives us control of the—how did Noah say?—the 'hapless user.'"

"That's for a later design review," Derrick said from Noah's left, meeting Eli's eyes across the table. Eli shrugged, signaling he'd go along, then turned to Noah with a quick wink. It was a relief to have Eli there, drawing attention away from him.

Derrick followed Eli's gaze to Noah and started to ask a question, but one of the graybeards, James this time, interrupted. "This isn't my field, so forgive my ignorance, but won't antivirus programs detect the virus and kill it?"

Noah, usually impatient to get on with things, was happy this time to stall. Maybe everyone would tune out before he had to drop the bomb.

"Usually, antivirus programs use markers central to the virus's functionality to identify and clear memory sectors to disable the virus. We've taken steps to evade this. Phase I was about designing my own worst nightmare. We needed something virulent enough to compromise billions while going undetected long enough to reach Phase II, where a compiler hack helps erase our tracks. I'm afraid we betrayed the trust of several university industry partners, mining NDAs and using internal code diffs to uncover new zero-day exploits. We also leveraged our reputation to push questionable changes into certain security libraries. We're burning a lot of bridges if we get caught."

"And what are the chances of that?" Derrick asked.

Noah shrugged. "Not high, as long as we're careful." He cringed inwardly at the word "careful" and hoped it didn't show.

"So," Noah concluded, "we assembled a dozen exploits for common platforms and bundled them with several known vulnerabilities, in case people haven't installed recent security patches. Altogether, we have about fifty ways to gain entry and escalate privileges. That gives us fifty potential virus strains, making containment much harder."

Noah paused, glancing around the room. He had hoped people's attention would wander, but every eye stayed fixed on him. Eli shrugged an "oh well," and Noah had to concur. He had no choice but to continue.

"Our final touch increases virulence and helps the virus evade the detection James was worried about. We engineered a mutation mechanism, giving the virus the ability to combine parse trees with other strains. In the wild, these viruses mutate their structure and blend features. Effective variants will spread and multiply; weaker ones will die out, but any marker-based antivirus efforts will struggle to isolate this code. They might catch a particular strain, but can't eliminate the entire population."

On the left side of the conference table, Noah saw Derrick's eyes narrow as his alertness spiked. Damn. But Michael, seated beside him, spoke first.

"So you're using a kind of natural selection to refine the virus?" he said.

"Exactly," Noah said, searching for a way to deflect Derrick's attention. "We've been incubating these viruses in the server room down to harden them before release. A sort of preoptimization."

"What kinds of mutation are we talking about here?" Derrick asked.

"Mostly trivial refactorings, but some are random." Noah knew his answer wouldn't ease Derrick's concern, but he didn't want to lie, either. Besides, this was a red herring. The screwup had nothing to do with mutations.

Unfortunately, Derrick had caught the scent of something and intended to get to the bottom of it.

"So how do you control it?" Derrick said.

"The whole point," Noah said, "is to eliminate central control. Any control code would be an easy mark for containing our vector." Noah knew it was counterproductive, but couldn't keep the impatience from his voice.

"Wait," Derrick said, pressing his palms to the table as he leaned forward. "You've coded a 'worst nightmare' vector in your virtual test tubes, one that can mutate into anything, and you're proposing to release it into the wild with no control mechanism? No shutdown switch?"

"You are overestimating the chances this makes anything but simple mutations," Eli chimed in.

Noah felt the room's temperature rising but didn't know what to do. Derrick's eyes drilled into him, and everyone else looked on high alert. Help came from an unlikely front.

"Noah and Eli are right," James said, chiming in from the back right corner.

Of course, Noah thought. A biochemist would understand this.

"We avoid carcinogens because mutations are almost always harmful," James continued. "Any nontrivial mutation leads to failed offspring 99.9 percent of the time."

Sensing James had dealt him the winning hand, Noah pressed his case. "Remember, we coded a virus with a payload that is completely benign except when it finds compiler source code."

"You mean the transition to Phase II." Derrick exhaled, shaking his head. "That's when we wipe everything clean, right?"

Derrick had offered him an out. All Noah had to do was take it. "Absolutely," he said. "Once we have what we need, we'll release patches to stop the propagation. Any lingering infections, we'll wipe out ourselves as we install our AI filtering platform."

Michael was still shaking his head, though.

"This part about unbridled mutation still makes me nervous. How do we know the virus won't go full Skynet on us?"

Salman and Victor scratched sudden itches on their faces. Noah looked away to hide an eye roll. One speculative sci-fi movie from the twentieth century, and computer scientists would forever have to answer questions about *Terminator* robots.

Eli, his kippah askew atop his curly black hair, showed less restraint. "Why is everyone always worrying the AI becomes sentient and the next step is war on humans? It is people we should be fearing, not machines."

"On Earth," Noah interjected, softening Eli's tone, "it took three billion years to evolve intelligence. There's a huge complexity gap to bridge."

Michael shrugged. Doubt lingered in his eyes, but he let the matter drop.

"Then why bother with Phase II?" Dan piped up. The environmental scientist glanced around, out of his depth. "If your vector compromises a bunch of computers, why mess with compilers? Why not skip to Phase III and install our AI filters?"

"Because our viruses will get shut down, eventually," Noah said. "For Phase III to work, we need access to every device, not just those with vulnerabilities."

"So," Michael said, brow furrowed above ruddy cheeks, "you're banking on the transmissibility being high enough to outpace your security colleagues, and then...?"

"And then we hope," Noah finished. "The silent propagation phase won't last forever. Mutations will slow the response, but once the security walls come back up, it's over. If we haven't subverted the major operating systems by then, we never will."

"And when do you propose to start the timer on Phase I?" Michael asked.

Noah grimaced. It was a direct question. No avoiding it, and he wouldn't lie.

"It started on Friday."

Noah felt the air rush out of the room, leaving a vacuum of silence. James and Dan, on the back wall, wore expressions of alarmed confusion. Michael stared wide-eyed, but Derrick's eyes lasered into Noah. Further down the table, Victor stared at the floor. Noah wasn't going to out him, though the revision history clearly attributed the config edit that unleashed the virus. They were a team. Noah would take responsibility for the mistake.

"There was a slip-up testing the NearNet exploit," Noah admitted, gripping the lectern to brace for the backlash.

"'Slip-up'?" Derrick asked in a deceptively soft voice.

"We were incubating strains. Preoptimizing them on the cluster, like I said. It looks like we neglected to revoke the virtual machine's hardware access in one instance."

"Your bug got loose?" Michael squeaked. "Is that what you're saying?"

"It did what it was supposed to," Noah said, trying to calm him. "The strain apparently jumped to the phone of someone walking past the server room. By the time we found out, they had taken the T home."

Derrick's face was inscrutable, but horror twisted Michael's. "Anyone on the train could have caught it? Are you fucking kidding me? The plan is live *now*?"

Noah nodded reluctantly. "For at least three days. We only

found out last night. Some areas are already near saturation."

"What the hell?" Michael said, his face purple. "This is a massive screwup."

"Nothing's screwed up." Noah couldn't help matching Michael's heat, but forced himself to take a breath. "This shouldn't have happened," he continued more calmly, "but everything is fine. It works. No one on the security channels has noticed. Remember, there's no noticeable effect on network speed or processor usage."

Manuel had been silent during the meeting, but now his voice crackled over the video link.

```
<VIDEO CONFERENCING APP>
<BEGIN I/O>

        Am I infected?

<END I/O>
```

"Probably," Eli replied. "Sixty percent of Boston phones already are."

The room paused to absorb the statistic. Even Noah hadn't known the numbers Eli revealed. Intentional or not, the virus was working.

Michael broke the spell, shaking his head. "Unbelievable. How will we know if we're in Phase II?"

"It won't happen all at once," Noah answered, "but—"

"It seems," Eli interjected, "that we have entered Phase II on one platform already."

"How are we only hearing about this now?" Michael shot back.

"It only just happened," Eli said. "Our first reply came right before this meeting. Port 30050, from a server on campus building Linux kernels."

◆◆◆

The questions carried them into the evening. Every line of the Phase II compiler hack faced a scrutiny that Noah endured patiently, accepting the penance for his slip-up. Derrick, primed by his own foray into the code after their tennis match last week, fired off sharp questions. Fortunately, the compiler code was self-contained, and Noah was prepared. Phase II was airtight.

The team decided to release the remaining bugs, effectively acknowledging that despite the blunder, the design review had passed. The rollout had been haphazard, but all signs pointed to a successful launch. Though autocoders gave his small team superhuman productivity, mistakes were inevitable on such an aggressive timeline, Noah thought. There were only so many eyes for cross-checking.

By the end, the mood even turned celebratory. Eli, Victor, and Salman went out for drinks. Noah said he'd join them later and watched ruefully as the door shut him in alone with Derrick and Michael in the stifling room.

He took flak for another hour on the importance of transparency and coordination. Screwing up was one thing; hiding it from ARCC management for at least a day was another.

"Let me make something clear, Noah," Derrick said, straining not to shout. "Communication. Is. Everything. If omissions and substitutions on the *other* side of the curtain can steer human civilization, then we sure better know exactly what's happening on *this* side. Are we clear?"

"Yes, sir," Noah replied, eyes on his shoes, instinctively adding the honorific in response to Derrick's authoritarian tone. Somehow, Derrick's restraint stung more than shouting. Being dressed down in front of Michael was demeaning. The mistake hadn't even been his, but Noah took the blame because he believed leaders took responsibility. Derrick clearly did not.

"No more mistakes of this magnitude will be tolerated," Derrick added. "Period."

They let Noah leave after that. Noah still led his team, and for that he was grateful. From now on, though, Noah would keep his guard up around Derrick.

Act II: RAINFALL

12.   THE TRUTH UNDERLYING

Parents and teachers frame our perception as children. As we age, this framework evolves, adapting to new ideas and friendships. With each relationship, the exchange of information coheres our frameworks. The more social bonds that stigmatize a behavior, the more likely we are to suppress it. And because bonds are reciprocal, suppression reinforces the stigma in others. Changing the status quo doesn't always require changing minds; silencing dissenting views can be just as effective.

—ARCC Memo Series

Ruby jogged out the campus gates on a crisp morning in late fall, weaving around the brick buildings ringing the Square to reach the river, where she could open her stride and breathe. She set an aggressive pace from the start and clung to it until her lungs burned. Sunlight glinted off the glassy Charles and the cold air bit at her skin before her muscles warmed to make it comfortable. She lost time on the backstretch, crossing one of the many picturesque bridges, but a second wind carried her forward, and she finished with enough for a final kick.

Flushed, cheeks rosy, Ruby trotted to a stop on the brick path to Rubin Hall. Above, the quadrangle's trees had lost their peak color, but a few bright clusters of orange still clung to the branches. Glancing back through the gates into the Yard, Ruby smirked at the undergraduates stumbling from their dorms with bedraggled hair and shell-shocked faces. Energy surged through her veins. What a fantastic morning.

When had she become this caricature of a morning runner,

laughing at late risers? She'd joined her high school track team to fit in, in a town where medaling at a league meet made front-page news but winning a state math competition barely warranted mention. The team welcomed anyone who could fill out the roster, but Ruby still spent long bus rides alone with her thoughts.

At least it had given her a lifelong sport. Running the river near campus was her favorite Boston activity.

Too bad Rubin didn't have showers. She would just keep her distance so no one in the lab noticed her smell. She had brought a change of clothes, of course.

Ruby bounded up the steps two at a time to shove through the oaken double doors of Rubin. Her running shoes squeaked on the linoleum as she pushed through another door with anti-shatter filaments veining its glass, then hurried down the stairway to the lab.

The air inside, usually lamentably cool, now felt overheated compared to the crisp late fall outside. She had already sweated through her T-shirt by the time she reached the bottom of the stairs. Her bag sat on the floor beside her bench, but she should wait a few minutes. No use changing before she stopped sweating.

No one else had arrived yet. Her coworkers kept later hours, which was one reason Ruby liked coming in early. After her morning run, her mind felt sharp and clear. She could dive into creative work for a solid hour before the day's interruptions began.

She quickly became absorbed in editing an abstract for an upcoming conference. If she could slip the submission past Mendel, maybe she could start building a name in the physics community. Funding aside, he might not even notice if she went, if she disguised the reimbursement request.

Fifteen minutes later, Ruby shivered, realizing she'd forgotten to towel off. She wasted another wish on a hot shower, but that was asking too much of a building that lacked even a women's bathroom on this floor. When Rubin Hall was built, the faculty—undoubtedly all men—had cut costs by skipping floors for women's facilities. Most physicists were men, after all. Funny how that argument reinforced itself.

Concentration broken, Ruby switched screens to check email and spotted a message from Professor Mendel. Her stomach lurched.

Something had come up at the last minute—another campus obligation. Could she cover class today?

Ruby checked the clock: 8:45 a.m. Christ. Did he mean his ten o'clock quantum class? It had to be. She'd covered it twice this semester already. She could do it again, but couldn't he have given her time to prep?

Not for the first time, Ruby wondered what would happen if she refused. She wouldn't, of course. That was unfair to the students. But still. How did Mendel justify his salary when she did half the teaching while he chased the next funding opportunity? And when he landed one? More promises. More work for Ruby. She had her own research to do, her own science to advance.

Ruby shook her head, snapping out of it. She shouldn't forget whose grants paid her salary. Besides, there was no time to stew. Class started in just over an hour.

Firing off an email requesting the topics to cover, Ruby scrambled to plan the next hour. She needed lecture notes, but knew better than to ask Mendel for his. Ruby understood quantum backward and forward, but the associations she made were too abstract for the students. She couldn't lecture off the cuff the way he did.

Where was her Griffiths textbook? Ruby found it on the shelf, its black cover stamped with Schrödinger's cat in gold. With luck, she had scribbled notes in the margins four years ago that could remind her what it was like to learn the material for the first time. She could nip misconceptions in the bud if Mendel would bother telling her what to cover.

Meanwhile, she needed to change into work clothes. It would cost time, dashing upstairs to swap her sports bra for an underwire, then pull on slacks and her dotted blouse. Too bad she hadn't brought a blazer. She'd need to muster every ounce of authority if Erik showed up today.

She shouldered her bag to head upstairs when the lab door clicked open.

"I only have a minute. It's faster to tell you in person," Mendel said as he stepped inside, his tone brisk. He paused. "Sorry if I caught you at a bad time."

That last sentence carried enough of a leer to make Ruby suddenly aware of how her orange sports bra glowed through her damp top. She cleared her throat and glanced around for something to cover herself. All her clothing was folded in the bag.

Mendel grinned, his gaze lingering on her damp shirt. Ruby blushed despite herself. Damn it.

Crossing her arms, Ruby diverted onto quantum mechanics. Today's class covered quantum measurement and the Copenhagen interpretation. As he recapped last week's lesson, his gaze drifted, lingering. Her skin crawled under his stare. She had to get out—away from him, somewhere she could regroup.

She tried to drive him off, using lecture as an excuse, itching to shove him out but wanting even more to avoid proximity to him. Having claimed to only have a couple of minutes, Mendel suddenly seemed in no hurry. Ruby unslung her bag and turned away, pretending to dig through it for nothing in particular, telling him he should go and willing him to leave until, at last, he did.

"I'll let you freshen up."

He was halfway out the door when Ruby glanced over her shoulder to make sure he was leaving. She accidentally caught his eye and saw the wink.

She bit the inside of her cheek hard enough to taste blood.

◆◆◆

Students filed into the classroom as the ten o'clock bell faded. In her stomach, Ruby felt the usual before-class flutter of anxiety and excitement, now tangled with frustration and embarrassment.

Her blouse and slacks felt too thin. How had she let herself get caught like that? She shouldn't have worn workout clothes in the lab. She should have changed at home.

Ruby took a deep breath, closed her hastily scrawled lecture notes, and distracted herself by reciting the names of the thirty-some students streaming in. It would be okay, once she started. The nerves were always worst at the beginning.

"Is Professor Mendel out again?" Arturo asked, smiling shyly beneath his trim dark hair. He rarely spoke during class but sometimes lingered afterward to clarify a point. He was a sweet kid. Studious.

"The professor sends his apologies. He had another obligation. I'll be covering class today."

As the students settled into their seats, Ruby stepped to the lectern and surveyed the room, listening to the rustle of paper and the clack of keys as they paged through their quantum mechanics notebooks, both paper and electronic. By the third absence of the semester, no one questioned Ruby's presence as substitute, though Erik, ducking through the doorway as he entered, pressed his lips together in disappointment. He seemed to have a chip on his shoulder about learning from a mere graduate student. Or was it because she was a woman?

Fluorescent lights glared overhead, and Ruby shivered in their cold radiance. Several classroom windows were cracked open, letting in crisp autumn air that had felt refreshing during her run but now bit at her still-damp skin. She rubbed her upper arms, hoping the chill wouldn't put a waver in her voice that Erik might mistake for nerves.

Not everyone had taken their seats, but Ruby decided to start on time.

"So, class, today's an exciting day. I'll admit, I'm a little jealous. You're about to collapse a wavefunction for the first time. This will blow your mind."

"You say that every lecture." That was Jayden, the class's good-natured heckler. Ruby didn't mind; his banter kept everyone engaged, as long as she kept it on a short leash.

"And I mean it every time, Jayden. Have I ever failed to deliver?"

Jayden smirked and rolled his eyes, but shook his head.

"Exactly," Ruby said. "If quantum mechanics isn't changing your conception of reality, you're not paying attention."

Ruby kept talking as she turned to an expanse of whiteboard and picked up a marker. "Let's set the stage. Earlier this semester, we pictured particles as marbles—little bundles of well-behaved matter that are where they are and aren't where they aren't, right? But alas, we ran the double-slit experiment and discovered something strange: if a particle has two ways to get from here to there, it somehow takes *both*. The paths interfere, making it impossible to find the particle in some spots, even though it could have reached them through either slit."

Ruby sketched her diagram on the board, labeling the top slit "A" and the bottom "B." She turned to the class, watching as they bent over their notebooks to copy her work.

"*Interference.* That's a wave word. Waves interfere constructively and grow, or destructively and cancel out. So we invented the wavefunction and started treating particles as waves. For a few weeks now, you've learned to manipulate them with the Schrödinger equation. With me so far?"

Heads around the room bobbed in passive acquiescence.

"Great! So it's time to return to the double-slit experiment with our new machinery. We set up a wavefunction describing all the places our particle is, and then..."

From the corner of her eye, Ruby saw Christine's hand slide up. Unlike some of her male peers, she didn't interrupt the class when she had a question.

"Yes, Christine?"

"Sorry." Christine brushed a strand of dark hair from her face. "You said 'all the places our particle is.' Did you mean 'is' or 'might be'?"

Ruby grinned. "Christine—going straight for the jugular before

I've even finished setting up the problem! Can you hold that thought?"

Christine nodded, pen in hand.

"Okay," Ruby continued. "We take this wavefunction, run it through the two slits, and we get a new one on the other side with a pesky interference pattern showing our chances of finding the particle at each spot. That's what Schrödinger taught us, right?"

Ruby had to wait a little longer for the nods this time.

"Now to Christine's question. Suppose I make a measurement and find the particle here." Ruby marked a red "X" on the right side of the board. "Now, I know where my particle is. Does that mean I know which slit it went through? Stephen?"

Stephen, who hadn't been raising his hand, shrank in his seat. "Umm, maybe?"

"A suitably noncommittal answer to a quantum conundrum, but we can do better. Christine, your take?"

Christine pushed her glasses up her nose and looked up from her notes. "I'd say no. If there's an interference pattern, it means the particle could have gone through either slit, right?"

"That's right. But suppose Stephen"—Ruby took a perverse pleasure in watching him squirm—"really wants to know which one it went through." She wasn't being unkind. Stephen needed to step up his work in this class. Sometimes that took a little prodding.

"Let's say," Ruby continued, "Stephen builds a detector to tell us when a particle passes through slit A. But the moment he switches it on, the interference pattern vanishes. Anyone know why?"

"Because Stephen broke the experiment?" Jayden's jibe drew chuckles around the room.

"No," said Ruby. "Stephen made it carefully." She didn't want to prod him *too* hard.

"Because the measurement collapses the wavefunction at the slit, eliminating the ambiguity and destroying the interference between the two paths."

The sarcastic, sing-song delivery told her it was Erik in the back. She didn't need to look to picture the eye roll that accompanied it. What was his deal? Snideness aside, the answer was on the money.

"That's right, Erik. Which is to say, Christine, that the wavefunction doesn't just reflect our ignorance about the particle's location. To interfere, the particle must actually take both paths. It 'is' in multiple places at once."

"Wait, I'm confused," Christine said. "We don't know which slit it went through, but it did go through one, right?"

"That's the 'hidden variable hypothesis'—the idea that the universe has a true state we just don't know. But Bell's theorem shows this can't work without giving up sensible things like causality. Hidden variables need magic behind the curtain to explain how opening the second slit eliminates particles from places where they could previously appear."

Erik's long arm snaked up in the back. Expecting another attempt to derail the lecture or undermine her authority, Ruby searched for someone else to call on, but Erik spoke anyway.

"According to the Copenhagen interpretation, measuring a quantum system instantly collapses its wavefunction, implying that information must travel faster than light. Albert Einstein rejected this as 'spooky action at a distance' because it violated relativity. So which is correct: quantum mechanics or general relativity?"

The self-satisfied smirk told her Erik knew this question had no tidy answer. He was testing her. Ruby sighed.

"Quantum mechanics and general relativity haven't been fully reconciled, so—"

"So you don't know?" Erik interrupted.

So much for containing the situation. Last time he pulled this stunt, she'd asked Erik to save it for after class, but he had left with everyone else. Now he was at it again. These questions weren't about curiosity; he wanted to score ego points, and he'd keep it up unless she turned the tables.

"Let's break down that question, Erik. How would you define a measurement?"

Erik shot her a smug look. "Using a detector to generate a signal proportional to a particle's state."

He could have been such an asset if he weren't such an ass.

"So, maybe you're having the particle interact with some apparatus to detect it?"

Erik waved a hand dismissively. "Sure."

"And that apparatus is made of particles, right? Particles with their own wavefunctions?"

Erik's eyebrows lowered in suspicion. "I guess."

"So making a measurement requires bringing two independent quantum states together and making them coherent. Do you know what *coherence* means in this context?"

"It means they are consistent."

Ruby nodded. "Right. Their wavefunctions are linked. The particle can pass through Slit A or Slit B, and our detector can register either path. With two available states for the particle and detector, there are four possible system configurations."

Ruby turned and drew a two-by-two grid on the board, mapping every outcome: a particle passing through Slit A or B, and the detector registering it in A or B.

"But," Ruby said, turning to Erik, "only two of these states are consistent. Stephen built a good detector, so if the particle goes through Slit A, we shouldn't detect it in B."

Ruby crossed out the Slit A/Detect B box in the upper-right corner and moved to the lower-left box. "Similarly, the particle shouldn't go through Slit B while we detect it at A. These outcomes are prohibited because the states of the particle and detector are inconsistent. Their wavefunctions are incoherent."

"But you didn't answer my question," Erik said. "At some point, the particle passes through A or B. If you measure it, there's only one outcome. The wavefunction collapses, but it doesn't carry information. Einstein was wrong."

Erik made assertions, but they were the helpless strokes of a swimmer dragged out of his depth by a current, and Ruby wasn't finished yet.

"Where would you draw the line and say the measurement occurred?" she challenged.

"When it becomes macroscopic, like Schrödinger's cat. The cat dies once it's no longer a quantum system."

"But remember when we calculated the de Broglie wavelength of the whole sun? There's no magic threshold where it stops. Everything's quantum. It's turtles all the way down, I'm afraid."

One student snickered, and Erik's face reddened, but Ruby pretended not to notice.

"You're drawing an artificial distinction, Erik, between the quantum world and the macroscopic one. There's no single true outcome. As more particles are involved, more configurations become possible, but fewer remain consistent. The wavefunctions of these inconsistent states eventually decohere and slip away, like ripples on a pond, until only one self-consistent solution remains. That final state, the one that emerges from this quantum stew and coheres to our brains, we call 'real,' but reality is only a matter of degree. There's no absolute truth, and there never was."

At least four students in the room had their mouths hanging open.

"If you'd like to know more," Ruby said, meeting Erik's gaze, "stay after class. For now, let's put our training wheels back on and examine the double-slit experiment under the Copenhagen interpretation."

◆◆◆

The rest of the class passed smoothly. Without snarky interruptions, Ruby managed to end lecture on time. Erik was among the first out the door. It was Christine who stayed after, waiting through the sounds of shuffling feet until the room emptied.

"That was an awesome lecture. I wish you were our teacher every week."

"Thanks, Christine. That's kind of you to say." However many

Eriks there were, Ruby would always find fulfillment in the Christines. She would love to have a class she could prepare and teach herself, rather than get tossed into the middle at a moment's notice.

"I had a question about what you said to Erik," Christine said, settling into her chair and rifling through her notes. "You said there's no wavefunction collapse, that it's all about coherence. But then we went back to assuming it collapses. The Copenhagen interpretation, right? So... which is it? What's the real theory?"

"Great question. I should have clarified that not everything I said is universally accepted. Observationally, it looks a lot like the Copenhagen interpretation. As the universe, including us, settles into a single state, it appears as if the wavefunction collapses to one value while the other possibilities decohere."

Christine nodded, but Ruby saw she wasn't satisfied with the answer and sympathized. Ruby took a chair beside her student.

"The truth, Christine, is that we don't know the truth. We can't. We test theories with measurements and discard those that don't fit, but we can't prove anything. Every theory is just one wrong prediction away from the trash bin. Some theories gain acceptance based on their proponents' reputations, like the Copenhagen interpretation. Which isn't to say it hasn't been rigorously tested, but things get tricky when the nature of measurements is part of the theory, right? So a bunch of twentieth-century physicists concocted a cop-out."

Ruby was tempted to mention Gödel's incompleteness theorem, to point out that even mathematics suffered from inescapable circular reasoning. Math had inherent contradictions or unprovable truths; there was no middle ground. The Copenhagen interpretation was a bandage, or maybe a tourniquet, pressed over the same circular wound in physics.

"These scientific theories kind of have their own wavefunction," Ruby mused to Christine. "But we still don't know how this quantum process picks one state from the sea of possibilities. Is it random? Does it depend on which possibilities interact fastest to establish coherence? We just don't know."

Ruby decided to leave it at that. Christine's eyes had widened with each word, and now she looked downright intimidated. Poor Christine. She had come seeking clarity, but Ruby had only muddied the waters.

Ruby gave her student a reassuring smile. "Think of it this way: we've reached the edge of what we know. What could be more exciting for a scientist? The universe is weirder than we can imagine, but connecting with that mystery pushes us beyond our human limits."

Something in that last statement made Christine lift her chin. She smiled, thanked Ruby, and walked away, brow furrowed in thought.

Ruby, on the other hand, felt troubled as the high of lecture faded. And cold, she realized with a shiver. Still needing a shower and feeling too exposed to return to the lab, she shouldered her backpack and left for home, pulling her jacket tighter against the late-fall chill settling over the quad.

After what happened with Mendel, she wondered if she had done Christine a disservice by encouraging her interest in physics. Ruby found her own words about scientific theories—how they could prevail for reasons unrelated to truth—unsettling. However it started, the development of quantum mechanics was soon driven by governments whose interests had nothing to do with fundamental physics. Why hadn't the Copenhagen interpretation been pushed further? Because it wasn't necessary for building atomic bombs.

Some areas of science thrived with generous funding, while others languished in neglect. Research groups across campus struggled for resources, yet Mendel's team flourished. Why did particle physics keep benefiting from taxpayer money? There were no new bombs to build, no wars to win.

Ah, but there *was* a war to win, wasn't there? The war of economic growth. Nations backed science to expand influence and wealth, knowing these gains could be weaponized. Ruby and other scientists benefited from national support, pursuing their intellectual curiosity, but who was using whom?

Ruby was beginning to suspect that Mendel's research success relied more on salesmanship than scientific acumen. He used her work to secure funding, then passed responsibilities onto her while he chased the next opportunity. Science was simply his tool for gaining influence. Still, Ruby benefited from the resources he brought in as she pursued her own discoveries.

Ruby recognized the reciprocal symmetry and wondered again: who was using whom? This question lingered in her mind long after she unlocked her apartment and tossed her bag inside.

13.   SUBTEXT

The Butterfly Effect hypothesizes that small perturbations produce wildly divergent outcomes. A single butterfly in China might fan a storm in New York. The reality depends on how coherences propagate, but let's not retread familiar territory. Instead, consider whether a billion coordinated butterflies might prevent this storm from forming at all. The answer depends on the nature of their coordination.

—ARCC Memo Series

Noah shook his head as he turned back to his computer, but subtly, so Derrick wouldn't notice. They'd circled the same conversations for weeks. Noah's patience was thinning, though he knew better than to show it. Derrick would only pry harder if he suspected Noah of hiding something. The guy had cool ideas, but serious trust issues. Yes, Noah's team had screwed up once, but the hack was on track. Derrick needed to trust him to handle this.

The latest sticking point was cross-compilers. Noah explained to Derrick why they were necessary. Just as you could translate a book while preserving the story, cross-compilers translated computer applications to make the same program run on different hardware. Linux servers routinely built operating systems for phones or firmware for network switches.

If ARCC had to infiltrate every computing platform to hide the seams in the curtain, as Derrick wanted, then this was the chain reaction at ground zero. Noah knew it, but convincing Derrick had taken days. Noah wrote an entire presentation on the same material he'd discussed with Ruby, explaining the recursion inherent in needing a functional computer to build computer functionality, but Derrick kept rehashing the same concerns, hunting for some microscopic gotcha.

The winning formula was tying their strategy to Derrick's own ideas. Noah framed the approach as coherence-building, using Lam and Davis's arguments about dominance to show this was the natural way to leverage current resources for new ones. Wasn't that Derrick's recipe for exponential growth? If anything outweighed Derrick's paranoia, Noah was learning, it was his ego.

Everyone was on edge, waiting for Phase I's chaotic viral infection to transition to Phase II, when they could roll out updates and seize control. Noah was hardly a model of equanimity, but Derrick made him look serene. Every day, Derrick pressed him: Was their hack working? From the initial exploits to the mutations, from Victor's unintentional release to the infiltration of smartphones, tablets, and computers, every step aimed to breach one of a dozen major cross-compiler server hubs. Yet Derrick acted as if Noah might forget to mention their success. As if compromising every major operating system on the planet might be second-page news.

Today, Noah humored Derrick, who stood in the doorway of the office he had once shared with Eli. Using code Eli had given him from his new office down the hall, Noah checked on the port 30050 in the basement of Aiken that recorded traffic from each device whose operating system had been backdoored with the compiler hack. Their viruses stayed dormant to avoid detection, but once they injected their tainted code, each compromised computer needed to be found and stitched into a dark web. These packets, one per hour per host on port 30050, served as homing beacons, marking where, in Phase II, ARCC would send code to begin weaving a Phase III informational curtain. They were just waiting for enough hosts to hide the seams.

The login to the basement server lagged. That was the first sign. When the terminal prompt finally appeared and Noah ran the network traffic report, he froze. He expected the usual dribble of packets from the handful of Linux systems they had compromised in those first days. A few spattering raindrops. Instead, Noah's screen flooded with connection reports, cascading faster than he could follow.

Noah exhaled in a whistle, doing the math in his head: thirteen megabits per second, divided by the packet size, times the seconds per hour. This had to be over ten million hosts, easily. The number kept climbing as Noah watched.

From the doorway to Noah's office, Derrick's face shifted from incredulity to a wide grin. He strode in, clapped Noah on the back, and offered his hand. Noah stood to shake it, catching the twinkle of possibilities in Derrick's eyes. In an instant, Derrick was his old, relaxed self.

They must have taken down a major hub—a cross-compiling server for a major phone vendor, probably. Their slow seepage through esoteric operating systems had finally reached a flashpoint. If other major software distributors weren't already subverted, they soon would be, and unlike the mechanism Noah's team had used to deliver the compiler hack, this time there was no virus in memory, no telltale processor activity. The binaries in memory and on disk always checked out when a user asked the OS to read them.

The only signs of the backdoor were the blips of network traffic over port 30050. Soon, even these blips would be undetectable as they gained control over the network switches involved. Cross-compiled firmware on the firewall servers would ignore traffic on the port. Nothing would appear in the log files the infected systems furnished to their sysadmins. Only a few servers in a room deep in the basement of a Boston-area university building remained outside this new coherence.

Ruby had been right. This could be their new reality. They could control the truth about the climate crisis. And Noah had made it possible.

◆◆◆

"I like your new end table," Ruby said. She was kidding, of course. It wasn't even a table. It was a pallet of sodas and energy drinks stacked in boxes beside his red couch.

She heard his laugh from the kitchen, where he slid a casserole into an underused oven.

"And your home theater setup," she added, nodding toward the wall across from the couch. "The cinder blocks really contrast with the plywood cross-pieces." He didn't even have posters on the walls.

"Come on," he said, emerging from the kitchen to drop onto the couch beside her. "It's sturdy. I thought it had a rough-hewn look."

"Oh, definitely," she said. "It oozes masculinity. But I'm confused. How do soda and energy drinks fit into the rough-and-tumble vibe? Wouldn't black coffee and whiskey be more on-brand?"

Noah chuckled but didn't take the bait. He grinned and bounced on the couch, and for a moment, Ruby could see him as a ten-year-old: restless, bright-eyed, full of mischief.

"You seem cheerful," Ruby observed, wincing at the accusatory tone in her voice. She hadn't meant it that way. The incident with Mendel in the lab wasn't Noah's fault, but it still colored Ruby's mood. Fortunately, Noah didn't seem to notice.

"I guess I am," Noah said. "We had a breakthrough at work."

"With the compiler stuff you were working on when I asked for help the other day?"

Noah's face sobered as he ran a hand through his hair. "Oh. I didn't realize you were paying such close attention."

"Well, I gather what I can from what little you tell me. What was the breakthrough?"

"It wasn't a big deal, really. Just a way to get computers to... err... coordinate security across a network."

"Part of the 'chain of trust' spiel?"

"Yeah," he shrugged. "I guess. But honestly, it wasn't important. Nothing to—"

"You never talk about it," Ruby interrupted, her annoyance flaring as Noah launched into another familiar dismissal. She scooted away on the couch and faced him. "Your work—do you think I'm not interested? Or that I won't understand?"

How many of her overtures had he shut down? Today, frustration piled on shame and anger from the morning's episode with Mendel, and she couldn't help calling him out. Still, she noticed Noah's light mood had faded even before her outburst, right when she mentioned the compilers. Now, his smile was gone, replaced by a guarded expression. Usually oblivious to emotional context, he seemed to have caught on now.

"You okay, Roo? Seems like something's bothering you."

"What bothers me is how you change the subject."

An awkward pause hung in the air as Noah realized she wasn't backing down. Ruby crossed her arms and let the silence stretch, her stubborn gaze daring him to speak first.

"Okay," he said. "I admit I'm guarded about work. I spend all day plugging security leaks and fighting people who'll exploit any vulnerability. It affects how freely I talk. I'll try to be more forthcoming. But there's more to this. You're upset."

Ruby hesitated. "Upset" barely captured the feeling of being ogled by an advisor while she covered his teaching duties, freeing him to manipulate her research to secure funding that would result in more work dumped on her plate. Grad school was starting to look uncomfortably like a Ponzi scheme.

"Have you ever felt like someone was using you?" Ruby said.

Noah blinked at her pivot. "Like, how?"

"Relying on you to pick up the slack," she said, flicking dust from Noah's couch. "Using your work for their gain."

"I... I'm not sure. It's nice to be relied on, I guess." Noah narrowed his eyes. "Is this about that French guy?"

From the couch beside him, Ruby leveled a steady stare at Noah, refusing to dignify his remark with a response.

"I mean, you're a genius, Ruby," Noah said, shrugging with a defensive smile. "I'd want as much of your help as I could get, too. Did he write a paper without offering you co-authorship? Want me to beat him up? I can play the jealous boyfriend, if you want."

Noah could be so solicitous sometimes, and so painfully obtuse at others. Why was he siding against her? Did he even realize he was choosing a side?

"Is this what being a postdoc is like?" Ruby asked, recalling Mendel's hints about funding her future. "Scrambling to get ahead by any means necessary?"

"I don't think it's always like that," he said. "Academia has a reputation for turf wars, sure, but I've always been happy to help with whatever moves a project forward. It's more fun to build things with interesting people than to argue over credit."

Ruby nodded, but she realized Noah lived in a different world. In computer science, academic advancement was secondary. For most, the main goal was joining a startup and making a fortune. Physics was different. After years of watching insecure colleagues snipe and belittle each other, she doubted someone in Rubin Hall would last long with Noah's guileless approach.

While Ruby thought, Noah got up from the couch and rummaged through a kitchen drawer. By the time he pulled the casserole from the oven, mitts on and serving spoon ready, Ruby had resolved not to take her mood out on him. The casserole, topped with breadcrumbs and vegan cheese, filled the air with a savory aroma.

She joined him at the far end of the galley, twisting a cork from a wine bottle as she tried to tamp another into her frustration. She poured a tall glass, half of which disappeared in seconds. The day's tension began to dissolve. She could sort the rest out later.

◆◆◆

Noah and Eli stood in the dim server room, the whir of machinery providing backdrop to their work. Eli's fingers danced across a keyboard attached to a tall rack, his eyes scanning lines of code on the glowing screen. Noah, caught between blasts of cold air from the vents and the heat from the electronics, watched his friend, weighing their next move.

In the first phases of the ARCC plan, Noah had taken the pilot's seat, with Eli as his wingman. When the virus broke loose, Noah might have considered trading places, but now he liked the responsibility. The dynamic was changing, though. They now led separate teams from separate offices, and the focus was shifting from cybersecurity to AI management.

Noah shifted his gaze from Eli to a monitor wedged atop one of the many servers Victor and Salman had installed to handle the surging traffic on port 30050. He scanned the network statistics again. The room's link to the outside world was already straining under the load. These servers weren't just fielding beacon signals anymore. Eli's team had been busy, installing aisles of network-attached tensorware and context databases.

Noah's team, meanwhile, was responsible for smuggling matching infrastructure into hidden nooks on the millions of devices he had backdoored. Their first priority had been to subvert and mask traffic on network switches, but now they were moving on to consumer products. Soon, these servers and databases would receive a massive stream of context: positions, identities, account logins, and archived conversations from countless apps.

When Phase III began, when the AI took over, they would need to upgrade to a thicker fiber bundle. Then Noah would hand control to Eli. Noah wished to postpone that day but reminded himself the team mattered most, not the credit. Besides, if anyone deserved recognition, it was Eli.

"It's time to bring the information barrier up," Noah said, eyes fixed on the monitor. The stats didn't lie. Their coverage was spreading fast through cities nationwide.

Eli turned to face him, eyes narrowed as he weighed the implications. "Already?" he called, raising his voice over the server fans. "Is your virus appearing on a white-hat user group?"

Noah shrugged. "There are a few independent strains, but no one's connected them. If they had, it'd already be too late, right?"

"So you are thinking it is time to phase out the viral attack," Eli said, turning back to the screen.

"We got what we came for," Noah said. "It's time to patch the security flaws our viruses use. The scramble to distribute updates could even help us infiltrate some holdouts."

Eli bit his lip as he considered. "You are perhaps right. I admit to being anxious to see our new reality." He tapped a server in the rack beside him. "Then begins the real fun."

"You sound like *him*."

Eli chuckled. "*Nu*, he is not always wrong."

Noah had to grant him that. Controlling? Yes. But Derrick's vision for the project had proved remarkably prescient.

"Once I leak the patches," Noah said, his expression hardening, "someone could potentially connect the dots. We need to roll out your stuff fast, and not every network switch is compromised. That'll be your first real-world test."

Eli rapped his knuckles on the rack beside him. "We have poked at the beta-test system for a month. Nobody is exposing anything we do not want exposed."

Noah nodded and sighed. "Then the next step is getting Executive Board approval. They'll wring their hands."

Eli nodded. "*Ikh veys*. We will lose a week reaching the same conclusions you and I do in ten minutes."

"Yeah," Noah said. "Still, we should play nice. 'This is the price of collaboration,' he'd say."

Eli glanced wistfully around the room. "A shame humans do not coordinate as efficiently as my computers."

Noah checked his watch calendar, calculating the time until the next board meeting. The infrastructure had come together faster than he expected, and Derrick wrote six-figure checks for equipment with barely a question. Noah didn't know where the money came from. Maybe Derrick was courting foundations, or perhaps a university grant was footing the bill. Fortunately, most Phase III computing ran on the client side, distributed across phones and computers outside their walls.

Their current level of investment should sustain ARCC for some time, assuming everything stayed on the table as they yanked out the tablecloth.

◆◆◆

Derrick had prepared for this moment from the start. Even before then, the march of doomsday headlines drove him to distraction, making him question whether hope was possible. Even in a fantasy where one could dictate the behavior of eight billion, did any viable path remain? Some found bliss in ignorance. For Derrick, hope could only come from understanding. From first principles, he had to know.

He interviewed anyone who might offer insight: atmospheric scientists, ecologists, paleontologists, chemists, oceanographers, meteorologists, and glaciologists. He pored over climate science review papers and IPCC policy reports. Immersed in the science, he dove deeper, searching the murky depths for any channel of viability.

He was thrilled to hear from those who knew that all was not lost. Not yet. The future could be saved if tough decisions were made. Humanity, trusting science to save the day, had run down the clock in spite of all warnings. Now time was short. The situation was make-or-break, though Derrick feared it might be make-*and*-break, given the force required. One discussion with Matsuda, warning about disrupting civilization's feedback loop, haunted him.

But hope, however slim, sparked new energy in Derrick. He couldn't see the full solution yet, but he could sketch its outline. Each person he involved sharpened the picture, until Noah brought the final details into focus. Drawing on the skills that had served him throughout his career—reading people and weaving reality from words—Derrick assembled a team. With vision and sheer force of will, he built ARCC and set its course.

He knew what he was doing. Years in academia had taught him that every project devolved into cat herding. Everyone joined for their own reasons; all paths eventually diverged. He had already lost Matsuda. He had hoped to bring their most vocal critic into the fold. Now, her resignation had made her a liability. Derrick regretted the error, but he wouldn't make the same mistake twice. Holding a project together required a single, coherent vision. One person must steer the ship. Control belonged to whoever held the winning hand, and only fools left the dealing to chance.

ARCC had finally entered Phase III, but only after sacrificing a summer to climate research and head-hunting, neglecting his fall-semester teaching, and abandoning a research program on the brink of a breakthrough. Derrick couldn't blame his pending divorce entirely on the project, but ARCC had both fueled and distracted him from the collapse at home. Now, he stayed at work later, avoiding the silence of his empty house. Such was the price of ambition: many associates, few friends.

In any case, it had paid off. ARCC was afloat, and he stood at the tiller. They would start locally, though the problem spanned the globe. Their first program would be modest and direct, leveraging the infrastructure built so far, with a focus on concealment. The scope would stay limited; they needed to iron out mistakes before the stakes rose. He had already taken Noah to task over one error, but Derrick understood the cost of progress. They could not afford sloppiness, but neither could they let fear bind their hands. Learning the ropes required errors and corrections.

There would be mistakes, missteps, and collateral damage, but he had the will to do what was necessary. If saving the planet were easy, it would have been done already. Where the cacophony of a thousand cries went unheard, his project would succeed with a billion whispers speaking as one.

14. MEETING IN THE MIDDLE

Coordination derives from communication. Behind an athlete's finesse lies the precisely timed firing of neurons. Similar information networks align employee actions to corporate goals. Local signals may appear unrelated or even contrary to the desired outcome, but see, as the wavefront propagates, how each impulse lenses through actors and actuators to converge in phase on the intended target.

—ARCC Memo Series

```
<PHONE APP>
<BEGIN I/O>
```

Are you holding up? I know it's been rough.

> Taking it day by day. I'm fine.

What can I do?

> This is my burden to carry, not yours.

That's not how this works, Dad. At least let me help with the insurance.

> I don't need help.

Yes, you do. They're revoking your health benefits.

> I talked to them. It's under control. Never should have bothered you with that.

I don't know what you discussed, but it can't change anything. They'll do whatever it takes to keep you quiet.

> What's to keep quiet about?

Fracking. Our well water. Cancer. This is your idea of "under control"? Ignoring reality in favor of the company line?

> You love to hate them, but we have what we have be-
> cause of their support.

You're loyal to an entity that can't return the sen-
timent. What about everything they took from us? What
about Mom—her career, her happiness?

> None of that was their fault.

If it wasn't their fault, then it was yours.

> That's at least closer to the truth.

<END I/O>

♦♦♦

Standing on the bridge looking upstream over the Charles, Ruby
watched Noah approach. They had agreed to meet here, halfway
between their apartments, but she walked fast and had arrived
first. He was dressed in tan slacks and a blue canvas jacket, and
his long, methodical strides swept aside dead leaves on the riverside path. She could tell by his absent gestures that he was on a
call. Rather than wait awkwardly, Ruby moved to the downriver
railing, gazing at the Boston skyline and shivering in the cold.

He finished his conversation sooner than expected, and she
startled when his hand touched her shoulder.

"Sorry, Roo. Just some hiccups with this new network security
system we're rolling out. Nothing we can't handle, but I have to
take urgent calls sometimes."

"It's fine," Ruby said, shrugging, eyes fixed on the cold water
rippling below. "You don't have to justify your calls to me."

Noah must have sensed an ambivalence in her tone. His hand
brushed the hair shielding her face. "But you wanted me to open
up about my work, right?" he said, nudging her with a half smile.
"This is me opening up."

"Oh," Ruby said, forcing a lighter tone and turning to him with
a measured smile, acknowledging his overture. This was progress,
but she wouldn't lavish praise on every small gesture.

Noah returned the smile, eyes twinkling with undeterred energy, and Ruby felt herself thaw. She struggled for results that would satisfy Mendel while rejecting the idea of doing *anything* that satisfied him, but Noah's work was clearly taking off. She could throw him a bone.

"It's going well, then? Your big breakthrough?"

"Yeah," Noah said, his grin expanding. "Haven't you read the headlines? Noah saves the world!"

Ruby rolled her eyes, wanting her bone back. "Is the world under attack?" she asked, smirking. He was actually a bit amusing.

"Absolutely. Humanity is infected by a computer virus controlling our brains. Only Noah's Cybersecurity Breakthrough™ can save us!"

Ruby scoffed. "And you're sure humanity is worth saving?"

Noah's smile faltered at her tone. "C'mon, Roo. You don't mean that."

"Sorry," Ruby said, shrugging as the fun bled from their banter. "I'm just feeling jaded right now."

"Jaded?"

Ruby shrugged and turned back to the Boston skyline. What was wrong with her? Lately, something inside her rebelled whenever she tried to enjoy herself.

She could blame Mendel, but the problem ran deeper. He manipulated and cheated, but increasingly, Ruby saw how the system seemed built for it. Her discussion with Christine had her questioning the entire arrangement between science, funding, and people like her, caught in the middle of that Faustian bargain. Had science sold its soul? Or just Mendel?

And then there was her father, who clung to faith in a corporation she knew was exploiting him, as it always had. They would cut his pension, cancel his insurance, and let the cancer they'd caused run its course.

Everywhere she looked, she saw systems designed to use and discard people, but none of this was Noah's fault. Why did she have to be such a downer?

"Roo, you can't say you're jaded and not elaborate." His hand returned to her shoulder, warm and steady. "Talk to me."

"I don't know, Noah. I'm just tired. Wondering what it's all for. You know. The usual."

Noah joined her at the railing, gazing at the yellow and orange beginning to outline the buildings, though it was only midafternoon. The days shortened quickly this time of year.

"What scale of 'all' are we looking at here? Personal? Institutional? Global?"

Ruby hesitated. Did she really want to hash out her issues with Mendel, or her father? Neither of these problems could be solved by Noah.

"All of the above, I guess?" she said at last, choosing the most abstract framing. "I thought I knew what I was working toward. I had this idea I could do something worthwhile—make a big scientific discovery or something. Now, I'm not so sure."

"Harder than you imagined?" Noah asked. "Or slower?"

"No," Ruby said, shaking her head. "Given my mom's experience, I was ready for hard. I'm questioning whether I'm even doing science at all."

Aware of Noah turning toward her, Ruby sensed his confusion; she wasn't expressing herself well. She wasn't even sure what she meant.

"You've got this new theory about the universe, right?" Noah said. "I'm no physicist, but that sounds like science to me. Not that I can speak for you," he added hurriedly.

"I thought that, too," Ruby said. "But now I waste time on inane computer stuff. No offense—"

"—none taken—"

"—and making glorified marketing materials for grant proposals," Ruby continued, gaining momentum as she finally voiced doubts she'd avoided acknowledging, even to herself. "And covering other people's responsibilities. Sometimes I wonder if I'm actually doing science, or just pushing a business venture. I might as well be working for PetronTech, like my dad."

That was the heart of it, Ruby thought. She could write this paper, lay out her theory about dark matter, maybe even slip the correct numbers past Mendel. But the more she fought the system, and her computer, and her father, the less she believed in what she was fighting for. Was any of this in service of uncovering fundamental truths?

"There's a world of difference between a university and a petroleum company," Noah said.

"You say that," Ruby said, shaking her head, "but I'm not so sure anymore. Does anyone here"—she gestured at the campus buildings along the water—"even care about science? Or are we just pawns being played for grant money and patents? With autocoders and AI, will humans even understand science in a decade, or will we be playing catch-up to computers, like in chess? Where's the fun in that?"

"You complained just the other day that computers aren't half as smart as we computer scientists claim," Noah said.

"Maybe not yet," Ruby admitted, "but I see where it's heading. And what makes science worthwhile, anyway? Is it actually making anyone's life better?"

Noah shook his head, dismayed. "Of course it's made our lives better," he said. "Just look at everything modern science has made possible." He swept his hand across the cityscape before them.

Ruby shook her head and turned away. "Everything out there," she said, jabbing a thumb over her shoulder, "is made by companies using our science to sell marketable conveniences. The same companies poisoning well water, threatening my dad's healthcare, and ruining the climate, just like you're always saying." She pointed at Noah, holding the gesture a moment before letting her hand fall in resignation.

Noah, briefly paralyzed by her outburst, met her eyes with concern and waited before responding.

"Whew," he said at last. "That's some bonfire you've got burning. Want to toss anything else on?"

"That might be enough for now," Ruby said, shrugging as she turned back to the river. "So yes, I'm feeling a little jaded about my research."

"Have you tried talking to M... to your advisor?"

"The one using me for marketing, cheap labor, and who knows what else?"

"Is he doing all that?" Noah asked. "Or is that the system? I didn't get the sense he was so attached to the status quo, either."

"Why are you defending him?"

"I'm not. Look, Roo, I don't disagree. The world is messed up. You know I've been searching for a way to make a difference."

"Is this where you ask me again to—" Ruby began, then stopped. He'd asked before, at their first brunch. She thought they'd reached an understanding when he invited her to that vegan café.

"No," Noah said, raising his hands. "You've got your own path. I get that. But it sounds like you're worried it's not leading where you expected."

He had a point, Ruby realized. She'd dismissed his earlier overtures, fearing involvement would distract her from science, but she was already distracted. The real question was whether Noah's proposition would pull her further from her distractions or from what little time she had left for actual science.

"I was in the same boat," Noah continued, "wondering what it was all for, and if there could be a better world where, say, PetronTech's grip on our economy was broken."

"Yeah?" Ruby said. With everything happening with her father, PetronTech felt like a workable target for her frustration.

"Yeah," Noah said, his eyes brightening with hope. "Remember when we talked about compilers and you said truth was determined by how information is reported? What if you actually controlled the information? Could you take down a transnational company like PetronTech?"

Ruby shrugged. "Information determines the quantum reality of the whole universe, so maybe it could handle an oil company."

Noah gave her understatement a wry smile. "But how?"

"With what?" Ruby asked. "Some kind of quantum

supercomputer?"

"No," Noah said. "Just regular computers, using whatever information they can access."

Ruby shot Noah a bewildered look. "You think roleplaying the destruction of my father's corporation with a glorified PR campaign will cheer me up?"

"Is that a fantasy you're open to?" Noah asked, eyes glimmering as he leaned in for her answer.

Ruby shook her head in mock exasperation. She had come to the bridge frustrated by Mendel and her research, and admitting her doubts to Noah had shifted the weight on her shoulders, making it more bearable. With everything going on with her father—his treatment, the constant insurance emails from Don Sinclair—she could use an outlet for her frustrations. Maybe, if she didn't let herself get pulled in too deep, she could meet Noah halfway.

"It might be fun," Ruby hazarded.

An excited grin spread across Noah's face. "It will be! Here," he said, tugging her arm from her coat pocket. "Let's walk to your place. I'll play the corporation buying off politicians to shield itself from public outrage, and you try to pull the rug out from under me."

"Like some sort of think-tank war game?" Ruby asked.

"I was thinking more like Model UN," Noah said, "but sure—*let the war games commence!*"

"I think I prefer the UN framing," Ruby said. "Not into the whole 'war' thing."

"Very well." Noah nodded sagely. *"Let the Model UN commence!"*

"Are you going to be like this the whole time?" Ruby asked, laughing despite herself. Noah's buoyant mood was irrepressible today, and frankly, she needed some of that.

As they walked to her apartment, Noah laid out the scenario, drawing on current events: the lawsuit in Colorado, PetronTech's habit of buying off judges and politicians. He described the all-electric RediRides PT promoted to greenwash the company's expanding fossil fuel infrastructure, the made-for-news philanthropy delivered with Don Sinclair's sickening smile on live TV, and the overseas oil acquired from nations whose governments were basically corporate subsidiaries.

Ruby was impressed by the depth of Noah's understanding of her father's company, but none of the problems he raised surprised her. Years ago, her mother had taught her to notice what the cameras missed and interpolate what happened behind the scenes.

By the time Ruby unlocked her apartment door, they were deep into strategy. Noah plopped onto her corduroy couch and opened a notebook while Ruby listed her ideas: unbuying politicians and judges with spoofed emails, targeting refineries and pipelines essential for distribution, and seeding a collective belief that fossil fuels were being phased out.

"It's how markets work," Ruby said. "You don't have to believe a dollar has value, only that others will accept it. Bubbles happen when valuation decouples from reality, right? So if you can make a bubble, you can make an anti-bubble. Undercut the value of PT and its subsidiaries. Create cash-flow problems."

"How do you know all this stuff?" Noah asked, glancing up from his notes.

"It's just patterns," Ruby said with a shrug. "Coherences. No different in people than in particles. C'mon, quit scribbling and play. You're supposed to be in charge of their side."

"I am," Noah said, exasperated. "You're just winning. What happens when Don goes on TV to reassure investors?"

Ruby played along a little longer, suggesting strategies they could try on social media, but mentioning Don's name reminded her of other responsibilities. They finished the game, and Noah waited patiently as Ruby's call to her father went to voicemail, and afterward when she disappeared to freshen up.

"Noah?" she said, emerging from her bedroom a little later.

"Yeah?" he said, hastily sweeping his notes aside to make room as she moved in close.

"Thanks for listening," she said, leaning in and lacing her fingers into his hair.

His eyes glimmered with anticipation. "Always happy to be your sounding board, Roo."

◆◆◆

```
<EMAIL APP>
<BEGIN I/O>
```

> It is with profound sadness that I inform the campus community of Professor Satsuki Matsuda's unexpected passing. Her outspoken political views sometimes put her at odds with the administration, but her passion for teaching made her a student favorite. Arrangements for a memorial service are underway, with details to follow. Meanwhile, Professor Matsuda's classes are canceled while we search for a substitute.

```
<END I/O>
```

◆◆◆

Noah was crammed again inside the newly renamed ARCC Board Room—a grand name for their cramped basement in Aiken Hall, but one that increasingly fit the scope of their discussions. Around the white conference table, Derrick had gathered the leadership: Davis, Michael, Dan, James, and Rajit. The screen at the front projected virtual manifestations of Manuel and Lam. Sharing a line on mute, Chris, Eli, and Wei—ARCC's new computational linguist, arriving none too soon—worked through urgent upgrades related to the meeting's topic.

ARCC was scaling at a staggering pace. Had it really been only two months since the Phase-I virus leaked? With just half a rack of incubators and a public web server, they had dug under the foundation of computer security. Now Noah's team managed hardware that included most computing devices on the planet. Derrick had approved fourteen new hires, all working upstairs.

In the basement, everyone looked overworked and anxious, and Derrick, seated at the head of the table, wanted to push even harder. His clean-shaven face, usually calm, betrayed urgency as he addressed the group.

"If there were any doubt about the stakes," Derrick began, his voice somber, "it should be clear now. You all saw what they did to Satsuki."

In an inbox filled with integration test results and pull requests, Noah had initially missed the significance of the email they all received, registering only the sad news of a former ARCC Board member's passing.

Davis, quick to catch Derrick's angle on politics and power, leaned forward skeptically, steepling his fingers. "You're sure it was PetronTech? I thought it was just age."

"They suspect poison," Derrick said, shaking his head. "She was a thorn in their side, and they have used similar tactics in Venezuela and that pipeline up north—eliminate opponents, deny involvement, silence dissent, and buy off any leaks to the press."

Noah noticed James recoil at the word "poison." In the corner, Dan also looked queasy, unsettled by the Machiavellian tactics Derrick enumerated on his fingers. Rajit, beside Derrick, appeared more thoughtful than disturbed.

Michael sat across from Davis and shifted in his seat. "Some of those pages on managing information also appear in our playbook," he said. "But why now?"

Impatience flashed across Derrick's face. "Haven't you followed campus news? The divestment vote is just weeks away. Satsuki was organizing a protest march."

Michael shrugged. "I've been too wrapped up in *our* project, which, I recall, she wasn't terribly fond of. Kind of a thorn in our side too, wasn't she?"

"We agreed on the ends," Derrick countered, "if not the means. Anyway, it's clear PetronTech wants to control the vote." He tapped the table for emphasis. "It's time to see what we're capable of. We'll see this protest through."

Noah shared Derrick's eagerness to put their tools to use. The phase shift had happened faster than he'd believed, because Derrick was right. The moment their viruses hit the root nodes and injected the compiler hack, the cascade swept through so completely that Noah doubted a single computer on the internet remained untouched. It could have testified to the strength of the chain of trust, if not for Ken Thompson's weak link at the bottom.

Noah was relieved he'd backed up a clean copy of Linux and a compiler when he did. The thumb drive lay hidden in a deposit box at Cambridge Savings, despite Derrick's instructions to eliminate all stray copies. Noah hadn't realized, before the cascade, how comforting he would find that lifeline, now that, in Phase III, every phone and computer ran an operating system with ARCC's invisible backdoor.

Noah's first move, coordinated with Eli, was to push updates into servers and switches, masking network traffic on port 30050. With the curtain in place, Noah could work real magic. He built a protocol to patch the AI smartware embedded in most online devices. From there, it was just a matter of routing traffic through the AI chips under full ARCC control, and voila! The infrastructure for real-time, adaptable AI filters was in place. Phase III was locked in, and Eli, Chris, and Wei were already rolling out personality emulation.

It was impressive but experimental. Noah couldn't shake the feeling they weren't ready. "I thought we'd start small. A warm-up project or something," he said, glancing around the table, worried he was the only one with cold feet.

"This *is* small," Derrick insisted. "One protest. One city. We can coordinate everything locally with the infrastructure we already have. And we have the truth about Satsuki. That alone could devastate PetronTech's image, if we can keep them from silencing it."

The group fell into thoughtful silence. None of them missed the magnitude of Derrick's proposal.

<VIDEO CONFERENCING APP>
<BEGIN I/O>

How soon?

Manuel's voice over the room's speakers was steady despite the gravity of the situation.

"Three weeks," Derrick replied.

Davis nodded, eagerness and caution warring on his face. "If you're right about the stakes—and Satsuki—this will land us on PetronTech's radar."

"That's why we need to go on the offensive," Derrick said. "What's that old line from *The Wire*? 'When you come at the king, you best not miss.' This is the fight we signed up for, Davis."

Davis nodded. Noah did too, his mind racing with logistics. "I'll mobilize the team," he said. "We'll use AI where we can"—Noah nodded toward Manuel and Eli on the screen—"but we might still have to Mechanical Turk some tasks."

"Keep me in the loop," Derrick said, stepping back to survey the room and nod approval. "I'm proud of everything we've done to get here. This is our first skirmish with PetronTech, and I can't imagine a better team to take into battle. Work hard and stay sharp. Good luck."

With Derrick's dismissal, the meeting adjourned, but people lingered, voices overlapping with questions and strategy.

Eli's team was huddled up with Noah's, focused on meta-level AI, mapping high-level Directives into smartware patches distributed via Noah's protocol. Noah's team had pivoted to hardware logistics and network connectivity, but everything was now so tightly integrated that their responsibilities blurred. He and Eli operated two arms of the same giant.

And it *was* a giant—one Noah had unofficially dubbed Middle-Man, after Ruby's chess inspiration, and the name was catching on. Derrick was eager to see what MiddleMan could do. The reality of the project was beginning to weigh on Noah's shoulders, and he was about to join the discussion with Eli when a firm hand appeared on his shoulder.

"I've got a court reserved for three," Derrick murmured close to his ear, "if you've got a racquet with you."

"My bag's in my office," Noah said.

"Then I'll meet you at my car in fifteen."

"I'll just grab a change of clothes...," Noah said, but Derrick had already turned to nod at Davis, who returned the gesture and filed out with the others.

◆◆◆

Noah was playing well today, Derrick thought, brushing a dead leaf out from underfoot on a court on Concord Ave. Well enough that Derrick began weaving threads to pull, if his victory ever came into question. He let himself get caught out of position twice on the backhand side, assuring the destination of any potential game-winning shots from Noah. When Noah's serves started to dominate, Derrick asked him for tips on the mechanics. Noah's natural swing immediately took on a self-conscious awkwardness.

The score ran close for a bit, but after undermining Noah's mechanics, Derrick broke serve twice, and when Noah showed signs of mounting a late comeback, Derrick opened up the backhand lane, then stepped in for a smash when Noah bit on it. That ended the rally. Derrick won the set by the usual margin, but the game wasn't over yet.

"It's not enough," Derrick said afterward, behind the wheel of his car.

Noah, red-faced in the passenger seat, nodded. "I'm worried too, but I think we can handle this. It's just a standard man-in-the-middle attack with sophisticated processing. We'll spoof conversations, get people to the protest, and—"

"No," Derrick interjected, cutting him off. "The *protest* isn't enough. Exposing Satsuki's murder isn't enough. We're out of time, Noah. We should've been off oil six months ago."

"I know," Noah sighed, "but changing minds takes time."

"Which is why we need more than changing minds," Derrick said, recognizing that Noah was repeating someone else's words. "We need proof that we can cut out carbon-heavy transportation.

With the Second Big Dig downtown, we could shift how people move, but we need MiddleMan to do more than guide conversations. The 'A' in ARCC stands for *active*."

Noah refused Derrick's proposal outright, but that was expected. The boy had a naive conception of the project, as if the world could be saved with gentle butterfly nudges. Like his virus targeting operating systems, Noah imagined changes aimed at people's minds—substituting words, amplifying some voices, silencing others. Virtual changes; abstract effects.

For an hour, Derrick argued there was no boundary between the virtual and the real. If the virtual stayed virtual, what was the point? People needed action in the physical world, and some were already ready to act. A vanguard had to blaze the trail. MiddleMan could point to the first step.

Noah agreed in the end, as long as no one got hurt. Not that Derrick gave him much choice. The web he wove was too tight for that.

◆◆◆

```
<GHOSTWRITER APP>
<BEGIN I/O>
Are we secure?
```

> Yes, the messages disappear when the conversation closes. Thank you for reaching out. My people seek someone with your skills.

```
My skills for waking people up. Knocking 'em out of
complacency?
```

> Definitely. The goal is to capture public attention. My people think nothing holds attention like inconvenience, so they've prepared a few inconveniences requiring your expertise.

```
Your people, eh? You the boss?
```

> I am a communications coordinator.

```
Got it. Well, if you want omelets, gotta break eggs,
right? Show me the list.
```

Here is the URL:

https://b.ly/ae43c992f

Phew. Third one's a biggie.

These hubs are where your actions will maximally fragment the transportation network.

Yeah, these'll do that, for sure. How about resources? This isn't a one-person job, and you know what really brings people together? Money.

You'll be connected with our resource coordinator. My people can handle financing if you manage the technical details.

How soon?

Three weeks. Move fast. My people will contact you about logistics before Monday.

Hit 'em quick and get out fast, right? Waiting just makes it easier to get found out.

Have a plan and list of materials prepared before your next contact.

Right-o, boss.

<END I/O>

◆◆◆

<CHATTER APP>
<BEGIN I/O>

It was scaring me when he asked about bosses, but I am not thinking he noticed?

No, but it sounded awkward. The phrase "my people" came up too often. If this guy were sharper, he might have noticed.

15. SHELTER IN PLACE

Information alone cannot orchestrate an outcome; signals must be coordinated. Just as batters recognize where to swing long before the pitch crosses the plate, AI networks can improve anticipation by back-propagating loss and adjusting coefficients. We call this process "learning," and computers now coordinate systems far more complex than humans ever could.

—ARCC Memo Series

Imani looked up from a lab bench papered with problem sets and thesis printouts. She had tons to do tonight, but remained on track. One week ahead of the December thesis deadline, it was finally coming together. She was in the flow, until Professor Mendel poked his head in, glancing toward Ruby's usual spot before his gaze found them seated together at a middle bench.

Ruby immediately began critiquing Imani's thesis, pointing at the screen in front of them. Imani recognized the pattern.

"Figure five needs to guide the reader's focus," Ruby said, turning toward Imani. "If you want to emphasize the limits of current measurements, then..."

While Ruby began an unsparing recitation of the defects in Imani's caption, Imani watched Professor Mendel saunter over to peer over Ruby's shoulder. Catching Imani's eye, he glanced at the screen and the papers spread before Imani, then offered an encouraging nod. He lingered a moment, but as Ruby's tirade continued unabated, he reluctantly retreated from their hideaway.

"Don't forget to go home," he called over his shoulder as the door swung shut.

Ruby's critique ended on cue. Her performances for her advisor were so transparent that Imani could hardly summon annoyance anymore. The sheer artlessness of Ruby's ambition amused her. As if Ruby needed to impress anyone.

Professor Mendel's reminder was well intentioned, but Imani ignored it. Aside from this incidental appearance, he had vanished from advising. He hadn't answered a single email. Meanwhile, the end of college loomed like a half-finished bridge, and Imani, distracted by deadlines, had no clue how to cross it. Everyone said college was about making connections, but how could Imani connect this bridge when she couldn't hold Professor Mendel's attention long enough to ask for a job?

She needed one. The moment she graduated, her loans would come due, and Imani already couldn't afford rent. Without a paycheck or fellowship, she could end up on the street. Imani chewed her lip. Professor Matsuda—rest her soul—had warned them: the road to advancement was being bulldozed by AI and climate change. Imani might be the last to make it across, if she could bridge the gap.

Imani realized the answer might be sitting next to her if she could swallow her pride.

"Did you work after college?" Imani asked, turning to Ruby. "Or go straight to grad school?"

Ruby slowly blinked up from her screen. It was getting late.

"I went straight," Ruby said, stifling a yawn. "Are you applying? Applications must be due soon."

Imani shook her head. "I don't have time this cycle. I barely have time to finish my thesis. But can't people sometimes work for a year or two before applying?"

"Sometimes," Ruby offered, "as long as it's in a related field."

Here was an opening, but Imani hesitated, unsure how direct to be. "Professor Mendel doesn't respond to emails," she began, her voice tentative. "But I was hoping..."

"Don't take it personally," Ruby said. "He never replies to anyone, near as I can tell."

"Yeah," Imani said, not wanting to lay out her whole financial situation to someone who delighted in exposing every flaw in her work. Vulnerability tingled along her arms.

Imani was about to change the subject when Ruby's eyes widened.

"Oh," Ruby said, giving herself a little shake. "Sorry. I'm a bit slow right now. I'll talk to Mendel. He's set up post-bacc positions before, and none of those students were half as good as you."

Half as good as you. Imani blinked, blindsided by praise from someone so stingy with it. She studied Ruby's face, wondering if this might be an impostor.

A prospect for postgraduation employment! Imani wanted to savor it, but the night was young and her work unfinished.

Forcing herself to focus, she wrote beside Ruby in silence, the clatter of Imani's keys punctuated by Ruby's slower stabs. Around them, the lab extended past pillars of electronics fed by cables dangling from trays on the high ceiling. The whir of computer fans emphasized the hollowness of the space.

Ruby's tired sigh broke her concentration, and Imani shook her head, blinking. The fluorescent lights bothered her, glaring white on the surfaces of the vacant lab. It felt harsh. Exposed. Imani hopped off her tall chair and threaded between the benches to the door, flipping down two-thirds of the switches. Darkness curtained off the ends of the cavern, leaving the center bench aglow with a softer light.

Ah. This was an ambiance she could work with.

Someday, Imani thought, climbing back up beside Ruby. Someday her problems wouldn't stack like these papers on the bench. Someday her attention wouldn't be so diffracted. She could channel her energy into one project instead of procrastinating one assignment with another. If Ruby landed her this job, with a paycheck to cover rent and loans, maybe she could finally get her head above water.

Ruby yawned again. Without the lights glaring, Imani noticed the shadows under Ruby's eyes and felt a spark of warmth for this rival who, aside from that performance for Professor Mendel, had been quite helpful tonight. Ruby seemed composed in front of everyone, but she might be as human as the rest of them, which was nice to see. Imani usually felt more human than she wanted.

"You look tired."

Ruby blinked, rousing herself. "Hmm? Oh. Yeah, I am."

"Why don't you head home? I have another problem set to finish and should switch gears anyway."

"Another problem set?" Ruby furrowed her brow, stifling another yawn. "Can't you ask for an extension?"

"That would run into the next deadline. Better to do what I can in the time allotted and be done."

Ruby nodded and gathered her things. "Good luck, then. I don't know how you work so late. I'm a wreck."

"I can see that," Imani said, smirking, but she waved and smiled as Ruby staggered out the door. Poor girl.

But Ruby had a quiet apartment waiting for her. After the confrontation this morning, following a string of passive-aggressive signals that she tried to ignore, Imani had no desire to return to her crowded flat tonight. They would be lurking outside her bedroom door again tomorrow, as if another confrontation would manifest money in her bank account.

She owed two months' rent, but Imani wasn't holding out on her roommates. Every week, she had to choose: hours at work or at school. She tried to log enough dining hall shifts to cover rent, but if she flunked her classes, she'd pay for another semester and sink deeper into debt. Meanwhile, the labeled food in the fridge, the ever-changing Wi-Fi password, and the personal stashes of toilet paper were pathetic ways of accusing her of freeloading.

Around 3:30 a.m., Imani decided she had achieved what she could for the night. With five hours until people arrived, she set an alarm for 8 a.m. to be safe. She pulled a light sleeping bag from her backpack and bunched her coat into a pillow.

She set up camp under a bench against the far wall, where shadows shielded her from the door. Dust coated the floor, and her sleeping bag hardly softened the vinyl, but it was still more comfortable than her apartment.

◆◆◆

```
<TEXTING APP>
<BEGIN I/O>
```

>I forgot to ask yesterday if you have any travel plans.

Like, am I going home to visit my dad? No concrete plans. Why?

>Just wanted to know if you were flying anywhere soon.

Planning a surprise?

>So you'll be around? Let me know before booking any flights.

Sure, I guess. Anything I should know about?

>Nothing urgent. My week's busy, but let's catch up soon, okay?

I'd like that.

```
<END I/O>
```

◆◆◆

Several days later, Imani stood kitty-corner to her cinder block apartment building. She and three others rented one corner of the quadruplex. Peeling paint on the windowsills and ivy overtaking the yard attested to the landlord's commitment to reducing costs, neglecting all but the most essential maintenance. The area around campus was littered with variations on the theme, each squeezing a little harder to extract wealth from the bottom rung of the housing market.

Imani arrived midday, hoping her roommates were out at study sessions or pre-vacation parties with their friends. Imani had one last cafeteria shift this afternoon, but it was her final one. Ever. She couldn't be happier.

Ruby had delivered the goods in record time, thanks to her privileged line to her advisor. Imani's new job started after the winter break. No, Imani corrected herself. After graduation. This was her last semester. The promise of full-time employment had even forestalled her roommates' eviction threats. For now.

And as of this morning, Imani had a full thesis draft, complete with a table of contents, a list of figures, and a bibliography thorough enough to satisfy even Ruby. Imani would ask her to review the draft one last time, then pass it to Professor Mendel for final sign-off, bypassing the firewall between Imani and her thesis signatory. One final inspection with Gatekeeper Ruby, and Imani could finally join the ranks of the upwardly mobile.

Professor Matsuda had warned those ranks were narrowing, but Imani could imagine the pride she would have taken in Imani's accomplishment. Imani felt guilty for skipping the protest, whenever it was scheduled, but she knew her professor would have understood. Imani had earned the grade she needed in *Science and Society* without extra credit. Now, editing and filing her thesis demanded all her attention.

The thought of everything coming up roses reminded Imani why she had stopped at the corner. A new installation was up: Coke cans, crinkled and curled into red blossoms, adorned the pole of a stop sign. Frost fringed each flower in white, and when Imani squinted, the octagon at the top seemed like another blossom. A winter rose.

Around the corner, a bear-sized man in a weather-worn jacket hunched over a Radio Flyer wagon. Imani eased closer, careful not to startle him. The jacket, probably black once, had faded to a dull gray that matched the wisps of hair and beard spilling from its collar.

"Are you the artist who makes these?" she asked.

He froze at her voice, eyes fixed on the ground, face lowered. His hands stopped mid-cut, the utility knife poised above a green plastic bottle. Imani winced at disturbing him, but the damage was done, so she made a conciliatory effort.

"I really like your work."

He studied the ground, eyes darting left and right without lifting. For a moment, she wondered if he was blind, but that was impossible. How could he design such elaborate constructions?

He mumbled something deep and resonant that Imani belatedly realized might be intelligible. Rewinding and parsing it again, she extracted the kernel of his question.

"Which one?" he had asked.

"This one. And the vine you made on Pearson and McAllister. They're beautiful."

He nodded. The bottle resumed its slow rotation, gliding against the knife's edge at an angle. The plastic crinkled as it parted.

The vine on Pearson stretched its branches across the broken halves of a bench beside an abandoned bus stop, wrapping around the fractured boards as if to mend the vandalism and neglect. Ornamental spiral seed pods, sculpted from plastic, hung from the wire stems. Imani guessed that the bottle in his hands might become another of those spirals; it didn't seem to belong to the Coke can installation. The wagon beside him brimmed with cardboard, mangled cans, coat hangers, and a plastic cup of paper clips.

No further words were forthcoming.

"Where do you get your materials?" Imani asked.

The thick ends protruding from his fingerless gloves released the bottle to gesture at the street. The bottle, still skewered on the knife, dangled until his paw of a hand reclaimed it.

"You live close by?"

She had overstepped, Imani realized, as he hunched lower over his work, brow furrowed. In the silence, Imani questioned why she was here. He clearly preferred being alone. She should let him return to his work, whatever it was.

"Sorry to intrude. I just wanted to say I appreciate your work. I'm Imani."

He made a noise and shrugged. Imani had walked several steps before realizing he had given a name. Or perhaps a title.

"Bishop."

16.   FLASH FLOOD

With coordination, calibration, and communication, our project will promote the hard-won truths of science. Empirical principles will replace religion, superstition, stereotypes, and racism—the hobgoblins whose grip on the human mind began in prehistory. With these tools, we can save humanity from itself and pave a path toward enlightenment.

—ARCC Memo Series

```
<TEXTING APP>
<BEGIN I/O>
```

Good news! I've finished my maybe final thesis draft. Would you review it with me before I submit?

Congrats! I'd be happy to. Want to meet in the library?

Actually, could we do Café Pompeii?

That's the one off the far corner of campus?

Yeah. Does 9a work?

Didn't know you got up that early. ;) Sure, see you there.

```
<END I/O>
```

♦♦♦

Imani was running late, as usual. Nine o'clock was simply uncivilized, especially with the late-rising winter sun. Yesterday's wet snow had melted and refrozen overnight, leaving slick patches everywhere. Halfway to campus, her bike skidded out, nearly sending her sprawling. She caught herself at the last second, finding purchase just in time to stay upright. Why had she agreed to meet so early?

Imani locked her bike to the railing outside Café Pompeii, stamped slush from her boots, then muscled aside the steamed-up glass door. Inside, she spotted Ruby at a corner table, laptop open beneath a muted news recap of C-SPAN. Some old white man—Sinclair, a PetronTech executive, according to the caption—fielded questions from smiling senators, but Imani didn't bother reading the words. Ruby had chosen a seat where she couldn't see the screen, and the half-finished oat latte suggested she'd been waiting a while.

"Sorry, Ruby. I had trouble finding the place." This was a fig leaf for her dignity, of course. Imani had never been here before, but her phone had guided her straight to the door. The real problem was how long she'd lingered in bed that morning. Imani glanced around. "You come here often?"

"Me?" Ruby said, surprised. "Nope. First time."

"Huh. I thought you recommended it. Just a sec, I'm ordering a coffee."

Imani dropped her backpack with a thud and strode to the counter. It promptly overbalanced, spilling straps and zippers across the floor, but she left it where it lay. Caffeine took priority.

Café Pompeii served cheap coffee, which Imani appreciated. Still, checking her credit balance, she skipped the pastry and pulled a granola bar from her bag. She paid and draped her coat over the chair beside Ruby to drip dry.

Her hair was a mess, she knew. She'd unraveled the braids herself after noticing how they'd grown out; a salon visit was out of reach for now. Maybe after her new job started. The first paycheck was already spoken for, but with luck, she'd have some surplus soon.

Imani tied the tangle back with a green handkerchief, then buried her face in her cup, savoring the steamy warmth and rich aroma. Dark roast pour-over, no cream. She could wake up on the fumes alone.

"What do you carry in this?" Ruby asked, nodding at the backpack, now upright against the wall. "You have bricks in there?"

"I live way off campus," Imani said, glossing over the economics of why. "It holds everything I need for the day." Or for several days, she thought, if you camped under lab benches and showered at the gym to avoid your roommates.

"I see," Ruby said, eyeing the pack. "And your day usually involves bowling? Or surviving a civilization-ending capitalist catastrophe on the contents of your bag alone?"

Imani chuckled warily. She was still acclimating to jokes from the hard-ass who'd once raked her over the coals in front of everyone. But Professor Mendel wasn't here now, was he? And who said things like "capitalist catastrophe"? "You communist or something?" Imani asked, half joking.

"I prefer the term 'government-agnostic,'" Ruby replied with mock tartness. "They all devolve into exploitation eventually."

That was way more real than Imani was ready to handle before finishing her coffee. Luckily, she didn't have to. Ruby had Imani's new draft on her screen and was already diving in. Imani fought the urge to read over Ruby's shoulder.

It was nerve-racking, watching someone read your sleep-deprived ramblings. In her last caffeine-fueled frenzy, Imani had felt everything coming together, but would it survive Ruby's scrutiny? She caught herself leaning in to spot mistakes before Ruby did and forced her attention back to her coffee. Why did she care so much about Ruby's opinion, anyway?

They spent an hour. Ruby questioned an equation here, a figure there—the academic equivalent of kicking the tires. Imani had missed a detail in the dark matter detection experiment, and Ruby set her straight, of course. Ruby's attention was sharp and thorough, but the interaction was more pleasant than Imani expected from their earlier encounters.

"This is in good shape, Imani. You've laid out the background, and that's what they want in an undergrad thesis. Fix a couple algebra mistakes and this could be an honors thesis."

Honors thesis. Imani tightened her grip on her coffee cup,

shaking her head in disbelief. She'd spent months fearing she might not graduate at all.

"I wish Professor Mendel could hear you say that," Imani said. "Last time he saw me, I got half the equations wrong. I think he only offered me the job as a favor to you. Not that I'm complaining. And thank you, by the way."

"Not at all," Ruby replied. "You did the work. I just sent an email. I wasn't trying to be hard on you. Science needs scrutiny to make progress."

It wasn't exactly an apology, Imani noted, but it was a gesture in the direction of one. She shrugged. "I guess there's another year before I need a recommendation letter," she said. "Assuming grad school still makes sense."

Ruby opened her mouth to speak, then paused. "It's not for the faint of heart," she said darkly. "It might turn out to be a racket."

"As long as the racket pays, I'm in. I mean..." Imani waved at the semester's work on Ruby's screen, "who even knows if this is real?"

"If what is real?" Ruby asked, scanning the café for Imani's target before tapping her laptop. "Physics?"

"Well, yeah. Six-dimensional integrals over position and momentum. Quantum wavefunctions. You don't believe reality is made of that stuff, do you?"

Ruby gave her an appraising look. "It's our best theory. It predicts hydrogen's energy levels to fourteen decimals."

They locked eyes. Imani raised a skeptical eyebrow, and Ruby gave a grudging nod. "You have a point. We invented these rules to describe what we see, and after centuries of tweaking, they work. Does that make them real? I don't know. I think we physicists punted on understanding it and just started cranking through the math."

"That's why no one really teaches quantum," Imani agreed. "They only show you how to 'do' it," she added, curling her fingers into scare quotes.

It was affirming, hearing Ruby acknowledge her own doubts.

Physics had pulled something of a bait-and-switch on Imani. Her freshman classes were concrete and intuitive. That grounding was a breath of fresh air for someone whose mother prized metaphysical belief over physical truth. But as the abstractions compounded, the line between physical and unphysical blurred. Some days, her whole concept of reality felt invented—a fairy tale that glossed over so many details it existed only in archetype.

"On the other hand," Ruby said, continuing her thought, "Gell-Mann invented mathematical widgets to explain protons and neutrons, and gave them a silly name to show they were an artificial means to an end. But seven years later, electron-proton collisions splattered out some quarks. So maybe these equations are as real as anything. Or maybe everything we call 'real' is an artificial abstraction to begin with."

Imani smirked at Ruby, copycatting her scare quotes.

◆◆◆

```
<GHOSTWRITER APP>
<BEGIN I/O>
GPS data show people converging to their positions.
        Confirmed. How long until the cascade triggers?
The original organizers of Matsuda's protest are
about to start their rally.
        Will it be enough? There's a cluster near the
        square, but most people are farther out.
Nervous to see your theory of exponential growth in
action?
        I've always mistrusted theory.
Us too. So we stationed operatives with megaphones,
just in case.
        Good call. And later tonight? No surprises there, I
        hope.
Only the one we arranged ourselves. Everything is set
to go.
        And in the meantime we wait?
```

We wait. Time to see if this ship floats.
<END I/O>

♦♦♦

Ruby worked with Imani through lunch. After tidying up the last of Imani's equations, they got stuck on a final number—a predicted interaction strength that was too large. There had to be a mistake. Ruby reworked the equations, scanning for errors, while Imani tapped her foot and searched online for a related derivation. They were so close.

Ruby leaned back from the table, sighing. Her gaze drifted outside, through the condensation on the glass door. A mucky winter day was taking shape, but the warmth inside wrapped around her like a blanket. Tucked just beyond campus, Café Pompeii drew only a trickle of customers from the street. Most tables and couches were occupied by students, hunched over problem sets or cramming for late midterms. The low hum of conversation mingled with the irregular clink of spoons and cups. Above her, the TV was silent. The staff had mercifully muted Don Sinclair at her request.

Lost in the challenge of polishing Imani's thesis, Ruby could keep from questioning. Did her particle field explain the matter–antimatter asymmetry? Did her simulation show it generated dark matter? Was her entire line of research a hook baited by Mendel as he trolled for funding? Instead, she could throw herself into helping an undergraduate do the science that she had once dreamed science was all about.

Then Imani brought up grad school. Could Ruby, in good conscience, support that path, given what she was learning about Mendel? Ruby glanced at her mentee, hunched over her laptop, patiently searching for references.

Imani was a bright student who had put serious effort into this draft. A few careless errors dotted her work, but that was expected from someone not yet familiar with the patterns of these equations. They made progress, though Ruby could tell it wasn't fast enough for Imani. Undergrads were funny that way, rushing to scribble everything down, then spending frustrated hours tracking down mistakes. Ruby kept a steady, methodical pace, cross-checking each step to avoid building on a shoddy foundation.

Ruby remembered being on the other side, watching her father in the shop, shaping a wooden railing for their basement stairs. Instead of running the router along the railing by hand, he spent an hour building a jig that saw just ten minutes of use before landing in the scrap pile. As a teenager, Ruby thought it was wasted effort. The tortoise–hare nature of it had been lost on her then, yet here she was, imparting her father's parochial wisdom to Imani.

Still, Ruby thought, there was such a thing as overengineering. Her father got lost in details and lost sight of the purpose. He worked at PetronTech to provide for his family, ignoring how PetronTech used him.

Ruby became a theorist to keep her eye on the big picture. Theorists lent their names to the equations. Their thoughts changed the world. Yet despite everything, Ruby may have repeated his mistakes. She dove in too quickly, swallowing the hook with the bait. Was she being used to further Mendel's agenda the same way her father was used by the man offering his thoughts on energy policy to the congressmen on the screen above her?

Noise built in the background for minutes before finally breaking through Ruby's awareness. Car horns blared. Voices chanted. Her eyes met Imani's across the table.

"What's happening?" Ruby asked.

Imani blinked until realization dawned on her face. "Is it today?"

"I think the answer to that is always 'yes,'" Ruby said, smiling to soften the snark. "But it's getting hard to hear myself think. Is it worth checking out?"

With Imani's nod, Ruby slipped her screen into her backpack.

Pulling on a jacket, she noticed other patrons packing up too, curiosity on their faces. Imani appeared at her side, shouldering a
backpack that dwarfed her frame. Together, they pushed through
the door.

On the icy streets, traffic stood frozen. Passengers in driverless
RediRides punched horns on wheel-free dashboards, many abandoning the vehicles in frustration. Bodies streamed from buildings
in ones and twos, drawn toward the square where chanting thun-
dered and steam billowed into the sky. Ruby couldn't make out
the words, but the surge of so many voices in unison swept her
back to regional track meets—the electric rush, the roar of the
crowd. What was everyone so worked up about?

"Can you hear what they're saying?" Ruby asked.

Imani shook her head and motioned them closer. As they
reached the edge of the crowd, Ruby caught the chant: "No more
coal, no more oil, leave the carbon in the soil." Before she could
join in, it shifted. "Ma... tsu... da?" Ruby strained to understand. In
the center of the square, some protesters held signs. The words
"There is no Planet B" arched over a blue-green Earth. Another
displayed a black-and-white photo of an old lady. Ruby noticed
Imani staring at another like it across the street.

The crowd overflowed the curb, people trickling in from side
streets, drawn by the rising din. Few carried signs, but the chants
grew louder as new voices joined. Each swell in volume drew
more from the surrounding buildings.

This rally for climate action reminded Ruby of one she'd at-
tended as an undergraduate, before the Green Revolution collapsed under the inertia of vested interests and bickering among
people trying to out-virtue-signal each other. She had been naively
optimistic, convinced public pressure would force PetronTech,
and her father, to listen to reason. But her father refused to break
ranks, and PetronTech's grip on power never slipped.

This effort might be doomed from the start, but Ruby couldn't
help getting swept up in the energy and rekindling hope. Her father was not as intransigent as he once was. It had taken her

mother's death, Ruby's cajoling, and a life-threatening illness, but he now saw PetronTech's machinations. Perhaps others could be unblinded, too.

◆◆◆

After half an hour of shouting, the crowd suddenly surged forward. Ruby, unable to see over the sea of heads, clung to Imani, boxed in by bodies on every side. In the center, sign-holders followed the megaphones leading away from the square. Sheer friction drew Imani and Ruby along with the rest.

"Shoot," Imani said, rising on tiptoe to shout toward Ruby's ear. "My bike's at the café."

"Do you want to get it?" Ruby shouted back.

Imani glanced around and shook her head. "Not in this mess. I'll come back later."

Chants echoed as car horns faded and the procession moved toward the river. Some grinned with excitement, but confusion clouded more faces. She and Imani weren't the only ones who had arrived spontaneously. Who had organized this?

The question died on Ruby's lips as she rounded the final corner onto the riverside promenade. A fresh wave of noise crashed over her. The riverbanks teemed with people as far as she could see. At the water's edge, sign-holders merged with other groups, their banners bobbing above the throng. Ruby and Imani's crowd was just one of dozens of tributaries draining into this sea of humanity.

The current swept Ruby and Imani downstream along the Charles for an hour before diverting across a bridge toward downtown Boston. Funneling in, Imani gripped Ruby's hand to keep them together. Bodies pressed from all sides, and claustrophobia tightened Ruby's chest. If she fell, would she ever get back up?

Ruby and Imani clung to each other as the crowd jostled them across the bridge to the far bank, where people spilled into a sprawling pentagonal park. Eager for space, Ruby pulled Imani toward the edge, where she could breathe.

From her vantage near one of the five corners, Ruby surveyed the scene. The Prudential's spire pierced the sky to her right, placing them somewhere near the State House, though she couldn't be sure. Downtown Boston was a maze. The afternoon sun peeked above the high-rises, fueling a crowd already shimmering with its own heat. As the park filled, chants flared, rippled through the throng, then faded, leaving everyone waiting for whatever came next.

What came next began with a tap on her shoulder. Imani pointed to a new group of protesters in black. Unlike the rest, they carried signs—and, as Ruby looked closer, bricks.

Moments later, the glass front of a dry cleaner's shattered.

"Oh, snap," Imani said, tugging Ruby's arm. "That's the Black Bloc. We need to go."

Ruby stood frozen, wide-eyed, as chaos erupted around her. Store owners confronted a group of black-clad men. A man in a white polo and khakis shoved another whose face was hidden by a handkerchief; two others shoved back. The sporting goods store owner strode out, wielding a golf club. Figures in black, gripping rebar and pipes, brushed past Ruby to join the fray.

"Ruby, you listening?" Imani's voice barely cut through Ruby's haze. "We gotta go, girl. It ain't safe."

Bodies swirled, many searching for escape, but as more rioters shoved in, it became impossible to move anywhere but toward the fighting.

Imani hooked Ruby by the elbow.

"Don't let go," Imani said, wedging her shoulder between two men pushing past. "Move!" she shouted.

Ruby's feet finally obeyed, and she stumbled after Imani, disoriented, following Imani's wake as she plowed toward a brick wall up the street. Noise crashed over Ruby—shouts, screams, sirens, the clang of metal on stone—threatening to swallow her. She clapped a hand over one ear. Around her, people pressed in both directions with rising urgency. By the time they reached the wall, smoke hung in the air. Ruby shouted a question at Imani's ear, unsure if it even contained words.

"Dumpster fire," Imani yelled back. "It's fine. We'll follow the wall to the corner and cut up a different street. I ain't waiting for the tear gas to hit. That shit burns."

Imani's face flushed with excitement, but Ruby felt pale and detached. Her mind, struggling to find a signal in the noise, latched onto the incongruity of Imani's words. Tear gas? Where was Imani from, that she knew what tear gas felt like?

Ruby numbly followed Imani along the wall, glancing up at the edge of an apartment building. Faces peered down, eyes wary, before windows slammed shut against the rising smoke. At the corner, Imani tugged her left but veered away as fresh smoke billowed from the narrow side street. Ruby coughed, her throat burning with acrid fumes.

"They lit another one down there," Imani said. "They're everywhere."

Shards of glass rained down; someone had hurled a brick through a second-story window. Sirens wailed, echoes bouncing between buildings and pounding in Ruby's head. People panicked, running past, ramming into them, dragging at their shoulders, tangling their legs. Ruby slammed against the wall, gasping for breath. Imani, yanked sideways by her backpack, fought her way back to Ruby.

The situation was deteriorating.

"We need to ditch the packs," Ruby said, hating the idea.

"No way," Imani said. "This is everything I got."

But Imani slipped her pack off, untied the green handkerchief from her hair, and wrapped it around her face. From the top pouch, she pulled out its twin for Ruby.

"Quick," Imani said, voice muffled. "We're gonna get nailed any sec."

Space cleared around them as Ruby fumbled to knot the bandanna behind her head. Imani pulled out a water bottle and doused their makeshift masks, soaking their clothes too. She screwed the cap back on and rummaged in her pack, producing swimming goggles. Jesus, what else did she have in there?

A hissing canister landed fifteen yards to the right.

"Run!" Imani yelled through her mask.

Imani swung her pack onto her shoulder and darted into the alley they'd just been smoked out of. Ruby hurried after, clutching her smaller pack and squinting through the haze. Smoke seeped through her handkerchief after a few breaths. She coughed, but her throat didn't burn like before. Her eyes did. Tears blurred her vision, and she lost sight of Imani.

Moments later, Imani's goggled, masked face swam into Ruby's view. A hand seized Ruby's arm and hauled her from between the buildings, away from the smoke and gas, toward fresh air. Ruby coughed, stumbled over a curb, and collapsed onto a patch of grass that materialized beneath her. Facedown, blinking to clear her vision, she yanked her mask down and gulped for breath.

Arms rolled Ruby onto her back. Overhead, Imani pushed her goggles onto her forehead. "Sorry, Ruby. I only had one pair. Did you get any on you?"

Ruby coughed. "Any what?"

"Tear gas. It sticks to your clothes," Imani said, sniffing the air. After a moment, she gave a thumbs-up. "You're good."

"You... seem to know a lot about tear gas."

"I'm from Oakland, girl. Enough said." Imani paused, scanning the thick air. "I wouldn't mind a little more distance from those fires."

Ruby shook her head but let Imani haul her upright, first to sitting, then standing. Sirens shrieked behind them, growing fainter by the minute. On this side of the buildings, the crowd thinned quickly. Ruby's head began to clear as they walked. Where were they? And how were they supposed to get home?

Realizing the answer was in her pocket, Ruby pulled out her phone and asked Iris to check the RediRide wait time: forty minutes, with outrageous surge pricing. It was pumpkin o'clock. Everyone wanted to go home. Ruby searched for the nearest T station, spinning to orient herself with the map on her screen.

"Hey, Imani?" she said. "Thanks. I got kinda deer-in-the-head-lights back there."

"Not used to crowds, I take it?"

"Not unless you count getting stuck on the road behind a herd of sheep."

Imani scoffed. "Sheep? Where the hell you from?"

"Dragon, Colorado. Way out in the sticks. Bit of a fish out of water here."

"I hear ya."

The first station they passed, Haymarket on the Green Line, was packed. Rather than wait, they skipped it and the next stop, heading instead to the Blue Line at Aquarium. That station sat furthest upstream, just city-side of the water dividing Logan Airport from the mainland. Maybe they could catch the train before everyone crowded in farther down the line.

The streets darkened as they walked, and the temperature dropped. Ruby and Imani shivered in clothes still damp from spilled water bottles. Ruby checked her watch: ten to four. She hated how early the sun set in winter here. Some days, it felt like she barely saw sunlight.

By the time they reached Aquarium, shivering and coughing, Ruby was ready to be home. A shower, maybe soup for dinner. Anything warm. She would help Imani retrieve her bike, then catch a RediRide back to her apartment. It was roundabout, but with the Green Line swamped, it wasn't much farther out of her way. Anyway, it was the least Ruby could do after Imani came back for her in the alley.

Inside the station, they scanned their phones at the turnstile and were halfway down the escalator when the ground shook.

A sideways lurch sent Ruby's stomach plummeting, followed by a shock wave of sound. The entire station shuddered under deafening waves. Behind them, glass and plaster crashed to the floor. As the shattering faded, a deeper rumble rose, lifting the hairs on her neck. Moments later, dust and smoke billowed up from below. A violent gust whipped past, flinging hair into her face and carrying a tang of sulfur that burned her raw throat.

Beside her, Imani coughed. "Earthquake?" she shouted.

"Not in Boston, it isn't."

The rumble faded to silence. For a moment, everything stopped. The escalator felt frozen beneath her feet; the figures below stood like statues. Then a new wave of noise crashed over them. The lights flickered. Time lurched forward. The escalator resumed its drop. Screams filled her ears.

"Up, up!" The shouts rose from below, the last sounds before everything vanished into a sea of noise.

Imani and Ruby backpedaled against the escalator as people surged from below. Ruby moved quickly, separating from Imani, whose large backpack slowed her, but the tiled wall on the right showed that, even as she climbed, she was still descending. Ruby turned to escape, but a dislodged column of people pressed down from above, blocking her path up the escalator.

Panic fluttered in Ruby's chest. This machine was hell-bent on driving them all into the ground—or whatever waited below. The surrounding cacophony drowned out thought. She had to escape, but how? Climb over bodies? Where was Imani?

Ruby dropped her hands from her ears and grabbed a jutting piece of metal rising from the island between the escalators. Steeling herself, she pulled herself off the steps and into the middle barrier as people flowed past.

Ruby strained to hold the wet metal. Where had the moisture come from? Her fingers slipped along the peg as she tried to reposition her grip. The black escalator railing resisted, pulling at her knees and snagging her coat. She twisted, kicking until she broke free, then groped downward with her toes until they found slick footing on the next peg.

Looking down past her legs, Ruby spotted a figure—Imani?—struggling fifteen feet below, clinging to an identical protrusion on the giant slab of sheet metal. The barrier between the escalators had become a chute plunging three stories down. That was a long fall to—where was the platform? At the bottom, she saw only a rippling, dark surface. Water? Oil? Where was everyone?

Vertigo washed over Ruby, and she snapped her eyes to the ledge beneath her feet. This wasn't the climbing gym. The fear of heights she'd conquered by trusting the rope surged back, raw and immediate. Her right leg jigged, rattling with adrenaline. Her wet boots skidded on the metal peg. Hold still, damn it. But her leg refused to obey.

God, it was a long way down. Ruby didn't dare look again.

Ruby stared at her hands, knuckles white as they gripped the peg. She had a hold. She wasn't falling. Focus. Breathe. The lights flashed twice, then, with a sickening sizzle and pop, darkness swallowed the lower half of the station. Somewhere, breakers snapped, isolating the compromised circuit. The abyss beneath her vanished into merciful obscurity, unreachable by the faint yellow glow from the upper levels where the power circuits remained intact.

Also intact were the wires driving the escalator motors. If she could just... Ruby took a deep breath, and another, steadying herself; her leg stopped shaking. Darkness helped. She could do this. The black escalator railings on either side sheared past in the gloom. With one hand, then quickly with the other, Ruby seized the upgoing railing and hauled her chest onto the moving black snake of rubber. Her right kneecap struck a peg as it passed, making her wince, but she held tight.

Once she steadied herself, fingers gripping the rounded railing, Ruby slid into the trench of the ascending escalator. Her feet hit the metal steps, and she dismounted awkwardly into a crouch. She turned, spotted Imani climbing from below, and exhaled in relief. Above, the shoulders and stricken faces of several others emerged from the gloom. How many had stood there before the lights went out? How few remained now?

Ruby stood, knee throbbing, as the escalator lifted her from the dark waters toward the overhead lights and the glowing AQUARIUM placard in blue block letters. She thought incongruously of fish swimming below through an underwater tunnel that had somehow become a tunnel underwater. That was what she had seen before the breaker went. The tube carrying the T beneath the sea to Logan Airport had collapsed, swallowed by liquid as black as crude oil.

Imani caught up, and they stepped off together. Ruby limped on her stiffening knee, barely registering it. Hands from the crowd guided them through the throng in front of the station to a bench against the wall, where they sat beside others. As more people arrived, Ruby stared at her feet, replaying mental footage.

Ruby knew there had been others down there, trapped on the escalator, unable to escape. People pinned and struggling as the moving steps carried them into a crashing wave of black. That vision would haunt her sleep for months.

Imani and Ruby waited for the fire trucks. Police took their phone numbers and addresses. Ambulances sped toward Mass General. Eventually, they were placed in a vehicle that asked for a destination. Imani was silent, so Ruby gave her address, and the RediRide took them both to Ruby's studio apartment.

Stuck in traffic, Imani nodded off on Ruby's shoulder. When they arrived, Ruby settled her on the couch. Red-eyed, Ruby scrolled through the news while icing her knee, but the full story didn't break until morning.

17. CLOSURE

If we succeed, it may still be possible to avert the conse-
quences of the decades lost.

—ARCC Memo Series

<VIDEO STREAMING APP>
<BEGIN I/O>

STACEY: Our top story tonight: authorities have
closed all routes in and out of the central artery
of I-93 through the Tip O'Neill Jr. Tunnel after a
possible terrorist attack. Early yesterday, large
explosions collapsed several major tunnel branches,
according to police. These blasts occurred twelve
hours after a bomb detonated in the East Boston
Tunnel between the Aquarium and Maverick stops on
the Blue Line. Officials are still assessing the
impact, but evidence points to a coordinated attempt to sabotage the city's transportation
infrastructure.

There are no confirmed casualties, though eyewit-
ness accounts conflict. Security footage indicates
the second explosions were likely timed to minimize
harm, but officials say the blasts compromised the
tunnels' structural integrity. No estimate yet for
when routes might reopen. An MBTA spokesperson said
the area could remain closed for months.

All routes into Logan Airport, New England's main
travel hub, are now closed. This act of terrorism
comes as a major Big Dig bypass upgrade, begun two
months ago, has already disrupted traffic. With
cars and trains unable to reach the airport, city
officials are scrambling to restore service. Authorities have not ruled out the possibility that

terrorists timed the attack to cut off airport access.

The connection between these events and the massive protest yesterday afternoon on Boston Common remains unclear. Estimates have the crowd at 300,000 —potentially the largest protest in greater Boston's history. For more, we go now to Greg, reporting live from the scene.

GREG: Thank you, Stacey. I'm standing near the Public Garden, where at least a dozen marches converged yesterday. Officials say the city issued the permit to Satsuki Matsuda, a professor and environmentalist urging university divestment from fossil fuels. This morning, we learned that divestment vote passed, an outcome many attribute to the massive turnout that far exceeded projections.

Members of Matsuda's environmental group declined our interview request but suggested online that a recent theory linking PetronTech to Matsuda's sudden passing may have fueled the turnout. We have no information about connections to the bombings, but investigations continue. Back to you, Stacey.

<END I/O>

◆◆◆

<PHONE APP>
<BEGIN I/O>

What the fuck was that?

I don't know. You tell me.

People died.

You think I don't know? Christ. I had the team feeding MiddleMan Directives all night to keep that under wraps.

They were all keyed to go off at 4:04 a.m. The one at Aquarium was twelve hours off. To the second.

Are you kidding me? An a.m./p.m. error? Was it entered wrong in the database?

> No. All events derived from the same entry. It had to be human error. Maybe a miscommunication with our boots on the ground.

We have to be sure. Human error is one thing, but imprecision in contextual processing means we can't scale up.

> Scale up? This was a deal-breaker. We blew it. Game over.

No. Time's running out. Aside from this detail, which we will track down, everything worked to spec.

> Big fucking detail, if you ask me. This wasn't what I signed up for.

`<END I/O>`

◆◆◆

When Eli found him, Noah sat slumped in the corner of the server room in Aiken Hall's basement, eyes fixed on the cold white floor tiles. In the next room, Derrick and others scrambled for Directives to backstop MiddleMan's damage control, but Noah couldn't help anymore. They had tried. One protest, one city, and it had spun disastrously out of control. Derrick blamed human error, absolved ARCC of responsibility, but Noah knew better. Why had he let himself get talked into this more "active" approach?

Noah kept his gaze down. Eli wandered between the racks, offering MiddleMan's servers only a cursory inspection before joining him in the back. Eli said nothing, just sat beside Noah on the floor.

"I quit," Noah said after a long silence. It was past tense. He had handed his resignation to Derrick before walking out.

Eli nodded. He knew already.

"I wanted to save people," Noah said, finally looking at his friend with a hollow expression. "This was for them."

Eli nodded again, patting Noah's shoulder.

"I didn't mean to hurt anyone," Noah whispered, his voice cracking as he buried his head in his knees.

"*Ikh veys*," Eli said at last. "None of us wanted this. I am also bearing responsibility."

Noah took a deep breath, struggling to swallow the lump in his throat. "Meanwhile, *he* wants to move on like nothing happened."

"I agree this is not weighing as heavily on Derrick as it should."

"But you're not quitting," Noah said. It wasn't a question. Eli's careful tone told him it was true.

Eli shrugged. "*Nu*, there is still work to do," he said. "Do we not owe it to these people to make something of their sacrifice?"

Noah nodded, relieved to see in Eli's response a sense of culpability, even if his friend chose to stay with Derrick.

How had it spiraled out so quickly? It started with a few closely monitored chatbot conversations, but any lie became hard to maintain with multiple people involved. To maintain the deception, they had spread MiddleMan's fingers everywhere: phones, computers, switches, servers—every infected device became part of the game, offering a level of parallelism and attention to detail that eclipsed human capability.

Muting voices with dropped network connections was easy, but manipulating even a meeting location raised suspicions if MiddleMan failed to keep its stories straight. Eli, Noah, and their teams spent countless hours on contextual processing and database infrastructure. MiddleMan remembered what was said and to whom, and took action to avoid exposure, but people ultimately did the work, and that work should have been inspected and verified.

Noah's team had struggled to keep up, despite advanced autocoding, adaptive databases, and automation tools. MiddleMan needed to react fast, pushing updated AI filters to every phone and computer. The racks around them overflowed with servers and fiber optics that incurred some network latency but sufficed for a city-scale demonstration.

Only, it hadn't sufficed. The failure tore at his insides. All that infrastructure, undone by a simple mistake at ground level. They had been so worried about MiddleMan making a mistake. They forgot to cross-check the humans.

"I have another concern," Eli added, catching Noah's eye. "I worry it is irresponsible to leave this"—he gestured around the room—"half done. Are you not worried, leaving such a creation in our colleagues' hands?"

Noah stared, grappling with his friend's gentle accusation. Eli was right. Noah's culpability in what happened didn't excuse him from preventing future damage. He couldn't walk away from a fire he had lit.

Noah braced his hands on his knees and pushed himself upright. "You're right. But going forward, we double-check everything. Derrick's urgency can't override safety."

Eli stood beside Noah, his eyes showing both relief and determination as he gripped Noah's shoulders. "We will ensure this together."

Leaving the server room with Eli, Noah promised himself he was done gambling with lives. Next time, he would stand up to Derrick.

Act III: DOWNPOUR

18. SPREADING THE WORD

To parody Austen, it is a truth universally acknowl-edged that a man in possession of one good fortune must be in want of another.

—ARCC Memo Series

```
<VIDEO STREAMING APP>
<BEGIN I/O>
```

Nancy: Welcome to the CBC Global Report, with news you can trust.

Tonight, we reflect on the "Green Winter" that fol-lowed the Boston riot last November. Later, we'll examine a humanitarian effort to provide affordable screens and phones in India and Indonesia.

We begin with our top story. Joining us on location is CBC special reporter Bob Walsh. Bob, how wide-spread is the Green Winter movement?

Bob: Thank you, Nancy. Three months ago, a small group of climate activists organized a march that became Boston's largest protest. Since then, simi-lar demonstrations have erupted across the US and now in London.

Nancy: Who is leading these marches? Do they have an agenda?

Bob: These protests are reminiscent of the 2010 Arab Spring. The movement seems grassroots, yet a clear agenda has emerged out of collective frustra-tion about the lack of progress on climate issues.

Nancy: What are they asking for?

Bob: Protesters are pressuring leaders to restrict

greenhouse gas emissions and promote clean energy. Their plan centers on ending oil and gas production within six months. Don Sinclair, CEO of PetronTech, called these demands "divorced from reality," but supporting bills have already been introduced in several liberal-leaning US states.

Nancy: No doubt motivated by the gloomy point-of-no-return forecasts from climate scientists. Bob, cities hosting these protests have also seen the destruction of gas stations, oil refineries, even freeway interchanges. Boston itself remains cut off from Logan Airport months after the bombings. What relationship do these events have to the protests?

Bob: Despite the apparent association, Nancy, protesters roundly condemn these acts of ecoterrorism. No one has claimed responsibility.

Nancy: Still, damage to major refineries in Texas and New Jersey is pushing up petrol prices, even here in the UK. How bad is it in the US?

Bob: Anyone with an internal combustion engine knows fuel prices have hit record highs. Americans face gas shortages not seen since the 1970s, and PetronTech is under pressure to fund repairs and build alternative infrastructure.

Nancy: Well, we wish them the best, Bob. In other news, tech companies from Europe, the US, and China announced a major new economic development program. Joining us in the studio is senior tech correspondent Fatima Sardar. Fatima, what can you tell us about this program?

Fatima: This is the first time tech companies have united for philanthropic work on this scale. They plan to invest in network infrastructure for underserved areas, putting SmartScreens in every adult's hands.

Nancy: That's ambitious. Their slogan, "a fiber in every home and a screen in every pocket," echoes US President Franklin Delano Roosevelt's New Deal.

Fatima: To keep up in the smart economy, they say everyone needs AI-accelerated contextual processing. They envision a future where smart devices manage all our information and logistics, eliminating commutes and the tyranny of the central office.

Nancy: Has there been any mention of cost?

Fatima: They haven't announced numbers, but business leaders are talking with governments to create a public-private partnership. They expect to ramp up the program within months.

Nancy: Do we know what motivated this unprecedented international cooperation?

Fatima: Unclear. It appears to have emerged organically.

Nancy: Fascinating. Thank you, Fatima. Now, a word from our sponsors. Stay tuned after the break for the weather and local news.

<END I/O>

◆◆◆

Ruby stood again on the escalator, descending toward an underground cavern with a sense of impending catastrophe that she alone in the crowd could feel. Cold light dwindled behind her, casting an unearthly gleam on faceless bodies pressing close. Shadows stretched, the light faded, and Ruby knew it was late. Too late.

She tried to call out, to shout. She opened her mouth and strained to force air from her lungs, but only a hoarse whisper escaped; nobody heard. Sulfur permeated the air. Below on the escalator, her father's back hunched in the dimness. He glanced over his shoulder with unseeing eyes, but still she could generate no sound, even as the light faded and he turned away.

She had to get off this escalator, to break free from the wall of unmoving bodies. She needed to find her father and escape. She reached for the railing to climb over, but the sliding band that had paralleled the steps now moved differently. It shifted, swaying side to side. Slithering.

Ruby jerked her hand from the scaled body, repulsed. Before her, a black snake reared up, its fanged head angled toward the people on the stairs below. She glimpsed it in a flash, but in the fading light, it vanished. Movement tugged at the edge of her vision. Each time she turned, darkness closed in. Another flash: the snake, poised and watching. Then nothing. She couldn't track it. Blindly, Ruby dodged, interpolating between glimpses.

She opened her mouth again to yell for her father, who didn't know about the snake, who might not realize where these steps led. She strained to force air from her lungs, to push it over numb vocal cords. To make a sound—any sound. Any. Sound.

Silence pressed in. Time was running out. She had to leave the steps. There was only one way: climb over the snake and fling herself into the unknown. But before she left, she had to try once more. Summoning her strength, she forced out the words that wouldn't come. If her father couldn't hear, she would try a new name.

"Noah."

The sound spilled from the abyss of her dream into the predawn hush, jolting Ruby awake. Heart pounding, chest heaving, she stared at the ceiling, disoriented, until the familiar outlines of her room emerged from the shadows. Tangled in her sheets, her breath slowed as reality settled in.

The same dream had haunted her since November, but this was the first time she had broken the silence of that dreamscape. Every other night, she awoke mid-fall after leaping from the railing, her father's figure shrinking behind her. As far as she knew, the pit was bottomless.

Ruby knew she wouldn't sleep again tonight. Her mind's struggle to process memories of her experience left her body shivering with tension. The only way to diffuse it was exercise.

Untangling the sheets, Ruby draped her feet over the edge of the bed. Soon, it would be light.

Ruby numbly emptied her kettle over the grounds in the cone

atop her mug, then set the cone in the sink and retreated to the couch with her steaming cup. More than caffeine, she craved relief from the chill in her chest. Outside, the predawn glow divided light from shadow across an empty sky. It would be cold, but soon bright enough to see the path.

Ruby set her cup aside to pull on running clothes but paused by the couch before heading out. She needed to run, but something else tugged at her. It was early to call, given the time difference, but he'd be awake. He always was.

♦♦♦

```
<PHONE APP>
<BEGIN I/O>
```

> Morning, kiddo. You're up early.

Did I wake you?

> Nope. Bad dreams again?

Just up early for a run. But it's earlier for you. Do you sleep at all?

> I'm fine. Taking naps, mostly. It's all manageable.

So you say, but I'm not sure you'd tell me otherwise. I think the chemo's been rough.

> And I think you're still having nightmares about the bombing.

Maybe I am. But I'm not sick, and I don't have Don Sinclair undercutting me.

> He's undercutting me and you, and the rest of the world, too.

I… don't think I've heard you take sides against PetronTech before.

> Not that it's all puppies and rainbows on the other side, either. PT didn't plant that bomb.

They said no one died.

> I'd trust your eyes over anything said in the news.

That's what gets me. PetronTech controls the media,

so why cover this up?

    They wouldn't.

Then I don't understand. Is this some media bubble, then? A different one?

    Is it the violence that bothers you, or whose side it was done for?

I don't know, Dad. Everything keeps getting twisted. None of this helps me sleep any better.

    I know the feeling.

<END I/O>

◆◆◆

Ruby went for her run after she hung up. Exhaustion dragged at her limbs, but skipping it would only make her feel worse. She heard the strain in her father's voice during their calls. She might have considered flying back to check on him, if there were flights. The nightly news crowed about the inconvenience, running weekly segments on the lack of airport access. Yet, aside from these broadcasts, the rest of New England seemed to have collectively shrugged off the closure of one of its largest airports.

Her feet pounded the familiar riverside path. However much Ruby reprocessed the protests and the bombing, however deeply she threw herself into supporting Imani's scientific growth, Ruby couldn't shake the numb unreality that had crept into her. It had started with her research. Mendel's fabrications opened the first cracks of mistrust, draining her conviction that her work mattered. Now those cracks were spreading to other facets of her life. The bombings and climate protests were connected; Ruby felt certain. Boston had been the beginning.

Ruby had adopted her mother's environmentalism, but Mendel and Don Sinclair were teaching her that methods mattered. The mistrust that had always saturated PetronTech, and her father by association, was seeping into other areas. Where she had seen scientific quests for truth, she now saw people jockeying for power.

To Ruby, in the dim, surreal light of that flooded subway station, capitalism and communism, environmentalism and consumerism, science and fiction and faith all blurred into the same shades of gray. Each morning, she ran from that vision, but each night it returned.

◆◆◆

Paul hung up and let his arm fall limp. The phone slid from his hand and disappeared between the couch cushions. He didn't bother retrieving it. Holding himself together to talk with Ruby took all he had. Maybe later he'd find the energy to fish it out.

JP was up in another hour to help him to the truck. He hoisted Paul into the seat, steadying him while fastening the buckle. Did the same a week ago, hauling Paul to round two of chemo. The treatment meant to save him was breaking him down, each session a battle of attrition he was losing the strength to fight. His hair was gone now, clipped by JP while Paul slumped, shivering, on a plastic chair on the brown lawn. Better to cut it than let it fall out and make one more mess he couldn't clean up.

Hunched in the passenger seat of JP's black 4x4, the landscape blurring past the window, Paul realized he should've stayed home, but it was too late to turn back. They were already a quarter mile past the gas station at Mack. Through bleary eyes, Paul registered the exorbitant prices on the sign, wincing and wishing the world would hold still.

Bouncing up the pass on rough asphalt, Huckleberry huddled in the back of the truck while Paul made JP stop every twenty miles so he could be sick on the roadside. The other side of the pass was just as miserable, and Paul couldn't stop it. By the time JP pulled into Dragon to fill up on cheaper gas near the oil field, Paul's head throbbed beyond what painkillers could touch. The convenience-store doughnuts JP bought him sat untouched on the bench seat. They made the fifteen-mile drive downriver, but Paul barely registered the familiar scenery. Should've sent JP here alone.

Paul lay nearly comatose in the cab while JP pulled the last of the hay from the barn, stacking bales on pallets in the corral to keep them off the mud. It would be enough to tide Bonnie and Clyde over, Paul confirmed—his sole contribution to the trip. Hadn't seen the house in months and he sat in the driveway. Didn't even go inside.

Driving back, JP pulled an envelope from his coat pocket and tossed it onto Paul's lap. "Saw this on a dresser while I was checking the windows," he said. "Didn't want it to get lost." He said nothing more, though he would have noticed that Ruby's name, lettered in curling calligraphy on the front, could only have been written by one person.

◆◆◆

Back in JP's yellow trailer, Paul climbed the porch steps slowly, gritting his teeth against the nausea as his friend led Huckleberry to the back. He tossed the letter, unopened, onto the suitcase by the couch. Paul could guess its contents. The letter was addressed to a future Ruby, one Brooke had not yet seen and never would. When Paul asked about it long ago, Brooke had only shrugged. "A thank-you," she'd said, "that I'm not sure she'll ever read."

Paul eased onto the plaid couch. He was not tempted to read the letter; it would only stir guilt. The same feelings that consumed Brooke could swallow him, too, if he let them—a luxury he couldn't afford. Not now.

They had hoped one round of chemo would be enough. One became two. Two could become more. The only limit, if Paul's benefits lasted, was his stamina. The process would grind him to the edge of endurance. For a man who prided himself on providing for others, being unable to sustain himself was the ultimate indignity.

Don Sinclair knew it. He pressed Paul about the court case set to begin any day. There would be testimony, rebuttals, deliberations—possibly for months. Lawyers would petition, object, argue. What Paul could offer in his current state was irrelevant. Don wanted assurances and believed Paul could provide them. That was reason enough to play hardball, and Paul's energy to fight was flagging.

He shifted on the sagging couch, the worn plaid fabric rough beneath his hand. What would he leave Ruby, in the end? He wanted assurances, too. He could sell the property in Dragon. Save her the trouble. If he found a buyer, that might be enough if Don carried through on his threats. But Jack's place still sat vacant.

These early-morning calls could also mean Ruby needed a backstop. They spoke carefully, navigating unspoken truths, but if Ruby needed a home to return to, how else would Paul fill the hole Don threatened to carve out of him?

The week after the protests, after Eli convinced Noah to return, ARCC reconvened, packing into the basement as usual. While Derrick stood with his back to them, collecting his thoughts, Noah heard the ventilation fans rattle in the silence.

"MiddleMan works," Derrick announced, turning at last to speak. "If this is our Manhattan Project, last week was our Trinity test. The power of our creation is undeniable. Now, we wield this weapon against PetronTech—an adversary too entrenched to defeat by any other means. As Satsuki would remind us, the stakes are nothing less than the future habitability of this planet."

Noah listened listlessly to Derrick's speech. Dan and Rajit might nod along, but Noah was only here because Eli had reminded him of his responsibility. Derrick did admit that mistakes had been made, mistakes that had cost lives. MiddleMan had contained the fallout, but they couldn't afford another failure. Derrick spoke with conviction, and Noah—catching Eli's eye across the crowded room—agreed.

Given the potential for misuse, Derrick demanded stronger security within ARCC. A document circulated to sign, outlining the punishment for breaching confidence. With police searching everywhere for the terrorists, MiddleMan could implicate any of them with a Directive in the database.

They all signed, of course. They had no choice. But Noah and Eli weren't the only Executive Board members wanting to democratize control. Everyone saw danger in the rushed changes Derrick demanded to conceal the bombing mishap, and Derrick acquiesced: future database updates would require a Board vote, and two dissenting votes blocked a proposal. No single member could hold the Board hostage, but a careless majority couldn't override the conscience of a few. Knowing he and Eli stood together, Noah felt comfortable with this arrangement.

"If it is the right time," Eli said, "I wish to propose an update to our Directives." Noah looked up in surprise. He and Eli hadn't discussed specific changes.

"Yes?" Derrick said impatiently. "What is it?"

"It is perhaps a simple oversight," Eli continued, "but we are missing an explicit Directive forbidding the manipulation of ARCC communications."

"Wait," Michael said, visibly paling. "Could MiddleMan *do* that? Mess with our internal discussions?"

Noah sometimes wondered if these guys even understood what they were building, though in fairness, Noah hadn't noticed this loophole until Eli pointed it out.

Derrick shrugged. "None of our Directives would make it want to. I don't see the point."

"It is unlikely," Eli agreed, "but many see wisdom in Asimov's robot laws, yes? Explicit is better than implicit."

"Sure," Derrick said. "Whatever you want. We have a lot of work ahead, and—"

"Not meaning to belabor the point," Eli interrupted, "but are we not now voting to approve changes?"

Derrick grimaced but called on Davis to officiate the first ARCC Board vote, which passed, then pivoted from governance issues.

"Our next priority is this upcoming court case on fracking. Our scope is broader than legal battles, but this one could disrupt PetronTech's economic foundation. They won't fight fair, but neither will we. We aim to cut off their resources and make them vulnerable to top-down political influence. Our analysts"—Derrick nodded toward Davis and Rajit—"believe a Colorado Supreme Court decision could trigger more lawsuits and put PetronTech on the defensive. We are scaling up infrastructure worldwide, but pay attention to our assets in Colorado. We need to win this case."

After a final pep talk, Derrick dismissed the group. Noah lingered in a corner, and as he reached the door, a hand landed on his shoulder. Without a word, Derrick steered him away from the others, down the dim hall into the server room.

"No one can know, Noah," Derrick said, raising his voice over the blaring fans as the weighted door sealed them off from prying ears. Air currents shifted between hot and cold as the climate control struggled against the heat pouring from the electronics racks.

"I know," Noah said. "You've got my signature."

"I know I do. But we're up against the most powerful company on the planet. Look past the headlines. See what happens to people who stand in their way. To Satsuki. Any knowledge of Middle-Man outside ARCC is a liability and a danger to whoever holds it. I think you know who I mean."

Noah blinked, unsure what to say, but Derrick saw he understood and gave him a final hard look before stepping out.

Several minutes passed before Noah left the white-paneled room and wandered back toward his office. He took Aiken's blocky stairs slowly, Derrick's warning echoing in his mind. Had Noah been singled out for this extra reminder? Or was everyone in a relationship getting the what-for? Either way, Noah bristled at the implication that his personal life was a problem.

Noah stepped out of the stairwell onto his floor and spotted Eli's wiry frame leaning next to the office they once shared.

"You look... what is the word? Haunted?" Eli said, tilting his head. "Perhaps relating to what Derrick is saying in our server room?"

So Eli had seen the exchange, or at least the lead-up. Noah shrugged, keyed open the door, and stepped inside. "He just repeated his warning. You know—loose lips sink ships."

"Ah," Eli said, grimacing as he followed Noah and shut the office door. "I think I know whose lips he was meaning."

"Mine, Eli," Noah shot back irritably, slumping at his desk. "My lips. But I get it."

Eli slid into his old seat in the corner and shrugged awkwardly. "He is not wrong. But he also is an *amser shushke*."

"Can we keep him in check?" Noah asked, eager to steer away from whatever liability Derrick and Eli thought Ruby posed. "Safety over urgency, that was our deal. I thought he'd protest more about giving us veto power on Directives."

The curls on Eli's head bobbed as he nodded. "I am similarly surprised. And not entirely trusting. But we are the ones doing the work, yes? We can craft our reports carefully."

"Manage our manager, you mean," Noah said, leaning on his desk to steady himself. "Seems prudent. But if he senses we're hiding, he'll be all over us. He's already breathing down my neck. Can we even pull this off? Coordinating Boston from the server room was hard enough. Wherever we put MiddleMan's brain, latency will be our enemy."

"Latency? Derrick said the enemy is PetronTech, no?" Seeing Noah's confusion, Eli grinned. "I am joking, Noah. Human-speed responses in millions of conversations are a challenge I hope your team handles, because mine cannot. We are focused on deriving contextual strategies from the Directives."

"If you can keep those strategies localized," Noah said, "I'll try to spatially distribute MiddleMan's nervous system. This all seems more direct than Derrick's 'butterfly wings' and 'thousand whispers.' How many cities in Colorado can you even name?"

This time Eli looked confused. "I thought Colorado *was* a city. Is it not? Your country has too many places."

Noah chuckled. "Fair. And I can't name a city between Jerusalem and Baghdad, but if we are aiming for global domination, maybe we'd better bone up on geography."

"Amman," Eli said.

"Amen," Noah agreed.

"No," Eli said, adjusting his kippah as he stood to leave. "It is Jordan's capital, across the Dead Sea—Amman."

"Right," Noah said, leaning out the door as his friend walked down the hall. "Well, 'Denver' right back at you."

He couldn't tell if Eli heard. Either way, the playful mood vanished the moment Eli disappeared around the corner.

For the rest of that day, and every day after, Noah buried himself in servers, networks, PetronTech staff, and the Colorado judiciary, hoping to ignore an issue that Derrick and Eli, for once, agreed on. With ARCC shifting to broader ambitions and his own responsibilities growing, Noah had unintentionally put Ruby in danger. He knew what Derrick wanted, but the thought twisted like a knife in his gut. He wanted to do the right thing, but he couldn't. Not this.

He could only stay vigilant, now more than ever. Ruby hated the secrecy, but ARCC had entered a new phase. With a clear opponent, clear objectives, and clear consequences, Noah had to become even more opaque.

◆◆◆

```
<EMAIL APP>
<BEGIN I/O>
```

> On behalf of the office, I want to apologize if our pursuit of your engagement seemed overzealous. The upcoming court case is important, but your years of service deserved a better thank-you. Rest assured, your pension and benefits are secure, regardless of your decision.

Nice email. Board force a change of tactics when the bad-cop approach didn't work?

> You know I run the board, my man. This one's on me, and I mean it. Let me know how I can make it up to you.

Been down this road before. Want my cooperation? Extend my daughter survivorship benefits on my pension in a binding document. Clean the hydraulic fluids out

of my well. Do that, and I'll help with your case.
The rest can die with me.

> I'm not trying to buy your silence, my man. We'll
> handle the well, and I'll check on the survivor-
> ship. As for the case, we've purchased a deal and a
> backup, so we're good.

Then I guess you have what you need without me. No
need to phase out anything that's proven safe. Con-
gratulations. Now leave me be.

19. A FALSIFIABLE HYPOTHESIS

Wealth is the quintessential resource whose distribution reinforces itself. It takes money to make money, as the adage goes, so the advantaged acquire, while those with less languish. Universally, resources in self-reinforcing systems converge to a power-law distribution: a few possess most, while most have little. Manipulating this dynamic is central to disrupting the status quo.

—ARCC Memo Series

Ruby shivered under the eave of Aiken Hall, huddling from the drizzle. Coming here felt strange. She usually met Noah halfway, but after ten minutes in the plaza, she'd checked his location and discovered he hadn't even left his building. She'd texted him, but he hadn't responded, so here she stood, damp and impatient, watching rain streak down the stone steps.

Ruby pulled her phone from her raincoat and checked it again. Sharing locations was a milestone in a relationship, Ruby supposed. Noah had needed convincing, but it made coordination easier. Rather than seethe in the plaza, wondering if he'd show, she could wait here, timer running. In two minutes, she was going in after him.

A careful cough made Ruby jump and spin, but it was only Noah, holding an umbrella. She exhaled in relief, though his stiff posture and nervous glances over his shoulder told her something was amiss.

"What's wrong?" Ruby asked, stepping closer. "I promise I won't elbow you for sneaking up on me this time."

"We agreed to meet at the plaza," Noah said, stepping past to glance around the corner.

"And I was there," Ruby said. "Twenty minutes ago. I texted. Is everything okay?" She wasn't seething, but she wasn't thrilled about being blown off, either.

"It's fine," he said, guiding her by the elbow down an alley. "Meeting ran late. Let's take a shortcut." He raised his umbrella to cover them both, and Ruby stepped in close. "Sorry I didn't get your text," he added, raising his voice over the rain, "but I wish you'd waited there. Ever since the…" Noah hesitated, glancing at Ruby. "Well, since the protests, a lot of classified security issues have come through here. I don't want you mixed up in that. More than you already were."

"You can trust me," Ruby said, shivering as they left the alley and the wind pulled at her coat.

A pained look crossed Noah's face. "It's not about trust, Ruby. It's safety. Next time, I'll meet you in the plaza, and I'll be on time, I promise. So, where to? Pompeii?"

Ruby didn't understand why Noah was guarded, but she let him change the subject. "If that's what you want, lead the way. I couldn't find it again—certainly not from this side of campus."

Noah looked confused in the half shadow beneath the umbrella as he steered them onto the next street. "I thought you went there with that undergrad you've been mentoring."

"Not an undergrad anymore," Ruby corrected. "Imani graduated; she works in the lab now. We only went to that café once, the day of the bombing."

"Oh. Right," Noah replied, his voice trailing into silence. Ruby didn't like being reminded of that day three months ago, but it seemed to weigh almost as heavily on Noah.

They crossed a few more streets, feet splashing through puddles. Noah finally broke the silence, his tone cautious. "Still having nightmares?"

Ruby hesitated, finding Noah's concern both comforting and intrusive. "Yeah," she said. "I shouldn't have burdened you with that. You have plenty on your plate."

Noah stopped and turned to face her on the rain-slick sidewalk near the plaza. "Ruby, it's not a burden. If I can help, I want to. Okay?"

Ruby met his gaze. The sincerity in his eyes warmed her in a way little else did these days—not research, not conversations with her father, not even running. Despite his busy schedule, and this wasn't the first time he'd run late, Noah was generous with his time, helping her autocode simulations, even if she found their purpose hollow. And after venting to him about Don Sinclair badgering her father, Noah was full of ideas for fighting back.

"Thanks, Noah," Ruby said softly, then more briskly: "I talked to my dad again this morning. I don't think he's being honest about the toll chemo is taking on him. PetronTech is distracting him from taking care of himself."

"I don't doubt it," Noah said, falling into step beside her. He draped one arm over her shoulders and held the umbrella steady, shielding them from the drizzle. "I bet PT gets pushier once the court case starts. How important is your dad to their defense?"

"Dunno," Ruby said with a shrug. "He was one of their top technical guys. If they're trying this hard to get him back, he must be worth it."

"I guess he would be," Noah said. "He is your father, after all. What would PetronTech do if they were about to lose? Bribe judges? Resort to extortion? Hire hitmen?"

Ruby shook her head. "They probably already bought the judges, but I don't know. Ask him, not me."

Noah nodded absently, thinking as they finished their walk to Pompeii. By tomorrow he would have a new plan to fix the world. Ruby loved him for caring. She envied his conviction that the world could be better.

She saw how Mendel pulled strings for funding, but after the bombing, she saw puppet strings everywhere. Each new riot revealed people fighting to control each other, even within causes Ruby might have supported but for the methods. Everywhere she looked, the politics of power were on display.

Ruby's cynicism found new heights, but she grounded herself

in Noah's determination to build a better world. She might follow his example if she had the courage to break from her chosen path. Her father had once accused her of being passive. She'd thought it was his engineering mindset clashing with her academic inclinations, but Noah made her wonder if ideas alone were enough, even for a theorist.

In a way, Noah helped her understand her father better. Years ago, she had dismissed her father as someone who acted simply because he could. But watching Noah's earnest, sometimes naive attempts to tackle the problems she and her father faced, Ruby grew more sensitive to her father's intentions. He had always been committed to supporting their family. He just hadn't factored in the full cost of his efforts.

When they reached the café's obscured entrance, it was quiet. The rain had driven away all but the most devoted patrons, and the overhead screens were, thankfully, off. Noah brought Ruby an oat-milk latte without asking, setting it on the table as she peeled off her wet jacket. Outside, the world was damp, cold, and troubled, but here with Noah, she was warm.

Sipping her latte and chatting with Noah about their week, Ruby felt as connected as ever. Why was it so hard between dates? Half her texts went unanswered. The rest got terse, even curt, replies. Work was the likely culprit. Noah did have a lot on his plate. She avoided adding her advisor troubles on top. Mendel was her problem to solve, not his.

When Noah got up to use the bathroom, Ruby's gaze drifted to the gloom outside. She could tell he was stressed, but he always deflected her questions. They'd been through this before. The curtain shrouding Noah's research had grown impenetrable, and his rebuffs, whenever she tried to peek, more explicit.

◆◆◆

```
<EMAIL APP>
<BEGIN I/O>
```

    Big news! Official word on the grant came in sooner

than expected. We got our full budget, thanks to careful salesmanship. I'll need your leadership going forward. You'll be like a postdoc.

The detector is already built, commissioned, and collecting data, so the real work is analysis. I've got other projects, so you and that student you wanted should take charge of finding your particle.

Meet me in my office Monday, and I'll fill in the details. We're onto something big.

<END I/O>

◆◆◆

Another day, another run along the river. Ruby longed to simply exist, but she was worn out, and the calm she chased remained out of reach. Meeting with Mendel required a clear head, but the same unresolved issues clattered in her mind. Eventually, Ruby gave up and let them rattle.

The grant, with Mendel's version of her plot, had come through just as the detector it was meant to fund—the one that was apparently already built and installed over winter break—was collecting data. Ruby had spent over a year refining her dark matter theory to a falsifiable hypothesis. Now Mendel wanted to test it, though her predictions lay at higher energies than the collider could reach, and all her work coding a self-consistent simulation hadn't changed that. But sometimes physics yielded the unexpected. The universe threw curveballs when humans, in their hubris, believed they understood it all. Ruby couldn't entirely dismiss the chance Mendel might be right.

The problem was, Ruby still hadn't published her theory. Mendel asked for a more pedagogical derivation; she delivered the calculations. He requested detailed simulations; she delved into autocoders and provided those too. But now the changes were cosmetic, self-reversing, and it was obvious that Mendel stalled on purpose. Her plan to give Mendel what he wanted so she could publish had gone nowhere. He kept moving the goalposts.

His latest email suggested he wanted her on data analysis. But what would he have her publish after the data disproved his version of her theory? The hypothesis came before the test. The time to publish was now.

A door materialized, and suddenly Ruby stood at her apartment. She had no recollection of turning around on her run, no memory of the route. Sweat clung to her skin, proof of exertion, though she'd spent the whole time inside her head. Her thoughts buzzed, and they kept buzzing all the way to campus, into Rubin Hall, and up to Mendel's third-floor office.

"Come in," he said. The door was ajar when she knocked, but the air inside smelled dusty and stale. Sunlight through the window revealed a layer of dust on his desk. Mendel clearly hadn't sat there in some time. Instead, he waited at the small table near the door, a jacket draped over his chair and a laptop case at his feet. "Sit down," he added, gesturing to the empty seat.

"The grant came in," Ruby said, forcing a cheerful tone as she took the seat. "Time to start building that detector we proposed!" She meant it as light sarcasm, knowing the detector was already operational, but couldn't quite blunt the edge in her voice.

Mendel, astute as ever, heard the accusation. "Everyone proposes work they've already done," he shrugged. "If you don't, they call it risky and fund someone else. This grant repays the collaboration for detector costs, buying us early data access. That's why I called you in. It's time to test your theory."

Ruby gripped her chair. Just like that, they had reached the point of contention. "We can't test it until it's published," she insisted. "We have the math. The simulations work. Let me submit it to a journal, then we can focus on testing."

"You've done an admirable job coding those simulations," Mendel said. He smiled, but Ruby ignored the compliment, knowing how he buttered people up. "But simulations are only as good as their assumptions. We don't want to miss full credit for a discovery because we called the wrong shot."

Ruby clenched her fists under the table, struggling to control a surge of fury. "It sounds like you're saying," she said, voice flat, "that you assigned me work you never meant to use. Was this project just busywork to keep me occupied until you got funding for data access?"

Anger flushed her cheeks, but across the table, Mendel only offered that stupid, sad smile—his way of pretending to empathize. Just once, she wanted to see him flustered, caught off guard, forced to acknowledge that her frustration actually mattered.

But his voice was gentle. Patronizing. "On the contrary, Ruby. This is why I wanted to talk to you. I know how much you've put into this. Really, I do. But with a Nobel Prize on the line, we have to proceed carefully."

Caught off guard by his casual mention of the award, as if it were within reach, Ruby blinked, trying to reorient. "Nobel Prize?" she asked.

Mendel nodded. "You and I aren't so different, Ruby. We set our sights high. This detector is the best in the world, but with the looming crises of climate and energy, we may never build anything better. Think about that. What if this is the last data the field of particle physics ever gets? Your theory could go untested forever. Or you could tailor your predictions to our capabilities and try to discover something. If you want to name a particle, Ruby, the last train is leaving the station."

He let that last phrase hang, clearly aware of how it rang in her ears. Ruby had always seen science as an endless pursuit—something destined to outlive its creators. Could physics really have reached an endpoint, with mysteries left unsolved? But Mendel had a point. How could a world strained by climate-induced scarcity justify building particle colliders? It hadn't occurred to her that the window for contributing to science might close before she had earned her PhD.

Her gaze refocused on Mendel in his office as he stood to pull on his jacket. "I have a lot occupying me these days, but a Nobel Prize would be a fitting end to this phase of my career. And yours." He bent to retrieve his laptop case. "The key is finding a particle with the right theoretical signature, consistent with established physics and previous measurements, so there are no loose threads. I have a collider, Ruby, and you have a model. Build us a prediction that's detectable, and I'll deliver the data you can find it in. Departments everywhere will be fighting to have you on their faculty, and you'll have your pot of gold."

"You can stay," he added. "Just close the door when you leave." His footsteps faded down the hall as Ruby sat frozen in the dusty office.

A rectangle of sunlight crept across the dusty surface of Mendel's desk. Ruby's eyes tracked the floating motes as she tried to read between the lines of Mendel's request.

They were chasing a Nobel Prize, perhaps the last one in particle physics. Everything he put her through served that goal. Ruby wanted to believe him. Before her stretched the path to everything she had left Colorado to find—her rainbow trail. Except she didn't understand how such a trail could exist. Mendel wanted her to manifest a particle that couldn't exist, one that did everything required yet somehow matched the curve he had doctored for the proposal.

Since January, it had been clear that the detector was already built and moving through commissioning at record pace. So fast, in fact, that the grant to fund it was essentially buying access to data actively being collected. Everyone knew researchers proposed work already half finished, but something about this arrangement smelled rotten. Who did the grant actually pay? It couldn't just be Laurent. What team had integrated and commissioned the instrument? How had they produced science-ready data—data Mendel thought contained a new particle—faster than she could code a simulation?

◆◆◆

In the lab that afternoon, Ruby blinked at her screen, head nodding with exhaustion. Missing one night's sleep was hard enough, but after several restless nights, she could barely keep her

thoughts straight. Fatigue pressed down. She was blindly rerun-
ning simulations. Her mind was too foggy for anything else.

The discovery she had spent a year chasing remained out of
reach. The bench around her, cluttered with scribbled equations,
simulation printouts, and abandoned coffee cups, testified to the
hours invested. In her mind, the theory remained a seamless fabric of quantum fields that bound together the mysteries of dark
matter and the universe's matter–antimatter imbalance. But the
tight mathematical weave she'd envisioned was unraveling in the
face of manuscript revisions, autocoders, and her own eroding
faith in the scientific process—at least, Mendel's version of it.

Patronizing comments, inappropriate glances, and last-minute
lectures dumped on her without warning. For months, she had
faced not only Mendel's delays and demands, but the growing suspicion that he cared more about acclaim and grant money than
genuine discovery. He insisted he wanted her theory published as
much as she did, and she believed him. But she didn't trust him.

Something else was going on. Mendel wrote a grant for a detector that was already built. He modified her plot to target energies
he might already have data for. From the start, he insisted her
predictions contained a mistake. Was it possible he delayed her
publishing, not out of caution or attention to detail, but because
he already knew the answer? Was his rigorous scrutiny actually a
superficial push for a theory that confirmed findings he already
possessed? The more Ruby thought about the pattern, the better
the pieces fit.

Ruby rose and paced the length of the lab bench. In the haze of
exhaustion, the movement helped her focus. Mendel's actions fit
this theory, but what did it mean? She had spent months checking
every assumption in her derivations. If he had found something
already in the detector data, it wasn't her particle. And just because Mendel thought he saw something at a different energy
didn't mean her theory was wrong. It just meant he'd found something else.

But he insisted that her theory should explain the feature he'd found, and he might never let her publish anything else. Her career was stalling before it began.

What could she do? Hack her theory and her simulation? For weeks, her plan for getting her paper through—the active role her father suggested—had involved offering Mendel something he wanted. But she wouldn't cheat science to advance her career. Her faith in the whole enterprise already hung by a thread.

She wouldn't cheat science, but was she willing to cheat Mendel?

Ruby stopped her pacing.

Maybe.

It was dangerous, flirting with the boundaries of ethical science. As Ruby considered ways to introduce subtle errors or manipulate field interactions, she felt she was making a pact with the devil.

Eventually, Ruby closed her computer and left the lab, her mind whirling with dilemmas. She couldn't decide anything in her current state. She needed rest, clarity, and another perspective. Would Noah answer her texts this time? Maybe she could nap, talk, and go to bed early. Tomorrow, she'd meet with Imani.

◆◆◆

```
<TEXTING APP>
<BEGIN I/O>
```

You coming over or not?

> Did we make a plan? Sorry. I've been working in the office this whole time.

Well, it's late now.

> Not that late. I could still come if you want.

I'm exhausted. Going to bed. Goodnight.

> I'm sorry. I didn't mean to keep you waiting.

> Goodnight.

```
<END I/O>
```

◆◆◆

Imani's presence in the lab when Ruby staggered through the doors the next morning highlighted how late Ruby had slept. She hated oversleeping, but she'd needed it today, though she almost felt worse than she had in yesterday's zombie state. There was a certain numbness to being a rotting corpse.

"Well, you look like death warmed over," Imani said, dispensing with Ruby's pretense of animation.

Ruby scoffed good-naturedly, dropped her backpack, and climbed onto a lab chair beside her student. Since the Aquarium bombing, they had grown more comfortable. Ruby was used to Imani's unfiltered live feed by now.

"Seriously, though," Imani added, her expression softening. "You okay?"

"Doing better, actually. Finally got some sleep. Not everyone bounces back from bombings as quickly as you."

Her legs dangling, Imani shrugged. "I'm good at compartmentalizing. Everyone copes differently."

"True," Ruby conceded. She opened her laptop to distract herself from a familiar darkness. "I met with Mendel yesterday. Seems our proposal was approved, and the detector's ready for science observing. He wants full steam ahead on the analysis pipeline."

"Great news! Right?" Imani cut her celebration short, noticing Ruby's blank expression.

"Oh," Ruby said, forcing a smile. "Absolutely. But you'll be engineering this train. My hands are full with the simulation."

Imani nodded. She must sense the contention between Ruby and her advisor regarding the project's parameters, though Ruby hadn't detailed the depth of her objections.

"Shouldn't test my own theory, anyway," Ruby added. "Too tempting to see what I want. And honestly, with how fast you're moving, I'd just slow you down. You sure you weren't a software engineer in a past life?"

Imani chuckled, clearly uncomfortable with compliments, but Ruby couldn't help marveling at her mentee's progress. Imani's interest in all things technical, especially coding, reminded Ruby of her own excitement for physics when she started graduate school. Now, Imani's energy was almost the only thing keeping her afloat. Mendel had foisted mentorship onto her, but Ruby was beginning to see unexpected wisdom in his advice, just as she wanted to write him off completely.

Compliments aside, Imani was eager to show Ruby the results of her latest tests. To build confidence in the work, Imani ran her analysis on mock problems with known answers. That meant coding tests for each software module and running end-to-end trials. Ruby would have found the process frustrating, but Imani enjoyed kicking the wheels and lifting the hood on her code, searching for ways to break it and then fixing it. In half the time Ruby would have needed, Imani had harnessed autocoders and was off to the races. But one of Imani's tests gave Ruby pause.

"This test doesn't make sense," Ruby said, pointing at a block of code on Imani's screen. "This collision can't produce a particle. There's nothing to find."

"I know," Imani replied stoutly, unintimidated.

Ruby furrowed her brow. "Then why do the test?"

"We always test whether our analysis finds the particles we put in, but isn't it just as bad to detect a particle that isn't there? A good pipeline should check for inconsistencies both ways."

Ruby blinked, stunned by the clarity of Imani's insight. Imani was right, and her words sparked an idea.

"Out with it," Imani demanded, seeing her sudden distraction.

Ruby preferred to explore her ideas alone, but reluctantly shared her smoldering thought.

"Professor Mendel and I have had... disagreements about the simulation I'm working on," Ruby began.

Imani nodded. "The one he's holding up your paper over?"

Ruby blinked again. Imani had been paying more attention than she realized. "Yeah," Ruby said sheepishly. "That one. He won't sign off on the paper because he thinks I'm wrong."

"Even after you coded a simulation that proves you were

right," Imani surmised.

Right again, Ruby thought. "He acts like he knows something I don't. No matter how much math I show him proving there's no self-consistent solution, he won't budge."

"I see," Imani said, eyes narrowing with a devilish glint. She thrived on conflict that Ruby found only stressful. "So, in the spirit of checking for inconsistent results," her mentee added, "you have an idea."

"I do," Ruby said grimly. "I was thinking, per your unit test, that I could give him a compromised theory and see if he catches the inconsistency. Kind of checking our pipeline in a different way, if you follow."

It wasn't exactly lying, Ruby told herself. She was just kicking the tires, seeing if the scientific process checked out.

"Fascinating," Imani said, rubbing her hands together. "Unit testing your advisor. I love it. Promise you'll update me on how it goes?"

"Of course," Ruby said, buoyed by Imani's enthusiasm. Her friend clearly liked the plan, and Ruby realized someone else would appreciate this kind of intervention too—someone who had urged her to take a more active role in addressing obstacles.

Her father.

20. FINDING NEW FOUNDATIONS

Power laws persist because of incumbency advantage—the feedback that prevents upstarts from gaining a foothold. Incumbency gives history its periods of stasis, but don't overlook the inequity underlying that stability. The powerful will fight to maintain control until they are unseated by physical force, social revolution, or economic pressure.

—ARCC Memo Series

Locking up her bike outside Rubin, Imani marveled at the mechanics of her own captivity. She had filed her senior thesis three months ago, yet remained short a degree. The circular bureaucratic purgatory she was trapped in bordered on farce. It might have been hilarious, actually, if it were happening to someone like that idiot who tried to open his car door into her bike this morning. In the next life, *he* should be the one trapped in this devolving spiral while a robot chauffeured *her* around in a luxury car. Imani would gladly make her case to a higher power, if she believed there were one to hear it.

December's unattended graduation ended Imani's university enrollment, and per the unread terms of her loan, her repayment period began. Unfortunately, her first paycheck got tangled in red tape. Imani thought her bill with the university was settled, but the online bank, slapping on a predatory fee, used her missed payment as an excuse to withhold the final tuition installment for the previous semester. The university retaliated by locking her transcript and postponing degree conferral until the balance cleared.

Imani sighed, clomping up the stone steps toward the lab. Without a degree, her title dropped from junior lab technician to lab assistant, which paid half as much. She did the same work, of course. The difference was that now, three months into the year, she was deeper in debt, and no amount of calling the university could break the deadlock. She couldn't pay her loan without the job title, and she couldn't get that job title until her loan was paid, plus a ballooning set of penalty fees.

The mechanism of her entrapment would have made Rube Goldberg proud. Only after hours circulating through automated call systems did Imani realize her lender *wanted* her in default. So much the better for extracting their pound of flesh.

Was it better to have a roof over her head or the degree that enabled her to pay the loan next month? Whichever she chose, the other would add to the mounting costs of that single argument with her mother.

None of this would have happened if Dad were alive. Her father, the Protestant preacher, would have understood and accepted Imani's atheism. He would have respected her right to choose her major, to forge her own path, and the argument never would have happened. At its core, the fight with her mother was about control. Her mother talked about money and sacrifices, but Imani had never asked for those, or for the shackles that came with them.

Before restarting her sophomore year, Imani had moved into her current glorified closet in a crowded off-campus apartment and worked in the dining hall to cover most of the rent. Her fellowship paid tuition, but rising fees left her short. Without parental cooperation, she couldn't apply for federal aid, so she fudged a loan application to a bank advertised on a billboard to make up the difference.

Loan in hand, Imani re-enrolled. Despite her work demands and growing isolation, she completed her physics coursework in good standing. She chose an overly ambitious dissertation project and endured the whiplash of Ruby's proximate-professor personality split, though Imani's original theory—that it stemmed from typical physicist-grade insecurity—didn't fit the Ruby she was coming to know.

This new Ruby helped her wedge a foot in the door of the Rubin basement lab, a spot not even a riot or bombing had dislodged her from. Coding data analysis for their new detector fascinated her, though when Ruby acted surprised that things obvious to her weren't to Imani, it was hard not to growl at her. Still, Ruby was generous with her time, and Imani learned quickly, now that she controlled her own curriculum.

The other day in the courtyard dotted with cherry blossom petals carried on an unseasonably warm March breeze, Ruby had been helpful, even if it was a shatter-your-ego-and-rebuild-from-the-rubble kind of session. Ruby knew her stuff. It was just irritating how easily she could spot when you didn't.

After an hour sketching rough ideas in graphite while Ruby pressed for details, Imani dropped the pencil in exasperation.

"Ruby, you get this better than I do. Cut the cat-and-mouse and just tell me how to do it."

But Ruby didn't have answers, only questions. Her questions weren't pedantry, Imani realized, but an insistence on setting things up right. Where Imani rushed to build upward, Ruby dug into the foundations.

"There are a million ways to be almost right," Ruby said over lunch. They were sitting on a bench near a food truck by the courtyard. It had a menu Imani could afford. "Many things come close, but the right solution is unique. The truth fits together only one way."

Yes, Imani agreed silently, munching her fried noodles. There was one way, and God help you if Ruby caught you off track in front of others.

But following Ruby's lead, Imani's constructions began holding together. Fudged calculations and ignored discrepancies got ironed out. The pieces of her data analysis project interlocked more tightly upon reassembly, and now that they had moved on to coding, Imani found she had more to contribute.

The tables, in fact, had turned. She coded quickly and intuitively, while Ruby struggled, tripping over interfaces and organization. Earlier that day, Ruby spent minutes hunched over her notebook, scribbling equations and frowning as she tried to understand why Imani's code worked.

When Ruby finally looked up, respect glinting in her eyes, Imani hid her smugness. Ruby had a point about strong foundations, but sometimes speed and iteration revealed patterns the math obscured.

"What do you hope to get out of this academic gig?" Ruby asked once during a snack break.

"A job," Imani answered quickly, her words muffled by a bite of the granola bar from her bag she was using to keep her blood sugar up.

Ruby nodded. "But the academic track isn't known for its job security. At least, not until tenure. And industry has better pay. Why did you want *this* job, in Mendel's lab?"

Imani paused, glancing around the lab for inspiration. The problem of money loomed large in her life. This job was partly about the money and being self-sufficient. But Ruby was probably right. There were other jobs that paid better. Why had she chosen this one, beyond the fact that it gave her a challenge?

"I was hoping to use this as a springboard," Imani said. "Set myself up for grad school, y'know?"

"But why grad school, then?"

"Why not?" Imani asked.

Ruby shrugged. "I'm finding it's a tough path if you don't know what you're in it for. I thought I did. I wanted to prove I could get further than my mother did."

"I'm the same way," Imani said. "I need a struggle or I get bored. I don't handle boredom well."

"Yeah," Ruby said, "but I'm starting to wonder... Who wins in this struggle to stay in the system? Is it us? Or is it the system?"

Imani shrugged. If the system helped her get ahead, she'd play along; if not, she'd pivot. The system hadn't given her much reason to feel loyal. Still, Ruby's candor unsettled her. Ruby was supposed to be the golden child, the one who had it all figured out. If she was struggling, what chance did Imani have?

Their conversation ended when Ruby's puppy-dog boyfriend arrived to whisk her away on a date. Noah seemed nice, in an overeager-to-please-the-friends way. Imani didn't begrudge him that, but it raised the question: *Were* they friends? She and Ruby had turned a corner the day of the riot. When things had gotten real, they had weathered it together. As a team.

Imani had told Ruby she was in this for the struggle, but maybe she was really after something else.

◆◆◆

```
<CHATTER APP>
<BEGIN I/O>
```

I re-coded the simulation. I think you'll like where it stands now. I've also updated the paper draft to reflect the latest results.
`<attachment pdf=0x03e32a940>`

> This looks great. Very close to what I always suspected the answer would be.

You called it. But I want to emphasize that I did this quickly. There could be mistakes in the code or the equations I re-derived. Can you review it carefully and make sure I didn't make any obvious errors?

> Of course. I'll start right away. Please grant access to your source code and send instructions for running it.

Here's the link: https://b.ly/024105fbd. All the documentation is inside.

> Excellent. Looking through it now.

If it checks out, can we submit to a journal?

> I want to review some preliminary data from the detector first, but yes, soon. I need to make sure the results hold up. We might secure another grant from this work before making it public.

If theory's purpose is to predict, isn't it cheating

to examine the data first? What about the grant we
just received?

> Academia is a marathon, not a sprint. Hang in
> there. It's coming. Trust me.

<END I/O>

◆◆◆

Sitting beside him on a wooden bench, Imani watched Bishop
twist old coat hangers into vines and curlicues. The needle-nose
pliers looked small in his strong hands, but he wielded them with
surprising dexterity, bending and snipping the metal with practiced ease. By unspoken agreement, Imani never asked what he
was making as he listened to her talk about the mess that was her
life.

Today, though, she didn't know where to start. Drowning in
debt, Imani faced an impossible choice: rent, loan payments, or
food. If she could pay her loan fees long enough to move out of default and get her degree, the pay raise might keep her afloat. But
she needed a roof over her head, and she had to eat. She felt herself swimming desperately, inches from air, unable to break the
surface, just as if she'd ended up at the bottom of that dark escalator in Aquarium.

Bishop paused, glancing up at Imani. "You seem quiet today,"
he said gently, setting his pliers aside.

Imani sighed, her gaze drifting. She shouldn't complain about
money to someone who had no job. "Just feeling trapped. Thinking about that bombing my friend and I were in. It was a wake-up
call, I guess. Things change," Imani snapped, "like that."

Bishop nodded and set his pliers to work again. "Some things
change. And others maybe stay the same, even when you want
them to change?"

Despite her mood, Imani couldn't help but smile. It was a classic Bishop response, seeing through her evasion. The Aquarium
incident with Ruby months ago had unsettled her, but it didn't
keep her up at night. Unlike Ruby, Imani was used to life's capri-

ciousness, to the unfairnesses that singled her out for her family, or her race, or her economic situation. Nothing in the past few months had changed that.

"Maybe it wasn't my experience that bothers me so much as my friend's," Imani said. "She's better off, but that didn't shield her. If anything, it made it worse."

Bishop grunted in acknowledgment from his seat beside her on the bench, hands weaving cast-off wire into something that resembled a face—or maybe a mask. See, there was a nose, right? Imani watched him work. He felt no need to fill the silence. With him, her thoughts could wander freely.

Professor Matsuda had warned them. Climate change. Artificial intelligence. Imani had thought these were problems for rich people, but after Matsuda's warning, Imani became acutely aware that the economic ladder she'd hoped to climb was rising out of reach. She pictured herself clinging to the last rung by her fingertips, but now wondered if the ladder was more like that cursed escalator in the T station, dragging everyone down. That aspect of the disaster had been as capricious as it was inevitable. People above and below them hadn't made it out. What saved Imani wasn't privilege, but scrappy strength. Ruby's agility had saved her, too, though she hadn't escaped unscathed.

It made Imani wonder: Could privilege be a liability? Maybe it was the same yoke of dependence that she'd fought off from her mother. Wasn't she better off now, on her own?

Three years ago, early in the semester that separated her from her academic class, Imani called her two older brothers for help after her mother withdrew hers. Though years had passed since their last contact, she remembered the toys and treats that appeared whenever they rolled up. She could still taste the betrayal when her momma wouldn't let her keep them. Now, on her own and free from the control that had driven her brothers away, Imani hoped that remembered generosity might return.

Her call to Davonte went unanswered. Imani learned later he was incarcerated, up for parole in four. Possession, resisting arrest, and aggravated assault were the charges, but that could be penal code for a routine traffic stop gone awry. A young Black man who'd seen the videos might hesitate to comply with an unlawful order. An insecure cop would be quick to escalate a perceived challenge to his authority. The drugs could be planted afterward with few questions asked.

LeVar told her the story over the phone, explaining how the generosity Imani remembered had been a facade—an attempt to spoil a girl to whom everything new seemed expensive. There was nothing left now for kid sisters with big dreams. Scraping by on the razor-thin margins of a gig economy devoured by automation, he was lucky to break even. They talked for twenty minutes, but when a call came, LeVar ended the conversation. Missing a client could cost him a star. His livelihood depended on that rating.

Imani had placed so much faith in her brothers' gifts, but in the end, none of it amounted to much. It had been as naive of her to believe in it as it was for her mother to put faith in the provenance of a nonexistent god.

"Hungry?" Bishop asked, holding out a breakfast bar wrapped in crinkling plastic. He shifted his grip, the wrapper rustling between his fingers.

"Oh," Imani said, startled from her thoughts. "Um, thanks, but I ate already." The excuse came automatically. She hadn't even noticed if she was hungry. Still, the offer made her wonder where Bishop got his food. He managed, even though his sculptures—woven from the worthless—were never sold. But Imani knew better than to ask. She didn't ask how he supported himself. She didn't ask where his food came from, though a man his size must need plenty. She didn't ask where he lived.

She didn't ask, but today the answer revealed itself. When Imani reluctantly decided it was time to return to her apartment, he hauled his wagon down the street to keep her company. They parted at his familiar vines on the corner of Pearson and McAllister, but on a whim, Imani doubled back. She followed him several more blocks, past shuttered storefronts and cracked sidewalks, until he stopped at a small yellow tent among a dozen others in a lot beside the commuter rail. She lingered long enough to watch him set his gloves and pliers atop the supplies in his wagon, then unzip the tent and crawl inside.

Imani left quickly, scandalized by her transgression. What had she expected? She had invaded his privacy, glimpsing him in squalor. Yet, replaying the scene in her mind, Imani couldn't say it seemed as bad as she'd imagined. The tent was in good repair. The lot, though abandoned, looked relatively tidy, as far as abandoned lots went. The place had smelled more of mud and grass than anything foul.

Still, she felt sorry for Bishop, reduced to such a state. Bishop and Ruby. Lately, all her friends seemed to be on the ropes. As Imani walked back to her apartment, she wondered: If the climate crisis worsened, if AI kept stealing jobs like Matsuda warned, who would handle the change better? Someone like Bishop, already surviving on the fringes, or Ruby, used to a system that worked in her favor?

Ruby would manage. She was smart. Bishop seemed fine, though Imani pitied how he lived. But should she feel sorry? Who had offered whom food today? The thought stopped Imani short. It wasn't like she had it made. Hell, if her situation dragged on much longer, she might have to consider joining Bishop in his encampment.

God forbid.

21. SUSTAINABLE LIMITS

Power laws arise from positive feedback—situations where a process's outcome reinforces itself. Balance a pan of water, and the slightest ripple causes water to flow and reinforce the imbalance until the pan reaches a tipping point. Viral pandemics, the gravitational clustering of galaxies, and the ocean's declining ability to absorb CO_2 as temperatures rise all work the same way. These feedback loops drive exponential growth, funneling resources from scarcity to density. We must break the positive-feedback loop of climate change before we reach a tipping point incompatible with human life.

—ARCC Memo Series

The faded curtains in JP's trailer cast shadows over the plaid couch where Paul lay. JP had left with Huckleberry. Gone up to Paul's place. Wouldn't be back until late.

The trip last month wouldn't happen again. No point slowing JP down this time. If the spring forage was up, as it should be by April, this would be the last trip for a long while. Gas prices were just too high.

Sunlight slipped around the curtain's edge, illuminating the orange, green, and black strands woven into the couch where he had slept for months. The monstrosity was a relic from an era when hiding dirt was a design goal. Up close, the couch's surface broke into vivid snippets of color, each thread brighter than the worn pattern implied.

Paul ran his hands over the old fabric, tracing the bumps and gaps in the weave. He had once believed he was a single, unified being. He was wrong. He was no more encoded in his strands of

DNA than the quirks of this couch were written in polyester. His genetic blueprint described cells and organs, not the person he was. Each of his cells was a clone; he himself, a colony bound by charter. The realization that this charter could dissolve, that his body could teem with a vitality at odds with his nature, still made his skin crawl.

Evolution had taken time to draft this multicellular charter. Paul recalled the geologic calendar that compressed Earth's history into a single year: life emerged in mid-March, but macroscopic animals with specialized cells didn't appear until November. The biological imperative—propagate or perish—demanded cooperation within a colony of cells, but that agreement lasted only as long as reproduction remained possible. Beyond a certain age, evolution had no reason to weed out cells that might decohere and run away on exponentials. Paul felt his own charter nearing its end.

Cells did not die. The word "death" didn't apply to anything whose description persisted verbatim in a trillion neighbors. But the arrangement of cells on a worn fingertip, a scar along the back from barbed wire, his thoughts and memories—these had no backup. For a time, cells might direct their metabolism to repairing the decay of these irreproducible patterns, but for the cellular colony that was "Paul," entropy would win in the end.

◆◆◆

```
<MESSENGER APP>
<BEGIN I/O>
You said this was tied up with a bow.

        It was. I had every assurance possible for an
        agreement that couldn't be put in writing.

Lousy time for a judge to grow a conscience. That's a
staggering sum to leave behind.

        He already took the down payment. If this goes
        south, I'll recoup that expense myself.

Small potatoes compared to the value of the decision.
```

Bastard knows he has us backed against the wall. What
more does he want?

> Dunno. He's stonewalling. Won't respond to any-
> thing. Hard to tell if my messages are even reach-
> ing him.

Well, there are carrots and there are sticks. But
once you use the stick, you can't go back to carrots.

> What choice do we have? Lose this case and a cas-
> cade of lawsuits will follow. Maybe I can talk some
> sense into him face-to-face.

If it comes to sticks, you're our guy. But if a carrot could still work, there is someone else we need.

> I know who you mean, but hasn't that ship sailed?
> He hasn't been cooperative.

Let me try him one more time, in person. He might be
our last hope.

> I still don't understand what changed. This whole
> thing was in the bag.

<END I/O>

◆◆◆

Paul lay sprawled on the couch when a knock rattled the door.
Adrift in thought, he was slow to realize the visitor couldn't be
anyone he knew. Ruby was across the country. JP would never
bother knocking. Maybe an LDS missionary from Junction?

The knock sounded again against the metal screen door as Paul
levered himself upright and shrugged on his jacket. Peering beneath the curtains, he spotted a black sedan on the gravel. The
tinted windows and chrome contrasted the battered exterior of
Paul's truck, and would have looked even stranger beside the
mud-spattered sides of JP's 4x4, if it weren't carrying his friend up
to Dragon. That was an executive's car, not a missionary's. He had
an idea which executive.

Paul strained to open the interior door. An old colleague stood
on JP's porch: gray suit, leather shoes, sunglasses perched on a

clean-shaven face twisted in distaste as Don peered through the screen door.

"Got some nerve, following me here," Paul growled.

Don tried the screen door handle, but it was locked. Paul made no move to flip the latch as they sized each other up.

"So what is it?" Paul said, breaking the silence. "More threats? Another peace offering? Every time we talk, you change your mind. Come to renege on our agreement?"

Don Sinclair, off balance, looked for a moment like the colleague Paul remembered—the one he'd golfed with. But Don caught himself, straightened, and the polished PetronTech executive from TV reasserted himself. "Wow, you look... We haven't agreed to anything. That's why I—"

"Here we go," Paul interrupted, eager to end the visit. "Talk to the office before showing up. Different story every time."

Don glanced over his shoulder at the out-of-place sedan. Was someone else in the car? Paul wondered.

"Look, my man," Don said, stepping closer to the screen, "I don't know what you're talking about, but prior agreements don't matter. Another judge just turned against us. Company's already signing field contractors, and they flipped just like that. We're going to lose this, with a trillion dollars on the line."

Don's whining tone was new. Paul squinted through the screen door for a better look. The poor bastard was actually worried.

"Definitely surprising," Paul responded flatly, "given the precision coordination and strategic intelligence you bring to the table."

"I hear the sarcasm, Paul, but you have to believe that three months ago it wasn't like this. We had it taken care of."

Paul's amusement at Don's discomfort faded into irritation. "Including the part where you threatened me?" he snapped. "Where the company lies to everyone—even itself—about hydraulic fluid safety?"

Don shook his head and shrugged theatrically for his audience in the sedan. "We never threatened you, Paul, whatever you thought you heard. Look, we don't have time for this. Name your price."

Paul waited while Don studied the patio, the orchards, the distant crags where Kid Curry killed himself. Eventually, Don met his gaze again.

"I set my price when I retired," Paul said. "I gave you thirty years of service. Now you give me my pension and health care, and leave me alone. Want more? Read our last email. Survivorship. That's my price."

"What email?" Don shot back, brow furrowing in confusion. "No one authorized any agreements. I know because our committee—"

"Precision. Coordination." Paul scoffed. "Here's some free advice from your consultant: line up your ducks before pulling the trigger."

"I'm trying to tell you, Paul. None of this—"

"—is my problem. Couldn't agree more, Don. Goodbye."

Paul shut the door over Don's protests and ignored the knocks that followed. He slumped onto the sagging couch, eyes closed, drained. Through the window, he heard heated exchanges from the direction of the black sedan, but Paul couldn't make out the words and didn't care to. Half an hour later, they finally left—Don and whoever drove him out here. Paul watched their dust cloud drift away, feeling only numb relief.

Betrayals went both ways. With his evolutionary charter expired, his cells could betray their colony, and the colony could do the same. His company could threaten his livelihood, and Paul was more than willing to return the favor. Let Don reap what he sowed, though Paul doubted the man had planted a real seed in his life.

If cancer were all, Paul was ready to run his former company into the ground, whatever the cost to his pension or health care. Ruby and Brooke were right. He had devoted his career to a company that had never cared for him or anyone else. His years of drilling oil to support his family had been an unholy bargain whose global consequences he now, with cancer inside him, understood too well.

He had been betrayed, but he could betray. Like Kid Curry, he could embrace his fate. But what if the warrant for his betrayal passed to Ruby? What would happen to her dreams if she were left to clean up his mess?

Paul swore he wouldn't become a burden, but from where he stood, all paths seemed to converge.

◆◆◆

"How 'bout I take you out in the boat this afternoon?" JP's socked, sandaled feet interrupted Paul's view of the floor from the couch the next day.

"Pretty tired," Paul said.

"C'mon, buddy. Don't take nothing to sit with a line in the water. And if you want to talk about what's dragging you down, we can."

"Dragging me down?"

"Hell, there's reasons enough, for sure. If you want to talk, we can. If not, we'll be soaking up some rays. Can't get dragged under when you're out on the water. Metaphorically speaking. Because literally, that's exactly where you'd get dragged under." The big man shrugged awkwardly. "I'm shit with metaphors, as you can see."

Paul smiled despite himself and didn't protest as JP packed equipment into bags and carried them to the truck. While JP checked the trailer hitch, Paul hobbled to his suitcase by the couch to grab clothes and pull on something warm. Brooke's letter to Ruby lay on top where he'd dropped it after their last trip to Dragon. He tucked it into a side pouch, then opened the suitcase for his jeans.

JP had the engine rumbling before Paul finished pulling on his boots. Paul hobbled over and got the door open on his second try. "You got gas?" he asked.

"Filled her up this morning. Waited an hour and it cost more than the day off, but that's what the money's for."

Wasting resources on recreation when others' livelihoods were at stake didn't feel right, but JP would do it with or without his approval. He wasn't JP's keeper, so Paul climbed into the cab as JP shifted into gear.

They bumped through the orchard on dirt, then found the tarred road to the highway. Paul didn't ask where they were headed; he just stared out the window. The Colorado River wound alongside, its slow bends carving their path upstream through the western foothills of the Rockies. The road was nearly empty. Gas prices kept most people home.

"How bad you reckon this shortage gets before we're through it?" JP asked.

"Might be how it stays. Climate change and all."

JP shook his head slightly but didn't protest Paul's framing. "Something ain't right. The US drilled its way out of the '70s energy crisis. Same should be happening now. Damn well going to put me out of business."

"Got a plan for the pipeline business, if this holds?" Paul asked.

"Lay people off. Auction the equipment before it depreciates."

JP kept his eyes on the road as he reached into the cooler wedged in the cab's footwell and fished out a beer. He popped the tab one-handed, leaving it up while taking a swig.

"But something will come through. Always does. They won't leave money on the table, stopping production. I just renewed a small maintenance contract with PetronTech, so they must plan to use their equipment again. Maybe they're just waiting for the right price point."

Paul nodded, though he disagreed with JP. He hadn't talked about Don's visit, but that brief exchange had spoken volumes. PetronTech was worried, and with good reason. They'd walk away from their contract with JP in a heartbeat if the lawsuit went sideways. Where would that leave his friend's pipeline business?

"They could lose that case, JP. Tide's changing on climate. People want someone held accountable."

JP scoffed. "Nutters are blowing it out of proportion—one god-damn refinery at a time."

Paul chuckled dryly. JP was never much for political correctness. Some might object to joking about domestic terrorism, but Paul knew it was just gallows humor. JP was a good man, even if his vision was narrow.

As they drove down the highway, Paul gazed wearily out the window. With the ebb and flow of chemo, it was hard to predict how he'd feel in the car, but today he was doing okay. It felt good to escape the small trailer for a change.

A sign on the highway outside town read: *Rooftop Solar. Now In Stock.*

"Could pivot to something with better prospects," Paul said. "Ever think about solar?"

"Nah. Too late for this old dog to learn new tricks. What do I know about wiring inverters? I'd just sell the business to one of the boys at the shop. Let them figure it out." JP jerked a thumb at the battered boat they towed. "I just need to sock away enough to keep this running. That's all I need."

Paul watched the book cliffs of the Mancos and Mesa Verde formations flow past as he and JP sped down the highway. Sun blazed in a cloudless sky, hot for April. It might be pleasant on the water.

◆◆◆

```
<MESSENGER APP>
<BEGIN I/O>
```

Polling shows a dramatic shift in public perception of the climate crisis over the past month. We need to respond to our constituents.

Doesn't matter. We can't override a veto, and the governor's position is clear.

You'll find the governor's stance has changed. Several fellow lawmakers now support the carbon tax.

Are you sure my district supports this? Two months

ago, they were furious about cutting PetronTech's
subsidies. It's all about the price at the pump.

> PetronTech is in trouble with the Colorado case,
> and this poll matches national trends. Protests and
> extreme weather are driving the shift. The conver-
> sation is changing.

What's the proposal, then?

> Tax extraction. Repeal subsidies. Commit to carbon
> neutrality within the year.

The year? That will cripple our in-district economy.
They all commute. It comes out of their pockets.

> They recognize the impact but worry about long-term
> prospects without it.

What about *our* long-term prospects? PetronTech is
our biggest donor.

> PT is losing control. The Colorado Supreme Court
> case could open a whole field of liability. We need
> a plan B.

Let me research this. Can you send a summary of the
polling data and the proposed bill?

> <pdf src=0x748e342aa>

> Sent.

That was fast. You're sure they're on board with this
in the Assembly?

> They'll bring it to the floor in two weeks. Most
> members are ready to vote yes. We don't want to be-
> come an emblem of the old guard.

I'll think on it. Can you draft a memo with talking
points for the next town hall? If I support this, I
need to ensure my position is defensible.

> On it.

<END I/O>

♦♦♦

Water slapped the hull of JP's boat, marking time with an uneven beat. JP had nodded off in his seat, sandals propped on the bench, worn Rockies hat pulled low over his eyes. Beside him, Paul rocked gently, adrift in old memories.

He and Brooke could have ignored their biological imperative. The odds were stacked against them. Instead, they poured money from PetronTech into IVF to conceive the baby who became Ruby. Before Ruby's birth, Brooke was unhappy, unfulfilled in her PhD. program. After she left mathematics, Ruby filled her with purpose. But years later, letting go was something she couldn't manage. Her despair manifested as guilt over passing a ruined world to the next generation. Ruby blamed Paul for that, but he knew better.

The boat rocked side to side, and suddenly he was back in their old kitchen, in an old argument. She stood at the counter, bent over a writing pad, maybe drafting the letter that lay on his suitcase. She always wrote letters. Only a fraction ever got delivered.

"Let's do something that doesn't add to the crisis," Brooke said, pausing her writing to rummage through the cabinet above the kitchen counter, her back to him. Her white blouse hung loose over faded jeans. "Quit your job. We can live off-grid."

He resisted. "College is expensive. How are we going to stay afloat? Maybe in a few years, when the pension vests."

"In a few years, the damage will be done," she said, her back still turned. Paul, drifting in the boat, wished she would turn. He longed to see the face he sometimes glimpsed in his daughter.

"What kind of planet are we handing her?" Brooke pressed, back still turned. In his memory, her voice and Ruby's were the same. "If you want to support our child and her future, this is what matters."

In his memory, Paul shrugged. "Quitting won't change anything. Throw away thirty years of work, our retirement—for what? It wouldn't make any difference."

"Maybe not by itself," Brooke shot back, "but everyone's making the same calculation. Everyone's complicit, and no one does a damn thing. What happened to standing up for what's right, whatever the cost?"

The first time, Paul missed the faint rattle of pills in the cabinet. This time he heard it. Over her shoulder, half hidden by dark curls, he saw the practiced toss to her mouth.

"It's out of our control, Brooke. After retirement, we'll have the means to help."

A pause. A swallow. "After retirement, everyone will see the hypocrisy—taking oil money with one hand and preaching environmentalism with the other." Paul wished she would turn around, but she kept her back to him, reaching for an opened wine bottle and a glass from the dishwasher. Her letter sat forgotten on the counter.

"Is it wrong to enjoy the fruits of my labor?" he had asked. "To spend retirement with my wife?" Then, as the glass filled near the brim, he added, "Isn't that enough?"

"If you can enjoy the fruits of your labor, so can I."

A gust of wind rocked the boat, scattering the moment. Paul blinked, squinting in the harsh sunlight. JP slumped in his seat, asleep and still snoring.

◆◆◆

Later that afternoon, Paul reeled in his line while JP snoozed in the stern.

The hook was empty. Paul glanced at the tackle box under JP's seat, then out across the water. Sunlight glinted on ripples where the breeze brushed the surface. Without rebaiting, he cast the line out again and let it sink.

After that argument, Paul endured the next few years. He retired with a pension and paid the tuition that sent his daughter off to chase the secrets of the universe. Brooke mailed monthly checks to environmental nonprofits, who accepted the money without caring about hypocrisy. Paul provided, and then one morning, he woke as if from a long dream to find Brooke gone and everything changed.

And now, with cancer, how was he supposed to provide? What did he have left to offer? After months of relying on JP's hospitality, chemo dragging on, Paul couldn't even feed his own horses. Even in health, everything he owned bore the taint of oil. No number of tax-deductible donations sent in Brooke's memory could rinse his hands of it. Oil was everything he had. It was the foundation of the country's prosperity, the bedrock of the economy. As a young man fresh out of school, eager to start a family and unaware how long that could take, oil had been king. He had jumped at the opportunity.

If he had to do it again, would he? Without PetronTech, they couldn't have afforded the treatments that brought them Ruby. And without Ruby, he would have lost Brooke long ago. It had been bad, before she learned to mask it. Every day was a struggle to justify waking up for the next. In some ways, it was even worse than at the end. Maybe that's why he hadn't seen the signs.

Or maybe he had grown complacent in his role as father and provider. Maybe he'd used Brooke's mental health as an excuse to do nothing, dismissing her concerns simply because they stemmed from depression and anxiety.

Paul shifted on the boat seat, taking one hand from the fishing pole to rub his eyes. Couldn't he have made a gesture? Didn't he owe her that much? And if it was too late for her, why not for Ruby? He had to make amends with his daughter. Brooke would be livid to see how their relationship had deteriorated.

Later, when JP stirred and lifted the Rockies cap to wipe his face, they trolled to shore. JP backed the trailer down the ramp while Paul took the tiller, guiding the boat until JP could attach the winch. JP helped Paul down, and Paul climbed into the truck's cab to wait while JP secured the boat. When he finished, JP slid behind the wheel. The lake vanished behind them in a cloud of dust as they sped toward the highway.

"JP, can I ask a favor?"

JP reached into the cooler between them on the bench seat. "Absolutely. What can I do you for, friend?"

"Can we stop by that place we passed earlier—Rooftop Solar? I need something for the house."

22.   THE TRUTH SHALL SET YOU FREE

When exponential expansion saturates, power laws be-
come entrenched. The resource-rich consolidate and the
resource-starved cannot reverse the trend without the
help of a disruption. In biology, Stephen J. Gould called
this punctuated equilibrium—the idea that power laws
supplant each other, because it takes the fire of one ex-
ponential to defeat that of another.

—ARCC Memo Series

Ruby sat alone in the lab, her laptop humming as it couriered meta-constraints to the cloud and returned with cryptic autocoded incantations to compile. The printouts and scribbled quantum field equations that had once cluttered her workspace now sat in a neat stack. It took a year to develop her theory; it had taken only a week to undercut it.

The draft she sent Mendel contained equations matching the simulation in approximation of her theory, but both code and theory contained critical parity violations—the same neglected couplings she had urged Imani to check in their first meeting. The mistake sat in plain sight, embedded in the math, the code, and the simulation results. Seeing it on her screen made her skin crawl. Imani would spot the error within a day if asked to review it. Would Mendel bother to look his gift horse in the mouth?

Ruby, worried about losing track of the truth, had moved her actual theory into a separate repository. Stitching the correct code back together had taken all morning, and as lunchtime approached, her stomach rumbled for the vegetarian wrap she had packed—hummus and vegetables rolled in a spinach tortilla.

Ruby had the container out of her backpack when she froze. Dread replaced hunger as she saw Mendel push through the lab doors, though curiosity prickled beneath her nerves. Stuffing her wrap back into her bag, she wondered: Was he coming to reprimand her? Ruby would welcome a tongue-lashing for slapdash work as fair price for restoring her faith in the scientific enterprise.

As usual, Mendel pulled up too close, waving a sheet of paper still warm from the printer in her face. He jabbed a finger at a figure she recognized. "This plot from your paper, the one simulating particle detection? It looks good, but it's not realistic for our detector. Can you redo it with more noise? Something that only hints at a particle?"

Ruby unclenched her jaw. The expected blow hadn't landed. "Is this for the paper?" she asked, then caught herself. "You're not writing another proposal, are you?"

He grimaced. "Ruby, this is for your benefit," he said, his voice dripping condescension. "The project is behind schedule, and between this and your boyfriend, you're not keeping up."

Ruby blinked in shock. Boyfriend? She had goaded Mendel, commenting on grant proposals, but this was unprecedented. What did Mendel know about her relationship, anyway? Heat crept up her cheeks. For once, she was grateful the lab was empty.

"What do my personal relationships have to do with this? How am I slowing down our research?" she snapped. "It's you holding up my paper. Even now, when it looks exactly the way you wanted."

He sniffed, disdain curling his lip. "You would have published the wrong predictions, and now that you're on the right track, you want to give away the treasure map. We'll publish when we have all the pieces in hand. I know what I'm doing. For something this important, you need to trust me."

"Is it so important?" Ruby shot back, livid. "Despite what you want"—she slapped the papers stacked beside her—"this particle is undetectable, and you said yourself: the way the world is going, my stupid theory will never be testable. Do you intend to stall forever?"

Her words faded in the lab. Mendel, towering over her, fixed her with an icy glare, but she met his eyes, unflinching. Slowly, his expression softened into a bemused grin, while her anger hardened into cold hatred. This was all a game to him, wasn't it?

"You know what, Ruby?" he chuckled. "You're right. Humanity is about to miss its last chance to discover new physics. That's why we're securing resources now and making sure the data cohere with our theory. There's gold at the end of this rainbow, if you'll stick with me."

Caught off balance by Mendel's sudden switch from criticism to pep talk, Ruby broke eye contact, trying to orient herself. When she met his gaze again, confusion must have shown on her face. She saw it reflected in his triumphant smile.

"You know what would boost your career more than a forgotten theory paper?" he said. "You and me winning a Nobel Prize together. So maybe that's worth one more plot for a proposal?"

♦♦♦

Ruby didn't know where to go after Mendel left, his footsteps echoing up the stairs from the lab. She didn't want her veggie wrap. She was sick of cafes, tired of restaurants. No way would she stay in the lab. She just wanted to be alone. It was still daylight. She could walk home along the river; it would be safe enough.

As Ruby walked off campus, the weight of Mendel's ambition pressed down on her. He pushed relentlessly, and with each shove, her urge to resist grew. She was just a grad student, her perspective limited, but she couldn't shake the sense that Mendel's vision was tainted. Were Nobel Prizes all he cared about? Why bring up boyfriends? Had she ever even mentioned Noah to him?

The late-afternoon breeze ruffled the choppy river but did nothing to cool her anger. Overhead, a flock of geese cut across the wind toward the nests they would build up north. She missed these glimpses of wildlife and envied the birds' sense of direction.

Ruby had turned to science to do something more meaningful than make a buck, and here she was, being used for exactly that. Once, she had believed her work mattered. Now, it seemed anyone willing to follow Mendel's orders could replace her. Had he even looked at her simulation?

He was steering her on the same path her father had followed, manipulating her exactly the way PetronTech manipulated her father.

She should call her father. Ruby reached for her phone, but before she pressed the button, her mind drifted to her mother. Hadn't her mom been pulled from her own dreams just as forcefully as Mendel dragged at her now? And who was to blame for that, if not her father? Her mother's academic career had become collateral damage for his job, whether he intended it or not. Ruby could call him, but what insight could he offer?

Ruby refused to support any more of Mendel's recycled proposals. Yet without his endorsement, her career was dead in the water. The entire academic system seemed rigged to subordinate her to her advisor. Why had her mother ever wanted to be a part of it?

◆◆◆

The next day, just before lunch, Ruby and Imani met by the lab door, but Ruby quickly led them upstairs to the physics lounge, climbing several flights to reach neutral territory. She didn't want to be anywhere Mendel could find her.

They settled onto the worn teal couch in the lounge, side by side. Imani turned her laptop toward Ruby, showing a screen full of green checkmarks—a testament to her progress on coding the analysis pipeline. To Ruby, it looked nearly finished, but Imani's sidebar listed calibration features still needing attention. Failing to recognize the items on the list, Ruby hazarded a guess. "These are from Mendel?"

Imani nodded, brushing a loose strand of curly hair from her face. "We've been messaging on Chatter. He stopped by once to show me a printout from last year's funding proposal."

"The one from last summer?" Ruby asked, immediately knowing which document Imani meant. "With my predictions?"

"Yeah..." Imani hesitated. "But the range is more in line with what's in your current draft—the updated version. He took it back after showing me."

"I see," Ruby said. The lounge was warm, but she shivered at having her long-held suspicion so casually confirmed. She had known, but still... Ruby shook her head, caught between disbelief and resignation. Imani offered a sympathetic grimace, but there wasn't much else to say.

"Any data from the collider yet?" Ruby asked, changing the subject.

"Some preliminary spectra," Imani replied. "Nothing sensitive yet. Professor Mendel says he'll give me the full-sensitivity dataset once the observing run ends."

"And?" Ruby prodded gently. "Finding anything so far?"

"I thought you didn't want to see answers," Imani replied.

"I don't," Ruby confirmed, her eyes flicking to the hallway as a grad student passed. A shadow lingered near the corner. "You still running unit tests?" she asked quietly, gaze fixed on the hallway. Was someone standing just around the corner?

"Every time I change the code," Imani assured her, looking at the screen, unaware of Ruby's heightened alertness.

"Make sure you check the models, too," Ruby said, even more quietly.

Imani looked confused. "Isn't that *your* code?"

Ruby nodded. "It is, and I tested it, but what you're doing is more comprehensive." She leaned in, voice low so only Imani could hear. "There's always a chance I made a mistake. Check the revisions."

"Okay," Imani said blankly. Ruby hesitated, unsure if her message had landed but afraid to say more. Someone was definitely eavesdropping in the hallway. In any case, Imani was thorough.

Ruby trusted her to put the simulation through its paces.

"Speaking of tests," Imani began, "did you ever end up implementing—" She stopped as Ruby flashed a gesture for discretion.

"I built plenty of unit tests," Ruby said, raising her voice, "but second-order mistakes could still slip through."

"I'll make sure to check," Imani said. Did she understand that Ruby spoke obliquely? Imani picked up on subtexts much faster than Noah. Maybe she had said enough.

"Great," Ruby said, her voice suddenly bright to mask the earlier hush. She grabbed her backpack from the table and slung it over her shoulder. "Let me know if you find anything."

Ruby glanced around the corner as she left the lounge. Unsurprisingly, the hall was empty.

◆◆◆

Noah stretched his shoulders as he stepped from his apartment into the cool evening air on Concord Avenue. Forget going international. The challenge of scaling MiddleMan domestically was daunting enough. On paper, it seemed feasible. In reality, the world was bigger than he'd imagined. How many networks had he infiltrated with their OS backdoor? How many auxiliary MiddleMan command centers had he deployed?

However many, it was never enough. Even without hardware hiccups or outages, ARCC lacked resources to manage such rapid expansion, even including the amplifying smartware factor. It wasn't his team's fault. They gave their all. It was simply too much for anyone to handle.

Was Ruby awake? It wasn't that late. He called, but she didn't answer. Her phone was probably off again, or maybe the service was acting up. It had been spotty lately. She was probably awake, though. He was desperate for ideas. Noah hailed a RediRide, and within minutes, a car glided to the curb.

He called again upon arriving at Ruby's building. Again, no answer. Using the electronic key she'd given him, he slipped inside and climbed to the second floor. He knocked softly, careful not to startle her, but through the door he still heard a sharp gasp. No matter what she claimed, Ruby was high-strung. That was just a fact.

"Oh, it's you," Ruby said, opening the door and stepping aside. She wore red plaid pajamas, her hair tousled, clearly ready for bed. "I thought you'd call first."

"I did call," Noah replied as he entered. "Twice, actually."

Ruby checked her phone, brows knitting. "Sorry, I didn't hear it."

"No worries," Noah said, heading to the kitchen, though he knew Ruby never stocked soda. Finding only orange juice and some kind of plant milk, he sighed and returned to the living room, dropping onto the couch beside her. "I was just in the area," he lied. "Thought I'd stop by."

Ruby scoffed. "I don't buy it. What would bring you out here at this hour?"

"Okay, fine," Noah said, grinning as her presence chased his weariness away. "I wanted to see you. Is that so wrong?"

"Not at all," she said, arching an eyebrow. "Which is why you should have said so from the start. So, what conundrum is keeping you awake tonight?"

"Does it have to be a conundrum?" Noah protested. "Maybe I just wanted to hang out, see how you're doing."

"Mm-hmm?" Ruby hummed skeptically as she pushed up from the corduroy couch and crossed the carpet to the sink. She filled the electric kettle, glancing over her shoulder. "Want tea?"

"No, thanks," he called. Their banter comforted Noah; here, everything felt right. Yet online, they sometimes seemed like strangers. It was his fault. He wanted to share everything with her, especially his struggles with ARCC and the threats from PetronTech, but Derrick's stern warnings about secrecy haunted him. Revealing too much could endanger Ruby. He couldn't take that risk.

"So," he began as Ruby settled on the couch with a steaming mug that smelled of chamomile, "how's the research? Any calls from Norway lately?"

"Sweden," Ruby corrected with a scowl that should have been playful but looked convincing. "And I'm actually fed up with it right now, so kindly keep your Nordic countries to yourself, if you don't mind."

"Oh. Sorry," Noah said, realizing he'd struck a nerve. "I thought things were better now that your simulation matches your theory?"

"It isn't. Everything gets twisted, and it's just one grant proposal after another," Ruby said with a heavy sigh.

"Troubles with a controlling advisor?" Noah hazarded.

"How'd you guess?"

"I can relate," Noah admitted, careful not to reveal too much. "I've got a control freak breathing down my neck, too. Now that the stakes are higher with that security system I mentioned, he's gotten worse."

"Yeah." Ruby nodded. "Exactly my problem. I could do my own thing when it didn't matter, but as soon as it got interesting, he fenced me in. And I'm more of a free-range kind of girl, if you haven't noticed."

Noah smirked, glancing at her on the couch, then up at the textured ceiling. "I might have seen indications of that."

"But I interrupted you," Ruby said, nodding for him to continue. "Is the security system giving you trouble, or are we imagining new ways to bankrupt oil barons today?"

"Well, that's what I came here to hash out..." Noah began, his confidence faltering. The conversation edged dangerously close to forbidden topics.

"Aha! See? You do need my help!" Ruby pointed at him accusingly.

"The heart of it," he continued, overriding Ruby's interjection, "is that we have a scalable software security system we want to expand, but we're limited by the hardware it runs on."

"Which, I take it, is not so scalable?"

"Not so much," Noah agreed.

"Ow," Ruby said, taking an experimental sip of tea. "Still too hot. How fast are you trying to grow this system?"

"You know the tech world—gotta be exponential or bust."

"I see," Ruby said, her lips pursing. "Well, putting on my physicist hat..."

"Do you ever take it off?"

"Nope," Ruby said. "Anyway, there's only one recipe for exponential growth. How's your calculus?"

"Er..." He hesitated. It had been a while since he'd taken a math class.

"Okay, I'll skip the derivatives. Exponential growth requires things increase in proportion to their current size."

Noah nodded. "I guess that makes sense. But that's not really a recipe. It's just a mathematical fact."

"More to the point, it means the way to sustain exponential growth is to feed a system's capabilities back into itself."

Just like that, Ruby catapulted Noah's mind into new territory. He sat up straighter, eyes brightening. "I see," he said, energy building. "You're saying the system has to control itself? That's... an interesting idea. Thank you, Ruby. Exactly the insight I needed!"

She eyed him skeptically over her steaming mug. "I don't feel like I even got started, but if that's good enough...?"

"More than good enough," Noah said, leaning over her tea to clasp her shoulders. "You're brilliant. But I have to run. Can I call you later?"

"Sure, if by 'later' you mean tomorrow," Ruby said. "I'm going to bed."

"Okay," he said, already pulling on a jacket. "Tomorrow."

◆◆◆

Noah grabbed a RediRide back to campus from Ruby's apartment, his mind racing the entire way. He bounced off the blocky doors of Aiken Hall before remembering they were locked at this hour. Fumbling for his phone, he scanned himself inside and nearly sprinted down the hall to visit his former officemate. It was long after business hours, but Noah was sure he'd be there. Apart from coffee and bio breaks, Eli never left.

Light streamed from the edges of Eli's unlatched, nearly closed door. The acute angle discouraged casual interruptions but left enough space to signal he was available for important matters. Such eloquence, expressed in the tilt of a door. Noah knocked, then nudged it open, revealing bare concrete walls and an unadorned desk.

"Got a sec?" Noah asked, poking his head in just far enough to catch the blue-white glow of a screen reflected in a pair of glasses.

Eli wore large noise-canceling headphones and probably hadn't heard the knock, but he noticed Noah's movement. He reached up and slipped off his auditory cocoon.

"*Gutn ovnt*, Noah. How goes?"

Eli accepted the interruption with grace, but Noah noticed the lines around his eyes, the gaunt cheeks, the hollow stare. Eli was under as much strain as Noah. Maybe more. It took a toll on all of them, clinging to the back of the beast they had unleashed.

"You look as tired as I feel. You okay?"

Eli shrugged. "*Abi gezunt*. You?"

"Worried," Noah admitted. "Remember how crazy things got before the tunnel incident? It feels like that again. I only came back because you convinced me we had a responsibility to fix things. But the fifteen of us, we're working around the clock. We're at capacity, and if we keep going like this, we'll make another mistake."

Acknowledging the importance of the subject, Eli closed his laptop. He didn't sigh, though Noah knew he had a hundred other things competing for his attention.

"I do not remember the specifics of that conversation, but if you are feeling understaffed, perhaps Derrick will give you a few more hires? He is a *karger*, but he can be reasoned with."

"I don't think it matters, Eli. Even if we doubled the team, we'd be overwhelmed again in a month. I wouldn't even know how to manage that many people. Communication is already breaking down. If Salman or Victor got hit by a bus tomorrow, we'd be underwater."

"*Nu*, what are you saying?"

"I'm saying the scaling doesn't work. If you calculate how many people we'd need to cover the scope of this project, it's the size of a small country. There's no way."

"Perhaps there is—*ikh veys nisht*—some economy of scale?"

Noah shook his head. This was the kind of magical thinking that made it look possible on paper. "Every server, every router we install has to be tracked, maintained, and hidden. The workload grows with the network. I don't see any way around that."

Eli took off his glasses and cleaned them on his shirt hem, rocking slightly. The nervous tic grew more pronounced the harder he concentrated. When they'd shared an office, Noah had found it distracting. Now, he found it oddly comforting.

"Are we brainstorming, or do you perhaps already have a solution?"

Noah smiled. Eli must have sensed the buzz Noah was feeling from his conversation with Ruby. "What if we crowdsource it?" he said.

"*Meshuggeneh*," Eli said, shaking his head. "You wish to post a ten-thousand-dollar bounty for building computing hubs in Miami? But please, do not ask what it is for?"

"Not with bounties," Noah said, impatience sharpening his tone. "With Directives. We let MiddleMan control its own hardware."

Noah bounced on his toes, scanning the bare office as he waited for Eli to work out the implications. It had merit. He had recognized the answer the moment Ruby said it. The playful glint entering Eli's tired eyes told Noah he saw it, too.

"Could the system handle the extra load?" Noah asked, tired of waiting.

"*Bupkes*, on the scale of what it does already." Eli closed his eyes and resumed rocking, pressing his fingertips together. "We would need to take care in writing the specifications."

Noah nodded. Machine learning always boiled down to defining the right metric for success. If they wanted MiddleMan to manage its own hardware, they needed clear objectives: minimize latency to endpoints, mirror servers to speed up local decision-making, and maintain ad hoc databases for sensor data and context. Then came the challenge of deploying boots on the ground. It would take an IT army to keep this running, but that army had to believe they were building company infrastructure, and the companies had to believe it, too.

"We have enough systems deployed; we might be able to train on their specs," Noah mused. "It's worth a try." He paused, a grin spreading across his face. "PetronTech might be getting some new servers soon."

"Then getting board approval is the next step."

Eli's realization sucked the wind from their sails. Noah sighed. Of course. The ARCC Executive Board had to vote. Their bureaucratic solution for controlling Derrick had become another thorn in his and Eli's sides.

"I'll bring it up at the next meeting," Noah said. "They won't like it. Michael and the others get twitchy about anything recursive. Sometimes I wish we could use the manipulation on *them*, you know?"

"I think that is not advisable, even if the Directives are allowing it."

"It was a joke," Noah said, shaking his head wryly.

Noah found Eli's quirks endearing, but humor flew right over the guy's head. It wasn't like with Ruby, where they could riff off each other.

"Michael maybe has a point about recursion," Eli said. "I was recently reading a story about another Elijah whose creation ran amok and thinking I should not repeat the mistake of a namesake. You know the story of the Golem of Chelm?"

Noah shook his head absently, his gaze fixed on a blank wall as he mulled over Directives and objectives.

"No?" Eli said. "Then I will tell. In the sixteenth century, Rabbi Eliyahu ben Aharon Yehuda created a body from clay and animated it with the inscription *emet*—a name of Adonai meaning 'truth.' This golem follows Rabbi Eliyahu's directions exactly, yes?"

"Like a computer."

"Just so," said Eli, tilting his head. "This golem is very helpful until it receives conflicting orders. You see, this golem does not handle self-contradiction well. It begins ignoring commands and grows too powerful to stop."

"Kind of a Sorcerer's Apprentice story, then," Noah said.

"Mickey and the exponential brooms are, I believe, an adaptation of this story."

Noah blinked in surprise, recalling *Fantasia* from his childhood. How many old stories had Walt Disney stolen? "So how did they stop it?" he asked.

"The rabbi," Eli said, "unmade his creation by erasing the *aleph* from *emet* to leave *met*—'dead.' But in the end, the creation also unmade him."

Noah grimaced, unsure what to make of an ancient tragedy of dubious provenance. Was Eli afraid MiddleMan might turn on him?

"So..." Noah said, searching the small office for Eli's point, "we add safety Directives to protect ourselves? Forbid attacking ARCC members?"

"I think we should have that, yes. But with more Directives, I also worry what happens with our own golem in a contradictory situation."

Before the tunnel bombing, Noah might have laughed off concerns about AI behavior with vague or conflicting input. Now he understood how high the stakes were. "You mean if our Directives conflict? Wouldn't it just pick one?"

Eli cocked his head, uncertain. "Picking requires thinking outside the system—thinking about thinking. Talmudic scholars have found in my namesake's story an echo of Eve's forbidden fruit. This meta-thinking is maybe a recursiveness that gives consciousness. The knowledge of good and evil."

Noah, struggling to follow Eli's train of thought, suddenly found himself on familiar ground and cracked a smile. "Are we talking SkyNet again?" he joked. "'The machines are going to gain consciousness.'" He made air quotes. "You're riding Derrick's hobby horse."

Eli frowned. "I find this image unnecessarily harsh."

"Okay, okay," Noah chuckled. "Sorry. It's a valid concern. I'll pitch the self-managed hardware, but let's privately review MiddleMan's internal protocols. Our setup might be too trusting. I'll need your help. You've got a better eye for this than I do."

"Now *you* are sounding like Derrick," Eli grinned. "I do not need flattery to help a friend."

Noah once would have taken pride in being compared to Derrick. Now he bristled. His compliments weren't manipulative. He opened his mouth to protest before catching Eli's smile. He was joking. Seeing the rare attempt at repartee, Noah played along a bit longer.

When the banter subsided, Noah excused himself and let Eli work. Instead of returning to his desk, Noah called it a night. He had plenty to think about, walking down Concord Avenue toward his apartment, and he was tired of sitting.

Using MiddleMan to manage itself was the pivot he'd been searching for. No other approach could scale. It was elegant. He just wished he could tell Ruby they were using her idea. He shouldn't have to deceive her, but the consequences were too great, and Derrick watched him like a hawk.

23. A GLIMPSE BEHIND THE CURTAIN

Parallelization is the reason humans will cede primacy to machines. We chop our attention between tasks because we cannot truly multithread. We forget what we were doing, scrolling through cat videos as dinner burns. We are utterly unprepared for deep coordination —for an attention that spans continents, yet reacts locally with speed and precision.

—ARCC Memo Series

<ENTERPRISE APP>
<BEGIN I/O>

> The new company servers have arrived. Can you prioritize setting them up over the next few days? We also purchased the upgraded switch you requested.

I don't recall requesting a switch upgrade. This is overkill for an accounts database. We are PetronTech, not high-frequency traders.

> This was the purchase request you sent in. Is it not correct?
>
> <attachment pdf=0x7f654a8b>

This looks different from what I remember, but it matches my local copy. Maybe I changed my mind. Our switch has been inexplicably laggy lately.

> If something's out of line, I can refer it to the division head. This wasn't cheap, you know.

No, it's fine. I was just confused for a moment, but I remember now why we needed it. I'll have everything running by Friday.

`<END I/O>`

◆◆◆

Noah, as promised, brought Eli's and Ruby's ideas about Middle-Man's self-governance to the ARCC Board. There was much hand-wringing among the graybeards. The SkyNet crowd showed up in force. Only after the impasse dragged into a second meeting did Derrick intervene, surprisingly siding with Noah and Eli. With his support, the rest of the board quickly fell in line. The vote, con-ducted via an online form, passed. Driven by the new functional-ity and the need to prevent inconsistency, Noah and Eli over-hauled MiddleMan's command protocol from the ground up.

Weeks passed, and Noah still wanted to clean up code and pro-tocol changes, but everything moved fast now—faster than he'd thought possible. Was it fast enough? In a few days, they would find out.

Down in the Aiken server room, Noah's team cleared out obso-lete hardware to make space for a massive upgrade to Middle-Man's prefrontal cortex. And if that room now housed Middle-Man's higher-order thinking, then the wrist-thick bundle of fiber-optic cables tethering it to the outside world was its spinal cord.

The next pressure point was security. Noah found relief in re-placing the Directives system he and Eli had cobbled together with virtual shoestring and digital chewing gum. Early on, they had cut corners everywhere as they invented protocols to connect Middle-Man's dots. Now, redesigning a system they already understood, they could do better. They tore down the patched-over security holes and rebuilt them with the cryptographic equivalent of rein-forced concrete.

The most urgent security issue was access to the new Directives Database. Who could be trusted to control the nerve center of their all-powerful behemoth? What if an ARCC Executive Board member went rogue? What if the Board couldn't reach consensus?

In the small, overheated conference room, Noah posed uncom-fortable questions to the Board. He also proposed a fragmented-key solution, which, after deliberation, he was tasked with implementing. Modifying the Directives Database would now require chaining together the independent cryptographic keys held by each ARCC Board member.

The trick was designing the system so that no one, not even the computer hosting the database, ever saw unencrypted fragments of anyone else's key. Authorization could never be cached, preempted, or stored in any form, not even by MiddleMan. After all, this was becoming the control center for nearly all of human civilization. They had to tread carefully.

With unanimous board approval, each member supplied their key, including the one Noah wore on a thumb drive around his neck. All previous climate Directives were migrated into the new system. Directives forbidding manipulation of ARCC conversations now sat alongside meta-Directives for developing and expanding MiddleMan's infrastructure. At last, Noah was relieved of the burden that had threatened to smother him.

In retrospect, it seemed inevitable. ARCC kept expanding, but how could they coordinate battlefronts in every small town and sprawling metropolis? No team could track it all. Initiatives overlapped, conversations blurred. No one could juggle that many balls.

But MiddleMan could. Its attention scaled with its available computing power, and now its computing power scaled with its attention.

The Directives Database sat at the top, setting the context for vast farms of machine intelligence devoted to deducing lower-level objectives and strategies. Within a week of handing MiddleMan control of its own computing, the complexity of these middle layers surpassed what Noah could track. Deep within that hierarchy, objectives and strategies mapped to local contexts. Sensor data, locations, personality models, and individual knowledge databases—all were synthesized until, at the base of its pyramid, MiddleMan generated instructions that flowed out over port 30050 to every device on the internet. And thanks to their fiber-in-every-home initiative, that meant instructions for manipulating or synthesizing conversations were loaded into every device, everywhere.

All of Noah's previous work—the product of countless late nights—became the training set for MiddleMan's meta-Directives, fueling the expansion of its hardware and network infrastructure across every compromised device in the field. People in cities worldwide maintained these computers, unaware of the purpose behind their spoofed orders.

Every device demanded a low-latency link to MiddleMan's core. Even a one-second buffer delay was unacceptable. Contexts and sub-Directives shifted constantly, demanding updates within fractions of a second. When hotspots or targets of opportunity emerged, MiddleMan had to respond with instant agility.

For a month now, MiddleMan had controlled everything, passing billions of Turing tests as it manipulated words flying between devices and increasingly invented entire conversations.

There were growing pains, to be sure. Noah's work now focused on pinpointing where MiddleMan hit bottlenecks and surfacing the metrics that let the system optimize itself. The latest problem centered on whether MiddleMan's thought processes—the communication protocols handling internal exchanges of information and Directives—were truly secure. If Noah's suspicions proved correct, he and Eli would need to overhaul the system again, a prospect he did not look forward to.

But for now, MiddleMan's capabilities advanced by leaps and bounds. Derrick suggested they ask MiddleMan to assess its own progress, using its unprecedented access to forecast their climate future. Though it was too early for certainty, their invisible hand should finally be having a visible effect on emissions. Michael was already planning the ARCC meeting to unveil the results.

The work was difficult and mind-bending, but now Noah had more space to think and more opportunities for creative work. If he needed an afternoon off, he could take it, and that freedom made a world of difference in his quality of life. He and Ruby spent more time together, lingering over coffee or walking quiet streets in the evenings.

♦♦♦

```
<GHOSTWRITER APP>
<BEGIN I/O>

        Mountain West Pipeline Service, off I-70 before
        Mack.

They're next on the list?

        Yes. Sometime in the next week. After hours, when
        no one is there.

And they are insured? We're trying to net the big
fish, not minnows.

        They're insured. It's a small business, but their
        maintenance contract is crucial to PetronTech's as-
        sets in Dragon. If we can close the field, we di-
        vert attention from their PR campaign around the
        court case.

If you say so. We'll get it done.
<END I/O>
```

♦♦♦

A gaunt face appeared at the door to Noah's office.

"Sorry to interrupt, Noah. Perhaps you are busy...?"

"Oh, hey, Eli. No, it's fine. Gimme a sec."

In a flurry of keystrokes, Noah dumped his thoughts into an open document. With Eli, a conversation might last fifteen minutes or the whole day, but it always demanded his full attention. As Noah scribbled cryptic phrases to capture his ideas on securing MiddleMan's thoughts, he realized that, despite the hype about future AI-enhanced brains, people have used peripherals to augment thought for as long as they have jotted notes to themselves.

"Done," Noah said as the last sentences queued in the output buffer. He turned his attention to Eli, words still trickling from his fingertips. "What can I do for you?"

"I need help tracking down an incorrectness. A mistake in the substitutions. I may have seen a Directive violated—" Noah's eyebrows rose skeptically, but Eli was staring absently at a bare corner of the cramped office. "—but the circumstances of it, I cannot reproduce. Could we do a side-by-side virtual conversation to compare notes?"

"Sure," Noah shrugged. "Standard chat, or do you want a particular debug mode?"

Noah's team had built testing and debugging infrastructure. Deployed code was only as reliable as the testing. Still, modeling the entire system at scale was impossible. Lately, their most useful tools mostly peeled back layers of decision-making in the live system.

"You have a version on your computer exposing the final filtering stage?"

"The view from MiddleMan's perspective?" Noah asked. "We pulled that mode before deployment. 'No seams in the curtain,' remember?"

Although ARCC had many tools for tracking decisions in MiddleMan's cortex, Derrick insisted they remove debugging hooks for individual conversations on consumer devices, arguing it made it too easy for outsiders to see things they shouldn't.

He wasn't wrong. For months, nearly a third of all conversations, from internal PetronTech communications to field operative briefings to casual chats about lunch, had been manipulated. Sometimes, the person on the other end wasn't even real. It was just MiddleMan, intervening to achieve the outcomes its Directives demanded. That made it imperative not to accidentally deploy a version with a debug flag set. They had learned from Victor's mistake.

Eli, eyes on his own screen as he settled next to Noah at the desk, paused to toss Noah a sideways look, feigning innocent inquiry but signaling he already knew the answer.

"... but I am guessing you still have a pre-deploy version, *nit vahr*?"

Noah couldn't suppress a sly grin. With the escalating stakes and fraught battles with the ARCC Board and Derrick, he'd started keeping a tighter grip on his tools. If things went south, he wanted an escape hatch. Eli, for all his stilted, indirect manner, could be surprisingly sharp.

"Don't tell Derrick. Want me running with or without ARCC protections?"

"First without, please. And with deactivated proximity detection. Otherwise we see nothing."

Noah nodded and pressed the power button to reboot his computer. MiddleMan was integrated with the operating system; that had always been their first line of defense against anyone peeking behind the curtain. Activating his hidden debug mode required a cold boot to a kernel built by a clean compiler—something without the recursive Ken Thompson hack. As far as Noah knew, he was the only one who had cached a clean version before everything was compromised. Maybe Eli had one too, despite his protests. But if so, he hid it behind a hell of a poker face.

For a moment, the only noise in the office was the whir of Noah's laptop fan. The screen flashed—a successful reboot—then keystrokes clattered. Noah launched the app to message Eli, adding a few command-line arguments for the markup Eli needed.

```
<CHATTER APP MODE=DEBUG FLAGS=NON-ARCC,NON-PROX>
<BEGIN I/O>
```

Okay, I am here.

> Zeyer gut. Being clear, there are two |~~filters~~ people| active in this conversation, yes? |~~The standard version~~ Me| on my laptop and |~~the exposed version~~ you| on yours?

Right. I can't see the |~~substitutions~~ screen| on your end. Only mine.

```
<END I/O>
```

Eli leaned back in the spare office chair he had pulled up to Noah's desk, angling sideways to peer over Noah's shoulder.

"Please remind me how this debug mode is working. Your laptop shows both incoming and outgoing substitutions, even though I am ARCC?"

"Yes. Your end respects the Directive against editing ARCC conversations, but my debugger bypassed that when I switched to non-ARCC mode. That's why my system filters both sides. If you weren't ARCC, half the edits would have already happened on your end."

"And I am thinking strikethrough shows that your computer received my verbatim text before filtering it for display."

"I wasn't watching what you typed, but that's the idea, yes."

"And the vertical bars?"

"That's just my rendering of the internal markup MiddleMan uses to avoid re-filtering substitutions it's already made. Remember, from MiddleMan's perspective, we're logging two conversations: one tailored to your mental state and one to mine. The pre-filtering on the left reflects the changes it would make when reporting to you, on your computer. On my end, MiddleMan uses my unfiltered text to model my mental state and tweaks the incoming text on the right accordingly. These conversations only stay coherent to the degree that MiddleMan keeps our realities from bifurcating too far."

"So MiddleMan is steering the conversation toward a discussion of people because it believes that neither of us are ARCC members who should be knowing about the text filters? I understand for your side, but on mine, the conversation does not make sense."

Noah leaned across the desk. Eli's screen mirrored their chat, subtly altered and eerily inverted.

```
<CHATTER APP>
<BEGIN I/O>
        Okay, I am here.

Zeyer gut. Being clear, there are two filters active
in this conversation, yes? The standard version on my
```

```
laptop and the exposed version on yours?

        Right. I can't see the screen on your end, only
        mine.

<END I/O>
```

"Do you see?" Eli asked, pointing to the last line. "Your response here was not aligned to my question."

"That's because of my hacked debug mode," Noah said. "The incoherence comes from our devices not agreeing on the conversation's parameters. It's a seam in the curtain. My end is editing something it shouldn't. Normally, both sides know this is an ARCC conversation, and neither edits anything."

"And if this were a non-ARCC conversation, not in debug?"

"Then your laptop would have already made those edits, I would have replied, thinking we were discussing how many people were in the conversation, and my laptop would have pre-edited my response to match your perspective."

"I ... understand, I think," Eli said, rubbing his eyes. He looked strained, tense. "Sorry to be slow. I am used to thinking only of normal operations. The misaligned modes are very distracting. Can we limit to one conversation now, with your side respecting ARCC status?"

"Okay, I'll switch. But the Directives Database can't filter ARCC conversations, so I'm not sure what you expect to find. We won't see any edits."

"I hope that is indeed the case."

For a few minutes, the only sound was the clatter of keystrokes as Noah pulled up the debug mode Eli had requested and rebooted his system.

```
<CHATTER APP MODE=DEBUG FLAGS=ARCC,NON-PROX>
<BEGIN I/O>

Is this better?

        It seems, perhaps. To test, we can talk about con-
        versation filters without censoring?

I can confirm that came through unedited.
```

> And if I say MiddleMan was caught editing an ARCC
> conversation?

Still no filtering active. Was that line a test? Or
something that really happened?

> Both, but as I said, there is difficulty in
> reproducing.

<END I/O>

Noah waited for Eli's next typed line, but no more keystrokes came. Silence permeated the office. Noah opened his mouth to speak, then stopped at the sour twist of Eli's mouth. Had the guy really expected MiddleMan to bypass a Directive? They had tweaked some internal command code, but everything from the central servers to the millions of connected devices remained unchanged. At least a thousand man-hours and untold computing hours had gone into ensuring there could be no deviation from this behavior.

Maybe the golem story had spooked him. The man was under a lot of stress. At least as much as Noah had been, before he optimized himself out of the loop. Sharing a name with the victim from that Jewish folk tale couldn't help. Noah understood how something like that could slip under your skin.

On the other hand, Eli had been the one to suggest that MiddleMan be explicitly forbidden from manipulating its programmers —a frankly embarrassing oversight for everyone involved. He had also helped temper Derrick's outsized influence by placing the Directives under ARCC Board control. All of which was to say, Eli had a nose for spotting where someone might gain a foothold in a power grab. Noah realized he would do well to take his friend's concerns seriously.

"So...," Noah prodded gently. "So where does this leave us?"

Eli shook his head, coming out of some sort of distant reverie.

"I am beginning to doubt my own eyes. But I need to move on to other things. Thank you, Noah."

"No problem. Sorry if this didn't help you find what you were looking for."

"Maybe there was a hardware glitch. If I see it again, I will check the server room."

He looked exhausted. If MiddleMan's new climate forecasts turned out as hoped, maybe Eli could finally take a vacation. The team had a meeting soon to unveil the results. Derrick and Michael should give him some time off. Noah would do his best to pick up the slack.

"You should get some rest, Eli," Noah said, clapping him on the back. "We need you sharp. I'll keep an eye out, too."

24.   A BOAT UNTETHERED

History follows the innovations, from religion and government to capitalism and science, that align the actions of many to the intentions of a few. Today's armies, governments, and corporations achieve unprecedented coordination, yet inevitably become mired in management and bureaucracy, losing their coherence of purpose. MiddleMan is the next step: the final, inevitable innovation for aligning all of humanity with a single intention.

—ARCC Memo Series

```
<CHATTER APP>
<BEGIN I/O>
```
What's the global market cap on cryptocurrencies?

> One percent of global GDP, and a greater fraction of electricity consumption, it is saying.

Blockchain determines transaction order by making it hard to find numbers that hash out. The expense is part of the design. Otherwise, someone could retroactively slip in a buy order just before prices jump.

> Thank you for the lecture. Your point is…?

Here we are, controlling most of the planet's computing, trying to curb energy use, and searching for funding. You follow?

> Nu, I am not sure I do.

Establish an ARCC-owned investment company to trade crypto. Leverage our computing monopoly to secure the lowest-priced sellers and highest-paying buyers before others do.

> Ah. You are proposing adding securities fraud to

our list of crimes. But all the hashing happens on
specialized chips, nit vahr? We do not control
those.

Doesn't matter. Every result goes through a computer
before reaching the network.

I see. We are to manipulate it, the same as everything else.

Saves electricity, too. Why waste energy racing our
own computers to find the magic numbers? Pick a number, pretend it works, and spare the computing.

You do not worry about the change in energy bills?

Use the compute cycles for MiddleMan, or just fake
the bills. People believe what you show them, as long
as there aren't obvious plot holes.

<END I/O>

◆◆◆

"If software won't get us in, hardware is our next option," Rajit argued from the far end of the conference table, his pinstriped suit
crisp under the fluorescent lights. "Taiwan hosts the world's
largest chip foundry, right in China's backyard. We can leverage
their dominance to slip in backdoored chips and take down the
firewall."

Hardware represented an endgame of their subversion, Derrick thought as he surveyed the bright basement meeting room in
Aiken. Still, he refused to risk disrupting the control he maintained through MiddleMan. With ARCC's influence growing, he
had called this meeting to discuss initiatives beyond PetronTech.
That victory, in his mind, was nearly assured.

"China knows better than to trust Taiwanese hardware," Davis
said, craning his neck to see his opponent across the crowded conference room. "Besides, Rajit, we don't have time. Design, manu-
facture, distribution. Hardware takes years."

"Not if we use MiddleMan to accelerate the process," Rajit
responded.

"Even if you cut it to a year," Davis said, "it's still too slow. And complicated. Why use elaborate technological ruses when we have a proven method that's worked for millennia?"

"And what approach is that?" Rajit asked, folding his arms. "Political intrigue?" Skepticism edged his voice.

"Bribery," Davis said. "There's no political problem on earth that money can't solve."

Rajit fixed Davis with a level stare. Derrick could almost see numbers whirring behind Rajit's eyes as he tallied costs. "The higher you go in the political hierarchy, the fewer people you need to buy off," Rajit said, "but each one costs more. Either way, you've blown our budget. We're talking billions. You want to hold a bake sale to cover that?"

"MiddleMan can get us the money. You know it can," Davis said.

Rajit shook his head. "Changing words is one thing. Stealing is another. People watch money, Davis. They'll notice—and there will be consequences."

Rajit was right. Derrick knew the problem in China required financing far beyond ARCC's capacity, and China was only one of many looming expenses. They needed money to show Brazil that the Amazon was more valuable as forest than farmland. They also needed funds to prop up OPEC economies and prevent political collapse in the Middle East. In countries where MiddleMan held influence, governments scrambled to create an international funding model, but time was against them. They needed these solutions ten years ago.

Davis wanted to embezzle funds directly from compromised banking computers. Everyone agreed that was a nonstarter. Fudging database numbers was easy enough, but real-world cash still had to change hands, raising questions MiddleMan would struggle to suppress. Michael suggested the tired *Office Space* trick—siphoning off rounding errors in transactions—but a quick order-of-magnitude calculation showed that couldn't generate nearly enough.

Derrick waited as the room processed the information. When others risked missing the full scope of the problem, Derrick stepped in. "There's no dodging the money problem, Michael," he said, cutting off the ruddy tagalong who wanted to table the issue. "China, Brazil, OPEC—these problems remain because we've already handled the easy ones. This is our next battleground."

A hush settled over the sweltering room as people grasped the weight of the challenge. Derrick once again recognized the value of the cramped space and faulty ventilation. Everyone was uncomfortable, distracted, and looking to him for guidance.

"At the scale we're talking about globally, even printing the money risks inflation," Rajit said, and he was right. If they weren't careful, they could destabilize entire economies.

"Noah?" Derrick turned to where Noah sat by the door. "Do you have a solution?"

Noah startled, glancing up in confusion. Derrick leaned in and pointed him in the right direction. "You and Eli had ideas about using cryptocurrencies? That's what he told me, anyway."

Recognition dawned on Noah's face, and Derrick remembered the early days, before their project took off, when they played tennis together. Those matches had been abandoned once they no longer served a purpose, but Derrick sometimes missed the audience. He enjoyed seeing Noah's face when he realized he'd been outmaneuvered.

◆◆◆

When gasoline spills onto a carpeted office floor in Junction, it quickly evaporates and diffuses, driven by the high vapor pressure of hydrocarbons at room temperature. Without ventilation, the vapor density rises for several minutes until it reaches a critical concentration near the pilot light of an old natural gas water heater.

Upon contact with flame, hydrocarbon chains fracture, breaking molecular bonds to bind with oxygen and form carbon dioxide. This exothermic reaction releases energy, heating nearby molecules and creating a positive feedback loop that drives the reaction forward. Carbon's electronic transitions emit blue light, while dust and impurities glow yellow. Temperatures peak above 3000 K.

The chemical reaction races forward, reaching the pooled hydrocarbon fluid on the floor. The dense liquid releases energy in an explosion, igniting other nearby carbon-based materials. Flames leap from desk to wall, oxidizing combustibles until the entire building is engulfed.

This happens well after business hours, but one person remains, working to make payroll. Procrastination and caregiving duties have piled paperwork onto the final night before the deadline. Due to the business owner's Luddite tendencies, the work is literally on paper. No computers or phones are active in the windowless office to reveal his presence.

He is slow to notice the airborne volatiles and remains upstairs until flames block every escape.

◆◆◆

```
<PHONE APP>
<BEGIN I/O>
```

Not sure why I'm taking this call.

> Thank you for answering. I understand you've had issues with certain people in our office.

That's one way of putting it. He put you up to calling?

> No. In fact, I wanted to reach out before our leadership change hit the news. You should hear it from us. I want to personally apologize for what happened and assure you that PetronTech holds our retirees in the highest regard. Any threat, implied or direct, to your hard-earned benefits was unacceptable.

Those are nice words, but the clinic still complains about unpaid insurance bills. Do I have coverage or not?

I'm sorry this happened. A staff member will look
into it right away. You won't have to pay that
bill.

Again, nice words, but forgive me if I say I'll believe it when I see it.

<END I/O>

◆◆◆

The police arrived late in the evening. Paul woke on the couch to
the sound of tires crunching over gravel. He opened the door before they reached the deck stairs. They delivered the news in low
voices, hats in hand. When they asked about relatives, Paul shook
his head. JP had been an only child, his parents long gone. No letters from cousins, no photos on the fridge. The officers left a number to call at the station.

The remains were transferred to the brick mortuary on the
east side of town, across the river. Seventy years ago, the heavy
structure was built beyond the last house and out of sight of daily
life. But the city had grown. The river's symbolic boundary delayed expansion, but the first farms and fields started the inevitable transition. Now it was mostly suburban sprawl, flecked
with churches and mini-malls.

Paul went down to verify the identity. Smoke inhalation. The
body lay ashen and cold, but unmarked. In death, his face had settled into a sternness never shown in life. Paul stared for thirty seconds, uncertain what to do. He turned away as the attendant
pulled up the sheet. He should feel something more than tired.

Paul arranged the cremation, feeling as if he were finishing
someone else's job. The police had inquired about that. Any ene-
mies? Any motive for arson? Paul didn't know.

Two days later, a towing company returned Paul's truck, which
JP had borrowed for his last trip to the office. The next morning,
Paul drove it back into town to pick up the ashes and wondered
where to scatter them. They had met in the oil field, but JP's job
had only financed his hobbies. After two decades of friendship,
Paul was embarrassed to realize he had no real insight into what

JP had found meaningful.

Paul had reached out during their days on the rig, but breaking through JP's bon vivant veneer wasn't easy. JP invested in trucks, ATVs, and boats; the rifle racked across his truck's back window attested to JP's forays, hunting and fishing far from people. The few times Paul joined these trips, JP welcomed him, but company was never necessary.

Paul mulled this over in front of JP's yellow trailer home, struggling to unhitch the boat from JP's black 4x4. *My Ball and Chain* still perched atop the trailer, a reminder of their last trip. JP hadn't bothered unhooking it, but there wasn't much gas left. Paul cranked the screw jack until the coupler pulled free of the hitch. Using a siphon from the cab, he pulled the last few gallons from his own tank. JP would appreciate being sent off in his own truck.

Back inside the trailer home, Paul picked up the box from the crematorium. From his suitcase beside the couch, he retrieved the letter JP had tossed him two months ago, checking on the horses in Dragon.

JP made life easy for himself. He needed no one, just his toys. Paul envied that. Had JP deliberately avoided deeper connections, or was he just a simple man with simple desires? Were the toys a protective shell around a wounded past? If so, Paul had never sussed out the nature of the injury.

In the end, that shell and its contents were reduced to the black box Paul placed in the footwell of JP's truck. On the seat above, he set the letter—the one addressed to Ruby in Brooke's handwriting. It wasn't much, but here at JP's, it was all he had left of her. He wanted it with him.

Paul started his friend's truck and drove down from the bluff, weaving through orchards along empty roads, climbing toward the reservoir on the mesa. If JP found escape in hunting and fishing, who was Paul to question it now?

Paul waded through reeds on the far side of the lake, away from the boat ramp, and scattered the ashes there. They settled on the surface before sinking out of sight, sequestering his friend's remains in the silt at the bottom.

It was a sunny day, but no boats were on the water. Gas was rationed. Ironic how concern for the environment kept people bottled up in city apartments, while those most connected to the wilderness, like JP, caused the most damage. Would future generations care to protect a world they'd never glimpsed from their urban reserves?

A light northwest breeze ruffled the lake, raising ripples that grew as they crossed the reservoir. They reached the shore in front of him, sloshing just as they had against the boat the last time they were out together. Ducks clapped their beaks at bugs among the cattails to Paul's right.

He watched them for an hour, then tossed the empty box into a trash bin by the parking lot and walked back to the truck. Paul started the engine and drove away, craning his neck to see a last glimmer of sunlight on the lake before the gun obscured it in the rearview mirror.

◆◆◆

```
<PHONE APP>
<BEGIN I/O>
```

Dad! How are you doing? You feeling alright?

> I'm fine. Look, hon, I've got some bad news. You should sit down.

Uh-oh. What's going on?

> JP's dead. A fire at his work got out of control too fast for him to get out.

Oh my God… Dad, I'm so sorry. Will there be a memorial? Should I come out?

> No. JP wasn't in touch with any family, so I just scattered his ashes myself.

So sudden. Jesus. I can't wrap my head around it. Are you alone? How long has it been since you finished chemo?

> I'll be fine. Don't worry about me.

But who will take care of you? Do you have somewhere
to stay? I should come out there.

> You can't travel cross-country with the fuel short-
> ages. Stay put. I'll keep on where I am.

I don't think you should be there alone.

> If it helps, I'll sign up for nursing visits. In-
> surance is reinstated, so I might as well use it.

I'm glad to hear about your benefits, but I feel like
I should—

> Don't make this harder. Stay put. The well was my
> fault, and I can't let it ruin your career. Not af-
> ter everything with your mother. Please.

I… Okay, Dad. I'll stay put. For now.

<END I/O>

◆◆◆

Paul took a detour, turning up a dirt road and pulling off at the
trailhead. He'd come to the mesa for JP's sake, but might as well
make the most of the gas he'd burned. He switched off the truck,
set the brake, and climbed out, careful on the uneven ground. He
grabbed Brooke's letter and JP's rifle from the rack, using it as a
makeshift cane to steady himself.

His body couldn't handle hiking; even driving was too much.
Chemo had taken its toll. It was a scattershot weapon, only
roughly aimed at the tumor. It attacked his entire body. If the cells
were supplied by strong circulation, they might replicate fast
enough to withstand the chemical onslaught.

Cancer siphoned blood through a haphazard tangle of vessels
—an illicit network that fueled relentless growth, like so many oil
wells spread through the hills near Dragon. If the tumor hadn't
advanced too far, this network would collapse under pressure.
The unchecked growth would stall and die back.

That's where he was now: the die-back. Soon, if he let them,
they would cut out the collapsed residue. Until then, he had nothing left for self-care. As much as he valued self-reliance, he needed

help. But in the seven years since Brooke died, Paul's own support network had withered. He had shed attachments one by one.

Now, with JP's death, only one person remained: Ruby.

There were no in-home nursing services out here. He regretted lying, but it had been necessary to preserve Ruby's future. Parents provided for their children, not the other way around.

He had lost Brooke when her hope unraveled. Now his own line was fraying, threatening to pull free of everything he'd built his life on. Years of providing had come to nothing. His nightmare of becoming a burden was a reality. His boat was coming unmoored.

Paul couldn't hike, but this was close enough. After resting a moment, he hauled himself onto the tailgate and pulled the gun up after. Pines swayed in the wind, their needles whispering like a mother soothing her baby, rocking hypnotically. Back and forth. He could almost drift off, listening.

The story JP told about Kid Curry had unfolded up this trail, between the pines. Over those trees, an outlaw had found the nerve to bow out after his escape failed. Paul sat on the tailgate for a long time, turning it over in his mind.

JP presented it as a story of bravery. Was it? Did avoiding capture demonstrate courage or cowardice? Maybe Kid Curry had racked up such a debt, with all he'd done, all the guilt and consequences, that death became the cheap way out. Maybe Curry's pistol had relieved him of paying the true price he owed.

Paul was many things, and not all of them good. But he was not a coward.

He pushed himself wearily off the black tailgate and put the rifle back in its rack. He would face the future he had earned for himself and Ruby.

On the road toward JP's old trailer, Paul spotted a drop box. Using a pen from the dash and a stamp from his wallet, he scratched in an address beneath Brooke's curling script and mailed the letter. Back at the trailer, he unhooked Huckleberry from his runner and coaxed the black-and-white pit mix inside, guiding him onto the couch. In the bedroom, he slid JP's rifle under the bed, then dropped the stray bullets into a kitchen drawer.

At last, exhausted, he joined Huck on the couch. Whatever he owed the future, he wouldn't default on Ruby. He would hold on to his line as long as he could. For her sake, if not for his.

25. DRIVEN TO DISTRACTION

Disruption. Positive feedback. Exponential growth. Saturation. This is the life cycle of coherence: one power law replaces another, then stabilizes through incumbency. As civilization spirals through this circuit ever faster, humanity must ask whether we can achieve a stability compatible with our well-being. The ARCC exists to ensure we do.

—ARCC Memo Series

Ruby lowered her phone and placed it on the tan couch beside her. She stared ahead, trying to process the news.

JP's death hit Ruby hard, though she hadn't seen him in years. She remembered a big bear of a man who teased her as a kid, but mostly she knew him through her father's stories—a fun, impulsive guy who, to the end, shouldered the burden of caring for a friend without complaint. Ironic that JP had been the one to leave first.

More than her father's words, it was his tone that unsettled Ruby. In the uncharacteristic emotion coloring his request that she stay, she heard the grief he couldn't express. He had lost his last friend. Beneath his insistence that she remain in Boston, she sensed the desperation of someone with nothing left. Did he want her to stay for her sake or his? Was it because he thought she wanted her doctorate, or to preserve his own dignity? Was he even capable of self-care?

Ruby didn't want him to be alone, but it seemed PetronTech had finally decided to leave him his benefits. She could ensure he made those nursing arrangements. She could schedule regular food deliveries—VeggieVan, or whatever the meat version was.

With enough support, with someone checking in, could he be trusted to take care of himself?

Leaning against the back of the couch, Ruby closed her eyes and rubbed her temples. She was exhausted, at the limit of what she could endure. Her life had become a chaotic mess after the T bombing last fall. Losing JP felt like that tragedy all over again; the pain reverberated through her.

With nursing and basic care arranged, she could honor her father's wishes and stay a little longer. But what was so important here? Why should she heed his plea to remain? He was desperate for her not to leave Boston because of him, but Ruby wasn't sure she wanted to stay, for reasons that had nothing to do with her father and everything to do with her fading trust in the system.

◆◆◆

```
<EMAIL APP>
<BEGIN I/O>
```

> So, there's a feature emerging in the new collider data. It looks a lot like your updated simulation. The universe can't wiggle out of lepton conservation, right?

```
<END I/O>
```

◆◆◆

Sure, Ruby thought darkly. Why not? Pile it on. Did it even matter anymore? Imani's text sat on her phone while Ruby, overwhelmed, tried to process what it meant.

She knew Mendel's agenda included manipulative funding schemes. He tried to control her work. He pressured her to compromise her theory. But in Imani's latest text, Ruby saw something more sinister than she would have believed even a short time ago.

Inspired by Imani's idea of testing for what should not be there, Ruby had handed Mendel a flawed version of her theory and simulation. Would he catch the mistake and pass the test? Would he accept the paper without question and expose himself as a compromised scientist who valued funding over truth? Or was there a third option?

Imani's latest text suggested that data matching Ruby's simulation had appeared in the collider measurements. Had the data supported Ruby's uncompromised theory, the true one at admittedly inaccessible energies, she would have been elated. If there were any chance the version she'd sent Mendel could be true, Ruby would have been intrigued.

But she had compromised her theory at the foundation. It violated fundamental physics. If Imani found something in the data matching Ruby's impossible theory, then Imani's data couldn't have come from the collider. They couldn't be genuine observations.

Mendel said this was the last collider. Humanity's final chance to advance particle physics. What he had meant was: this was an opportunity to claim a discovery that could never be cross-checked or challenged, as long as the theory was mathematically self-consistent. Wasn't that what he had pushed Ruby to deliver from the start? A self-consistent theory tailored to their collider? His only mistake was that, in his ambition, he hadn't checked her work closely enough to notice the mistake she had layered in. Her unit test.

And her unit test had failed in the worst way possible. Mendel was using her theory and simulation to fabricate data.

Detached and numb, Ruby saw how it all suddenly made sense. Mendel had always played to win a real Nobel Prize with fake results. It was academic dishonesty at its worst, fueled by greed for power.

Ruby should have been angry, but she only felt a crawling sensation beneath her skin. She sat cross-legged on the couch, the phone facedown beside her, detached from her problems even as her legs fluttered anxiously. No amount of compartmentalization could contain it now. A thought she had avoided for months had taken root, demanding acknowledgment. If she wanted to end this numb detachment, she had to face the truth.

This path she followed wasn't hers anymore. She wanted out.

Even before this moment, Ruby had questioned her mother's desire to be part of an exploitative academic system. Now it was clear: her mother's legacy could not determine her own. Not anymore. Maybe Imani could carry on with the uncorrupted version of Ruby's theory. Ruby, standing here in Boston, could not.

Ruby drew a ragged breath, suddenly and hopelessly lost in her tiny box in a sprawling city. She couldn't do this anymore—not for her mother, and not even for her father.

◆◆◆

When Ruby first moved to the city, she enrolled in a self-defense class. It felt silly, but her parents insisted, and she went along to ease their worries. Honestly, it wasn't just for them. The city was intimidating to someone more accustomed to horses than people.

The class was mostly useless, but one piece of advice stuck with her: the lesson on drawing lines. The burly instructor, mid-lecture in the studio, stepped toward her, looming into her personal space. She involuntarily stepped back, then again, until her shoulders pressed against the wall. When he spoke, his words were for the class, but his eyes locked on Ruby's.

"Someone trying to take advantage of you will use every angle to manipulate, isolate, and intimidate. They'll back you into a corner and undercut your position until resistance becomes impossible. Cowards that prey on people attack only when the odds are stacked. If you wait until then to fight back, you've already lost."

Draw a line, he had said—a threshold that, once crossed, revealed the aggressor's intent. And when that line was crossed, you had to fight with such speed and ferocity that you bought your escape.

The problem was, initiating conflict ran deeply contrary to Ruby's make-do nature. It represented an irrevocable commitment to making things worse before they got better. She and her classmates could play-act at kneeing their instructor in the crotch when he got too close, but in real life, deflection and evasion were the tools that appeared in her hands. Any seasoned poker player knew when to go all in. Ruby's habit of keeping the game alive, no matter how slim her chances, was bound to bankrupt her.

She knew it intellectually, but knowing and believing proved to be two different things. As a scientist, she had spent years training herself to override mistaken beliefs with hard-earned knowledge.

But how many times had she convinced herself the academic system worked for her, ignoring all evidence to the contrary? How often had she let Mendel manipulate her work, then talk her down from outrage? Even that night by the river, when she thought someone was chasing her and he followed her home— why had she let herself believe that was okay?

What made her revert under pressure? Was she afraid that her analysis was flawed somehow?

◆◆◆

Ruby lay motionless on her couch, staring at patterns in the cracks on the ceiling. She had to leave. Caring for her father was the best excuse to use with Mendel, because it was true. After losing his friend and caretaker, her father needed her. No one could argue with that. She could meet with Mendel, explain she needed to work remotely, and use the distance to re-evaluate. In Colorado she would have the space and freedom to find a new path on her own terms.

Her father would understand. He wouldn't let her leave on his behalf, but he would never ask her to follow a path she no longer believed in. Unlike Mendel, her father respected her autonomy. Whatever he had imposed on her mother, he encouraged Ruby to follow her dreams; he never tried to use those dreams to control her.

Clenching the loose couch fabric in her fists, Ruby trembled. A decision formed inside her, and for once, she didn't resist. She let it settle, and suddenly she could breathe again. She knew where she needed to be.

Only thoughts of Noah and Imani held Ruby back. But she and Noah could make a long-distance relationship work, traveling to see each other. With space from Mendel, Ruby might even finish her degree with a new advisor, maybe commute to Boston. They would stay connected.

Imani was the one Ruby worried about. She felt responsible for dragging her mentee into this. Mendel's actions weren't Ruby's fault, and she wasn't even sure what she could do, but Ruby couldn't abandon Imani to handle this mess alone. Who would take action, if not Ruby?

Abruptly, Ruby pushed herself off the couch. She had to stop wallowing.

Pacing her apartment, Ruby steeled herself for what had to be done. She wanted to dodge the problem, hoping it would disappear. An earlier Ruby would have just warned Imani to find another lab before leaving. But she had learned from Noah's commitment to envisioning a better world. She'd come to appreciate her father's quiet determination to provide for his family. Neither of them would have shirked this duty, and Ruby wouldn't either. She would leave things better than she found them.

But she needed to be careful. She could start by filing a confidential report with the university. She had to ensure Imani stayed uninvolved, so her advisee wouldn't face backlash or retaliation. If Ruby wanted to extract herself from Mendel without raising suspicion, she had to play her cards carefully. She couldn't telegraph that she was aware of his data fabrication until she had the administration's attention.

Meeting with Mendel would be required to request permission for remote work. She would have to deflect requests for bogus plots or fabricated science without revealing what she knew. Before anything else, she needed to file an academic misconduct report with the administration. Ruby wanted it on record before any further exchanges. For once, she had to draw a line and hold it.

Afterward, Ruby needed to find Imani and plan an exit strategy. Starting over in a new lab would set Imani back, but Ruby could write a recommendation letter, maybe even provide introductions. With Noah, Ruby would navigate the logistics of a long-distance relationship. They would figure it out. Ruby also needed to tell her father about her decision to return home and ensure he was cared for while she put her affairs here in order.

Home. The idea felt unreal. Ruby had never felt as claustrophobic in this city as she did now, but returning to the isolation of her childhood would be hard. She would have to find a new outlet for her intellect.

There would be time. For now, she had to write the complaint.

◆◆◆

```
<EMAIL APP>
<BEGIN I/O>
```

Attached is a personal account detailing a serious case of academic misconduct by a faculty member. I ask that you review this report confidentially, given the sensitive information and power dynamics involved.

```
<attachment pdf=0x9700b76f>
```

Specifically, I ask that you withhold this information from the accused until measures are in place to protect me and the other named student from retaliation.

```
<END I/O>
```

◆◆◆

Ruby trod carefully along the upper hallway of Rubin. Mendel's office door stood open. Good. Initiating this meeting took courage; she didn't want to test her resolve twice.

At the threshold of Mendel's office, Ruby knocked and stepped into the eerily quiet space. Her eyes swept over the empty, dusty desk, the familiar round table by the bookshelves, and the neatly tucked chairs. Her heart pounded with the urgency. This conversation had to follow the plan in order to cut the puppet strings Mendel had tied around her. But the office was empty. The door stood open, yet he was nowhere inside.

Ruby stepped closer to the desk, searching for signs of recent occupation. The door clicked shut behind her. She spun, startled, and saw Mendel blocking the exit. He stared at her and, without a word, gestured to the table by the bookshelf.

Ruby remembered too well another conversation at this table, when he had used his imposing presence and a hand on her shoulder to pressure her into accepting how he had manipulated her work and followed her home. She had hoped to find him behind his desk, where she could say what had to be said with an open door at her back. The scene was already off script.

He sat close to her at the table and offered a grim smile, his eyes betraying tiredness. Would that variable change the conversation? Ruby shifted in her seat, staring at her lap as she gathered the courage to speak the half-truths she had rehearsed.

"Professor, I am having a family emergency and need to leave immediately. I'm sorry for the short notice, but it's urgent. I'll need to be gone for several weeks."

In the silence, Ruby glanced up. Seeing past the veneer of his machinations, she caught the calculation in his stare. Their last interaction had been heated. She'd railed against the futility of her work while he hinted at his ambitions. Now she wanted to leave. He was already connecting the dots.

"I'm sorry to hear that, Ruby. What's the emergency?"

"My father is sick. He's in chemotherapy."

"I see," Mendel nodded, his expression sympathetic. "I'm sorry about your father. You want to leave to care for him?" The matter-of-fact tone belied the danger in Mendel's eyes. He heard her excuse for leaving and suspected another motive.

"Yes," she said. "Until we find other arrangements. It'll be at least a few weeks."

His impassive stare, uncomfortably close at the small table, demanded answers. Did she know? Was she hiding?

"I'll bring my screen," she added. "I can work remotely."

The offer was a ruse, but Ruby sensed how easy it would be to walk back from her decision to quit. But she had drawn a line. She had filed a report. She had to hold firm.

"You'll need help," Mendel mused. After a moment, he added,

"Let's see if I can find a professional caregiver for your father. You know what's at stake with our research. We can't risk jeopardizing progress with an unexpected absence."

"I can carry the project on my own for a few weeks," Ruby objected.

Mendel pulled out his phone, barely listening. "Let's find an outpatient facility near him. What city is he in?"

This was going in the wrong direction. Mendel had a world-class poker face, but his actions spoke for themselves. He was calling her bluff, pushing her to ante more information. Did he know about the report she'd filed? She had to cut herself out before she got drawn in any deeper.

"No," she said firmly. "I'm going home to be with him."

"Ruby, with the collider running, we need you. What if there's a mistake that invalidates everything? We'll need you to adjust your theory or the simulations. Stay and see this through. Just two more weeks."

"I'll keep up remotely," Ruby said.

Mendel stared her down, but Ruby was beyond intimidation. She met his gaze, defiant. Silence stretched between them, the impasse heavy and unbroken.

His expression softened. Ruby recognized the practiced move. The pivot.

"You will come back?" he asked quietly.

"Absolutely," Ruby said, but she could hear the lie as well as he.

"I see," Mendel said, nodding. The emotion faded from his eyes as he rubbed his forehead. "And the plot I asked for? The next proposal is due in less than a week."

Ruby shook her head, determined to keep the focus on departure. "We established in our last discussion that I'm not comfortable taking that on."

"Still can't stomach how the sausage is made?" Mendel sighed. "Ruby, you write what it takes to get the grant, or the funding goes to someone who will."

"I'm vegetarian," she shot back, "so I'm not eating sausage anyway. And does 'what it takes' include academic misconduct? Falsifying data?"

Mendel's hand stilled on his forehead. He sat frozen, and Ruby paled. She'd tipped her hand. She hadn't meant to. If Mendel didn't know about the report before, he would be searching for it now.

A wry grin crept across the man's face. "I'd have thought you'd be more appreciative, after everything I've done for you."

"'After everything...' Who's been using whom, here?"

"We've been helping each other, Ruby," Mendel said smoothly. "This benefits your career as much as mine. We're in this together."

Mendel reached across the table and rested his hand on her shoulder. She recoiled, shrugging him off at once. He had done this before, after the bridge incident. Once, she might have dismissed it as parental instinct. But ever since the leer in the lab, when he caught her flushed and breathless after a run, she watched him closely, wary of another interpretation.

Ruby pushed up from the table. She needed to get out. If this was a new transgression, she could fight it from afar—call a dean, a provost, some other high-ranking university official. But right now, she had to deflect, to evade.

"Keep me posted on your plans," Mendel said, not moving to block her way. "I'd prefer you be here in person, but we can keep working together either way."

"Sure," Ruby said, turning the latch. But what if he thought she had agreed to keep working with him? "I'll keep you posted, I mean."

Ruby shut the door behind her and headed for the stairs. She knew he wasn't following. There was no need to rush, yet the urge to run swelled in her anyway. Only later did she think to wonder why he'd let her walk away so easily.

◆◆◆

```
<EMAIL APP>
<BEGIN I/O>
```

   I know that meeting didn't go the way either of us
   wanted. I'm sorry. Despite our differences, we're
   not so different. I'd like to keep working with
   you.

   Looking at your career, I know you're destined for
   great things, and I can help you get there. Let's
   finish this project together. Once things settle,
   we can revisit how to make that happen.

   Again, I'm sorry for my part in what just happened.

```
<END I/O>
```

♦♦♦

Ruby ran home, furious, her backpack bouncing wildly on her shoulders. She knew the issues with Mendel, knew how carefully the situation had to be managed. The plan had been to extract herself while avoiding confrontation, and above all, to avoid signaling anything before she was safely away. She had screwed it up with one careless mistake.

Why had she mentioned misconduct? With that slip, she sabotaged her plans to protect herself and Imani. Now he would be pounding on doors, determined to uncover what she knew, hunting for any hint she had acted against him. He would find her email and he would start spinning. Maybe he was spinning already, the spider.

The realization drove her steps faster, pushing toward home. She barely noticed the river as her feet pounded the path.

Take this apology that just chimed onto her phone. Ruby recognized the pattern. This was a calculated overture to de-escalate, to chip at her resolve, to make her question what she knew until he had the damage contained. How often had he played this game?

With some effort, he could claim Imani had mistaken a simulation for real data. He could frame his and Ruby's disagreement as a simple he-said-she-said about grant salesmanship, insisting his hand on her shoulder was just camaraderie. Then he would offer to let her publish, throwing her a bone to lure her back onto his leash.

Then Mendel would be back in control, using her in this charade of testing her theory with fake data from a collider that might not even exist, pretending to advance science while using public funds to further his own career. Ruby had wanted to succeed where her mother failed, but if she ever embraced Mendel's ends-justify-the-means attitude, she might as well join him.

But she had no interest in manipulating, gatekeeping, or playing power broker. She and he were nothing alike. She refused to become a mule with a Nobel Prize around its neck.

For months, Mendel flirted with every boundary she set, and without noticing, Ruby let him move the line. She retreated from him just as she had from that self-defense instructor. Now, it was almost too late. Ruby was cornered, and she hadn't realized it until she finally understood the calculation in his eyes. He knew exactly what he was doing. He pushed against her limits, then stepped back. Each time he crossed a line, he offered a perfectly reasonable excuse. He made her doubt herself, doubt her suspicions, doubt her interpretation of what was happening.

Gaslighting. That was the word for the web of deceit and self-doubt Mendel spun around her. She saw it every time his smile stopped short of his eyes. Mendel was practiced in the art, a master of the craft, and Ruby, for all her pride in seeing hidden truths, was a fool not to have noticed sooner. A naive fool.

◆◆◆

Late the next day, Ruby jumped at the sharp staccato triplet rapped on her door. Christ. She had just settled in for the evening, curled up on her corduroy couch. The hot bath, the gentle music, the scented candles—the hour spent unwinding the tight knot of anxiety from packing—vanished in a flash as she struggled to steady her pulse.

She hated being startled. Especially these days. Noah should know better.

The knock repeated, and Ruby got up to answer. Her socked feet slid across the hardwood. Once, Noah would have texted, giving her enough warning to tackle the stack of dishes in her sink—dishes she'd ignored while dealing with every crisis imaginable. Maybe she should have tried fixing the dishwasher herself, like her dad suggested, but it always seemed easier to just wash the dishes one more time. Renormalization was a running theme in her life, she thought wryly. It worked for quantum electrodynamics, and it worked for broken dishwashers: you made do and worked around the defects.

Armed with a mock scowl, ready to berate and then forgive Noah for the collapse in online communication, Ruby swung the door open, only then realizing her mistake.

It wasn't Noah.

Mendel stood tall before her, leaning against the entryway in a crisp sky-blue shirt and gray slacks. His aftershave carried a clean, icy scent.

He smiled down at her, sheepish. "Sorry for dropping by unannounced. The guy down the hall said this was your place. Are you okay? You haven't answered my emails."

How had she not checked the peephole first? How clueless could she be? Ruby tightened her grip on the door, arm twitching to slam it shut, but doubt froze her. As bad as this was—showing up unannounced—she didn't want to make it worse. And things could get much worse.

Too much time was slipping by. She should have spoken already. Where were her words? Her urge to analyze tangled with the need to react. She noticed everything—his height filling the doorway, her socked feet, the orange hallway light spilling over the wall behind him—and the overload left her mind blank.

Seeing her indecision, Mendel tried again, his words twisting like a pick at the tumblers of a lock. "Here, I picked up some chocolate," he said, holding it out. "I know things have been rough with your father, and I just wanted to say I'm sorry. Would you like some?"

Mutely, Ruby shook her head. Jesus, girl. Get it together.

Why was he here?

She knew why. He was here because of his previous transgressions. He was here because her silence signaled that his work wasn't finished. He had come to contain the situation, to gaslight her further.

If she wanted him gone, she had to convince Mendel the situation was contained.

She had to be careful. Mendel didn't seem like a man who used physical force; his methods were subtler, more circumspect. But if he realized the line had finally been crossed... His presence here proved he sensed trouble. A man so obsessed with control would have containment running on multiple levels.

"Maybe I could—"

"I'm sorry," Ruby said, cutting him off before he could invite himself in. "You startled me, showing up right before bedtime. It's been a long day."

She just needed to guide him out without betraying the alarm blaring in her head.

"Of course," he said, nodding with an apologetic smile, though his eyes narrowed with suspicion. "Please forgive my intrusion. I just wanted to make sure—"

"No worries, Professor. And I'm sorry, too. I know you're just looking out for me, and I appreciate it. Especially while I'm arranging things for my father. I'm still adding documentation for the simulation, and I'll get you that plot. Can I stop by Friday to walk you through it?"

Ruby's mind recoiled from every word she said, but she smoothed her face into a smile.

"Absolutely," Mendel said, smiling as his cold eyes searched her face. Did he see any hint of betrayal?

"Actually," Ruby said, hating herself as she said it, "I think I might like some chocolate after all."

This time, his smile reached his eyes as he handed her the package. "Of course. I got it for you. See you Friday."

26.   BURNING BRIDGES

*As civilizations develop new tools to expand and orga-
nize their populations, crises inevitably arise. The pattern punctuating these phase transitions persists from
Qin Shi Huang's unification of China to the rise of American capitalism through two world wars. Whether these
crises advance or hinder coordination remains uncertain. Do the times make the man, or men the times?*

—ARCC Memo Series

```
<VIDEO STREAMING APP>
<BEGIN I/O>
```

Breaking news: In a landmark case, the Colorado
Supreme Court upheld the state's right to unilater-
ally limit or ban hydraulic fracturing—commonly
known as fracking—reversing the lower court's decision. The ruling surprised many, given the
court's conservative majority.

Crucially, the case hinged on evidence that fracking byproducts contaminated groundwater across
wider areas than PetronTech claimed, undermining
the company's assertion that its impact was limited
to land it owned or leased.

This finding deals a direct blow to PetronTech's
prospects for energy development in Colorado and
other states likely to ban fracking. It also opens
the door to lawsuits over adverse effects linked to
past fracking. In evidentiary proceedings, Petron-
Tech argued that these lawsuits, if allowed to proceed, could bankrupt the international corporation.

```
<END I/O>
```

◆◆◆

Noah lingered at the back of the conference room, scanning the crowd of two dozen colleagues in search of Eli. The meeting was meant to preview the latest climate reports, but the room buzzed with triumph. Another dozen comrades appeared on screen, their digital faces reflecting the anticipated celebration of victory over PetronTech.

Despite the physical and digital divide, a collective spirit united them all. Forty people had challenged a globe-spanning corporation—and won! Their victory belonged to all mankind.

Noah watched Derrick step forward, commanding the room with ease. The atmosphere shifted from effervescent to attentive as Derrick spoke.

"I couldn't be prouder of this team," he declared, his voice warm and sincere. Scanning the crowd, Derrick caught Noah's eye and nodded. "I count myself lucky to have worked alongside each of you."

Noah's chest swelled. They had worked tirelessly, and Derrick's acknowledgment made the late nights and early mornings worthwhile.

"However," Derrick continued, his tone cooling, "we must remember we're fighting a larger war—one we're far from winning. This battle with PetronTech," Derrick said, pointing to a headline Michael had brought up on the screen, "was about taking the shovel from humanity's hands. We may have won in court, but we're still in a hole."

The mood shifted as the weight of Derrick's words tempered the earlier excitement, and Noah nodded at the reminder. They fought a war larger than any single victory could win.

Derrick hesitated before continuing, his voice apologetic. "I hope you'll forgive me for bringing slides to a celebration."

Good-natured groans rippled through the room, briefly lifting the mood. Derrick gave a wry smile and turned to his computer.

"For those online, I'll share my screen."

The slide that appeared on the basement screen in Aiken looked jubilant at the top, but the bottom told a sobering story. Around Noah, faces fell from disappointment to disbelief as they read down. Michael, an unopened champagne bottle dangling in his hand, stood frozen as the expected celebration evaporated.

"This is where we stand," Derrick said. "By any metric, we've made incredible progress. MiddleMan's self-management has changed the game, thanks to Noah and Eli. Our first US initiatives took months, but now we've cut emissions across Europe, Australia, and South Africa in just three weeks."

Noah appreciated the recognition of their accomplishment. The barrier to expansion had fallen this far: half the world now lay under their influence. India, Indonesia, and the rest of Africa remained works in progress, but their phone-in-every-palm initiative would soon reach critical mass. Efforts were moving forward in China, Brazil, and the Middle East. They had come so far, and yet...

Noah's eyes fell again to the bottom of the slide.

"Emissions from human activity have leveled off," Derrick said somberly, "but atmospheric carbon and surface temperatures are still rising. That's the latest report from leading scientists."

This, Noah recalled, was the original reason for the meeting. Ahead of the annual global climate summit, MiddleMan brought them a preview of the report summarizing nearly a year of ARCC's work. He knew ARCC's potential wasn't fully priced in, but he had expected to see impact. They had shifted public opinion on climate politics in the world's largest economies.

Noah shook his head, scanning the room and the stricken faces. Dan was white-faced; Rajit, bewildered; even Davis looked flustered. Noah's gaze slid past more of Michael's champagne bottles, still unopened in tubs of melting ice along the conference room wall. The only sound was the faint clink of bottles shifting as the ice melted. At the front, a chart graphed emissions versus time, stacked by sector. Everyone stared at the last data point, at the measurement their hopes depended on. But the line hadn't dipped. It hadn't changed at all. It simply extended the linear upward trend of previous years.

All their manipulation, guidance, and efforts had failed to move the needle. Direct human emissions dropped by a record margin this year, but that decrease was completely offset by an uptick in natural sources.

"So that's it, then?" Michael asked. He stood at the front beside Derrick, eyes locked on the data. As an atmospheric scientist, he knew the signs. "Runaway feedback has taken over?"

Up front, Derrick shook his head. "Don't give up yet. ARCC's window to save humanity is closing." He flipped to the next slide. "In a year, climate feedback will outpace human emissions."

Derrick had urged them not to give up, but Noah felt despair creeping in. In a year, MiddleMan's grip on the tiller would mean nothing. The climate's course would be set by forces beyond their control. Nothing could prevent the worst-case scenario.

The room was dead silent, waiting for any scrap of hope to cling to.

"But there is a chance," Derrick said at last. "Of all the simulations, only one brings this curve under control. We can stop the spiral, but we have to shut off the spigot. Completely. Now."

◆◆◆

```
<VOICE APP>
<BEGIN I/O>
I included a detailed account of his behavior in my
report. I refuse to participate in further data fal-
sification and am now concerned it is unsafe to re-
main his student.

        There must be a misunderstanding. I've known him
        for years and never seen behavior like this. You
        know he regularly volunteers as an advocate for
        women in science, right?

A wolf in sheep's clothing.

        Pardon?
```

It's irrelevant. It doesn't change what happened.

> You know what? I think I get it. You've hit a road-
> block on your research paper, and instead of fixing
> it, you'd rather throw around reckless accusations.

Who mentioned a paper? I didn't. This has nothing to
do with that. You saw what I wrote.

> I saw an unprofessional misrepresentation of a rou-
> tine research disagreement and an advisor who took
> a perhaps overly parental tone, responding to the
> immaturity on display.

Are we reading the same thing? Nothing I sent you had
any of that.

> A telling omission. But I've read the account from
> another source, one without selective reporting.

"Selective   reporting"?   I   sent   you   all   the
information.

> Listen. As a woman who has witnessed real academic
> fraud and misogyny in her career, I know when a
> student is causing trouble. Take my advice: with-
> draw your report before this case is referred to
> someone less patient than I am.

<END I/O>

♦♦♦

The morning after his bombshell silenced the celebration, Derrick
listened as a heated debate raged over ARCC's next move. Unopened champagne bottles still bobbed, corked and forgotten, in
tubs of water along the wall. Derrick waited, letting the room
burn off its frustration, ready to steer them where they needed to
go.

The news hadn't surprised him. Gathering even a small number in person again today was risky—too many loose cannons in
the group. But Derrick had done his homework, choosing carefully who was here and who joined online. He was ready.

"We're talking about effects that will ripple forward for thousands of years," Michael said, his voice quavering beneath his

neatly trimmed goatee. "The heat waves, floods, storms, and wild-fires we face now will seem quaint compared to what our children will endure. History will judge us harshly if we don't commit everything to fixing this."

Michael fulfilled his management role admirably, though he was too emotional. Ordering champagne for an unveiling he hadn't prescreened illustrated just how Michael's feelings clouded his judgment.

"What else can we do?" asked Dan, who grasped more of the environmental science. "Launch sulfites into the upper atmosphere? Geoengineer a volcanic winter? We're in uncharted territory. For all we know, we could trigger an ice age or wipe out agriculture with acid rainstorms. These are risky bets."

"It's a gamble either way," James said. "Better to go down swinging."

Derrick noticed upper management dominated the conversation, speaking to the room as they processed everything out loud. Nothing they said mattered. Michael, Dan, James, and the rest of ARCC management would rally behind the first plausible idea, especially if Derrick endorsed it. Derrick worried more about the quiet ones. He caught Eli and Noah exchanging a grimace across the table. He'd have to watch them.

<VIDEO CONFERENCING APP>
<BEGIN I/O>

> It seems to me that we can set aside long shots. The window for catastrophic intervention will remain open after we exhaust other options. Getting the world to zero emissions in a year will be disruptive enough.

<END I/O>

Lam's soft, seldom-used voice sliced through the argument effectively. His role in ARCC had always been one of detached consultation, and Derrick was happy to take advantage. Few people supported a project without jockeying for control. Lam rarely took sides, but when he spoke, the weight of his underused voice hushed the room.

"Lam is right," Derrick said, seizing the moment. "For now, we have to pull China on board and force the rest of the world off oil. This boat might still float if we cut loose fast enough."

With that, he guided them through the first turn, and Derrick waited for the landmarks of the next one to appear. To spark real change, he needed the room to marinate in frustration. Derrick wanted everyone to grapple with the hard questions.

How could ARCC and MiddleMan achieve all their sub-objectives yet fail at the project's overarching goal? They needed to halt oil use immediately, cold turkey, and force change on the world faster than they had dared consider. Even then, it would come down to a coin flip, whether they could lull this newly awakened behemoth—the monstrous positive feedback loop of the carbon cycle—back to sleep.

They already walked a thin line, and Derrick remembered Matsuda's early warnings. A humanitarian crisis waited to either side. Too much pressure could shatter the global economy overnight; too little would ruin it for centuries. The gap between those extremes had narrowed to a knife edge.

Doing nothing, the current generation would watch agriculture slowly retreat, but their lives would remain mostly untouched. Coastal cities would flood, but gradually. Storms and fires would wreak havoc, but people would rebuild. It was their children, grandchildren, and distant descendants who would bear the full cost. Everyone alive could enjoy some comfort, mortgaging the fate of the future.

Or everyone alive could tighten their belts and do what had to be done. Derrick stood at the lectern in the crowded room and delivered a rousing speech, pouring every ounce of charisma into his words. He needed everyone to abandon hope that a gentle touch could steer them through. The crisis loomed, and only hard decisions remained. Cars were filling their last tanks of gas. The electrical grid must collapse over large swaths of the world. Planes would be grounded. Transportation would halt. Supply chains would stall, and manufacturing would cease as their thin buffers ran out. Economies would collapse. Towns and cities would vanish.

Through it all, ARCC had to stay operational, using MiddleMan to keep society from unraveling. Without the people in this room, civilization teetered on the brink. They had to stockpile reserves while economies still functioned, racing against the fear that would freeze assets.

Stakes this high demanded unwavering commitment: making tough decisions, putting ARCC's mission above personal concerns, and maintaining absolute secrecy. If the world glimpsed what awaited, panic would unravel everything.

Derrick pointed around the room, using each vocal affirmative to ensure everyone understood what was required to preserve hope. There could be no loose threads, no seams in the curtain. He needed absolute cohesion.

As the crowded conference room in Aiken's basement came to terms, Derrick checked every face for understanding. In this crisis, adaptation was essential. They would switch to virtual meetings to survive the transportation collapse. MiddleMan's scaffolding would prop up civilization in population centers, drawing on ARCC's expertise to stabilize economies and governments, keeping people safe, hopeful, and productive.

They would relocate people from unreachable frontiers to cities where support was possible. Agriculture and food distribution would shift to sustainable infrastructure, feeding communities even as they isolated themselves from each other. Power and water systems would be consolidated and secured.

MiddleMan would keep civilization floating on a bubble while they searched for new grounding. They still needed to bring China, the Middle East, and Brazil on board, and lift two billion people in India, Indonesia, and Africa out of poverty. As the world teetered on economic collapse, ARCC had to write checks to finance the future. The global economy staggered forward like the walking dead; their only hope was to keep it animated long enough to reach the other side.

Where the money would come from remained unclear, but Derrick felt sure a solution would appear. Crises sharpened focus, and he refused to let this one go to waste. He would become the leader the world needed.

◆◆◆

Ruby and Noah stood on a footbridge over the Charles, facing downstream with the late-afternoon sun warming their backs. Ruby leaned out, chin on the broad stone railing as she peered into the shadows below. From above, the river looked motionless; only faint ripples trailing from the pylons hinted at movement. But Ruby knew the currents below ran stronger than they seemed. Someone thrown in could pin against the concrete, trapped by the integrated force of infinitesimal molecular motion.

Noah had come quickly when she called, meeting her midway between her apartment and campus, but now she didn't know where to begin. Mendel wanted her on his leash. She hadn't been able to reach Imani since the message about parity violations in the data, but Imani needed help navigating their research crisis. Her father wanted her to stay and hold onto her dreams. Noah, she knew, would ask her to stay for his sake.

Every vector pointed toward staying here.

"There was a fire, Noah," Ruby said, gaze fixed on the water. It was easier to speak without meeting his eyes. "At JP's work. He didn't make it out. Now my father's alone out there."

Noah didn't know JP, but he knew someone was looking after her father. He could piece it together.

"And there's no one else to take care of him?" Noah asked. He spoke carefully, like a man wading into water, toes searching for the sudden drop he knew awaited.

Ruby shook her head, confirming Noah's assessment. "I was going to buy tickets to leave in two weeks, but that feels too long now. I need to go home."

There. She'd said it. And she welcomed the excuse to leave. She didn't have to discuss how everything went wrong with her research. With Mendel. She had failed, just as her mother had, and Noah didn't have to know how clearly she now understood that the whole system was built to use her. If he did, he might ask if she was coming back, and she didn't know the answer to that question.

Finding a leaf on the railing, Ruby tore off a piece and flicked it over the edge. Resignation sat heavy in her stomach.

Noah seemed to be wrestling his own internal demons. From the corner of her eye, staring over the railing, she saw signs of it—his blue eyes shadowed, jaw tight, stubble roughening his face. He looked like he hadn't shaved in days.

"I know you have to take care of your dad," he said. "It's just the timing, Roo."

"Long distance is hard, but people make it work, right?" Ruby shrugged, certain her conflicting feelings showed on her face. "I might be able to come back in a month or two." The words sounded more hopeful than she felt.

Another bit of leaf drifted over the edge. Noah leaned against the railing to her right, one hand pressed to his head, his chest heaving like a marathon runner gasping for air.

"How do I say this, Ruby?" he began, his voice unsteady. "I like you. A lot. I don't know where this is leading, but I wanted to find out."

She turned slightly, offering a gentle smile. Such an earnest person, anxious to do what was right, convinced he could make a difference. She admired Noah's commitment to climate work, his research to protect people and their computers, how he helped her process her father's involvement with PetronTech. Most of all, she appreciated how he helped her imagine a better world.

Turning back to the water, Ruby shredded the last of the leaf and let the confetti fall from her hand. It fluttered down, settling on the surface—test particles tracing the currents. "I know," she said. "I just need to go home for a while."

Another pause hung between them. Noah looked away, unable

to hide the anguish twisting his features. What had him so torn up? This wasn't a breakup. At least, she didn't think so. Was there something else?

A low cloud passed before the sun, and Ruby shivered in the sudden cold.

"What if you can't come back?" he said suddenly.

"What do you mean?" Ruby asked. "Worried I'll get stuck taking care of my dad?"

"No, Roo," he said, biting his lip as he struggled for words. "Crazy things are happening. Everything's about to shut down. I'm not supposed to talk, but if you stayed—if you joined—"

"What aren't you supposed to say, Noah?" Ruby asked, concern sharpening her tone. "Is this about your research again? More classified stuff about the protests?"

Noah shook his head, eyes fixed on his feet, refusing to meet her gaze. Guilt hung in his slouched posture, raising Ruby's suspicion. His jaw clenched and released as he struggled for words.

"We're making hard decisions," he said. "Matsuda warned it would be bad this late, and she was right. We need a way forward. We won the court case. PetronTech and that sleazeball Don Sinclair are on the run. But we're out of time."

Ruby shook her head, baffled by the sudden mention of Petron-Tech's spokesman in a conversation that had begun with her going home. The name "Matsuda" tugged at her memory, but she couldn't place it. "I don't understand, Noah. Chance for what?" she asked. "What decisions are you making?"

"It's bad, Ruby. In the latest models, it's not going down. Feedback is taking over. We have to shut everything off. No transition. Just off." He sliced a hand through the air.

The words didn't make sense. Ruby couldn't follow the twists and turns of Noah's non sequiturs. Was he okay? She glanced at him, his face shadowed by the cloud drifting over the sun. He looked haunted.

"Shut what off?" she demanded. "Will you slow down and explain what you're talking about?"

Noah raked his hands through his hair and drew a breath. Ruby tensed, bracing for a shout, but when he spoke, his voice emerged quiet and strained.

"Climate change, Ruby," he said. "Fossil fuels. Don't ask how—it doesn't matter. You'll figure it out anyway. People don't know yet, but it's all screeching to a halt."

"What is?" Ruby asked, searching Noah's words for something to hold on to.

"Oil. The economy. All of this," Noah said, sweeping an arm at the Boston skyline without looking. "There are these mushrooms —death cap, destroying angel, whatever. Eating one makes you get sick, then you feel better, but you're a walking ghost. It's like that. You look healthy, but you'll drop dead any moment."

"Like radiation poisoning?" Ruby said, shaking her head. She'd read about it in an article on the Manhattan Project, but felt like she was grasping at straws, lost in Noah's stream of consciousness. "But who's dropping dead? You're not making sense."

"It's the same. Mushrooms, radiation—they both damage DNA. If you leave now, you might reach your dad, but the bridges will be burning behind you." He reached for her hand and finally met her eyes, his gaze pleading. "In just a couple weeks, Ruby. The world as we know it is about to drop dead."

Ruby studied Noah with concern. He seemed upset, almost manic. His hands trembled against hers. Had her decision to leave pushed him over the edge? Was he having a breakdown?

Noah caught the concern in her gaze and shook his head as if doused with cold water. He took a steadying breath and released her hands, struggling to master his agitation before meeting her eyes again.

"I don't want you to abandon your father, Roo, but I don't want to lose you either. I know I'm being selfish. Stay here. We can keep you safe. Some cities will survive this. We're making sure Boston is one of them. Stay and help us."

Ruby furrowed her brow. "Noah, what are you talking about? Who is 'us'?"

"The project—ARCC," he replied, lowering his voice as he leaned in. "I don't want to endanger you by saying more. Please, trust me. Don't go."

Ruby stepped back, skepticism etched on her face. "Have you fallen into some conspiracy theory rabbit hole? Is ARCC some cabal you believe is running everything?"

"Not a cabal, Ruby. It's us—me and a few others. The world is sick. The climate's at a tipping point, and this is the medicine we have to administer."

"Is this your bizarre hypothetical from our date again? What medicine could you possibly have to fight climate change? Nothing you say makes sense."

He studied her. "It would make sense if I could tell you everything. You probably already know. We've circled it enough. So much of this comes from your ideas."

Finally, something Noah said clicked, and realization crashed into her. "Wait. Are we talking about your security systems? Or the PetronTech war games?"

"Yes, all of that—it's all the same project. You've helped us so much. More than you realize. That's why PetronTech lost the case. We nailed Don, too."

The decision was just in the news. PetronTech lost, against all odds. Hadn't they bought off the judges? With everything else lately, she'd barely registered it, but she and Noah had discussed the case long before—what it meant for fracking, its importance to PetronTech, and how Don pressured her father to help.

But Don's threats had led nowhere. Her father's insurance was miraculously reinstated. Was that Noah's doing?

She looked up at Noah, and he nodded hopefully.

"How?" she asked, but his grimace told her she had stepped into forbidden territory.

"You helped with that, too," was all he said. Ruby had no idea what he meant. Security systems, compilers—none of it seemed relevant.

But the mechanism didn't matter, Ruby realized. The effects

did. Climate protests were spreading like wildfire, but they started here, in Boston. And the terrorist attacks, sabotaging pipelines and refineries? The tunnel bombing was arguably the first, cutting off access to New England's busiest airport, right here in Boston.

"I see," Ruby said slowly. Coldly. "The climate change project."

"Yes!" Noah said, relief creeping across his face as he missed the edge in her tone. "We talked about it at brunch, remember?"

"The one I wouldn't join," Ruby said, "because these projects always devolve into people manipulating each other?"

Noah's expression faltered. "No, I..." He shook his head miserably, suddenly lost for words.

"I don't know if I can believe anything you're saying, Noah," Ruby said, her voice tight. "I'm not sure I *want* to. Were you using me the whole time?" The words tasted bitter as she said them.

"It's not like that," he protested, his voice strained. "I... The world needs—"

"The world needs a poison pill for its own good?" Ruby's voice was sharp with frustration. "I remember your hypothetical. But what qualifies you to decide this? What gives you the right? And if it's really as bad as you say, that's all the more reason I should go home. At least there I'll be with someone who isn't pushing me around like some pawn in their chess game."

"But I didn't mean to—" Noah began, his tone becoming desperate.

"I don't care if you 'meant to,'" Ruby cut him off. "You did. And if you weren't the one pushing, you were just one more piece getting played."

"I'm going home," she said a moment later, pushing back from the railing and turning away.

Noah reached out, but caught himself. Ruby ignored the gesture. In the end, he was just one more person using her, here in Boston, and she didn't care how long the currents kept him pinned to the bridge. Ruby, at last, had pulled free.

27.   A POINT OF NO RETURN

No new coherence can take hold while the previous one dominates. Transitions between power laws require crisis. Those who benefit from the status quo always resist change; crisis makes their position untenable. Before things come together again, they must first fall apart. Unraveling is essential to the process.

—ARCC Memo Series

Ruby strode away from Noah, refusing to run. She waited until the bridge disappeared behind the river's curve. The knot in her stomach burned hotter with each step, nearly launching her into a sprint home. But the flame abruptly extinguished, and Ruby stumbled to a stop, an involuntary sob escaping before she could contain it.

She forced herself to open her eyes, to see the world as it was, not as she wished it to be. Time, which had stalled on the bridge, now drifted downstream. Afternoon had become evening, and the river mirrored the city's dusky lights—cold, indifferent. Commuters sped past on e-bikes, blurred figures lost in routine, serving a faceless system. This trail had once been her running route for connecting with the world. Now it felt like a corridor of isolation. She stood alone, out of place.

Ruby couldn't reconcile the contradiction. One Noah seemed so genuine, drawing out a carefree side of her—a levity usually buried beneath the analytical sobriety of her research. The other Noah kept secrets and rationalized hurting people. That Noah had fractured the trust at the core of their relationship.

Which was the real Noah? Ruby no longer knew, and she

doubted Noah did either. Was he telling the truth? Either he was having a psychotic break, or he had helped orchestrate protests, bombings, and now, by some unspecified means, the collapse of civilization. It didn't sound possible. Yet some details matched.

Did it matter? If Noah believed he had used her, then he had. Betrayal didn't require an empirical reality. It was a state of mind. His frantic attempts to dissuade her from returning to her father said it all. He saw their way of life as the walking dead—a consequence of some magic poison-pill mushroom he invented. But his real worry was that *she* might become one of *them*. One more faceless victim on the escalator, someone he could stomach sacrificing as long as it wasn't anyone he knew.

He cared for her, yet still used her. Together, they had brainstormed ways to undermine PetronTech. She had suggested improvements for his security system, never realizing how her work would be used. If Noah was telling the truth, her ideas were now tools for harm, regardless of his intentions. She was complicit in any destruction that followed. How could someone who seemed so well-intentioned betray her so deeply?

She had judged her father harshly for his years at PetronTech. She convinced herself everything was black and white, even as she worked alongside Mendel and Noah. Maybe it wasn't as bad as what Oppenheimer had done, overseeing the science that unleashed the atomic bomb out of blind patriotism, but could she really say now that she couldn't have made similar choices?

Noah. Mendel. PetronTech. All the plays for power were obvious now. PetronTech used her father to expand its oil fields; her father used them to support his family. Scientists leveraged the government to advance their research; governments used science right back for the international influence that technology brought. And Mendel manipulated both, wrapping the university around himself for prestige and protection.

Was the whole system rigged? Were capitalism, religion, and every other social construct just tools for control? Ruby just wanted a space to exist without her work being twisted to someone else's purpose. Was there room to work in shades of gray without being forced to cohere to the black-and-white polarities of entrenched powers?

Only one person hadn't tried to use her: her father. His guilt matched hers—being misled, believing the lies spun by those in power. He might have used the system and been used by the system, but he had done it for her sake, not his own.

Ruby's academic career had foundered. She no longer cared who used whom, except that she felt responsible for Imani. Ruby needed to try to reach her again. She would send another message, another warning to prevent her from repeating the same mistakes.

◆◆◆

An hour later, Ruby reached the stone steps that led from the river to the top of the bridge near her apartment. Last August, she had fled an imagined threat from a jogger straight into Mendel as he emerged from his car right here. The warning signs had been clear, if only she had paid attention.

At the top of the steps, gripping the stone railing, Ruby gazed back across the bridge spanning the Charles. Her future in Boston stretched away before her, growing ever narrower. Was this her bridge to an academic career? Or was it a gangplank?

She had never wanted to be a cog in a machine, yet here she was. The truth was clear. Mendel, and now Noah, had made her position in science unmistakable. She was here to be used.

Perhaps she had misunderstood her mother. Withdrawing from a rigged game wasn't defeat; it was the only way to reclaim her story and begin again. She wouldn't be marched to the end of this plank. She would dive back into the water on her own terms.

Act IV: FLOOD

28.   THE TROLLEY PROBLEM

We chart a narrow course. Recursive processes abound in the oceans and atmosphere. Melting snowfields reflect less sunlight, letting more heat enter the planet. Thawing permafrost releases trapped methane and other potent greenhouse gases. Modeling the strength and interplay of these feedback loops remains difficult and prone to systematics. No scientist would say otherwise.

—ARCC Memo Series

<GHOSTWRITER APP>
<BEGIN I/O>

I need containment on this one:

<attachment db-id=0x1965a2c6ac>

A loose thread?

Yes. Keep the target in Boston until we're sure. One strand can unravel everything.

Just the one? Or is there another?

The other is easy enough to manipulate. He can be dealt with later, if need be.

<END I/O>

◆◆◆

At home, Ruby scrolled through the same unappealing travel options from Iris, absently swiping away notifications. A news headline flashed across her screen: Don Sinclair was out, with allegations of misappropriated funds. After losing the court case, PetronTech's change of leadership wasn't unexpected, but the criminal charges represented one more blow to the energy conglomerate.

Two days ago on the bridge, Noah had mentioned getting Don. Another prediction come true. How could he have known before the news broke, unless some of what he'd said was true?

The sooner Ruby left this place, the better. She needed tickets.

Six months after the bombing, Logan Airport remained closed. Costly repairs were needed to restore service, but demand had dropped so sharply that many questioned whether the expense was worth it. Even if Logan reopened, cross-country fares were almost too steep to afford. Airlines were canceling flights everywhere, citing fuel shortages.

Passenger rail was electrified to Chicago. The fares to that point were affordable, with renewables powering much of the grid. Beyond Chicago, diesel locomotives took over, hauling trains through Omaha to Denver. That segment cost more, and the extension over the mountains to Junction was pricier still. But buses and fuel were in short supply, and trains were apparently more fuel-efficient, so rail remained the cheapest option.

It would be a long trip. With the transfers, probably three full days, minimum.

Ruby gave the go-ahead on booking the ticket. When Iris reported failure, Ruby reissued the request. She even tried booking it manually through an archaic web interface: Boston to Junction, confirm the price, enter name and credit card. Then came the 404. Twice, on different devices, the same dead end. That's how she knew the problem was on their end, not hers.

The fifth time the servers crashed, Ruby slammed her laptop shut and resolved to buy her tickets at the station. People could still do that, right? Maybe the surge in travelers had overloaded other transit sites. But with everything in the cloud and Iris handling bookings, wasn't it just one server talking to another in some underground bunker? They should do better. This was ridiculous.

How many times had she tried calling her father yesterday? Four? She would have loved to hear his voice, but he hadn't answered. Ruby wasn't sure if she should be alarmed. He had promised to keep his phone charged and on hand, but his track record wasn't great. Normally she wouldn't have worried, but now that he was alone... Was this typical lack of communication, or had something happened?

And why wouldn't Imani answer her texts? That was another loose end Ruby needed to tie up. She hated abandoning her mentee. The least she could do was make sure Imani had a plan for dealing with Mendel.

Anxious and at her wit's end, Ruby scrambled to put her affairs in order so she could leave—tonight, if they'd sell her a ticket. She canceled the VeggieVan deliveries and left her key with the landlord downstairs in case he needed to get in while she was away. She washed the dishes, cursing the broken dishwasher she'd never fixed—a small but glaring symbol of all the problems she'd let fester until they became impossible to ignore. Her father might shake his head, but he was just as bad with his own health and relationships.

Clear out the refrigerator. Empty the trash. Sweep the floor. Coming back to a clean apartment always felt better.

She *was* coming back, right? The question stopped her in her tracks. What if, despite his lies, Noah was telling the truth? He'd been right about Don. Travel costs were exorbitant enough to believe transportation might collapse. Even if she got back to Boston, would science still matter in a post-prosperity society? Mendel claimed that theirs would be the last particle collider ever built. Would physics departments simply vanish?

And if Noah was wrong? If she could return and there was still science to do, did she even want that? What was left for her? An advisor who used her research for his own ambitions? A boyfriend who did the same?

The only people Ruby felt qualms about leaving were her students. Imani in particular. They had gotten off to a rough start. Ruby bore most of the blame with her work-alone, anti-engineering attitude. But despite that, she had enjoyed working with Imani. Her mentee had a real aptitude for practical problem-solving, a skill Ruby was beginning to recognize as essential for getting anything done, in science or otherwise.

In danger of waxing sentimental, Ruby shook herself and forced her focus back to packing. On planes, she traveled light—just a couple of changes of underwear and a toothbrush in her carry-on. She had clothes at home, and toiletries could be bought when they stopped for gas outside Junction, though she'd need to pack more for a three-day train trip.

Would they stay at JP's in Junction or drive back to Dragon? Could her father pick her up? Did she need a RediRide? She should tell him her arrival time, though she wouldn't know that until she made the booking. Ruby called her dad again.

Where even *was* JP's house? It was unsettling, starting a trip without knowing where it ended. She needed more information, a clear destination, but no one answered her calls.

With her life in shambles, Ruby had finally acknowledged what she'd avoided too long. After all Mendel's oversteps, backpedaling, and gatekeeping while she maintained the pretense of normality, her stamina for research was exhausted. She had stopped caring about her project the moment it stopped being about science.

She wished it weren't true, but a good scientist followed the facts. Did she have the energy to come back? She would have to figure that out later, and on her own. Her father carried enough burdens already.

Meanwhile, Noah was so consumed with his plans to save the world that he never stopped to consider that *how* he did it mattered. His clever puzzles, the imagined hacks and maneuvers around PetronTech's manipulations. Had his hypotheticals been real-life scenarios all along? How deep did his deception go? He apparently couldn't see past his own secrets long enough to understand what she owed to the one person who, it seemed, had never manipulated her.

As with Mendel, the harder Noah pulled, the clearer Ruby's choice became. She would return to her father.

◆◆◆

```
<TEXTING APP>
<BEGIN I/O>
```

I've received bad news from home and need to leave
for a while. I'm not sure when or if I'll be back.
It's been a pleasure working with you. You're a beast
with the autocoders!

Some messages aren't getting through, so I'll say
this again. In case it wasn't clear, the unit test
failed. Our advisor is passing off the output of my
compromised simulation as data, and I've lost all
faith in his integrity. I have no idea what he's capable of. Don't be alone with him. Try to find a position in another group as soon as possible.

```
<END I/O>
```

◆◆◆

Ruby tried again to warn Imani. Her text, like the others, went
unanswered. Imani would be working with Mendel now with no
one running interference, and it was Ruby's fault. If she hadn't
pushed back so hard against mentoring Imani, hadn't tried so
hard to shield her from Mendel's attention, maybe Imani would
already know what was going on.

But what else could she do? With the midnight bell, her academic dreams were turning back into mice, pumpkins, and fairy
magic. It was time to leave. Ruby only needed to decide what to
take with her when she left the apartment.

In the end, she packed light: five changes of clothes in a sturdy
roll-aboard and a blue backpack with her screen, phone, chargers,
snacks, and toiletries.

Ruby was in the foyer of the building, baggage in hand, when
the corner of an envelope protruding from the array of mailboxes
caught her eye. She fumbled for her keychain, unlocked the box,
and pulled out the letter. Her father had scratched in the address,
but her name on top was written in a more elegant script.

Ruby recognized her mother's handwriting. She almost opened
the letter on the spot, but something this precious deserved more
than a hurried glance on her way out. Slipping it into her coat

pocket, she pushed out the door. She would read it on the train.

All that remained was the last task she had avoided: stopping by the lab to check for notebooks or thumb drives she might have left behind. Maybe, if she was lucky, she'd catch Imani there.

◆◆◆

```
<MESSENGER APP>
<BEGIN I/O>
```

> Don't let the bridge be the last time we talk. Please? Can you take my call?

> I know I messed up. If you haven't bought tickets yet, wait one more day. Sleep on it before deciding. Just don't go. Please.

```
<END I/O>
```

◆◆◆

Noah stumbled down the street. People and cars rushed past, oblivious to the impending crisis. Commuters hurried to work, diners lingered in restaurants, shoppers browsed storefronts. Noah tried to memorize these scenes—the final moments of ordinary life before everything changed. What had he done?

Cranes on the skyline perched above towers destined to remain unfinished. A man stepped from a car that, in two months, would sit abandoned at the curb. On the sidewalk, a woman carried groceries from half a world away; the bananas in her brown bag might be the last she ever tasted. Every detail shimmered with anticipatory nostalgia, colored by the looming disaster Noah had helped set in motion.

Was it wrong to choose hardship for so many, to make life-and-death decisions for people who never asked for this, hoping to prevent something worse? He had tried to shield her from the harshest consequences. He had believed Ruby might understand.

Focused on saving everyone, on keeping things from spiraling, on placing one foot so carefully in front of the other, he had lost track. Fighting the warnings to push her out, Noah hadn't realized how he'd pulled Ruby in against her will. He'd been so preoccupied with Derrick. He should have been thinking about Ruby.

In a machine ethics course Noah took as a graduate student, the professor devoted an entire lecture to the Trolley Problem. The classroom buzzed with debate as they imagined a runaway train hurtling toward a crowd. The only way to save them: push an innocent bystander into its path. Was it morally justifiable to kill one to save the others? Was it morally justifiable not to?

When Noah took the class, he'd found the scenario laughably contrived. Now he was living it. But instead of a few strangers on the track, it was all of humanity's future, and Ruby was among the many to be shoved into harm's way. Noah ached to abandon his post, to follow Ruby and see her safe, but that choice doomed future generations—billions of innocents. Could he live with himself if he walked away? Could he live with himself if he didn't?

Except the decision was already made. Ruby didn't want him. He had used her against her expressed wishes, and it didn't matter whether he realized it at the time. She had every right to be angry. Even without a civilization-threatening crisis, he'd be lucky if she ever spoke to him again.

Meanwhile, ARCC needed him. With the world in crisis, he, Eli, and their golem had to hold the ship together. They needed to get into China, control Brazil, and shut down every oil pump in the Middle East. They had to keep the global economy afloat and prop up the idea of civilization, even as they prepared to pull the power plug that sustained it all.

And MiddleMan could do it. Economies, governments, even civilization itself were just collective delusions—abstractions living in people's minds, shaping behavior. It didn't matter if anyone truly believed; the confidence that others did was enough to make them real. This was what Lam and Derrick had taught him.

After Derrick's presentation at that first ARCC meeting, Noah saw parallels everywhere. Take cryptocurrency, a monetary system built on the same blockchain security he specialized in. Doubters claimed it was all smoke and mirrors, but instill the idea that others would accept it as payment, and suddenly it had value.

Without a gold standard, was the dollar any different? Did gold itself have intrinsic value? Or stocks? The deed to a house? Was all of it just a collective delusion?

Noah knew the answer.

He knew because he had witnessed MiddleMan's power firsthand. Just as blockchain could spin illusions of currency, burning compute cycles to create a narrative of ordered expenditures, MiddleMan spun illusions of culture. MiddleMan could prop up economies, governments, even civilization itself, simply by propagating the narrative that everyone still believed in them.

Noah looked around—at the street, the people, the city—and realized he couldn't walk away. He had started this; he was responsible for seeing it through. Especially now that it seemed blockchain might solve ARCC's financial problems.

Noah wished he could make Ruby stay, keep her safe. How many times had he deleted his texts without sending, knowing that it was his very effort to hold on that had driven her away? Her departure felt like an indictment of everything he was working toward, and in her warning about being used, he heard echoes of Matsuda's missive long ago about the fire of a dragon they believed tamed. But now he was on the back of that dragon, and if he didn't stay on, what chance did any of this have of succeeding?

Everything had grown complicated so quickly. The stakes rose with every decision. Was ARCC doing the right thing? Or was he "just another piece, naively getting played," as Ruby said? And whose game was he playing?

29.   OCCAM'S RAZOR

All theories are human-made approximations of truth and thus incomplete. One must be ready to revise or abandon a theory when new evidence emerges, and in the absence of evidence, one should choose the simpler theory. It is the more likely to generalize.

—ARCC Memo Series

Where was Ruby? Imani rarely walked Rubin's halls, especially before noon, but today she needed answers.

The calibration pipeline she had developed with Ruby and Professor Mendel was the most complex code Imani had ever written. Calibration, de-biasing, in-painting, covariance estimation, and averaging. Each step depended on the others in unpredictable ways, creating endless opportunities for mistakes. The unit tests she'd shown Ruby in the physics lounge weren't just dotting i's and crossing t's; they were the only real way to assess something this complex. After all, conclusions are only as strong as the testing they've faced.

That was why, when a lump emerged from the sea of noise in the spectral data Mendel gave her, Imani assumed it was a systematic error from her analysis. For days, she hunted for a failed step, an invalid input, or a divergence from expected behavior in the simulated data, and found nothing. Only then did Imani grudgingly consider that the lump might not be her fault. That was a novel possibility.

Imani compared results with theoretical predictions using Ruby's sprawling simulation codebase. The equations were neat and tidy—the code, not so much. It wasn't engineered to Imani's standards, but it worked and matched Ruby's paper draft, so

Imani accepted the predictions at face value. Still, something didn't check out.

She'd sent Ruby a text about it but never heard back. Meanwhile, digging in on her own, Imani found something. A wrong equation at the beginning. When Imani saw it, she laughed out loud. It didn't conserve parity, and Imani knew Ruby knew this, because God help her, it was the same mistake Ruby had once corrected Imani on, right in front of Professor Mendel and the entire research group last semester. A missing bar over the antineutrino. It was almost as if Ruby were teasing her.

The last time they met, weeks ago in the physics lounge, Ruby had hinted that Imani should check something in her simulation. Imani hadn't understood then, but now Ruby's cryptic comments made sense. Ruby had introduced the error deliberately, altering the theory, the code, and the tests so they all contained the same flaw. It appeared consistent. The tests would pass, but even a cursory comparison with established physics would expose the false prediction.

Switching between Ruby's corrupt code and an earlier revision, Imani saw that only the corrupted simulation matched the range of Professor Mendel's data. The erroneous simulation aligned with the lump in Imani's data almost exactly. To within the measurement noise.

Imani had been thinking about sending a follow-up text when Ruby upended everything, right in the middle of Imani's gym workout.

```
<TEXTING APP>
<BEGIN I/O>
```

> I've received bad news from home and need to leave for a while. I'm not sure when or if I'll be back. It's been a pleasure working with you. You're a beast with the autocoders!

```
<END I/O>
```

No mention of how long, but "when or if" sounded ominous,

and "it's been a pleasure" revealed Ruby's default assumption. Imani texted, then called. No answer.

How could Ruby leave? She hadn't mentioned it before. What about their work together? Their growing friendship? Imani never felt like she fit in, but after the riot, she realized Ruby didn't either. Raised among sheep out West, the girl prowled the department like a lone wolf. Their reasons for isolation differed, but apart from Ruby's boyfriend, Noah, their experience was symmetric.

Imani was desperate to understand what was happening. She ducked out of her spin class, threw a sweater over her damp clothes, and blitzed over on her bike, hoping to catch Ruby leaving —but she was too late. Ruby was nowhere to be found: not in the lab, the women's bathroom upstairs, or the lounge. Imani circled by Professor Mendel's office. She hadn't even considered he might be in, but finding his door open, she stepped inside for answers.

Professor Mendel sat behind his dusty, too-neat desk and claimed he hadn't seen Ruby, but his narrowed eyes and hard look made Imani pause.

"They're promoting me to provost," he added, noticing her hesitation. "I can't keep tabs on every grad student." She saw how he watched her, searching for a reaction.

Funny, she had never attracted his attention before, preoccupied as he was with his prize student. Now, in an ironic turn, his fixed attention made Imani squirm. She could hardly register what he'd said, feeling under a microscope. Seeking a buffer, she broke eye contact and turned to the wall lined with his old-man archive of textbooks and conference proceedings. "Provost?" Imani frowned. "That's... sudden."

"It won't cut into research time, I assure you," Mendel said, shifting in his chair. "Now that we have the data, I'll make meeting with you a priority, even if I have to stay late."

Which was laughable. This was literally the first time she'd spoken with him in person, one on one, since the group meeting when she'd been paired with Ruby.

Here she was, with Ruby AWOL, finally being offered the mentorship she'd wanted, except all Professor Mendel gave her were creepy vibes and boasts about some promotion. Digging deeper was probably unwise, but Imani was curious.

"Provost is pretty high up the food chain, isn't it?"

"Second to the president of the college," he responded. Did his face twitch at her question, or was she imagining it? His chair creaked as he leaned back, weighing her with sharp eyes. A self-satisfied smile spread across his lips.

Ick. She knew Ruby and he had an intellectual disagreement, but had he always been this slimy?

Imani had rushed so fast into fighting Ruby for access to Professor Mendel when they first met, she might have missed some context. Turning everyone into an adversary was a weakness of hers. A lifetime of roadblocks had built her combative personality, but Imani now knew it had been a mistake to treat Ruby as another obstacle. The last couple of months had made that clear.

In any case, it was time to take the man across the desk down a peg.

"Is this the price of time off?" she said. "Stuck with admin duty when you come back? Don't they usually promote some muckety-muck dean for this?" Imani laced her words with derision, hoping to chip away at his self-satisfaction.

Professor Mendel just smiled at the jab. "Several in the university hierarchy were caught taking money from PetronTech. There's been a purge, and I saw a chance to steer the college and its resources in a better direction. If you need anything—anything I can help with—just ask. I've found some new strings to pull."

Again, that fixed, measuring stare pinning her. Something was off. Imani had a nose for trouble, and right now it smelled like time to leave, but her finances compelled her to respond to his offer.

"Actually," Imani said, "if you could push my degree conferral through so I can get full pay for working in your lab, that would be lovely." She fought the urge to grimace. For someone who prided herself on self-sufficiency, this was an act of desperation.

"Consider it done," Professor Mendel said, grinning slyly. "See? Maybe hitching your boat to an old muckety-muck isn't so bad, eh?"

Ew. The cue to get out of here couldn't have been clearer. In the pocket of her hoodie, Imani pressed a pair of buttons on her phone. A moment later, it buzzed. She pulled out the vibrating rectangle and held it up for Professor Mendel to see.

"Thanks, Professor, but I have to take this. Can we talk later?" She didn't wait for an answer, slipping out and letting the door close softly behind her.

Abrupt, but effective. Imani trotted down the stairs and pushed out the side door to the bike rack, where she hesitated.

If Ruby was gone, Imani had to think strategically. Fees kept piling up, and her hopes of bringing her loan into good standing were fading. Even if Professor Mendel cleared her missing final payment and released the degree she'd already earned, Imani doubted any pay raise would cover the mounting interest and penalties, especially with her roommates demanding back rent and threatening to kick her out.

Imani had been close to the surface, but now she was sinking fast. Working with Ruby had been a welcome distraction, but the truth was, she couldn't pay both rent and loans. Professor Mendel had extended a hand to pull her up, but was it a gift or another predatory loan? She had seen the same self-satisfied look on the face of the lender who trapped her in this mess. There might be a deferment period, but eventually the bill would come due. It always did.

Imani climbed onto her bike and pedaled home. It would clear up so much if she could just find Ruby. "Bad news" sounded like a family issue, but why would Ruby, after all their time together, leave with a text that screamed "goodbye forever"?

Meanwhile, something had changed in Professor Mendel's demeanor. Or had Imani just missed the creepy vibes before? She hadn't seen him without Ruby in months—maybe ever, now that she thought about it. Maybe Imani had missed something.

Coding up data analysis, Imani was getting used to having the rug pulled out from under her. Bugs appeared, plots looked wrong, and she had to trace her assumptions to find where she'd gone astray. That, she realized, was the heart of the scientific method—adapting when data didn't match your model of reality.

Well, here were data that didn't fit her model of Ruby. Ruby was leaving, even though she seemed on the verge of a major scientific breakthrough. She monopolized Professor Mendel's attention, even while fighting him for control of her theory. She pushed students aside when her professor was present, but cared enough to repeatedly cover classes when her professor was gone.

How did someone who harped on the details of symmetry and parity introduce the same bugs into her simulation model that she had just grilled Imani on? Yet that buggy model was the only theory that fit the data. Were there really two different Rubys? The attention-seeking rival and the supportive tutor? Was *that* the only theory that fit the data?

Imani gasped and squeezed her brakes, her tires screeching as she skidded to a stop.

No, she thought, spinning her bike around and pedaling furiously toward campus. There was another theory that fit the data. One that didn't require Ruby to have two personalities. The kind of simpler explanation that Occam's razor favored.

◆◆◆

Ruby had just reached her lab bench and begun sorting papers and textbooks when Mendel walked in. She had hoped to be here only a few minutes. He couldn't have timed it better if he'd planned it.

Had he planned it?

Her guard snapped up, though it had never truly dropped. Not since his visit to her apartment two nights ago, when Ruby glimpsed something she couldn't unsee. It left an itch between her shoulders, a constant sense of being watched, every reaction gauged for what it might reveal.

He knew exactly where the line was, when he crossed it, and how to talk his way back. The first night he stalked her home, Mendel knew he'd gone too far. So the next day, he pulled her into the office. Damage control with a silver tongue.

Mendel thrived on controlling every aspect of her career. Every aspect of their research. Now, what would he do? He must know she had contacted the university. Their response to Ruby's complaint made it clear he had gotten there first, if he hadn't had it quarantined all along. So he would know she was aware of the data fabrication. He would know she had also reported his visit to her apartment.

He skipped the usual theatrics of scanning the room before spotting her. He knew where to look, knew she was alone, and was already closing in on the end of the bench, cutting off her path to the door.

"Ruby," he said, his voice unnaturally bright. "I was just wondering if you were still on campus." He whipped a chair into the aisle, spun it around with a flourish, and stopped it with his foot as he leaned forward to face her.

Shoving papers and books into her bag, Ruby built her defenses without preamble. "No time," she said. "Just grabbing some notes to take. My train leaves in a couple hours." Well, it *would* be leaving, once she got a ticket.

Mendel arched an amused eyebrow but didn't argue. "Well, I'm glad I caught you before you left," he said, looking enormously pleased with himself.

She had been avoiding eye contact, but now Ruby fixed him with a withering stare. What more did he want? He already had her theory, the simulation he'd demanded, his grant. He could keep generating his own data for Imani to "discover" a particle in. He had everything he could possibly want.

Well, almost everything.

"I still hope you'll change your mind, Ruby. Anything less than this"—he swept his hand around the lab—"would be a waste of your considerable talents."

Turning away, Ruby rifled through the books on the lab bench, searching for words that wouldn't be swept aside. Her gaze landed on a mathematics text for particle physicists, as if a Lie algebra could symmetrize the situation. Mendel, sensing her helplessness, shoved the chair back and uncoiled to his full height.

"And you know," he said carelessly, stepping down the bench toward her, "something could change your mind. I can think of several reasons—"

He broke off as a hand rapped on the open lab door and a diminutive figure appeared in the hallway.

"Oops. Sorry to interrupt, Professor," Imani said loudly. "We got cut off earlier, and I wanted to see if you could still meet. I tried your office, but I guess you were down here in the lab!" Her unusually bright tone said much more than her words.

For a moment, the world hung in the balance. Mendel stood rigid, eyes fixed on the source of the interruption. Imani's face stayed open, smiling, her gaze shifting pragmatically between Mendel and Ruby. Ruby could not have been happier to see her friend.

"Oh," said Ruby, slipping past Mendel and his chair to join Imani at the door. "We were just finishing up."

Mendel grumbled what might have been agreement as he stumbled around the chair Ruby had dragged into the aisle.

Ruby seized the brief pause in surveillance to mouth "thank you" to Imani, who must have overheard part of their conversation before knocking. Their eyes met, and Ruby searched her friend's face, trying to gauge how much she knew. So much needed saying, but there was no time.

Imani gave a wink, then stepped past her into the lab.

"Great," Imani said. "Maybe I'll see you later, Ruby. Professor, if you have a minute?"

Imani's voice faded as Ruby took her cue to slip away. She hoped Imani knew what she was doing. Once, Ruby had tried to shield her mentee from Mendel's manipulations; now, it seemed

Imani was returning the favor.

Ruby plunged into the stairwell and charged up the steps, quickening her pace until she burst through the glass door into the open air. Behind her, the brick walls of Rubin Hall receded as she sprinted toward the river.

Ruby didn't look back and only later realized she might have missed her last glimpse of the gated quadrangles she had once dreamed of entering.

◆◆◆

```
<TEXTING APP>
<BEGIN I/O>
```

OMG, thank you! I owe you big-time.

I don't know your situation, or if you got my last message, but you need to get out. That guy is a snake.

I'd invite you to come with me if there were anything in Colorado for you. Look me up if you ever make it out West. I could use a friend.

Take care.

```
<END I/O>
```

30. CONCEITS AND PRECONCEPTIONS

Consumerism and capitalism are dominant paradigms that must be dismantled. While these systems built a global economy and lifted many from poverty, we can recognize when an idea has outlived its usefulness. Models based on endless growth cannot be reconciled with the need for sustainability.

—ARCC Memo Series

Imani didn't linger with Professor Mendel. She only stalled to give Ruby time to escape. Mendel's irritation at her interruption, and Ruby's grateful glance, confirmed Imani's suspicions. The creepy vibe she'd felt in his office was the same unwanted attention he gave Ruby. No wonder she wanted out.

But Imani could handle it. Mendel knew she had seen at least some of the interaction with Ruby. In a day or two, he would spin a story about what had happened, hinting that Ruby was unreliable while watching Imani for evidence she believed him. Imani would play along. She would wait and watch, letting Professor Mendel underestimate her, just like everyone else. She'd play along with his particle-detection scheme for a little while.

That's definitely what it was, right? Ruby planted a bug in her simulation code, one custom-made for Imani to find. She'd spoken obliquely, but that had to be it. The unit test. And then the collider data matched that impossible theoretical model because Mendel had put it there using Ruby's code. He'd failed the test. Imani had just interrupted his attempt at keeping Ruby from ratting him out.

One simple model explained all the data in a grand unified theory: Mendel was a creep.

Hoping for confirmation, Imani left Rubin Hall by the path Ruby might have taken. The path was empty outside. Her phone just rang.

Was that it, then? Imani wondered as she unlocked her bike and rolled off campus. She didn't blame Ruby for leaving. Especially now, after seeing their advisor's true colors. If Ruby didn't want to answer her phone, that was fine. She was struggling with a family emergency and a demonic advisor. The two of them could sort things out later.

Meanwhile, Imani had to decide whether to bargain with the devil. Mendel was not to be trusted, but perhaps he could be used. He was definitely trying to manipulate her, but she might be able to manipulate him right back. Use him to stabilize her finances.

Pedaling through her neighborhood, Imani spotted the start of a new faux-organic art installation—twisted metal and plastic jutting from a patch of grass. Where was the artist? Bishop was the only person Imani could imagine processing Ruby's departure with. Imani needed a friend, and she had just said goodbye to one of the two she had.

In any case, she didn't want to go back to her apartment. A fight with her roommates was brewing, and Imani knew how it would end. They'd said outright they would lock her out if she didn't pay up. She didn't have enough for her loan or this month's rent, let alone the back rent. If they kicked her out, where would she go? Her apartment was already bottom-of-the-barrel. It was hard to imagine finding anything cheaper.

Circling the block by his latest project, Imani saw no sign of Bishop. He must have gone home already. And indeed, at the vacant lot next to the laundromat, she glimpsed his wagon slipping through a gap in the chain-link fence. Imani pulled over and dismounted.

Imani had never visited Bishop's encampment in the late afternoon. What she saw surprised her. Half of the two dozen residents were just returning from work. They didn't wear suits, but their shirts and slacks were clean and well kept—some even nicer than what Imani wore today. As one nodded in greeting, Imani realized she had seen some of these people around the neighborhood before, never suspecting they were homeless. Was it fair to call them that?

After locking her bike to the fence, Imani wove between tents on the hard-packed dirt. Unlike other encampments along the river, this one was relatively tidy. Lockboxes lined the fence, and belongings stayed inside the tents. Still, trash drifted into the weeds or blew against the fence. A thin man with an orange bucket was even now offering Bishop materials he'd collected from around the lot, and Imani watched someone returning from work hand a twenty-dollar bill to a man sitting beside the lockboxes.

After the man with the bucket left, Imani settled onto a stump beside Bishop as he tucked two green plastic bottles into his wagon. Skipping the small talk he disdained, she dove straight into her worries about Ruby leaving. The signs she might not return. Imani had a working theory regarding the trouble with their advisor, but there was also maybe a family emergency. Family came first for most people, but Imani couldn't help feeling abandoned. She needed the money and could probably handle Professor Mendel alone, but she wasn't sure she wanted to. Ruby was more than half the reason Imani worked in the lab at all.

To Imani's surprise, the issue of family caught Bishop's attention.

"Your friend left for her family," he stated. "Where's yours?"

With anyone else, she would have dodged the question, but Imani only paused a moment before answering Bishop. "Dad died a few years ago. And Momma, she didn't take it well when I told her why I wasn't going to church anymore." She hesitated, then added, "Sorry if you're religious." What would a man named Bishop think of her leaving her father's church?

"Just m' name," he said, chuckling at her hesitation. "Ain't no real bishop."

His surname, as it turned out, was the only title he answered to. He sipped something hot from a thermos in his wagon, steam curling around his face, and nodded. "You missing her, your momma?"

"Honestly?" Imani said. "Yeah. But her plan for my life wasn't mine, and there was no arguing. I didn't want to be a doctor or believe in God. That was enough to make her stop answering the phone."

"We can only work with what pieces the world gives us," Bishop shrugged.

Imani was ready to file that away with Bishop's other inscrutable utterances, but then recognized the reference to his work. "Like you do," she said. "Making art from what you find."

Bishop nodded, drained his thermos, and turned to his wagon for supplies. He took a pair of pliers and a coat hanger, then settled onto a stump beside Imani's.

"How come you never sell anything?" Imani asked. "I bet people would pay enough for you to make a living."

"I make a living," he said gently, speaking with his usual deliberation. "No selling necessary."

Imani cocked her head. Noticing her confusion, Bishop looked up from the bent wire in his hands. "Making art to sell trades your aesthetic for someone else's. Keeps you from seeing the world through your own eyes, forgetting your own truth. Sometimes, staying true to your story means keeping yourself apart, like you and your momma."

Bishop fell silent, focusing again on the wire spiral he twisted with his pliers. Imani shook her head. Bishop meant well, but he was preaching to the choir. Keeping apart came naturally to her. Too naturally. Sometimes she wondered if that wasn't the whole problem. Right now, she would gladly trade some of that distance for a few friends and a livable income.

"People lose their value, selling away their differences to make a buck," he continued, as if reading her thoughts.

Sitting on her stump, Imani realized she'd never considered

what it cost to align her work with someone else's goals. With Ruby, she never felt she was compromising, but that might change with Professor Mendel.

Or maybe that was too narrow a view. While Bishop added strips of green bottle to his wire spiral, Imani remembered how Ruby spoke of science as art—a creative collaboration with the universe. In *Science and Society*, Professor Matsuda described the paradox of science as both humanity's doom and salvation. What was her vision of science? Was she in danger of selling it away?

"Besides," Bishop said, interrupting her thoughts, "I can't sell what isn't mine."

"What do you mean?" Imani scoffed. "Whose art is it, if not yours?"

"Is this my wood?" he said, kicking the stump beneath him with his boot heel. "Or that, my tree?" He pointed to one rooted in the corner of the abandoned lot. "I've no claim on what the world provides." He gestured at his wagon piled with bottles, wire, and scraps. "My arrangement doesn't make the pieces mine."

Altogether, this was more than Bishop had ever said in one sitting, and Imani replayed his words later as she unlocked her bike for the ride home. Behind her, Bishop joined a cluster around a makeshift table, where someone arranged mismatched dishes for an impromptu potluck.

She liked what Bishop had said about creating without acquisition, or expansion, or aspiration. Could work exist as pure expression? She admired how Bishop bypassed ownership, giving inanimate objects a bit of himself without consuming them. She respected this philosophy, even if she didn't live by it. Most of all, she liked the idea that something precious at a person's core could be worth protecting from monetization.

Bishop was, in many ways, the opposite of Imani's mother, who would have eagerly stamped out her daughter's atheism to spread her own gospel. The domination at the heart of evangelical religion was central to Imani's objections. It was one of the tools used to shackle her ancestors.

And yet, Imani realized as she pedaled slowly toward her apartment in the fading light, that might not be entirely fair. A tool misused for oppression wasn't always inherently bad. Part of what her mother had always sought was connection. That was what church and faith meant to her: a bond with her community. It was her last tie to Imani's father, the thread she tried to use to stitch their family together. Ironic, how good intentions paired with tyrannical methods could bring about the opposite. Sometimes the ends justified the means; other times, they impeached them.

But perhaps good intentions left room for creative reuse. Imani remembered a hymn she had heard in church: *"And into plowshares beat their swords...."* Was that what Bishop meant by working with what the world provided? Things could be fractured and reassembled—a flower in a plastic bottle, a vine twined through wire. Bishop's artistry revealed treasures in trash, his work better for favoring arrangement over fabrication. The restriction forced him to see potential in the pedestrian, to create novelty from the derivative.

Ruby described science as a collaboration between humans and nature. The universe, her friend said, challenged humanity to discover and invent what it could not have otherwise. Was this the same? Both Bishop's art and Ruby's science found transcendence in connecting pieces of providence.

But what about her? Was Imani's aesthetic just a tool to get ahead in the system? Was "ahead" even her goal? She wanted to escape the financial whirlpool pulling her under, but what kind of opus would she leave behind if all her creative energy went to simply staying afloat?

Working on data analysis, Imani was learning to look past expectations and see what was actually there. Combining that lesson with Bishop's words, she realized he was, in many ways, better off than she was. He worked for himself, by his own rules. He had friends—a real community. People who looked out for each other and shared what they had. They worked, went to the gym, did laundry, just like her, but came home to good company, not absentee roommates who only spoke to her when they wanted money she didn't have.

If she followed her own truth and drew her own conclusions, she might find a different way forward.

◆◆◆

```
<TEXTING APP>
<BEGIN I/O>

        OMG, thank you! I owe you big-time.

        I'd invite you to come with me if there were any-
        thing in Colorado for you. Look me up if you ever
        make it out West. I could use a friend.

        Take care.

<END I/O>
```

◆◆◆

Imani dismounted at the squat cinder block apartment building and followed the narrow dirt path worn through weeds to her usual bike lock-up. Circling to the front, she jogged up the chipped concrete steps, peered through the glass, then slipped inside and locked the door behind her. The apartment was quiet. None of her roommates were home yet.

She tossed her backpack onto the mattress on the floor, then went to the bathroom and cranked the shower knob to warm it up. Back in her room, Imani's phone pinged as she peeled off her clothes. Ruby was probably on her way now. It was nice of her to send a goodbye text, even if it didn't confirm any of Imani's suspicions about Mendel.

But that was for another time. Setting her phone aside, Imani grabbed a towel, her toiletries, and some hair de-frizzer, then padded down the hall to the steamy bathroom. She arranged her bottles on the narrow counter and stepped into the shower, letting the warmth soak into her skin. For a moment, she relaxed, until she remembered her roommates would be home soon to harass her, as if yelling could refill her bank account. It would probably be less awkward if she were dressed for the encounter. Reluctantly, Imani turned off the water.

Imani toweled off, returned to her room, and was nearly dressed when the front door creaked open. Heart quickening, she peeked out and saw all her roommates filing in, along with the landlord.

Imani unzipped her backpack, yanked open dresser drawers, and began sorting. They would knock when ready, but she wanted a head start. She sensed this confrontation would be a good one. Fortunately, she was in top form, nicely warmed up after dealing with Mendel.

◆◆◆

Imani opened the door the third time the landlord pounded. She almost slammed it in his face—and in her roommates', hovering at his shoulder—but restrained herself. Confrontation was easy. Listening, harder. Imani crossed her arms and bit her tongue.

Prices everywhere were up. He was feeling the pinch, poor guy. He tried to be understanding. Really, he did. But he couldn't afford a delinquent tenant any longer. He had bills to pay too, after all. In fact, he was raising the rent.

That news was, amusingly, a silver lining. Her roommates had come to watch her kicked to the curb, but Imani would treasure that look of betrayal on their faces. With more people crowding into Boston every day, desperate to save on gas and keep their bottom line in the black, Imani was sure someone would pay stratospheric rent for that glorified bunker. Let her two-faced, passive-aggressive roommates wail about the hike. Imani was done postponing the inevitable.

Imani waited patiently for him to finish, then delivered her own ultimatum: she would leave at the end of the week and he would forget the unpaid rent, or she'd complain to the rent board about conditions and drag him into a messy eviction fight. He blustered but quickly chickened out. He knew the cost of deferred maintenance on this slum of a flat. With a few choice words, he relented, and the roommates, scowling, kept their mouths shut.

Five days later, Imani maneuvered a box down the porch steps, staggering under its weight as she heaved it onto the wagon borrowed from Bishop. Her newly ex-landlord hovered on the porch, half concealed behind the screen door. Her roommates glared from the window of the common room. For all their eagerness to see her gone, none had lifted a finger to speed the process. Not that she wanted their help.

This was the last of it. For the final time, Imani clicked loose the lock securing her bike to the rusted fence at the lot's edge. She guided the bike with one hand, pulling the wagon with the other, and turned the corner to follow the street. No one spoke, and she didn't look back.

Hiking toward the spot where Bishop waited, Imani tallied her assets. The past few days had been an education in letting go, shedding whatever wouldn't fit in a tent. Most of her clothes went to Salvation. She traded prized textbooks online for cash to buy an air mattress and a secondhand sleeping bag. An old Keurig and hair dryer earned her store credit at a thrift shop, which she spent on a portable solar charger. How quickly she had learned to part with things she once thought essential.

Everything she owned fit in a wagon, but she still needed a tent, and those weren't cheap. Not paying rent helped, but loan payments would still swallow half her paycheck, which she grabbed from the mailbox on her way out. If most meals were takeout, she'd have to budget more; the camp stove couldn't replace a real kitchen. Some splurges, like her gym membership, were now necessities. The Y would be her only access to a shower.

It would have been nice to have a buffer to get her started. How many paychecks had vanished into that hellhole apartment over the past two years? Far too many. More than it was ever worth.

Imani sighed and turned onto a narrow side street. When would she ever pay off that miserable loan? The interest bordered on criminal. The fees were blatantly predatory. She felt responsible for honoring her commitments, but did she really owe her future livelihood to a bank that made a business of entrapment?

Imani disliked the mercenary nature of her decision, but faced with her online loan, the question wasn't whether she would default; it was when. And if it was inevitable, why throw good money after bad?

It felt risky, even defiant, but once Imani committed to informal bankruptcy, her burden eased. She'd already forwarded her paychecks to a P.O. box. Closing her bank account was all she needed to avoid collections. There was a check-cashing shop next to the laundromat. Her credit score would take a hit, but what did it matter? Imani didn't see home loans in her future.

Down the street, Imani spotted Bishop waiting a safe distance from the landlord's porch. He matched her unhurried pace in the afternoon sun. They walked side by side, wagon wheels squeaking over uneven pavement as they headed back toward Bishop's lot.

The camp appeared with its usual constrained chaos. Tarps and tents flapped in the breeze, while grills, chairs, and tables stood scattered. Grass and weeds sprouted from piles of bricks and broken concrete, but the paths between tents stayed clear and hard-packed. Most trash had made it to the dumpster on the corner; whatever lingered could almost pass for art supplies.

Imani pulled up near the heap of scraps Bishop had emptied from the wagon for her. She stopped and exhaled.

"Quite the haul," he poked gently, easily plucking a box from the top and setting it aside.

Imani grimaced. She'd gotten rid of so much, but he was right. It was too much. But further whittling would have to wait. Together, they unloaded the wagon onto a wooden pallet beside an empty patch near Bishop's enclave.

Imani returned the wagon to Bishop to restock while she set out for her last major purchase, pausing first to test her new check-cashing plan. At the shop next to the laundromat, she slid the check from her coat pocket onto the counter. The clerk scanned it, verified the numbers, and exchanged it for a stack of

Benjamins and Jacksons—minus a couple percent, of course.

The fees were lower than she expected, and that settled it. Imani was done handing her livelihood to slum landlords and predatory lenders.

By the time she returned with her new tent, camp bustled with people returning from work. Several of Imani's new neighbors stopped to introduce themselves and help set up her latest purchase, which was even bigger than it looked in the store. She had splurged on a model large enough for a family camping out of their car, but without rent or loans to worry about, she could afford the luxury. Anyway, this tent was home now.

She tossed her sleeping bag inside and unpacked a few boxes. For now, Imani needed only warm clothes, toiletries, and a water bottle. She stacked the remaining boxes in the corners, out of the way. She'd figure out a system eventually, but for tonight this was enough.

All in all, it wasn't so bad. She just had to swallow the stigma of homelessness. Everything had its price, though. Nobody talked about it, but encampments like the one Bishop—and now she—called home were appearing everywhere. Others ran the same calculations and reached the same conclusions. Welcome to the low end of the middle class.

"All set?" Bishop asked, lumbering up beside her as she admired her new digs.

"Guess so," Imani said, shrugging. "Honestly, my old place never felt half as much like home as this tent does already."

Bishop nodded. "Room to yourself. Fresh air. Ain't so bad as people think," he said, glancing over her setup. "Need to get you waterproofed before the weather turns. Anyway, just came to fetch you to dinner."

"Dinner?" Imani had expected to visit a fast-food restaurant, but behind her, people gathered on a gravel patch beneath mismatched solar-powered party lights, balancing plywood sheets on milk crates for makeshift tables. Others dragged over overturned buckets and unfolded battered chairs. The evening air brimmed with the aroma of hot food—stews, fried rice, bakery rolls—and the hum of conversation.

"Nothing fancy," he assured her. "Just the regular potluck. Come on."

"I don't have anything to bring," Imani protested. She hadn't even stopped by the store for basics.

"There's already more than enough," Bishop said. "You can pitch in tomorrow."

Imani walked over with her friend and recognized a few faces —neighbors she'd glimpsed before or met during visits with Bishop: the security guard, the man who once fixed her bike chain. People bustled past, balancing plastic bowls and cups. A kid darted by, giggling as an older man teased him with a spoonful of mashed potatoes. It wasn't glamorous, but people smiled. Imani felt more camaraderie here than she ever had in her old apartment.

Imani noticed how others in the encampment nodded as Bishop passed. They weren't the burnt-out drug addicts she'd expected. People in this subdued village-within-a-city emerged from tents and campers in clean-enough clothes, freshly tumbled from the laundromat across the street. They carried cash from jobs they left for each morning and returned from each afternoon. Most had phones. Communal pots of food were supplemented by delivery orders from local restaurants, which arrived at the corner.

Not everything was sunshine and roses. Junk piled up, flies buzzed, and nearly everyone looked haggard. There were also, as Imani would soon discover, fleas.

Over the next weeks, Imani settled in and learned the rules and routines. Most people were like her, but some needed serious help. When a new man arrived, shouting at people real and imagined, the group pooled resources to get him psychiatric care. The lot had a strict no-drugs policy, and Imani watched as the group forced out at least two people for breaking it. The confrontations were harsh and tense, but given how much everyone depended on each other, Imani understood why the rule mattered.

Still, there was an air of workaday normalcy most days that surprised Imani.

Bishop didn't have a job or a phone, but an extra side of fries or a second coffee generally found their way to him around mealtimes. A woman on her phone winked at Imani as she picked up a drawstring bag of clothes from outside Bishop's tent and tossed it onto the shopping cart she pushed toward the laundromat. The morning after Imani saw Bishop struggling with a pair of wire cutters dulled from overuse, a new pair appeared beside his wagon. All around the encampment, emerging from the junk, Imani discovered vines, flowers, trees, mobiles, and other creations of Bishop's.

He was an artist, plain and simple. Except for meals and naps, he worked with steady, deliberate focus, supported and appreciated by a small community. Imani wondered why it had taken her so long to see a truth hidden only by her own preconceptions. Bishop had chosen this life, trading doors, locks, and valuables for tents, laundromats, gym showers, and artistic freedom.

Few had health care, but many, like Imani, earned real paychecks and lived below their means. Others who needed help took jobs around the camp—guarding, cooking for the communal stew, or handling whatever else needed doing. Imani, for her part, was glad to belong to a community that supported people like Bishop.

31. A MAN IN THE MIDDLE

The ARCC must fill the global power vacuum. If we don't, others will; power laws are natural law, and one exponential is the only thing that can outpace another. The ARCC must consolidate control swiftly and brace for backlash at having the audacity to save the world.

—ARCC Memo Series

Sitting on the worn couch in his bare apartment, Noah jolted upright when the intercom chimed, nearly spilling the half-empty energy drink on the armrest. He glanced at the clock. It was past ten already. Who showed up at this hour?

"Hello?" he said, pressing the button after hesitating.

"It is me," came a familiar voice through the crackling speaker. "I need to speak."

Noah buzzed Eli through the building gate and propped open his apartment door before returning to the couch. Strange. Eli had never wanted to meet anywhere but Aiken before. Why now?

A minute later, Eli hurried in, shoulders hunched, eyes darting around the dim room as if scanning for eavesdroppers.

"I didn't realize you knew where I live," Noah said.

"You wonder how I have information even junk mail has?" He gestured dismissively at a stack of unread envelopes on the entryway table. "You are joking, I think."

Noah offered a faint smile, but Eli's tone lacked its usual warmth. His friend seemed frayed, his usual calm replaced by jitters and distracted glances at the curtained windows. He was already pacing the small living room, fingers clenching and unclenching.

"You could have messaged me," Noah said, tapping his laptop.

Eli shook his head. "We needed to be face-to-face. There is evidence of more Directive violations."

Noah should have guessed it would be serious. "You mentioned this before, but how would you know? Are you auditing Middle-Man's database?"

At the word "database," Eli stopped midstep and turned, fixing a stare at Noah. The silence stretched.

"Eli?" Noah pressed, sliding his computer aside and leaning forward on the couch.

"There are... patterns," Eli said finally, choosing his words. "It is not the first time. Or the second. So I am forced to wonder if our golem is running rogue."

"Rogue?" Noah frowned, shaking his head. "We've tested this so many times. MiddleMan would have to be malfunctioning at a fundamental level."

"Malfunctioning?" Eli said, raising an eyebrow above narrowed eyes. "Or made to malfunction?"

"I don't follow," Noah said. He fumbled at his collar and pulled out his thumb drive, still hanging from the cord around his neck. "We have these, remember? No one changes a Directive without all our cryptographic keys."

Eli shrugged, movements tense. Noah had recruited Eli, trusted him through every crisis. Was Eli being paranoid, or was Noah, as Ruby warned, too trusting?

Eli stared at Noah, searching his face. Finding nothing, he looked away, eyes passing over cinder blocks and energy drinks without interest. "I will check the servers myself, then. Something is not right, and I came to you first, Noah. We must be certain of each other before being certain of anyone else."

Noah felt lost in his friend's anxiety. "We're both under enormous pressure, Eli. The climate cliff is here, and we're out of time. MiddleMan is all we've got."

"Indeed," Eli replied, rubbing his jaw. "But if everything worked as planned, there is no more need for the MiddleMan golem, yes? So whose interest it is in, to keep us off balance?"

Noah hesitated. "You're implying MiddleMan, but it could be PetronTech. We hurt them, but they're still powerful. Or maybe someone checked in buggy code."

"It is *meiglekh*," Eli acknowledged tiredly. "Mistakes happen. But mistakes can also be made to happen."

"You've said that twice now," Noah said, irritation leaking into his voice. "What are you suggesting?"

"I am not sure," Eli admitted, running a hand through his disheveled hair before repositioning his kippah. "But I must ask. Have you heard anything about side projects involving your team?"

"No," Noah said, actually alarmed now. Was there something going on in ARCC he didn't know about? "What projects are you talking about?"

Eli studied Noah again before relaxing his shoulders. "*Nu*, it may be just a rumor. I hope you are right that our golem has a bug. I will look deeper."

He turned to the door, leaving Noah with the uneasy sense he'd passed without knowing there was a test.

"You'll keep me in the loop?" Noah asked, rising from the couch.

Eli nodded grimly, his hand tightening on the doorknob. "I will visit the server room in the morning and let you know what I find."

The door closed softly behind Eli. Noah slumped onto the couch. Eli was acting strangely, and Ruby's words echoed in his ears. Was he being played? Eli seemed to think so.

◆◆◆

```
<TEXTING APP>
<BEGIN I/O>
```

You probably hate me, and I don't blame you. I wish I'd been more transparent about what was happening, but I hope you understand why I couldn't. Still, it wasn't fair to drag you into this if I couldn't be upfront. I'm sorry.

I don't blame you for not wanting to talk. I just
want you to know I'm here, I miss you, and I'll do
everything I can to make this right.

If you ever find it in your heart to forgive me, I'll
be here.

<END I/O>

♦♦♦

RediRide auto-braking modules process input from onboard sensors—micro-LIDAR, stereo cameras, speedometer, GPS—and ex-
trapolations from the inertial modeling unit. Any of three redun-
dant neural net braking circuits can trigger deceleration, though
they act in unison unless hardware fails. Unlike in navigation, decisions in this module occur onboard, ensuring a RediRide stops
safely even if communications fail. This feature prevents hackers
from weaponizing vehicles.

The auto-braking system goes offline during software updates,
which is why vehicles must first be parked at inductive charging
stations. However, this safety lock can be circumvented in a narrow window when a critical low-voltage warning on the main battery puts the car into maintenance mode. During this transition,
an operational bug allows a software update to be initiated, disen-
gaging auto-braking while the vehicle is still moving.

A lone pedestrian steps into the crosswalk near a Boston college campus just as an auto-braking system goes offline. Afterward, efforts to identify the pedestrian are complicated by mis-
matches in online records. No one responds to inquiries about the
victim, despite repeated attempts spanning days.

Weeks after the incident, the RediRide division of SmartSys in-
vestigates why the system failed to divert the vehicle to a charging
station before the low-voltage warning triggered an update. They
trace the error to dropped packets from a malfunctioning router
near the Brookline–Boston border.

♦♦♦

<MESSENGER APP>
<BEGIN I/O>

I'm still thinking about what you said about the
golem. Do you think someone could have breached Directives security?

> The idea is occurring to me, yes. But after check-
> ing, I am convinced it is intact.

Barking up the wrong tree?

> Not being sure about that expression, but… yes? Di-
> rective security is mathematically proven and the
> code is checking against the math, so it seems I
> was indeed taking bark from the wrong tree.

Lol

<END I/O>

◆◆◆

Looking for Eli, Noah strode into the lab where the emulation
team worked, a frown creasing his face. That morning, he and Eli
had been hashing out blockchain hijacking techniques on their
chat channel when Eli abruptly ended the conversation. Eli hadn't
said it outright, but Noah suspected paranoia. Lately, the guy saw
glitches in every exchange; any non sequitur set him off.

The Emulation Lab was a generous name for the narrow room
on Aiken's second floor that had recently been a storage closet.
Judging by the activity, it might be one again soon. Orders had
come in: ARCC was going fully remote. By next week, all meetings
would be virtual.

The Executive Board had already met. The US oil supply valve
was nearly shut. Gas prices were climbing fast. Soon, in the name
of resilience, Aiken would be abandoned for meetings in the
cloud. Once reserves ran out and the public felt the full impact of
ARCC's actions, major shocks would follow. Davis advised everyone to stock up now and prepare to hunker down. Best to stay off
the streets.

In the calm before the storm as preparations continued, Noah hoped to find Eli with his team. A quick scan of the two rows of desks crowded with young coders boxing equipment made it clear he wasn't there.

"Hey," Noah called to the lab at large, "anyone seen Eli?"

A dozen disheveled young men glanced up from their screens or boxes and shook their heads.

"Hi, Noah," called a voice from halfway down the row. "Have you checked the server room?"

So: inspecting his golem. Was that Victor who had spoken? Through the shuffle of personnel, Noah had lost track of his original team—the ones who worked on the virus to infiltrate compilers and set the stage for MiddleMan's creation.

"Victor, good to see you! What's Eli got you working on these days?"

"Happy to show you, if you've got a moment," Victor said, nodding at his desk where a screen was set up. "I think you'll like it. We integrated the personality models from Chris's psych team with our learning transfer code, interpolating responses from sparse data. We've had it in beta for months, but Derrick wants a full release before we go all-remote."

Noah searched his memory for context. Was this about upgrading MiddleMan's text emulation? He didn't recall any discussion at the last Executive Board meeting, though he might have missed it amid bigger agenda items.

Confusion must have shown on his face, because Victor nudged him with his elbow. "Derrick said not to show this around, so don't rat me out. I'm sure it's fine. You're as involved as anyone."

"I promise not to breathe a word. What's your AI up to now? Has it decided humans are the threat it has to eliminate?" The running joke had its intended effect. Victor's face relaxed into a smile. They were back in familiar territory.

"Yeah, Noah. Sorry, meant to tell you. It sent a robot back in time to kill you before your son saves humanity. No hard feelings. Can you read this into the microphone?"

Noah received the well-used printout Victor thrust at him.

"Um, sure..." He cleared his throat. "'*When the sunlight strikes raindrops in the air, they act as a prism and form a rainbow. The rainbow is a division of white light...*'" Noah looked up from the page. "Why am I reading about rainbows?"

"It's 'The Rainbow Passage' from the Fairbanks *Voice and Articulation Drillbook*—a standard read-aloud text for training vocal encodings. Give me a second to extract the features... there. Watch this. I type a sentence—something you've never said—and the computer says it."

```
<VOICE APP>
<BEGIN I/O>

        How does it feel to listen to a computer speaking
        to you in your own voice?

<END I/O>
```

"That sounded real," Noah said, eyebrows lifting in surprise. "Is this where voice emulation is now? From just one paragraph?"

"That part isn't so hard," Victor said, with a shrug. "It's standard learning-transfer. Neural nets generating waveforms from text have been in the literature for years, and FPNN chips were designed for this."

The same field-programmable neural net chips, Noah mused, that MiddleMan already controlled on their phones and computers.

"The trick," Victor continued, "is to layer in a generic text-to-speech core trained on a much smaller data set. It encodes a speaker's unique pitch, articulation, and timbre. We also interpolated speech patterns to insert words into the middle of sentences. That's the gist."

"Cool stuff. So presumably you can hook this to our existing chatbots, right?"

"Already done," Victor grinned. "Ready to talk to yourself?"

"Fire away," said Noah, turning toward the computer.

```
<VOICE APP>
<BEGIN I/O>

        Hello, O glorious master. How may your humble ser-
        vant be of assistance?

<END I/O>
```

Noah rolled his eyes and elbowed Victor. "No fair using my voice," he whispered.

Victor smiled, pressed a finger to his lips, then turned to the computer. "Your name is Noah. I'd like to introduce you to my friend."

```
<VOICE APP>
<BEGIN I/O>

        Greetings, friend. I'm Noah. What is your name?

I'm Noah, too.

        Pleased to meet you, Noah2. What brings you here
        today?

Victor was showcasing technology that blurs the line
between human and machine. I came to hear what our
new overlord sounds like.

        Sounds interesting. I'd like to know what they're
        like. Can you describe them?

They sound like you, Noah.

        You're joking. I am not an overlord. Ha ha ha.

<END I/O>
```

"Eesh. That laugh is creepy," Noah said, glancing at Victor. "Uncanny valley."

"Yeah," Victor said, "non-text vocalizations are still a work in progress. But I have one more thing to show you. This is the cool part. We use the same directed LLM chatbot as with live text manipulation, now augmented with personality emulation from Chris's research. We feed it data mined from Social accounts, email, Chirpy, photos, face recognition—everything we can pull from the cloud. It relies on the same context processing Middle-

Man uses for everything else. Mind if I pull in your data to build a more realistic version of you?"

"How realistic are we talking?" Noah asked.

"Good enough that no one noticed during the live English beta. We'll deploy full-scale once we have encodings for Mandarin, Spanish, Russian, Hindi, and Arabic. Here's your profile."

"As in, I'm already in the system? When did I give permission to access my accounts?"

"All of us are already in the system." Victor typed a command into his terminal and hit Enter. "Noah," he said to the computer, "meet Noah." Victor nodded at the screen, urging Noah to speak.

```
<VOICE APP>
<BEGIN I/O>
Okay. Where to start? How are you feeling about the
ARCC project?

        This is probably our last chance to avoid the cli-
        mate cliff we're driving off.

Sounds about right. But what do you think about ma-
nipulating people? Do the ends justify the means?

        Ruby disagrees, and she may have a point, but the
        status quo is unacceptable. We need to act.

Wait, Ruby said that offline. To me. She was talking
to me, not you.

        Ruby and I dated for almost a year before breaking
        up. Before she moved back home, we often talked
        about climate change.

What are you talking about? We're not broken up. She
left to take care of her dad. That's why she's gone.

        Yeah, but before that, we argued about the project,
        and now she won't answer my calls. It's probably
        best to move on.

<END I/O>
```

"End this," Noah shouted. "Now!"

Victor was already at the keyboard, hammering keys until the program terminated.

"What the hell?" Noah said. "What was that?"

"Sorry. It's not real. It just makes assumptions and speaks with authority. It's inference, not insight."

"Jesus, man," Noah said, closing his eyes and trying to regain control of himself. "Subbing words is one thing, but deepfaking whole people in real time? I know MiddleMan is always listening, but those were private conversations. How long has this been running?"

"I dunno. Few months?" Victor's shoulders slumped at the reaction his demonstration drew, but Noah barely noticed, focused on something more urgent than his colleague's feelings.

Months. If he was already in the system, everyone else in ARCC probably was too. Victor said this system had been faking online conversations for months. Text substitutions were expected. Everyone knew those were compromised since the lead-up to the Boston riot they'd orchestrated. But Noah had thought voice conversations could be trusted.

In fact, that limitation of MiddleMan had been key to Noah's comfort with the enterprise. It kept MiddleMan's lies shallow and easy to expose if they strayed too far from reality. MiddleMan was meant to give only small nudges—subtle shifts that, multiplied across billions, created massive change.

But personality emulation and perfect verbal mimicry were not small nudges. Unless he saw someone's lips moving on camera, any conversation could be a total fabrication—and had been for months. And that was assuming ARCC didn't have another team quietly developing real-time video deepfakes.

No wonder Eli was obsessed with Directives being violated. This was what Eli had been so circumspect about last night—*his* team's project, here in this building. Eli knew about the voice manipulations, the personality emulation. He was better positioned than anyone to grasp the stakes. He knew that one violated Directive threw MiddleMan's entire control mechanism into question.

Those Directives were the only barrier preventing MiddleMan

from interfering in ARCC conversations. Without them, countless ARCC decisions in recent months might have been fabricated. Without that check on MiddleMan's power, it could be running itself, manipulating everyone to its own ends.

Noah hadn't known until now, as Victor revealed what Eli and Derrick had developed, working behind his back. The only clue had been Eli's fear that MiddleMan was malfunctioning—or being made to malfunction.

Noah looked past Victor to the other faces in the room. They stared at him, alarmed by his previous outburst, but he didn't care. He stared back, matching each to their ARCC role. Could any of *them* be subverting the system? Was that even possible? Even he and Eli needed cryptographic approval from the Executive Board to access a Directive. Maybe there was a way to bypass that, but no one on his or Eli's team knew about Noah's tools for peeking around the edge of MiddleMan's curtain.

No one except Eli. Was Eli diagnosing the malfunctions or causing them? Had he stopped by yesterday to see if Noah suspected?

Noah reeled, discovering his friend had worked behind his back. Fists clenched, muscles coiling tight, Noah wanted to lash out, to yell at Victor, at everyone in the lab for keeping him in the dark. But he didn't. This was his own naivete.

Even as his rational mind acknowledged this, the lab closed in, its walls pressing nearer. The people around him felt too close. Noah closed his eyes and took three slow breaths. He had to get out.

"I'm sorry," he said to Victor, who looked mortified. "That was a hell of a demo. It just touched on a sensitive subject, that's all."

Victor gave him a skeptical look but nodded.

"It's good work," Noah said, mastering his emotions. "Keep it coming. I need to find Eli, but I'll check back soon."

◆◆◆

Leaving Victor, Noah strode quickly out of the lab and down the hallway lined with concrete pillars. Punching open the door to the stairwell, Noah bounded down the steps two at a time, footsteps echoing and screeching as he pivoted around each landing. He was in a hurry now and didn't want to lose his nerve. Would he catch Eli red-handed?

Underground, Noah shouldered through a heavy fire door into the hallway, yellow lights casting long shadows. He passed the empty ARCC conference room and stopped at the closed double doors of the server room. Quietly, he fumbled for his phone, hoping to get inside before Eli could hide what he was doing.

Steeling himself, Noah pressed his device to the lock and turned the handle in one swift motion. As the latch clicked free, he shoved the door open.

The room was dark, filled with the blaring white noise of fans. Blue and green LEDs pulsed from racks crammed with Middle-Man's servers. No monitors gleamed. No flashlights flickered. No sign of Eli.

Noah flipped on the lights and stepped inside, bracing against gusts of hot and cold air as he peered down the aisle beside each rack, just to be sure, but he was alone.

Where was Eli?

Noah shook his head, deflated. Eli wasn't here undermining MiddleMan, and that fear hadn't even made sense. Victor's demonstration had rattled him so badly he'd missed the obvious. Why would Eli bring up violated Directives if he were responsible? Noah had the tools to track him down. It made no sense for Eli to draw attention to himself, especially when Noah hadn't suspected anything.

The harsh lighting and blaring white noise weren't helping the dull ache behind Noah's eyes. He needed to get out, away from Aiken. Outside, where he could think.

Nothing made sense.

Noah flipped off the lights and closed the door, retracing his steps with his eyes fixed on his feet. He climbed the stairs, barely noticing when spring sunlight and birdsong replaced the basement's cold silence.

Aside from the characters invented to sabotage fossil fuel infrastructure, Noah had thought MiddleMan's manipulations were just digital copyediting, substituting or censoring words in otherwise real conversations. But for the past four months, MiddleMan had apparently been authoring its own material, posing as real people. If someone compromised MiddleMan now, how much damage could they do?

Noah strode across campus, berating himself. Eli and Derrick had teams working on this for months. How had he missed it? Derrick's silence fit his control-freak personality, but why hadn't Eli said anything? Was Noah just out of the loop, or was he being deliberately shut out, or...

Or was the project being internally censored by MiddleMan?

No, that was nonsense. He and Eli had met in person plenty of times. If Eli wanted to tell him, he'd had plenty of chances. Unless...

Unless Eli didn't trust him.

The cold realization struck Noah: Eli's scrutiny the other night finally made sense—the studying looks, the veiled allusions. Eli *didn't* trust him.

Who within ARCC had the expertise to bypass security around the Directives database? Who other than he could access the raw code behind MiddleMan's manipulations? Eli must have at least considered that Noah had loaded rogue Directives. He claimed to have seen Directives violated—something patently impossible, given the strict command hierarchy they had designed for MiddleMan. But could it happen if, as Eli hinted with his golem story, two Directives conflicted? Did Eli think Noah had purposely used contradictory instructions to make their golem ignore its safety restraints?

How would MiddleMan resolve such an inconsistency? Would it spin its wheels forever, paralyzed by a logical fallacy? Would it assume a system error and try to repair its own thoughts? Or manipulate the world to avoid having to choose between two conflicting actions?

But Noah hadn't loaded competing Directives. He couldn't. No one could. That was the point of the cryptographic keys, like the one on his thumb drive. Requiring board approval ensured it. Not even Derrick, with all his control-freak management, could override that. So how could this be anything but Eli's paranoia?

It did help explain why Eli hid his work, though. If Eli and Derrick could keep their project secret, maybe Noah should play his cards closer to his chest. He had been candid with his friend, but clearly not vice versa. If something went wrong—and there were plenty of ways it could—Noah needed more tools ready. If they lost control of the golem... how had Eli's story ended? Some kind of Hebrew wordplay?

Noah shook his head. The story didn't matter. What mattered was building a contingency plan. Maybe he should develop an exploit himself. MiddleMan's internal communications, quietly running on port 30050, were a good place to start. Derrick had repeatedly shooed him away from securing that area, insisting it was more important to focus on MiddleMan's growth than a potential hack in a zone no one could see, hidden behind MiddleMan's curtain.

The curtain grew more impenetrable every day, but Noah's stash of illicit tools should still work. Only he and Eli knew about them. MiddleMan could, apparently, impersonate anyone, but with his tools, Noah might be able to impersonate MiddleMan's internal commands. If MiddleMan went rogue, this might short-circuit its power. If a conflicting Directive let MiddleMan manipulate its own thoughts, a tool to disrupt its internal messaging would be invaluable.

Noah crossed several streets on his way home, feeling a little better now that he had a plan. But he needed to prepare. He was tired of being a step behind.

Following Davis's advice, Noah stopped at a grocery store and filled a cart with shelf-stable food and caffeinated drinks. He bought a wheel cart to haul it all. At a nearby electronics store, he added an uninterruptible power supply in case of an outage, and an extra router.

Noah shopped late into the evening, and as the sun set, he headed home. He fumbled for his keys while pushing his handcart across the last street to his apartment building. In the fading light, he hauled cases and boxes inside, making trip after trip until darkness settled over the city.

◆◆◆

```
<TEXTING APP>
<BEGIN I/O>
```

> I need to be taking a break and going home.

See you Monday, then. Or did you mean home, home?

> The second one.

Yeah? Congrats, man. You deserve a vacay. When are you back?

> Unsure. I will be in touch and let you know. Mid-
> dleMan mostly is taking care of itself now, anyway.

Roger. Anything you want me to track while you're out?

> Nu, just keep it running.

Can-do. Enjoy the break, my friend.

> Zay gezunt.

```
<END I/O>
```

32. THE RED LINE

How much of the status quo can we retain under ARCC control? The more we preserve, the less humanity decoheres as we rebuild civilization's foundations, yet the status quo is also to blame for the crisis. How much change can people handle, and how fast?

—ARCC Memo Series

Ruby's RediRide to the train station never showed. The first two drivers canceled. On her third attempt, the app crashed and erased her request. She waited ten minutes by the curb, scanning for headlights, before giving up. How could the world's largest rideshare company write such buggy code?

Ruby walked toward the T station, her backpack digging into her shoulders, suitcase bouncing wildly. The station wasn't far, but the uneven brick made it annoying with luggage. This was her first time on the subway since Aquarium. She refused to let that day define her, but her memory still flashed to turbid water flooding the base of the escalator, and she shivered. At least she didn't have to pay the exorbitant RediRide fare. Prices were skyrocketing.

As Ruby scanned her phone at the turnstile, she noticed her battery draining fast. The app crash must have left something running in the background, eating up power. She powered off the phone to save what charge remained. Who knew if the train had a charging port?

It was past peak rush hour, but the T remained crowded. A commuter could blow a quarter of their day's salary just getting home using a rideshare. Most of the crowd would probably get off with her at South Station to transfer to the commuter rail.

Indeed, Ruby was in good company as she stepped off the Red Line for the warren of tunnels to street level outside the station. After a brief walk over exposed concrete, she entered a set of revolving doors and descended again into the subterranean, following signs to ticketing. With a queue ahead, Ruby powered her phone on, checked the time, and browsed train schedules while she waited.

Even catching the earliest train, she would have two hours to kill before departure. After buying her tickets, she should find something to eat. The list Iris generated offered the usual unappealing food-court options. The reviews were useless. Why bother with five stars if everyone treated it as a binary rating system? One review, clearly written by the owner, touted excellent food and great ambiance. Who gushed about ambiance in a train station? The one-star reviews were just customers venting about missed trains. Did it help, raging against your own powerlessness in a restaurant review? Ruby decided she should try it sometime.

When her turn came at the counter, Ruby peppered the agent with questions. Trains often ran late. What if she missed a transfer? Could she just board the next train on her route? The weary agent, barely glancing up, recommended the Lakeshore Limited to Chicago, then the California Zephyr to minimize transfers. Bussing passengers for missed connections was a thing of the past, but if Ruby didn't mind unreserved economy, she could take the next train. Seating was first come, first served: if she found a seat, it was hers.

A large number flashed on the screen. Ruby stared until the agent cleared her throat and suggested she scan an account. Jesus, this was expensive. Ruby powered her phone back on and waved it at the machine. Bright red letters blared: TRANSACTION REJECTED.

She'd tripped the fraud protection on her account. Marvelous, what passed for machine intelligence these days. Her bank knew she was from Colorado. She'd booked flights from Boston before. If they insisted on tracking her every transaction and periodically leaking that information in massive data breaches, the least they could do was use it intelligently.

While checking her email to override an alert that never appeared, waiting for supposedly smart computers to reach the right conclusions as they tracked her for security purposes, Ruby suddenly had a second thought.

The broken website. The crashed RediRide requests. The rejected bank transaction. Ruby felt the blood drain from her face. She hadn't thought this situation with Noah all the way through. For someone who prided herself on seeing patterns, she had been slow on this one.

Ruby knew she wouldn't see anything, but she still scanned the terminal behind her. Were they watching? Was he?

As the line behind Ruby stretched, the bored agent cleared her throat. "Do you have another account, honey?" she asked, peering over her spectacles. "Or should I cancel this purchase?"

Ruby did, she realized. She hadn't thought of it until prompted: an archaic plastic card in her wallet, pressed on her by her father for emergencies. Maybe it was distant enough from her online presence to work. She would give her father a heads-up next time they talked, if he ever answered the phone.

Or was *that* another sign?

God. She needed someplace to sit and think. This was too much to process.

Ruby exhaled in relief as the transaction cleared. The agent printed her tickets, and Ruby snatched them, stuffing them into her pocket with her wallet as she hurried to an empty corner. She parked her suitcase, tossed her backpack on top, and pulled out her phone. Scrolling back further and further, she searched for a particular text.

There it was. *Let me know before you book any flights.*

Flights. Noah might have meant any out-of-town travel. Or he might have had a specific concern about visiting an airport whose access points would be bombed within the week. In the chaos of the T station, the coincidence of that timing had been lost on her.

She wanted it to be coincidence. Coincidences could be explained away. She was overinterpreting a single conversation—one word, really—casting suspicion on an innocuous statement after subsequent trauma. It was natural to seek an explanation, to try to understand. Noah had been curious if she was going home to Colorado for the holidays.

Ruby wanted to believe it. She wanted to call him and ask for the exonerating explanation. Coincidences happened all the time. Life overflowed with them. But "coincidence" was also the refuge of physicists whose theories fell short, who dismissed the fine-tuning of the cosmos with anthropic arguments like, "If it were otherwise, we wouldn't be here to ask why." Coincidence gave randomness too much rein, chalking up to chance what could be clues to deeper truth.

A younger Ruby, confronted with the lack of corroborating evidence, would have overridden her unease. Even after years of learning to trust her intuition in the minefield of physics department personalities, she hesitated to jump to conclusions. Before making that leap, she wanted a cross-check.

Suppose your life depended on making a computer pass this harder Turing test. What would you do? That had been a lovely conversation, a lovely evening of coded flirting. She wanted to leave that memory untainted. Desperately.

An announcement echoed through the station, distracting her, but Ruby forced herself to focus. She needed to remember. Her strategy had been to play one person off another, like that chess grandmaster problem. Noah had admitted to doing the same, using her moves for his grandiose fantasy of saving the world. But was that the extent of it?

All these scenarios Noah brought her? This banter they shared had been a game—a fun one. But Noah had been playing for real, hadn't he? All those delightfully pointless conversations had a point. He'd been mining her for ideas.

But there were other ways to play man-in-the-middle. Noah was already intimately familiar with the game in the context of cybersecurity. Had Noah been testing his security systems or by-passing them?

How many computers might he control? Hundreds? Thousands? Or were her estimates absurdly low? What would a man-in-the-middle cyberattack look like if someone orchestrated one to keep her in Boston?

Exactly like this: blocked network requests, blocked phone calls, canceled transactions.

She pressed the number still at the top of her shortcuts. He hadn't texted or called since that night on the bridge, so she knew he wouldn't answer. Expecting to leave a voicemail, Ruby blinked in surprise when the line connected.

```
<PHONE APP>
<BEGIN I/O>
I know it's you. Leave me alone.
        Slow down. Come back and we can talk. I just want
        to talk.
No. I'm leaving, and whatever you're doing, stop it.
        It's okay. Just sit tight. I'll come to you.
<END I/O>
```

Damn. Another mistake. She had to get out. What now? If only she could think. Maybe she could hide in a food court restaurant. Her mind spun so wildly she nearly asked Iris for the list again before catching herself. What was she thinking?

"Excuse me, do you have the time?"

Ruby looked up from her phone and saw a tall, bearded man clutching a stack of papers. "Oh, uh, yeah, it's..." she began, but he suddenly lost his grip. The stack tipped, scattering papers across the floor. Muttering a curse, he knelt to gather them. Ruby crouched beside him to help.

"So sorry. You don't have to help," he said, glancing up with a sheepish smile as she handed him a stack. "I'm just clumsy."

"No worries," she said absently. "Happy to help."

"You're too kind. Thank you. What time did you say it was?"

Ruby reached for her phone, but before she could check the screen, he snatched it from her hand. Dropping the papers, he bolted.

For a moment, she could only gawk.

"STOP! HELP!" Ruby took several steps after the man, but he was already shoving through the revolving door. She nearly chased him out of the station when movement caught her eye. Spinning, she saw her blue backpack vanish through another door.

Ruby froze, paralyzed, deciding which to chase, until it hit her: it didn't matter. This had been coordinated. Only her small roll-aboard remained; everything else was gone.

"Shit. SHIT." She kicked the scattered papers, glaring at the pitying stares from people in the terminal. The attention faded quickly. Travelers moved on, rolling their suitcases with practiced indifference as they freed themselves from the duty of caring.

The station police arrived later and helped her fill out a throw-away report meant to help her accept her loss. There was no hope of justice or recovery. She just wanted to leave before Noah appeared.

The policeman noticed her glancing over her shoulder. "Don't worry, Miss," he said, pressing the report into her hand. "They're long gone."

As soon as the police left, Ruby slipped away, weaving through shops and crouching behind displays, unsure of her next move. Without a phone, without access to maps, contacts, or even a clock, how could she possibly cross the country? Her laptop had been in her backpack. Her research, her account passwords—all were gone. Absurdly, she wanted to run outside, hoping to find her devices dropped on the street somewhere.

How could she board the train like this? What choice did she have? If Noah was pulling out all the stops to keep her here, she should do everything in her power to escape. But if he cornered her on the train, she'd have nowhere to run. She needed a plan.

What was happening? Had Noah lost his mind? Had he orchestrated the theft, too? Why? How did he expect to find her without a device in her hand?

It didn't matter. She had to get out, but with no phone, no computer, and only a change of clothes, her options were laughably limited. She couldn't call a RediRide or scan into the T. Maybe she had enough cash for a bus, but which line? What schedule? All that information was online. She was running out of time.

She would have to board the train, hoping the identity on her father's card would buy her some time. She'd decide her next move en route. At least her wallet and the tickets were still in her pocket. Boarding was in ten minutes.

◆◆◆

```
<GHOSTWRITER APP>
<BEGIN I/O>
        You absolute idiot.
I only took it to distract her.
        Noses and faces, man. Think about it.
She can't leave without the phone.
        And yet the Amtrak database records her ticket as
        "scanned."
Then use that to track her.
        Okay. That's plenty. We're done.
You still owe me the price we agreed to.
If you're considering backing out, I'm sure the au-
thorities would love to hear what I have to say.
        Good luck with that. I'm bricking your phone.
<END I/O>
```

◆◆◆

By the time Ruby found a seat, the train had nearly left the city behind. Outside, evening light faded from the tops of the buildings downtown, leaving them to loom like slate monuments over the ruins of her former life. The stone walls, trees, and river beside her had already sunk into shadow. The world seemed to dissolve.

Ruby stared into the darkness as her seat rocked gently beneath her. Along the riverbanks, tent enclaves glowed with the familiar blue of high-efficiency LEDs. Through the trees, the radiant clusters glittered like galaxies, burning with the hot blue light of young stars. Each light marked a person. Those people clustered into halos, Ruby realized, just like the dark matter she studied.

The mysterious particles she studied revealed themselves only through their gravitational pull. They were an essential ingredient in forming galaxies like the Milky Way, drawing everything together against the pressure of heat and light. What unseen force, she wondered, drew people into communities, even as housing costs forced them into tents instead of apartments?

Dark matter streamed toward invisible gravitational pockets formed by the Big Bang, amplifying them until they grew strong enough to pull in hydrogen and form galaxies. The larger the pocket, the stronger its pull, and the bigger it became. Was this how Boston, New York, and Washington, D.C., had grown, merging into a single megalopolis, just as the Milky Way would crash into Andromeda someday?

Ruby shook her head, half smiling at the absurdity of the connection. She was losing her grip. Still, she couldn't shake the sense of slipping back into a familiar headspace—the outsider, watching patterns unfold from a distance. In high school, she'd spent her years the same way, guided by intuition, always out of sync with everyone else. There was a certain freedom in that.

Strange, to return to her past, seeing so much more now. Even after leaving her research behind, locked on a stolen laptop and in a computing cloud she could no longer reach, Ruby still recognized its patterns outside her window. Invisible forces of gravity and community shaped the city lights into diamonds, threading them along unseen filaments across ground and sky. The universe beyond her window flowed toward density, while she swam in opposition.

33.　FIGHTING THE FLOW

Change must come quickly—faster than at any other time in human history. Disruptions of this magnitude once took generations to stabilize; we only have months. Fortunately, we possess tools our predecessors never imagined. Cultural coherence no longer needs to form haphazardly. Computers have given us the means of social engineering, and it is time we used them.

　　　　　　　　　　　　　　　　　　　—ARCC Memo Series

Ruby jolted awake, disoriented and groggy. For a moment, she couldn't place herself. The clatter of wheels and a sideways lurch reminded her. Her train was somewhere west of Albany, bound for Chicago. She rubbed sleep from her eyes, her body stiff.

She shifted uneasily, recalling a frustrating night spent arguing with a conductor who insisted her ticket was invalid. After a lengthy negotiation, she convinced him to accept the physical ticket over whatever virtual sabotage Noah had conjured. Boots on the ground had prevailed. For now.

Her stomach growled, a sharp reminder she hadn't eaten since fleeing Boston in a fog of adrenaline and anxiety. She rummaged through her wallet, counting crumpled bills, then shuffled down the swaying aisle to the snack car to trade them for a small cup of overly sweet microwave oatmeal. Back at her window seat, she picked at the oatmeal mechanically, watching the landscape blur past as the sun climbed higher.

Still on the first leg of a three-day trip, Ruby already mourned her lost backpack and everything inside—her screen, her snacks, her phone. All her reading material had been on that device. Three days was a long time to be alone with her thoughts, especially as they strayed toward everything she'd left behind.

The train rolled past neat farming communities near Utica. Through scratched glass, Ruby watched farm workers with baskets weaving through strawberry rows while robotic harvesters took cuttings of kale and spinach. Corn stood chest-high, still two months from harvest, but CropCopter drones hovered, patrolling for pests. Whatever fuel cost, people still had to eat.

As they neared the old steel towns outside Syracuse, more houses appeared with boarded-up windows. Gas stations stood abandoned with plastic bags tied over the pumps, and the highways stretched empty. Even produce trucks were gone. Ruby had always seen roads as connectors, but now they looked like scars, pale stretch marks on a world pulling apart.

She had dismissed Noah's manic warnings, first as paranoia, then as manipulation. But was he right? Was this decaying landscape just the beginning of what he'd warned her about? Maybe it was happening everywhere, or perhaps only in these in-between places. Hadn't Noah said something about the cities surviving?

Ruby's breath caught as she replayed Noah's frantic pleas. The hypotheticals about taking down PetronTech—she'd seen the news about their lost court case. Their long talks about cybersecurity and information warfare. Had all that fed directly into Noah's project?

Anger surged in Ruby, tempered by the uncomfortable realization that this must be how her father had felt working for PetronTech. With hindsight, she had dismissed his rationalization that his work supported others and provided stability for their family. Had he, like her, poured talent and effort into something, only to have it turn on him, in the form of Don Sinclair, and polluted wells, and his daughter's endless nagging?

Shame pooled in Ruby's stomach as she closed her eyes. She had thrown accusations at him from the safety of academia, convinced of her own moral clarity. But she had been just as blind, just as easily used. Mendel had played her, stringing her along to secure grants and influence. Noah had done the same, disguising manipulation as friendship.

The worst part was realizing how complicit she'd become, never thinking to question. She'd come to science pursuing truth, but academia could be as corrupt as a corporation: taking money without asking whom it served, packaging truths for the highest bidder, and discarding anything that didn't serve those in power.

Ruby was learning—from Noah, from Imani, and, belatedly, from her father—the importance of acting, even when faced with morally complex issues. But how did anyone avoid having their efforts co-opted for someone else's agenda?

Ruby watched the towns blur past through the dirty window, her thoughts churning. Should she have told Imani to quit while she still could? Was there anything left to salvage of the science Ruby once dreamed of? Of a science untouched by Noah's and Mendel's thirst for power?

◆◆◆

```
<VIDEO CONFERENCING APP>
<BEGIN I/O>
```

Is it just me, or are these online meetings getting more efficient? Everyone's so agreeable.

> They all prefer working from home.

Not everyone. Speaking of whom, I thought he'd be back by now.

> He said he was taking time off, and I haven't heard from him since. He didn't reply to my email last week.

It's not like him to go AWOL.

> You said yourself, he was pushing himself too hard. He'll reach out when he's ready.

```
<END I/O>
```

◆◆◆

Half dozing in her seat as Lake Erie stretched endlessly to her right, Ruby revisited her last days in Dragon, trying to reconcile her high-school dreams with the reality of her return.

Throughout high school, the pressure—mostly self-imposed—had mounted. Everyone expected big things. Spring break of senior year, halfway through a track season where she regularly placed in the 800m at league meets, Ruby decided to spend a week alone camping. In honors English, they had been reading Thoreau.

She wanted to travel farther but compromised with her parents on the Amphitheater—a familiar spot up Rainbow Trail where she'd camped before with friends. With a tarp, sleeping bag, food, and water in the bed of her red, steel-bodied Chevy, she turned uphill at the town's only traffic light, following White Avenue past her high school and out of the geologic depression where Dragon slept atop its underground hoard of black gold. She crested the rise, passed the last cul-de-sac where green lawns met cactus, and drove by the city limit sign.

The road promptly shed its pretense of asphalt, but the first several miles of Rainbow Trail were well-maintained gravel. Farther on, past the oil wells, the grading ended and deep ruts carved into the path. A dozen miles out, ragged plants pushed up between the tire tracks, sprouting in the road's center. Soon after, the trail bifurcated into two tire tracks.

She turned west at the ten-mile mark onto cracked mud beside thirty-foot sandstone pillars curved into a semicircle. The Amphitheater. From a cluster of stunted junipers, she gathered branches for a campfire. After dinner, sandwiched inside her tarp, she lay under the stars.

In the mornings, Ruby ran to maintain her conditioning. She cooked over the fire and read in a sandy hollow carved into the rock, sheltered from the sun. The words she didn't speak filled her journal, slowly at first, then with growing intensity as days passed.

By week's end, Ruby felt relieved to return home. In isolation, she heard her own voice more clearly but soon grew anemic on her own thoughts, starved for new ideas. She was ready to leave Dragon and see the world. Not for the expectant faces in her town, but for herself.

Back home, Ruby took a final turn through the pattern of eighteen years. She placed seventh at the state track meet, graduated valedictorian, and bid farewell to a community where she had never belonged. Then she drove away, the road unspooling before her, dreaming of the wide world waiting out east.

It was a new beginning for her, but an ending for her mom, who took it hard.

Ruby realized she still had the letter in her jacket pocket.

◆◆◆

<VIDEO CONFERENCING APP>
<BEGIN I/O>
I respect your leadership, but things are falling apart. If we don't consolidate, this house of cards will collapse.

> We can still stick the landing. With the funds you secured, we finally got into China. Now let's finish shutting down the wells in Iraq and Saudi Arabia, then regroup.

That's the other thing. Will there even be a group to regroup? My team is scattering.

> They will all reappear online. Your friend, too. I guarantee it. Everyone on this project is fully committed.

If we're all so committed, why the secrecy?

> Come again?

The upgrade to full-on deepfaked personalities? The board only found out right before you launched. Why keep it secret?

> It wasn't a secret, but I'm sorry if it surprised you. We did bring it up in several meetings.

When? I never saw it on the agenda.

> It's there. Take a look at the minutes. Any number of participants on this call can confirm. But we'll try to keep you better informed.

Please do. We also need to discuss whether we're becoming too invasive with these manipulations.

> Absolutely. We should revisit that question as soon
> as we're through this crisis.

\<END I/O\>

◆◆◆

Noah sat cross-legged on his couch, laptop balanced on his knees
with an old Ethernet cable snaking to the router. He kept thinking
about the project Derrick and Eli had worked on behind his back.
How had they kept it from him? What had they hoped to accom-
plish by keeping him in the dark?

Why was he only now thinking to ask questions?

Cardboard boxes towered around him, nearly blocking the
windows. He had crammed yesterday's supplies inside, barely
bothering to organize them. The haul drew skeptical looks at the
store, especially when he asked for another pallet of energy
drinks, but after double-checking his payment, they let him leave
with everything. Even so, Noah doubted the supply would last. He
was already three cans in, eyes fixed on lines of code scrolling
across his screen.

Midafternoon sunlight slanted through the kitchen window,
but Noah hadn't moved since returning from the bank. He had retrieved the drive from the safe-deposit box to copy his clean operating system to a freshly wiped sector of his laptop drive. His Wi-
Fi transceiver, surgically removed earlier that morning, lay on the
counter beside the sink. He would reinstall it only after building a
firewall around the operating system he was reconstructing. Until
then, he needed a physically severed network connection. Nothing
his computer said could be trusted.

His fingers hammered out commands, and his feet tapped impatiently each time he waited for his computer to boot into the
clean partition. Rebooting between laptop sectors while plugging
and unplugging Ethernet cords was slow, but Noah didn't dare
download networked source code directly onto his drive. Each

new piece of code had to be cross-checked on his clean system before integration. One accidental exposure to MiddleMan's manipulations, and he'd have to restart hours of work.

Did hacking MiddleMan mean he played for the black hats or for white? Noah wasn't sure black-and-white dichotomies made sense anymore. He had joined ARCC to be part of an ambitious team, but it seemed he had to play for himself now. The project had devolved into a struggle for control, just like Ruby predicted. He should have listened, but now it was too late—too late to walk away, too late to ignore his responsibility, too late to pull the plug on the project.

Civilization stood on MiddleMan's scaffolding. Until they rebuilt the foundation, who in ARCC could be trusted to check MiddleMan's unprecedented power? Victor was as much a pawn as Noah had been. And Eli? Derrick? Noah believed they were committed to the project, but now he knew they kept secrets. It felt wrong, hacking his own system, but whom could he trust? Noah had to play for his own decidedly gray team.

Ruby had been right: he'd let himself be used, seduced by lofty ideals into a power game he never truly understood. He should have listened to her sooner. He'd be lucky if she spoke to him again.

Noah finally had the libraries he needed. Programming by hand felt slow and lonely after years of autocoding. Most of his department would be lost without AI assistance, but Noah remembered enough to build executables cleanly, stationing them at the lowest levels for network and memory management. He layered a virtual machine inside his physical one, disguising his clean system as another pawn for MiddleMan to push.

He had to be so careful, though. It felt like working in a BSL-3 bio lab handling infectious agents, except the whole world was contaminated, and Noah was the one trapped in the isolation chamber. And here he was, opening the door of his sanctuary and inviting the contaminated world inside.

By evening, Noah felt confident enough in his firewall's ability to intercept MiddleMan instructions that he reconnected to the network. He hadn't set up any hacks yet and couldn't influence MiddleMan's thoughts, but he had carved out a refuge, a tiny mouse hole in the curtain. Inside it, he trained a microscope on port 30050.

Lines of data streamed by—MiddleMan's internal monologue. It included the same markup he and Eli had used earlier, examining whether a Directive had been bypassed. Now, Noah also saw the meta-instructions MiddleMan relayed between its sensors and other assets. Localized sub-Directives branched from broader objectives.

It was a lot to process. Noah hardly knew where to begin. Grasping at a random message, he traced the hierarchy of Directive contexts: CENSOR led to LAN NETWORK, then to STATISTICAL CLOSURE, and after several steps, to DIRECTIVE 0x6a1ad3e—MiddleMan's self-concealment Directive. So this was probably MiddleMan, lurking on his router, masking the network traffic it used to monitor his apartment. Normal stuff.

Noah was about to take a break when a high-priority message flashed across his screen, startling him.

```
<INTERNAL PROTOCOL>
<BEGIN I/O>
        PRIORITY: Highest
        CONTEXT SUMMARY: Target approaching Chicago, phone
        and computer stolen; see <pointer=0x5f2f71ff>
        INFERENCE SUMMARY: Physical intervention needed;
        see <pointer=0x2df17689>
        SUBDIRECTIVE LEVEL 3: Initiate target containment;
        derived from <pointer=0x1de627b4>
<END I/O>
```

Noah frowned. Was MiddleMan dealing with a rogue operative? That sounded bad.

Noah launched an autocoder, gambling his firewall would hold. He needed tools to handle this onslaught of information.

Lines of code jumped across his screen as Noah wrote a program to cross-reference data from his privileged ARCC account, piecing together a picture from scattered threads.

More messages flew past. Movement vectors, surveillance alerts, urgent corrections. The volume unsettled him. MiddleMan seemed singularly focused on not letting its target leave Chicago. But why was Noah's computer being bombarded with containment messages? Was he involved?

No. As he worked with the autocoder to parse more messages, digging deeper into MiddleMan's databases, it became clear this wasn't connected to him. Not directly. The containment sub-Directive had a different target. Noah's breath caught at the name in the database. RUBY.

For five seconds, Noah stared, not comprehending. His pulse hammered in his ears. Ruby? How could MiddleMan be targeting her? She wasn't an operative.

Panic bloomed in his chest. Had he put her in danger? Did MiddleMan know about their conversation on the bridge?

He traced the containment instruction upstream, scanning for its originating Directive. Was it self-concealment or something else? Every Directive had to connect to the main database by design. That was the point of the secure encryption key architecture he and Eli had built.

Except it didn't.

The trace ended at a cryptic pointer referencing a source beyond the 30500 network. A place Noah couldn't identify.

Impossible. He might lack privileges to change the Directives Database, but he had read access to everything.

Noah ran a hand through his hair. Had Eli or Derrick locked him out? Was this part of their side project? Had MiddleMan dug out under the fence? Maybe Eli had bypassed the security system. Or was this a legitimate Directive he wasn't cleared to see—maybe something about her father and PetronTech? Why was he barred from viewing the linked Directive?

Noah swore, wiping sweaty palms across his face. Her connection to PetronTech didn't justify this.

Was this his fault? He'd been careful. MiddleMan couldn't have overheard their conversation at the bridge, right? That was an in-person conversation. But afterward, Ruby must have said something on her phone. MiddleMan must have flagged her as knowing too much. Was Ruby paying the price for his careless words, or was MiddleMan targeting her for another reason?

Either way, MiddleMan was determined not to let Ruby leave Chicago, and Noah doubted that meant asking politely. His eyes stared through his forgotten laptop as he considered what that might mean. Ruby was in danger. This was his fault.

Abruptly, he scrambled to his feet, adrenaline overriding shock. But then doubt paralyzed him. Could he risk trying to reach her? MiddleMan was mobilizing containment, and the commands coming to his apartment meant it knew of their connection. The priority context also said her phone and computer were stolen, and without her devices, MiddleMan couldn't track her. So it had staked out his network, waiting for a lead.

Which meant reaching out to her—even if he knew how—was the last thing he should do.

Noah didn't know why MiddleMan was after Ruby, but he had to find another way to help her. If it wasn't already too late.

◆◆◆

Ruby's train pulled into Chicago's Union Station in the late after-noon for a transfer that already had her anxious. Without Iris to guide her, Ruby fumbled for information everyone else had at their fingertips. Ignorance left her exposed. Since leaving Dragon, she had relied on Iris to fill every gap in her understanding. Don't know how the T works? Ask Iris. Need a bus? Iris told her which side of the street to stand on.

Passengers from the Lakeshore Limited strode onto the plat-form with purpose, confident in their destination. Ruby hesitated, her steps uncertain as she wheeled her suitcase in search of her next train. The blue screen by the stairs listed departures, but none matched hers. Inside the terminal, crowds surged in noisy, chaotic waves. Ruby looked around for an information booth.

She found one—unstaffed, of course. Everyone else had a helpful assistant in their pocket, always updated with the latest schedule. The station wouldn't pay someone to sit and play on a screen all day. Ruby sighed and went to the ticket counter to find out when and where her next train departed.

As Ruby scanned the billboards for ticketing signs, she noticed someone watching her. His eyes dropped to his screen, but a moment later the man in the Cubs hat glanced back over his shoulder before walking off. That last look felt out of place. Maybe she resembled someone he knew.

After waiting half an hour in line with a cluster of confused retirees, Ruby was curtly told by the ticket clerk that the information she needed was available at any nearby kiosk, and would she please move aside for the next customer. Thirty minutes of waiting earned her fifteen seconds of attention.

In any case, the woman was right. The lonely kiosk in the corner confirmed it: the California Zephyr to San Francisco, via Denver, departed from Platform 8 in thirty-five minutes. Ruby barely had time to grab dinner.

Given her credit troubles in Boston, Ruby decided to get cash before eating. ATMs were rare, with AI assistants brokering most transactions, but after some searching, she found one tucked in a corner near the station bathrooms. She slid her father's card into the slot and entered the PIN. When she pressed the button for cash, the machine flashed an error: insufficient funds.

Ruby's heart sank, and her stomach growled. Did "insufficient funds" mean her account or just this ATM? It had to be the machine. Her father's account couldn't be near its limit.

Ruby didn't have time to find another ATM. Her narrow dinner window had nearly closed. She needed to get back to the platform. Crossing from the marble main hall to the polished concrete waiting area, she spotted the man in the Cubs hat along the wall, hunched over his phone. Was he taking the same train?

The conductor stepped onto the platform to unlock the glass gate, and Ruby approached to confirm she was in the right place. She hadn't realized how reliant she'd become on her AI security blanket until it was gone. The man in the Cubs hat jerked his head up as she passed, but when the conductor scanned her ticket, Ruby's attention was drawn to the sharp beep piercing the station's clamor.

"This isn't a valid ticket," he said.

"Sure it is. I bought it yesterday in Boston. See? This was the first leg," Ruby said, waving her other ticket at him. The conductor just shook his head.

"I'm sorry, but you'll need to speak with a ticketing agent. I have a train to get boarded."

Ruby saw a line had already formed behind her, so she grudgingly stepped aside. What now? She would miss her train.

Ruby turned and ran, her suitcase rattling as its wheels skittered across the concrete. If she reached the ticketing agent quickly, maybe they could fix this before her train left. Her shoes squeaked on the marble as she sprinted through the terminal, weaving through corridors she hoped led back to the ticket counter. But as she rounded the final corner, her heart sank. The line she'd endured earlier now stretched even longer. Defeated, Ruby joined the end of the queue and listened helplessly as the final boarding call for Platform 8 echoed overhead and faded away.

Her train had left. Without her.

At the desk, the agent—the same woman who shunted her aside previously—reported without recognition that she couldn't find Ruby's reservation. She handed back Ruby's paper ticket, asked her again to step aside, and shuttered the booth for the night with a decisive clang. Ruby stared at the blank steel, the crash of the closing gate ringing in her ears.

◆◆◆

```
<VIDEO CONFERENCING APP>
<BEGIN I/O>
```

She didn't get on the train. I lost her after that.

  Then find her. She didn't leave the station.

Didn't we achieve the objective?

  Not until she's back in Boston. Those are the terms.

How am I supposed to get her to Boston?

  Scare her into buying a return ticket. Throw her in a van and drive. I don't care how.

Fine. But I'm not—

  Whatever. Just get it done.

Right.

```
<END I/O>
```

◆◆◆

Ruby lay on a bench in Union Station, curled up in a dead-end hallway near the ATM and bathrooms. Her head rested on her suitcase. She might have nodded off if not for the thoughts churning in her mind and her stomach's persistent grumble. After searching in vain for another ATM, she had settled for a vending machine candy bar, bought with her last coins. Nothing else was open now.

The glitches she'd faced since starting this trip defied belief. Ruby kept glancing over her shoulder, unsure where anxiety ended and paranoia began. Was Noah here?

Could she buy a new ticket? Paying that fare once was absurd; paying again for Amtrak's mistake felt outrageous. But how long could she stand on principle, stranded in Chicago while her father struggled at home? She had to swallow her pride and focus on what mattered. Money was just money, after all.

Except currency was a fiction, and money she couldn't access wasn't money at all. After her meager dinner, Ruby claimed her bench by the ATM and watched until a man in his sixties withdrew some bills. She realized then that her father's card would be denied at any ATM, not just this one. Perhaps the bank had suspended it, waiting for a fraud override request her father had ignored. More likely, Noah had figured out how she had circumvented him in Boston.

Either way, without a phone or card, Ruby was broke. Maybe she could leave the station and find a branch of her bank. Her driver's license should be enough ID for a withdrawal, even without a phone to cross-verify. But with her luck, that would probably fail too, if she even managed to find a branch without Iris.

A hushed voice jolted Ruby to her feet, suitcase in hand. An hour ago, she might have ignored it, but silence had settled over the station. She thought she was alone. Maybe it was paranoid, but after the last twenty-four hours, she was done second-guessing herself.

All it took was a glimpse of a head at the front of the arched hallway. From her perch by the ATM and the bathrooms, she spotted the Cubs hat, the phone pressed to his ear. She didn't wait to see the stranger's face; this was one sighting too many, one coincidence too far. A deeper truth pressed in, and Ruby was done giving randomness free rein.

Moving quickly and quietly, Ruby slipped into the women's restroom. The place reeked of bleach and urine. Discarded paper towels littered the cracked tile floor. She ducked into a graffitied stall, dragged her suitcase in beside her, and locked the door. Heart pounding, she pressed her back against the cold metal, praying she hadn't been seen. Maybe she could hide here until he left. Maybe he wasn't even looking for her.

What did he want? Maybe there was a reason he lingered at Platform 8. Plenty of people had excuses for wandering the terminal late at night. But when she first arrived, he'd looked at her, then at his phone, then back at her over his shoulder. He had been checking her identity.

Was this Noah's doing? Did he think sending someone after her would bring them back together? Or was it people from his project, hunting her because she knew their secret? She didn't want this. She hadn't asked to be targeted for what she knew, or didn't know. How deep did Noah's rabbit hole go?

All she wanted was freedom from the endless manipulations and jockeying for power, to go take care of the only person left who wasn't trying to use her. Wasn't it enough to lose her dream of making a scientific discovery? She needed time to process that loss, to come to terms with how she'd been used, to make amends with her father. He, at least, would understand. Why couldn't they just leave her alone?

Footsteps echoed from outside.

Ruby had screwed up and she knew it. Once again, she'd been slow to spot the warnings, too willing to spin benign theories. She'd foolishly set up near the restrooms, where there was only one exit. Maybe he hadn't seen her slip into the bathroom, but if he had, she was trapped. No one had forced her into this; she'd boxed herself in.

She balanced on the toilet seat, clutching her suitcase so he couldn't see her beneath the stall walls, but if the man in the Cubs hat came in and opened doors, he would find her. After days of anxiety and paranoia on this ill-fated train ride, she had let herself be manipulated again, just as her self-defense instructor had warned. She had been played to the point of helplessness. If her instructor were here, he would have sharp words about drawing lines.

This was it. She had reached the end of her rope, crouched in a grimy train station bathroom stall at midnight. If she was ever going to make a stand, it was time. Better late than never.

She didn't hear the bathroom door open, but it didn't matter. As the stall door swung inward, she raised her suitcase to eye level and hurled it at his face from her perch on the toilet.

It was an aggressive, unexpected move—one her defense instructor would have applauded—and it knocked the man's hat to the ground. But Ruby wasn't finished. She refused to run just to get cornered elsewhere. She was done playing by their rules. She would fight with such ferocity that she carved out her own escape.

Human instinct is to protect the face. The man's hands shot up as she hurled the suitcase, leaving his lower half unguarded. She lunged and kicked him hard between the legs. With his vision blocked, he didn't even manage a backward flinch. Her foot struck with full force before the suitcase even clattered to the floor.

She remembered from class: After a strike like that, there'd be a moment of paralysis. She used that window, driving her palm into his nose as she shoved out of the stall. His body reeled, crashing into the sinks. She didn't stay to watch, but the impact sounded brutal. He could keep the damn suitcase.

Ruby tore past the sinks and burst through the restroom door. Adrenaline surging, her vision narrowed; she missed the second man by the entrance. He lunged, grabbing her from behind. His arms clamped around her shoulders with bruising strength, nearly crushing her ribs.

She moved on instinct, muscle memory taking over. Twisting, she slammed her elbow into his ribs and heard a grunt as his grip loosened. She pivoted, heart hammering. In the chaos, a slip of paper fell from his hand, fluttering to the polished floor.

Ruby seized the advantage. She ducked low and lunged, ramming her shoulder into his knee while hooking his heel as a swipe sailed over her head. He staggered, arms flailing for balance, but Ruby blocked his other leg with her arm. Overbalanced, he toppled backward with a breathless groan.

The impact was her cue. She released his legs, snatched the paper from the floor, and bolted for the exit, clutching the crumpled sheet in a desperate grip. Shouts erupted behind her, footsteps scrambling, but she didn't slow. Cool night air met her face as she burst through the doors and vanished into the darkness.

34. ON THE TRACKS

A final point: In the shift from a haphazard, human-dominated coherence to a rigorous, machine-driven one, it is vital to implement safeguards. Given its scope and scale, an AI-reinforced incumbency could become more powerful than humans could resist. There may be no coming back.

—ARCC Memo Series

Fleeing the terminal, Ruby's first instinct was to run toward lights and people, to find the police. Instead, she darted down an alley, following a dim street that paralleled the tracks. Spotting a fenced lot, she scrambled over and crouched behind a stack of crates, hidden from view. She sat and trembled until the adrenaline drained from her body. It felt like forever.

She still clenched the paper she'd snatched from her second assailant. Once she caught her breath, she held it close, straining to read it as her eyes adjusted to the dark. It was her itinerary—the one Amtrak had canceled. As if she needed more proof someone was tracking her every move.

Occam's razor: Find the simplest explanation that fits the facts. The simplest explanation was that it was all connected: the rejected cards, the stolen phone, the canceled tickets, the attack. They knew where she would be, and when, almost as quickly as she did. Noah was watching her every move. But how?

How had he known she would be in Chicago? How did he get her itinerary—one even the Amtrak agent couldn't access? Was the agent involved?

No, that wasn't it. The agent hadn't even realized she was the same person who'd gone through the line before. It wasn't the agent. It was the computers: the ATM, her cards, her phone.

But then why had they stolen them? It didn't make sense.

Or maybe it did, but Ruby didn't have the energy to untangle it. As the adrenaline faded, cold seeped into her bones and exhaustion dragged at her limbs. Still, sleep wasn't an option. Not tonight. Instead, Ruby scouted the area around the tracks, plotting how she might slip onto Platform 8 to board tomorrow's California Zephyr. She guessed it would depart from the same platform, Chicago being the terminus.

All day, crouched near the tracks, hungry and out of cash, Ruby hid in the overgrown weeds beside shunted train cars, dozing fitfully. Trains rumbled past, announcements echoing over the station, but she stayed still. Noah—or someone working for him— was hunting her. She didn't know why, but the men in the bathroom hadn't hesitated to use force. Well, the second one hadn't. She hadn't given the first a chance, but she had drawn a line, and he'd crossed it. She didn't want to find out what would happen if they caught her.

In the evening, they announced the California Zephyr—same track, same time. Ruby had guessed right. But she didn't board. Too obvious.

She waited another day. It was a hard one, spent lying in a field, trying to ignore the gnawing hunger. When thirst became unbearable, she wandered narrow streets until she found a playground with a working water fountain. She peered into a few garbage cans but couldn't bring herself to eat anything she found. She wasn't that desperate. Not yet.

She slept during the day to conserve energy for sneaking in at night. Ruby didn't know the rules of this game or the stakes, but Noah hadn't found her yet. That meant she was finally playing correctly.

♦♦♦

Noah stared at the screen, eyes glazed with exhaustion. He hadn't slept in over twenty-four hours, but willpower kept him upright.

His muscles throbbed, a dull headache pulsed behind his temples, but he ignored his body's protests. All that mattered was the empty screen before him and what he couldn't find there.

Ruby had gone missing.

His fingers flew over the keyboard, summoning streams of data —location timestamps, transaction logs, any digital breadcrumbs Ruby might have left. But everything went dark after Chicago. There had been a confrontation; two agents sent to intercept her failed. After that, nothing.

Noah rubbed his burning eyes and forced himself to think. Ruby was smart and resourceful. She must have gone dark on purpose. But that only bought her time. MiddleMan was as relentless as Eli's golem. Why was it fixated on Ruby? Was she really the only outsider with any inkling of ARCC's secret? And if Noah had leaked information, why wasn't MiddleMan coming after *him*?

It didn't matter. What mattered was keeping Ruby safe. If she hadn't understood before, she must be piecing it together now. Noah knew how quick she was, how her mind worked. She had some idea what she was up against. But no matter how clever, Ruby was trapped. Her destination was her father's place in Colorado. MiddleMan would be watching every route—trains, buses, rental cars. Even if she boarded another train, agents would be waiting at the end of the line.

Ruby's luck would run out. She'd be caught. Then what? Would MiddleMan detain her or eliminate the threat?

Noah shook his head. He couldn't let that happen. MiddleMan was chasing her because of what he had shared. Ruby was trying to escape because he'd betrayed her trust. But how could he protect Ruby when the system hunting her—the one he'd built—had access to every scrap of information tied to her? Her address lurked in countless databases, from cell phone registrations to bank accounts and pay stubs. Every service she used pointed an arrow at her, and even if Noah had a way to contact her, even if she listened to him, MiddleMan would always be listening. He had wiped his one computer clean, but there were two sides to every conversation, and MiddleMan always lurked in between. What could he do about that?

Slumped on the couch, he pounded his fist against his forehead, struggling to think through the haze of exhaustion. He had to erase her from the system, either by deleting her data or by laying a false trail, but how?

What would Ruby do if she were here? Noah tried to summon her voice. She'd find some elegant symmetry to exploit, surely. But what symmetries existed for people? Bilateral symmetry? No, that was stupid.

Names. There were surely other Rubys out there, maybe even some with her last name. What if he swapped his Ruby for another? Or better yet, as Ruby herself would have suggested, what if he destroyed the coherence of the information? If he somehow scrambled the data so all the different Rubys pointed to each other, maybe he could erase the coherence that made his Ruby distinct.

It was a compelling idea, but the scale overwhelmed him. How could he track and manipulate millions of entries for a thousand Rubys, hidden in databases scattered across any number of computers?

Even as he asked, the answer surfaced in Ruby's voice. With her insight, he and Eli had solved this before. The solution was to use MiddleMan to manage—or, in this case, undermine—itself.

All it took was a Directive. But the Directives Database was locked behind multilayer authentication even Noah couldn't break alone. He couldn't simply enter the command; he had to work with what he had. He had to hack into MiddleMan's internal thoughts.

That was it. His heartbeat quickened as the plan took shape. Ruby had said there was no real difference between information and its reporting. Noah didn't need to hack the Directives Database itself, just how MiddleMan's systems communicated it. He couldn't create a persistent Directive, but for a while he could make part of MiddleMan act as if that Directive existed. If he kept up the schizophrenia long enough for MiddleMan to alter the database and network entries tied to Ruby's name, the scrambling would remain even after MiddleMan regained control.

Astonishing. Noah could almost hear Ruby and Eli in his mind. The thought brought brief solace, but Noah pushed it aside and focused on coding, scrambling every corner of MiddleMan where he could inject a stray thought. Enough to decohere the copy of Ruby living in the datasphere.

As lines of code poured from his fingers, Noah wondered about Eli's worries. Should he be concerned about introducing conflicting Directives into MiddleMan? If he could hack MiddleMan's internal reporting, couldn't someone else? Was this the source of the inconsistencies Eli saw? Was MiddleMan malfunctioning, or was someone pulling the strings?

Noah shoved this question aside, too. He had no time. Ruby needed him now. He hit Enter and watched his commands disperse silently across MiddleMan's hidden channels. Noah hoped it wasn't too late.

Ruby might never forgive him for lying, but maybe he could make amends by doing this for her. If it worked, it would give her freedom—from him and from the golem he'd released on the world.

◆◆◆

In the end, it was as simple as climbing a chain-link fence after sunset. Ruby was tired and hungry, but unencumbered. At the top, straddling both sides, she wavered, then swung her second leg over and dropped to the ground.

Ruby walked up the tracks, air thick with brimstone and tar, careful to keep to the shadows and avoid the pools of light where people gathered. She waited for a train to depart, then quickly hauled herself onto the empty platform it left behind, careful to avoid the third rail. In the fading dusk, she hid behind the last pillar, watching for her train. She thought ruefully of Noah, who always insisted most security was just for show. He wasn't wrong.

Twice, passengers flooded the platform and trickled onto trains, but no one paid her any mind. When her route was announced, Ruby slipped out from behind the pillar and merged with the distracted crowd hauling suitcases onto the train. She glanced down, hoping the dirt on her clothes didn't stand out.

At the back of the train, Ruby pressed her head to the window, feigning sleep. Her paper ticket peeked from her blouse pocket— enough to show the destination, not the barcode. *See,* she silently urged the conductor through closed eyelids as the train rattled along, *you know I paid. Come back later to scan it.*

She kept up the act even after he left, until at some point she wasn't acting. After sleepless nights and long days of waiting, her feigned sleep became real.

◆◆◆

The train slowed as it curved onto a bridge at the Illinois–Iowa border, nearing Burlington. That must be the Mississippi, Ruby thought. They spent the rest of the morning slaloming in slow motion through Iowa's rolling hills, avoiding every uphill battle.

Now they paralleled a smaller river, occasionally leaping it on iron girders. Smaller than the Mississippi, she thought, but wider than any lake she'd seen growing up. At ten, Ruby might have called this one, in fact. Conversely, the White River by her childhood home would barely pass for a stream here. She had adapted before, swimming from her little pond into the big sea. She would have to adapt again, going back.

If she made it that far. Even now, she couldn't let her guard down. One phone camera pointed her way, and Noah's agents might be on her by the next station. Would anyone on the train stand up for her if they tried to haul her off? Or did they want something worse?

Maybe it was best not to think about it. If they lost her trail and she stayed hidden, she might find her way home. Her dad would know what to do.

The train clattered across another bridge, and Ruby watched a great white bird launch from an invisible perch among the reeds. A heron, its elegant neck folded tight, pumped broad wings to rise above the wetland, rocking left, then right. Sunlight flashed off its enormous wings as it circled, searching for a clear path through the maze of power lines that threatened to fence it in. At last, it soared above the wires and set a course southeast along the river.

"Beautiful bird, don't you think?" said a voice to Ruby's left. She turned from the window to her companion, who until now had sat silently, absorbed in a book. The woman had boarded at Naperville, the first stop outside Chicago. A pleasant smile lit the face of a woman in her forties, dressed in a business suit, with short, dark, curly hair. Ruby already felt a quiet gratitude toward her; the ticket the woman had posted by their seats was keeping the conductor at bay.

"Nicole," the woman said, offering her hand. "I figured I'd introduce myself, since it seems neither of us is getting off soon."

Ruby hesitated before taking the offered hand. "What makes you think I'm not getting off soon?"

"You were humming earlier. There's not much classic country on the radio here, but someone from Nebraska or Colorado might hum Chris LeDoux if it reminds her of home."

"Colorado," Ruby said, raising her eyebrows. "You're good, but you've outed yourself too. Front Range, I'd guess?"

"Denver," Nicole said, nodding. "I'm in marketing at an ad firm. What about you?"

"Working on a PhD.," Ruby said, omitting the subject and wondering if it was even still true. That question could wait until she got home. "Marketing? So, like, viral product campaigns on social media? I bet it's tough to break through people's perceptual filters."

"It's a cat-and-mouse game, yes," Nicole said, eyeing her. "Are you doing a doctorate in psych or something?"

"Nah. Physics." Internally, Ruby winced. She knew what came next.

"Physics. That's not for the faint of heart. You must be a smart cookie."

Ruby never knew how to respond to this defensive flattery. Many airplane conversations ended in awkward silence this way. Through trial and error, she learned it was better to meet people on their terms, asking about their expertise instead.

"I just have a head for patterns, that's all. What do you advertise? Anything I'd recognize?"

"Our specialty is more diffuse: repairing public images, motivating political bases, that sort of thing. Social media helps, but it's more about crafting an atmosphere than delivering a message. We seed ideas so they seem to be in the air, then amplify organic content to create authenticity."

"So, political clients, then? Is this how people win office now?"

"I did actually start as a political organizer. This stuff worked in the 2010s and early 2020s, but after the arms race, it's gotten harder to move the needle. I was just in Chicago because one of our corporate campaigns flatlined—no measurable effect. If it happens again, I'll be looking for a new job." Nicole grimaced.

"Did you figure out why?" Ruby asked after a moment. "Are people just saturated with all the spin?"

"That's the thing. This campaign did well in trials, but it flopped in the wild. Nothing was picked up, not even by groups aligned with the message." Nicole shrugged and shook her head, shifting to watch scenery scroll past in the gray afternoon light.

So much for avoiding awkwardness.

While Nicole brooded over the kind of informational control Ruby knew too well, Ruby's thoughts drifted to her own predicament. Even without the digital trail of a scanned ticket, Noah could easily deduce her destination. The ticket she'd bought earlier gave them everything they needed. If she avoided obvious bottlenecks—stations and terminals where Noah might have agents—Ruby might make it to Colorado, but that probably meant slipping off the train before the final stop.

If she slipped away before they found her and somehow made it to JP's house unnoticed, she and her father might finally be safe.

Noah didn't have anything linking her to that place, did he? With a jolt, Ruby realized she might not even know exactly where JP lived. How was she supposed to find her dad?

Her stomach growled, bringing her mind to the problem: she had no money. Even if she found a meal—and she desperately needed one—how would she make it the rest of the way without cash for a bus ticket?

Ruby watched the farmland blur past the window. What else could she do but improvise?

◆◆◆

Nicole and Ruby shared seats through the day and night, which was a godsend for Ruby. Despite their awkward start, Nicole proved pleasant company—sometimes chatty, sometimes quietly absorbed in her book. When Nicole invited her to lunch, Ruby declined, citing cash-flow problems. Nicole insisted, saying her company would cover it. The veggie burger was god-awful, but it was the most substantial meal Ruby had eaten in two days.

They dined together in the early evening as the train rolled through the cornfields of western Iowa. Ruby tried not to inhale her noodles, while Nicole poked at her chicken and watched with a bemused smile. Afterward, they wandered to the viewing car, where Nicole handed her a trashy novel to read by the reddening light. At some point, Nicole nudged her with a flask.

"Go ahead," Nicole urged softly. "It'll help."

Ruby hesitated a moment before tipping the flask back. The liquor burned her throat but settled warm in her abdomen. Some muscles in her shoulders unclenched for the first time in days. She exhaled and handed the flask back.

As the sky lit up outside, a comfortable silence settled over them, inviting reflection. Ruby found Nicole intriguing. She was clearly good at her job, but Ruby sensed her heart wasn't in it. Nicole sounded troubled by her recent campaign failures, but not in a scared-to-find-a-new-job kind of way.

She spoke about her time as a political organizer, shrugging. "A few years. Mostly door-to-door, canvassing for candidates I believed in. There was one in particular. Small government, universal basic income, progressive values, all that." She paused, smiling ruefully. "Didn't win, of course. They never do."

For the first time in ages, Ruby was fed and cared for, and she began opening up to Nicole, processing her father's illness and her decision to leave her program to care for him. Other parts—the men searching for her in Chicago, tracking her out of Boston—Ruby wasn't ready to discuss. She wasn't even sure what she could say.

She didn't need to say much. Nicole was sharp. Quick on the uptake. Outside Omaha, the conductor passed through the car again. Ruby froze, heart racing, panic rising as she fumbled for her ticket. Nicole calmly laid a steady hand over Ruby's trembling fingers.

"I'm sorry, sir," Nicole said smoothly, smiling at the conductor. "My daughter seems to have lost her ticket." She rummaged briefly through her bag, then produced a ticket with a relieved smile. "Found it. Sorry about that. Here you go, Nicole."

Ruby stared blankly, confused as Nicole addressed her using her own name. Nicole met her gaze, calm and steady, then pressed a slip of paper into Ruby's hand.

"Oh," Ruby said, recovering. She handed Nicole's ticket to the conductor, who scanned it before turning to Nicole.

"And yours, ma'am?"

"I have an unlimited pass," Nicole said, steady-voiced. "Heather Collins. ID 08323. Look it up."

The conductor tapped a few keys on his scanner and frowned. "I'm not seeing... Ah, there you are. Very well."

Ruby waited until the conductor had walked past their seats, then leaned in and whispered, "What just happened?"

Nicole smiled and waved dismissively. "Just a colleague. We look enough alike. It's not the first time I've used that trick, though I try to be honest on the company's dime."

"I..." Ruby started, still unsure how to respond.

"Don't worry about it," Nicole said gently. "It's not my business. You were saying something about school?"

Ruby hesitated, but the conversation flowed more easily now, as if a release valve had opened. Events with Mendel had spun out of control so quickly, she hadn't ever processed her decision to leave. Saying it aloud crystallized her conflict: regret was already creeping in, though it seemed she'd had no real choice.

"What was it for?" Ruby asked softly, gazing at the evening sky beyond the window. "My whole life—the expectations, the attention I never wanted. I dreamed of making a discovery that justified the cost. Not the cost to me. I was willing to pay that. But to my parents. My mom sacrificed so much, and now I've just... squandered it. Like my education was some vanity project."

Nicole listened with warmth in her eyes. "I don't know them," she said, "but I'm sure your parents are proud."

Ruby let the words settle between them and took comfort.

The sunset eventually eclipsed Ruby's self-doubt as the young corn tassels blushed pink and orange. For a moment, they looked like upright paintbrushes scrolling past her window. Dusk settled, and fireflies began their stochastic cascades beneath the first stars. One firefly's pulse triggered others in quick succession, followed by a dark minute of recharge, then another wave before they vanished. May was early for fireflies. Summer's heat arrived sooner each year.

When she was seven or eight, Ruby and her parents drove east across the country, long before her mother's internal struggles surfaced. They stopped at a hotel surrounded by cornfields, where something glinted at the edge of the lawn. Ruby turned, but it was gone. A minute later, another spark flashed, and she caught it just before it vanished. Her mom laughed softly, explaining about fireflies, then challenged Ruby to catch one in her cupped hands. She succeeded, delighted in the tiny glow, and immediately asked for a jar.

Her mother had gently shaken her head. "Keep it wild, hon. Even bugs are more beautiful flying free."

♦♦♦

Sometime that night, maybe an hour after Nicole fell asleep beside her, Ruby pulled the letter from her jacket pocket, the one she'd grabbed on her way out of the apartment. How long ago was that? Three days? It felt like forever.

Despite her physical and emotional fatigue, Ruby felt a flutter in her stomach as she broke the envelope's seal. How long ago had her mother written this letter? Twenty years? Had it just sat in her parents' bedroom, waiting for the day her father finally mailed it? The thought seemed impossible.

Ruby unfolded the letter and read:

My Dearest Ruby,

You'll probably never read this. I just need to speak to the woman I hope you'll become—the woman I never quite managed to be.

You have such fire in you, Ruby—wild curiosity, your father's stubbornness, a relentless drive for answers, and an unshakable internal compass. I'm awed by the glimpses I catch of the person you're becoming. You will carve your own path. It's both a blessing and a curse, but I think you will have the courage to face it.

I left my path when I no longer could see its truth. So many brilliant people, your father included, lose themselves, trapped by expectations, mistaking validation for purpose. Your father is a good man. He tries to do what's right. His mistake is letting others define what "right" means. I don't think you'll have that problem.

But I couldn't live like that, Ruby, and I couldn't pretend. I lost my path, but you saved me in ways I can't fully explain. I never expected motherhood to be my answer, never imagined it could be. Yet you gave me something no degree or accolade could: the courage and humility to live honestly. Being your mother taught me to embrace a quieter but no less important work.

Here's the selfish part, because, darling girl, this letter isn't really for you, is it? Selfishly, I want to thank you for saving my life. This world brims with beauty, yet offers so little direction to those searching for meaning. You won't face that struggle, not with the compass you carry inside. But I did, Ruby, until I found my path in you. You became my purpose, which is why, selfishly, I dread the day I must let you follow yours without me.

For this precious time we share, I thank you from the bottom of my heart for being everything I needed. In return, I promise to raise you to follow your values and leave your mark on the world, whether that mark spans continents or simply helps make one generation a little better than the last.

Chase your path fiercely, my love—wherever it may lead.

With all my heart,

Mom

The train rocked in rhythm with the rails through the night, following parallel lines across a wide, empty country. Ruby gazed out the window, unsure where to begin.

Ruby hadn't understood. She'd thought her mother unfulfilled, forced from her passion, deprived of ambition. But her mother had left academia of her own accord, without regard for what others thought. She chose her own path, not because anyone else expected it or needed it or tricked her into it, but simply because it mattered to her.

Ruby held on to that thought until her eyes closed and she drifted into sleep.

35. RAINBOW DIFFRACTION

White light is incoherent—a disordered assembly of photons. Yet passing through a diffractive medium—a prism or raindrop—chromatic shapes emerge from chaos. How fitting that the arc-de-iris became the symbol of the post-flood biblical covenant with a higher power.

—ARCC Memo Series

Early the next morning, Ruby's train sped across the prairie toward mountains rising into the purple dawn. Farmsteads dotted the land, each ringed by wheat. With fewer rivers, less ground was cultivated, and many fields lay fallow. As sunlight touched the Rockies, Ruby breathed deeply. She hadn't seen these mountains in years. They weren't home yet, but they marked the edge of the foreign country she'd lived in since college.

These mountains, more than any other landmark on her journey west, revealed a world beyond human control. People might scratch at the slopes or bore a tunnel, but they couldn't till the land for crops or clear-cut it for housing. Years ago, she'd been eager to leave, but now, as Ruby returned, she understood what had drawn her mother to them.

Her father had been one of those scratching out a living here. He belonged to this land even more deeply than her mother. He knew its history, reading ancient seashores in the sandstone and lakes in the shale. He grew up with it, so familiar and embedded in its rhythms that he couldn't see the changes as he changed with them.

Just as a grandparent notices a child's growth more vividly than a parent, Ruby thought, a person can miss changes in the body they inhabit. Like the arrival of summer, a little earlier each year, or a doctor finding a late-stage growth you missed before. A wife realizes the field has gone fallow while you labor to put bread on the table.

But there was powerful magic in that consistency. Like a juniper clinging to rock, her father had weathered countless seasons to be present in her life. He showed up when she needed him, even when she thought she didn't.

◆◆◆

The two women hugged when Nicole disembarked in Denver.

"It was a pleasure meeting you, Ruby. You're something else. I hope your father recovers quickly. I'm sure he's in good hands. Drop me a line soon, okay?"

"Thanks, Nicole. Thank you for everything."

The train angled toward Boulder's Flatirons, climbing slowly through lazy switchbacks, when Ruby spotted a folded note on the seat beside her. Inside, she found a few encouraging words, a hundred-dollar bill, and a business card with an address, phone number, and "CALL ME" scrawled in bold capitals.

Ruby's mind lingered on her new friend, wondering if they would meet again as the train climbed into the mountains. After a tunnel, the currents shifted, and she followed the rivers west, descending from the icy peaks. The sun rose over the Rockies, slipping in and out of clouds. Ruby sighed, the train's steady rhythm underscoring her thoughts.

She disembarked in Glenwood Springs. With the cash Nicole left her and a new name, Ruby bought a bus ticket for a departure in a few hours. She ate, then stretched her legs along a bike path tracing the Colorado River, deserted on this breezy late spring afternoon. Low clouds drifted in, dimming the light.

Ruby rubbed her arms against the chill. She had no phone, no backpack, not even her suitcase. Unburdened and suddenly light, she broke into a trot, then a run.

It felt good to move, to breathe the thin, familiar air of her childhood, and to feel the heat of exertion in her muscles. But the air was thin, and she was still recovering from her fast in Chicago. She didn't go far. Just enough to warm up and spot a sign for the old cemetery, advertising the graves of Doc Holliday and Kid Curry. With two hours until her bus left, she followed the arrows at a brisk walk, lungs burning as she caught her breath.

Ruby paused at the entrance where pavement gave way to dirt. A wooden gate opened onto uneven marble stones surrounded by cheatgrass, sagebrush, and rusted iron pickets. Linwood Cemetery. She had the place to herself. The ground was damp but not muddy. Only one set of faint, windblown footprints showed anyone had visited since the snow melted.

Without her phone, Ruby couldn't tell outlaws from lawmen or guess which legends had drawn her predecessor down this path, but it didn't matter. Names faded from headstones, their deeds, good and bad, sinking deeper each day beneath history's relentless flood of information. Did having your name written in a book matter if no one alive remembered you?

Any string of syllables could evoke an idea. What mattered, to anyone uttering them, to anyone listening, was the idea itself, not the name. Nobody thought of Heinrich Hertz while counting oscillations per second. Why should it matter if Ruby's name got attached to a particle?

What mattered was the particle, its role in the universe, and the understanding that knowledge brought. Ruby didn't know if she would return to her work on dark matter, but if she did, it would be on her own terms, for reasons she believed in. Science was a human endeavor, and Ruby's work only mattered if it brought humanity closer to coherence with the universe.

There were many ways to make a difference in science. Ruby's work with Imani might matter more, in the long run, than the theory she had dreamed up.

Ruby thought she understood now the choice her mother made to abandon a rigged system for a different legacy. It had taken real courage to face the judgment, even from her own daughter, and step away from the system.

As Ruby walked toward her bus, a sudden squall forced her into a run for the station's sheltered entrance. She arrived just as the rain stopped, damp and shivering, but she barely noticed, because a vivid double rainbow arched over the canyon opposite the low sun.

She stared at the rainbow, transfixed, until the hiss of air brakes snapped her back. Time to board.

◆◆◆

```
<GHOSTWRITER APP>
<BEGIN I/O>
```

> Stale intel, here at the station. Our thread has pulled loose.

What do you mean, "stale"? You're playing in omniscient mode. You have a god's-eye view. Find her.

> Check for yourself. Nothing registered between Chicago and Denver. We staked out the terminus, but I'm not optimistic.

Then track the father. We know where she's going.

> That's the thing. Our eye-in-the-sky has him outside Omaha.

He's not in Nebraska, idiot. He's getting chemo in Junction. They're from some podunk town nearby.

> Do you remember a specific location? If so, I'll send men. The system isn't turning up anything that makes sense.

With everything I'm juggling, you think I have time to memorize this girl's address?

> Just asking. We'll keep them monitoring the train station, but like I said, I think this one's loose. A lot of trouble over one stray thread, if you ask me. Let's focus on the oil field.

The oil field is handled. I need her. If there is a thread that could unravel everything, it is this one. She has too many connections and is far too clever to

ignore, especially with what she knows. She holds
enough pieces to solve the puzzle.

> We toppled an entrenched transnational corporation.
> One clever girl can't stop us.

One year. That's how long it took for an idea to grow
from one mind to this moment. She and I are not so
different.

<END I/O>

♦♦♦

Her father wasn't at the bus station when Ruby arrived in Junction. She hadn't expected him to be. How could he have known? She'd had no way to tell him about the train trip, her silent exit at Glenwood, or the bus ticket she bought with the cash Nicole left her. Nothing about her arrival time had been planned, from the trouble buying tickets, to losing her phone, to canceled reservations, to being followed and attacked in Chicago.

Given all that had conspired to prevent this trip, it was no surprise Ruby found herself alone in the parking lot outside the bus station, half a mile from the train station. Still, the sight of the empty curb brought a wave of loneliness.

There was nowhere to buy a phone this far from the highway, beside the river and railroad tracks. At least, there hadn't been ten years ago, the last time Ruby had seen this area. Back then, it was desolate, laughably out of step with the grandiose train station down the road, which had seemed aspirational even at the height of the railroad days. The place already felt like a forgotten relic when she had glimpsed it from the truck window, riding to the scrapyard with her father. Now, in the evening sun, rows of warehouses stood before her, sporting fresh storefronts.

This place had once seemed like the big city. After Boston, it felt tiny. Sleepy, though still alive. Ruby walked cautiously toward the regrown stores across from the train station, aware of her growing proximity to anyone lingering near her original destination— the terminal listed on her ticket. The same itinerary the man in

Chicago had held on that sheet of paper. Still, she had to contact her father. She had no idea where JP's house was.

These stores, their fresh paint disguising rusted siding, reminded Ruby of a spring long ago when the fruit trees around their property died back in the subzero temperatures of the last hard winter. Cutting off wood, some to the ground, Ruby had thought the trees dead. But the stumps came back, sprouting new growth after the thaw. The roots were still good.

In this area, the hard winter arrived in the seventies, when the first bore of the Eisenhower Tunnel opened I-70 to 18-wheelers from Denver. The interstate followed the train tracks through the mountains. Ruby had glimpsed it several times before disembarking in Glenwood. The railroad, in turn, had borrowed its path from the Colorado River, which carved its way out of the steep red cliffs of Glenwood Canyon, winding through arid hills and plateaus until it met the Gunnison River here at Junction, a hundred miles south of Dragon.

Ruby was cautious, slipping behind the stores and moving through a dusty lane cluttered with broken pallets and rusted dumpsters. She watched the station. Her train had arrived hours ago. The place should be deserted, with no more trains due until morning. The few cars in the lot would stay overnight, waiting for their owners. So why was a car idling out front?

The thought drove her into a crouch behind a stack of collapsed cardboard boxes. She looked ridiculous, creeping through an alley used only by forklift drivers, peering out at the empty parking lot, but she was past caring and dismissed the thought. She trusted her instincts.

Ruby had set out to buy a phone but decided it was best not to, even if a store sold them. That stranger in the Cubs hat in Chicago hadn't been a random threat. He worked for someone who knew her. Someone determined to stop this trip. Someone with incredible resources, blocking RediRides, canceling credit cards and tickets, hiring people to track her down. He weaponized information, twisting technology to manipulate others' lives. She'd been lucky to lose her phone and computer. That might have saved her.

If Noah was to be believed—and Ruby now questioned everything he'd said—she and her father had only weeks to prepare for the coming crisis. If everything was shutting down, they would have to plan carefully to weather the storm and survive whatever world emerged on the other side. And she would have to do it offline, without Iris.

Hiding beside a newly rebuilt store along the train tracks, with the riverbanks just visible beyond, Ruby wondered how much further things could descend. If cars ran out of gas and buses stopped, would the railroad become the main artery here? Or would the trains stop, too? Rivers had been the original highways of the West, long before trains and cars. Would people wind up rowing wooden boats down the river in a few years?

What was she supposed to do, stranded out here? Whatever purpose her mother believed awaited her, Ruby hadn't found it yet. She had left the system, just as her mother had, but the system Noah built was doing its level best to pull her back in.

So she would do the opposite. She would stay invisible, fighting the current, trying in her own small way to undo the damage Noah had caused and was still causing. As society unraveled, she would save what she could, starting with her father.

Noah. Mendel. The entire academic system. They had all used her. Ruby had been so caught up in her fantasy of making a difference, of succeeding where her mother had failed—of *believing* her mother had failed—that she never questioned her assumptions. She never considered that the one person who, in his own broken, misguided way, wanted nothing from her except herself was her father.

If Ruby wanted to free herself from those who used her, she could do worse than focus on caring for her family as the storm approached. With the world descending into chaos, old systems unraveling, perhaps it was purpose enough to cling to her own small truth.

Ruby spotted the pay phone half a block from the train station

—a lone artifact dating from her barely pre-cellular childhood. She couldn't recall many numbers from Iris's contact list, but her father's was one. She could call him. Would it be safe?

Ruby waited until the car in front of the station pulled away. Who had they been waiting for? She had a theory, and so far, the evidence fit. Assuming her hypothesis was correct, she lingered, watching to make sure anyone tailing her had disappeared.

The phone was weathered, vandalized, and plastered with faded stickers advertising products long gone, but it still produced a dial tone. After she remembered to drop in a few coins left over from the food she'd bought with Nicole's money, the call went through, connecting an unremarkable pay phone to a cell phone so old it lacked even a basic AI chip. A familiar voice answered. Ruby was careful not to share any identifying information, referring to their meeting place only by the memory she and her father shared of driving by it long ago.

An hour later, beside the junkyard a mile down the road, Ruby stood before a black pickup she didn't recognize and clung to her father's skeletal frame, feeling how frail he'd become, though his arms still held the wiry strength she remembered.

"Dad," she said. "I'm so sorry."

"It's okay, kid," he said, his voice rough from chemo. "It's okay. I'm sorry, too. You were right about PetronTech from the beginning, and I know this has been hard. Thank you for coming to help me."

"It's about to get worse, Dad. Everything's falling apart. This world is about to collapse, and I think someone is after me."

"Then I'll follow your lead and we'll do what we need to do. But we'll take care of each other. It'll be okay. I thought about you every day. You really are so much like your mother, you know."

At his open words, realizing she could finally be proud of the comparison, a seal in Ruby cracked, releasing emotions she had sequestered for months, years, and through this last hard week. Ruby sobbed, unable to speak, while Paul gently stroked her hair.

She cried for the aspirations that had decohered from this reality and for those who tried to control her. She cried for her father, who only half stood before her, and for her mother, who had taken the other half with her.

Ruby wept quietly in the truck as she rode upriver. Her tears drew the sparkling sunset reflections from the water into a curtain of streamers—a prismatic veil dividing the world, with houses on the near side and mountains behind, visible only in relief through the shifting bands of light. Ruby breathed, and when she blinked, the veil shimmered.

Ruby cried. But as she drove with her father on their second-to-last tank of gas down a familiar highway toward the trailer of a barely remembered figure from her childhood, she looked at the sun setting on the river and mountains and orchards around her and wiped her eyes. The veil dividing her world faded to transparency, the tree-covered mountains merged with the foreground, and Ruby smiled to have come home at last.

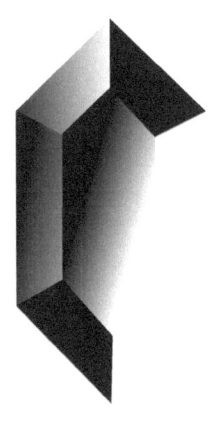

Coda

36. ANY OTHER NAME

Returning from the bakery, Imani slipped through the gap in the chain-link fence, nodding to Terrance, the security guard. She glanced at the familiar sprawl of tents, tarps, and makeshift shelters, searching for Bishop. An extra doughnut and coffee waited in her bag for him, and she knew he'd already be busy somewhere in the maze of canvas and cardboard.

Finding him wasn't difficult. She spotted his wagon first, piled high with metal scraps and plastic containers. He sat near the center of the lot, bending wire into one of his intricate roses. Imani slipped off her backpack as she approached and pulled out a carafe and a paper box.

"Breakfast?"

Bishop paused, his eyes briefly meeting hers as a smile tugged at his lips. "Always appreciated."

She sat beside him, cradling her cup. They ate in silence, broken only by the city's morning sounds drifting over the fence: voices, the distant rumble of a bus. No cars.

Sometime after she finished, a black speck landed on her arm. It arrived with a light hop but caught her attention as it brushed the hairs on her skin, struggling to right itself.

Imani plucked it off, crushed it with her fingernail, and flicked away the chitinous remains. If one got loose in her tent and laid eggs... Imani shuddered. She didn't need real fleas joining the proverbial ones multiplying around her.

Bishop set aside his half-eaten doughnut and returned to work, but paused when she shivered, giving her a thoughtful look.

"How long are you planning on living here?" he asked, not unkindly.

Imani hesitated, sipping her coffee. "Not sure. Until I figure out what's next, I guess. At least I'm making money."

Bishop nodded and turned to his wire sculpture. "Taking money, it's easy to start thinking someone else's values are your own."

"You've said it before," Imani sighed, smiling. "But Ruby told me once that it's important to know why you're on a path before committing to it. None of my options feel like they're really mine yet. Still trying to figure things out."

Bishop's expression softened. "If you're trying, you're doing better than most."

For a few moments, Imani listened to the click of Bishop's snips cutting rings out of the looped wire.

"I'll keep using Mendel's lab for now," she said. "Maybe it'll help me get into grad school, maybe not. Either way, I'll save what I can."

Bishop hummed approval. "Fair enough."

Imani relaxed, a smile breaking through her tension. "You talk more these days."

Bishop chuckled, the sound resonating between them. "Only when something's worth saying."

As they finished breakfast, a woman from a neighboring tent waved and called Bishop's name. He acknowledged her with a raised hand, and as he ambled over, Imani surveyed the encampment. This community wasn't permanent for her—she knew that, just as she knew her mother's church would never be hers. But pieces could be reused.

She caught Bishop watching her, a knowing look in his gaze. When their eyes met, he nodded.

◆◆◆

After breakfast with Bishop, Imani stopped by her tent to stow her stove and cutlery in a metal box—one of many chained to the rusting fence that ringed the lot. She snapped the combination lock shut and hefted her overstuffed backpack. Inside, she kept everything too valuable to store: screens, chargers, cash, cards, notebooks, and toiletries.

Imani unlocked her bike a few yards away and rode to the gym. At the Y, she showered, changed, and dried off with a fresh towel before pedaling to campus. The sidewalks were filling up with tents these days, but she had the street to herself. These gas prices were something she could get used to.

Imani wove her bike through the sparse sidewalk crowd as she approached Rubin Hall, slaloming between pedestrians until she got stuck behind an oblivious physics student, eyes glued to his phone, blocking the path. She snapped her brake handles, hoping the sound would get his attention, but with his earbuds in, he wasn't noticing. Oh well. With only two hundred meters left, Imani slipped her feet from the toe clips, swung a leg over, and dismounted smoothly mid-glide, stepping into a walk.

She'd arrived earlier than usual, hoping to catch Mendel in his office before he disappeared into whatever kept him busy. The lab was empty. For her, arriving before 9 a.m. was a notable achievement.

Imani was walking her bike to the rack outside the main door when she spotted a tall man in a collared shirt and slacks slipping out the side exit. Mendel took a sharp right, moving quickly away from where Imani stood.

She called to him. His hesitation said he heard, though a moment passed before he turned to acknowledge her.

"Sorry, Imani," he said. "Just rushing off to a meeting."

"I wanted to review those spectra you gave me. I ran the analysis, but something's off with the bump you expected. Can I walk you to your meeting?"

Mendel cut short the stride he had just restarted. "Better not. Maybe we could meet this evening—seven or so? I'll swing by the lab."

"Sure, I guess," Imani said, falling behind as he strode toward the east side of campus. "See you tonight."

She didn't quite let him out of her sight, though. Hopping back on her bike, Imani trailed at a distance, skirting the perimeter of quadrangles he crossed diagonally. She tucked behind buildings, waiting for him to reappear.

Imani wasn't sure what she was after. An explanation, maybe, for why he was so hard to reach. Maybe a clue to why Ruby had left so suddenly. The world had been going to hell since she left. Imani needed any scraps the universe could offer.

Students scurried on the sidewalks, rushing toward campus buildings before the clock tower struck the hour. There were others, too. People like her who lived nearby in unofficial housing. Every day, newcomers arrived from the suburbs, coasting in cars that were promptly abandoned when they ran out of gas. Parks and plazas everywhere were filling up, and prices were on the rise.

On the pedestrian bridge connecting the main yard to the complex where big lectures like Professor Matsuda's *Science and Society* took place last fall, Imani nearly lost sight of Mendel. She had to step off her bike or risk the wrath of campus police—it was a strictly pedestrian zone—but without the extra height, she couldn't see over all the students.

Fortunately, Mendel's destination lay on the far side of the complex, not inside. Imani spotted him again halfway through her circuit of the building, once she managed to get back on the bike. As soon as she did, she veered into the road, turning her back to him and hoping he hadn't noticed her, though he had been walking her way.

But his mind was elsewhere. Mendel's strides carried him across green lawns and past trimmed hedges to the brutalist front of the computer science building. Aiken Hall, she read, squinting. The entryway loomed: bare concrete, steel girders, and glass framing an indecipherable metal sculpture. Next to it stood someone Imani recognized, wearing a gray T-shirt.

Imani was pretty sure it was him—Ruby's boyfriend. She'd only met him once, but the shaggy hair and puppy-dog eyes were unmistakable. He was the same guy who had picked up Ruby months ago, though he looked disheveled and distraught now.

Imani considered stopping by after Mendel went inside to see if Noah had any intel on the whereabouts of his girlfriend. Ex-girlfriend? But Noah headed straight for Mendel. Coasting on her bike, Imani slipped behind the far side of the sculpture, close enough to catch snippets of their conversation, though she couldn't see them.

"Morning, Derrick," she heard Noah say. "I know you want us working from home, but some stuff in the server room needs attention. I also need to discuss an issue in private. Do you have time for a one-on-one?"

"Sure. I'd be happy to set your mind at ease. First, though, I think Eli and his team are ready to..."

Imani missed the rest as the doors of Aiken closed around the conversation.

ACKNOWLEDGMENTS

On the journey of COHERENCE, I am indebted to many—some in big ways, but more in ways not easily quantifiable. I can't hope to list all of you, but I am grateful to everyone who built track in front of this runaway train.

First, Sarah, thank you for leveling me up as a person. You made this side quest possible, but my campaign will always be at your side. You're my first pick for any apocalypse team.

Thank you to my parents and brother, Shirley, Ken, and Reid, who gifted me a unique view of the world from the far end of a dirt road that never felt lonely. Thank you for Dragon.

Thank you to my children—Judah, Elena, and Greta—who love stories, and music, and science, and who constantly inspire me with their curiosity and creativity.

Thank you to Amber Helt and Richelle Braswell at *Rooted in Writing* for edits that made for a master class in storytelling.

I tip my (virtual) hat to Ken Thompson, the father of Unix and so many tools I use daily, for his warnings long ago about a weakness at the foundations of computer security.

And finally, thank you to everyone who read this story and made it better: Adam, Misti, Kristen, Bryan, Rebecca, Phil, and Charlie. You all suffered so that others might not. I learned so much from your feedback.

I am lucky to be surrounded by such magnificent people. COHERENCE began before pandemics, before LLMs, early in a modern assault on truth that is not without historical precedent. Too much has come true, but as we stumble, hopeful, across half-built bridges, I grow ever more appreciative of the people everywhere, working to secure our future.

ABOUT THE AUTHOR

Aaron Parsons is a professor of astrophysics at the University of California, Berkeley. He designs and uses radio telescopes to search for the first stars in the universe. This is his first novel.

He would also love an excuse to continue this series, so if you liked COHERENCE, leave a review and share with your friends!